FOR NEVER & ALWAYS

"Once again, Greer has written a gem of a book. FOR NEVER & ALWAYS is equal parts romantic and heartbreaking, perfectly capturing the experience of growing up and growing together, and of true love finally finding a right place and a right time. Could not be happier to be back at Carrigan's."

—Rachael Lippincott, #1 *New York Times* bestselling coauthor of *She Gets the Girl*

"FOR NEVER & ALWAYS is a story about a love that doesn't let go, doesn't ask questions, and doesn't listen. Which means Helena Greer does a masterful job, penning characters you believe will do all three as they fight for themselves and the happy ending to their story they deserve."

—Stacey Agdern, author of *History of Us*

"FOR NEVER & ALWAYS is an absolute dream of a second-chance romance! The pining and the tension leap off the page and will grab you right in the feels. Helena Greer has crafted a gorgeous sophomore novel with the most relatable characters and the most charming setting. Once I started reading, I couldn't put it down!"

—Falon Ballard, author of *Just My Type*

"FOR NEVER & ALWAYS captures the vibrancy of a 1940s black-and-white screwball film and displays it in bright, dazzling, inclusive color. Hannah and Levi's love story is a jubilant reunion romance that deftly balances heartfelt angst and aching sweetness. A second trip to the enclave of Carrigan's was just what my queer heart wanted!"

—Timothy Janovsky, author of
Never Been Kissed

"Take the history and angst of both a marriage-in-trouble and second-chance romance, wrap it in the warmth and complications of found family, and you'll have just a little taste of Hannah and Levi Blue's epic love story in FOR NEVER & ALWAYS. It always feels like a special privilege to read a book like this one that clearly lives so deeply in its author's heart. Visiting Carrigan's feels like getting wrapped in a huge, queer, Jewish hug, and I cannot wait to return."

—Anita Kelly, author of *Love & Other Disasters*

"Helena Greer's second book, FOR NEVER & ALWAYS, packs a major emotional punch. It's got a lovestruck, pining hero and a heroine who takes no crap but still can't help falling hard. The book is delightfully queer and with small-town charm—and complications—aplenty, there's a lot to sink your teeth into. Every page is a revelation of emotions and readers will find themselves completely lost in Hannah and Levi's swoony love story."

—Jodie Slaughter, author of *Bet on It*

"This book made me so happy. It was an absolute fire hose of angst and drama, but in the sparkliest way—I love that our prickly asshole chef Levi is also pining so openly, and our clinically anxious hotel manager Hannah is a font of strength when the chips are down. I love how complicated and messy people are in this book: they make mistakes and they misinterpret and it's all part of the roller coaster. I love the food and the side characters and the emotionally resonant haircut. Can we get a Carrigan's book for every major holiday?"

—Olivia Waite, author of *The Hellion's Waltz*

SEASON OF LOVE

"[This] love story is by turns heartbreaking and delightful."

—*Library Journal*

"There's plenty of fun to be had... like frothy eggnog amid the holiday bustle."

—*Publishers Weekly*

"A warm, queer romance with holiday cheer and emotional depth."

—*Kirkus*

"A holiday mash-up of epic proportions... Greer gives new meaning to making the yuletide gay."

—*Entertainment Weekly*

"A heartwarming and inspiring story about letting go of the past to find your joy and being open to love."

—Abby Jimenez, *New York Times* bestselling author of *Part of Your World*

"If you are like me and completely obsessed with Hallmark and holiday movies, then you don't want to miss Helena Greer's debut novel, SEASON OF LOVE. This book hits on all your favorite Hallmark tropes as it weaves a beautiful journey from hate to love for Miriam and Noelle. A cozy, queer, heartfelt holiday romance that will have you grabbing a blanket, a cup of hot chocolate, and snuggling down to read this charming book."

—Rachel Van Dyken, *New York Times* bestselling author of *The Godparent Trap*

"A warm, cozy holiday romance, SEASON OF LOVE is a vibrant exploration of embracing that which is most unexpected in life...and in love. Best read under the glow of rainbow twinkle lights and a cup of cocoa."

—Ashley Herring Blake, *USA Today* bestselling author of *Delilah Green Doesn't Care*

"If you need the cozy feel of a Hallmark holiday movie in book form, visit Carrigan's! SEASON OF LOVE has all of the warm, queer, Jewish holiday vibes you could possibly want. It's a cup of cocoa with the perfect amount of marshmallows, it's a sweet kiss under the mistletoe. Helena Greer creates characters and settings that I never want to leave behind."

—Jen DeLuca, *USA Today* bestselling author of *Well Matched*

"Satire and romantic holiday magic in equal measure, SEASON OF LOVE is a sly, bighearted book that will have you laughing even as it makes your heart grow three sizes."

—Jenny Holiday, *USA Today* bestselling author of *Duke, Actually*

"SEASON OF LOVE is a warm and witty romance with characters that leap straight off the page...Greer's writing is vibrant and she handles grief and complicated family dynamics with tenderness..."   —Alexandria Bellefleur, bestselling author of *Count Your Lucky Stars*

"SEASON OF LOVE uses the magic of the holidays to do what romance novels do best: convince its main characters (and its readers) that the healing power of love is something every single person deserves. This heartwarming debut has everything you want in a holiday romance—and I can't wait to recommend it to my friends."

—Therese Beharrie, author of *And They Lived Happily Ever After*

"Stepping into this book is like stepping into an eccentric winter wonderland—exactly the kind of holiday escapism I crave. Come to Carrigan's for the loveable cast of kooky characters, but stay for the meaningful reflections on grief, family relationships, and identity. At turns a holiday confection and a deep character study, SEASON OF LOVE filled my heart. I can't wait to visit Carrigan's again and again!"

—Alison Cochrun, author of *The Charm Offensive*

"Greer has crafted an idyllic setting I want to whisk away to for Christmas (but then stay all year) and a charming cast of characters I want to befriend. Readers are going to lament that Carrigan's isn't a real destination they can jet off to."

—Sarah Hogle, author of *Just Like Magic*

"Greer's debut simply sparkles. It's so easy to get lost in the magic of Carrigan's with Miriam and Noelle and a stellar secondary cast that includes a fat cat named Kringle. This delightful Christmas Chanukah mash-up will have you braiding challah by a Christmas tree."

—Roselle Lim, author of *Sophie Go's Lonely Hearts Club*

ALSO BY HELENA GREER

Season of Love

FOR NEVER & ALWAYS

HELENA GREER

FOREVER

New York   Boston

Copyright © 2023 by Helena Greer

Cover design and illustration by Leni Kauffman.
Cover copyright © 2023 by Hachette Book Group, Inc.

Forever
Hachette Book Group
1290 Avenue of the Americas, New York, NY 10104
read-forever.com
twitter.com/readforeverpub

First Edition: November 2023

Forever is an imprint of Grand Central Publishing. The Forever name and logo are trademarks of Hachette Book Group, Inc.

The publisher is not responsible for websites (or their content) that are not owned by the publisher.

Forever books may be purchased in bulk for business, educational, or promotional use. For information, please contact your local bookseller or the Hachette Book Group Special Markets Department at special.markets@hbgusa.com.

Library of Congress Cataloging-in-Publication Data

Names: Greer, Helena, author.
Title: For never & always / Helena Greer.
Other titles: For never and always
Description: First edition. | New York : Forever, 2023.
Identifiers: LCCN 2023020941 | ISBN 9781538706558 (trade paperback) | ISBN 9781538706565 (ebook)
Subjects: LCGFT: Romance fiction. | Novels.
Classification: LCC PS3607.R4726 F67 2023 | DDC 813/.6--dc23/eng/20230508
LC record available at https://lccn.loc.gov/2023020941

ISBNs: 9781538706558 (trade paperback), 9781538706565 (ebook)

Printed in the United States of America

LSC-C

Printing 1, 2023

For Joe, who made me believe in fate.
And for all the weird gay kids who grew up
weirder and gayer out of spite.

Content Guidance

This book contains mention of past homophobia as experienced growing up in a small town in the late nineties/early aughts, anxiety that manifests in symptoms similar to agoraphobia and treatment thereof, and grief from the past death of a family member (not on page). I have tried to treat all of these as sensitively and honestly as possible, however, if any of these are pain points for you, please treat yourself with care.

I hereby officially declare a Shenanigan.

PART 1
April

The Carrigan's All Year Calendar

☐ Passover Matzo Ball w/ Rosensteins
☐ Delilah Davenport visit
☐ Tax Help clinic
☐ Miriam's Glitter and (Glue) Guns class
☐ Book Club: *Get a Life, Chloe Brown*

Hannah, Age 7

Hannah Rosenstein was seven when she made her first Big Life Plan: never be separated from Blue Matthews.

The travel trailer that Hannah's parents called home was bumping down a dirt road somewhere in the badlands of Montana. Hannah tried to let herself be lulled by the motion. She was supposed to be sleeping in the back loft bunk, her parents driving through the night to meet a filming deadline on the other side of the dawn. Instead, the pale glow of her cheap flashlight lit the tiny nook just enough to read the xeroxed, stapled newsletter she'd smuggled to bed: the *Carrigan's Christmasland* circular, several months out of date because it had taken a while for it to be forwarded from their PO box.

Hannah's parents—documentarians whose lives were all over the world, wherever there was a story they felt compelled to tell—might have called the trailer home, but to Hannah, her real home was in the Adirondacks, at Carrigan's Christmasland.

Her dad's aunt Cass owned Carrigan's, which was both a tree farm and Christmas-themed inn—an admittedly eccentric career choice for someone in a Jewish family, especially one that made a very comfortable living running a chain of bakeries. Hannah's parents used Carrigan's as a base when they needed to stop somewhere for a while, celebrate the High Holy Days with family, or when Hannah simply got too miserable traveling.

Blue got to live at Carrigan's all year, because his parents, Mr. and Mrs. Matthews, were the handyman and cook there.

It wasn't, Hannah knew, exactly her parents' fault that she hated traveling and only wanted to stay in one place, go to school, make friends, but it wasn't exactly not their fault, either. She wished she loved what her parents loved, but she couldn't.

She smoothed a hand over the cover of the Carrigan's news-letter, the black-and-white print on the front showing Cass, in a turban and swing coat, posing next to a pine tree. She had already read the descriptions of the upcoming events a dozen times. Even if she hadn't, she had the Carrigan's calendar memorized. In the back of her head, whatever was going on, wherever they were in the world, she always knew what they would be doing if they were at Carrigan's, with Blue.

She loved everyone there, Cass, Mr. and Mrs. Matthews and the twins, Blue's younger brother and sister. And her cousins who sometimes visited with her, especially Miriam. But if she were really honest with herself, Blue was the reason she couldn't stop thinking about Carrigan's. He was the only person who always made sure she was having fun.

In the envelope with the circular had been two other pieces of paper: an airplane napkin with Cass's neat block handwriting and a Polaroid with Blue's wild scrawl. The airplane napkin was an old habit of Cass's— she wrote on them when she was flying, tucking them away to send whenever she remembered, often finding them in coat pockets and putting the notes into the mail a year or three after she'd originally penned them.

The Polaroid was not of Blue. It was of a soufflé Blue had baked. She was proud of him, she knew he'd been working on the recipe, but she wished he'd sent a letter with it, or anything to make her feel more like she was there. She barely had any pictures of him and she hadn't seen him for months. Who knew how much taller he was now?

Blue was her best friend, but he was a terrible pen pal. He was always busy. He was always up to shenanigans that were more interesting than writing letters. She, Blue, and her cousin Miriam were a trio when they were all together. They were the ones who'd given him his nickname. His real name was Levi, and when they were little, the girls thought it was funny that he was named after blue jeans. They were all the same age, and they all needed friends. (Technically, Blue was almost a year older than her, but for part of the year, they were all the same age, which was what counted.)

So, the dream team of Hannah, Miriam, and Blue was born. Blue was reckless, Hannah planned everything, and Miriam could turn anything into a scheme, a project, art. Miriam had ideas, Hannah handled logistics, and Levi had no fear.

When they were apart, she was logistics for nobody. She hated it. Her real life blipped on when the trailer drove through the gates of Carrigan's, then back off when she left, and she was always waiting while everyone at the farm was having their real lives all the time.

When she was a grown-up and she got to decide where she lived, she was never going to leave Carrigan's again. Then she would be real all the time. And she was going to redesign the advertising because what was Cass thinking? It was so out-of-date. She was going to get Carrigan's Christmasland with the times.

And she would never go weeks or months without seeing Blue again.

Chapter 1

Levi

I t had been four years and change since Levi Matthews had last crossed the threshold of Carrigan's Christmasland, demarcated by giant filigree wrought-iron gates and by, he'd always suspected, some kind of boundary magic that allowed the pocket dimension of his wayward home to exist slightly out of sync with the outside world. He'd left right after Rosh Hashanah, when the apples were ripening and the woods were leaking the last of summer through their fingers. It was spring now, Passover week, the birdsong a cacophony on the old state highway up to the farm. He lifted his face to feel the sun as he turned his motorcycle off the road and drove up to the gates.

He'd expected to feel a rush of resentment at the sight of the wrought-iron twin *C*'s, the symbol of Cass Carrigan, who was—or had been—the soul of Carrigan's Christmasland. The woman had presided like an empress over this place where he'd grown up, where his family lived but that had felt as often like a prison as like a home. He'd both never meant to stay away this long and never meant to come back. No single thing in his life was as fraught with complications as his feelings about Carrigan's, unless it was his feelings about Hannah, and it was impossible to tell where one ended and the other began.

What he felt instead was a bone-deep sense of readiness as he rode onto the grounds. It was time. He'd gone out into the world, to find and prove himself, destroying the thing that mattered most to him in the process, and he had done it. He'd made himself into something.

He was coming back as a man with a rising career and a sense of self he could never have found in this stifling old inn. He was ready to show everyone who he'd become—well, almost everyone. Cass Carrigan was dead six months now. He'd never be able to show her she'd been wrong about him.

The farm was beautiful against the icy bright sky of the early April day, one hundred sixty acres of evergreens nestled up against Adirondacks National Forest, spread out behind a rambling old Victorian inn squatting picturesquely at the back of a big front lawn. He didn't follow the drive to the front porch, with its big carved wooden doors that led to the foyer and reception desk. Instead, he turned toward the back of the house. To the servants' entrance.

He kicked off the bike he'd borrowed from a chef buddy, because his had been left here when he fled and was now probably long sold. He moved to roll it into the shed behind the kitchens where his dad kept the lawn mowers, but the doors pushed open before he could, a familiar gray head following.

When their eyes met, Levi dropped the bike and his dad dropped the wrench he was holding.

His dad stood looking at him, wary, as if Levi were a feral cat and he was afraid if they got too close, Levi would hiss and run away again. He'd earned that. He'd always been a prickly little shit. He might wish things were different between them, but he had only himself to blame. Just pile his relationship with his dad on the mountain of things he should have done differently.

Levi needed to make the first move, wanted to take away the distance in his dad's eyes, but he was lost.

"Dad," he said. His father nodded, as if in acknowledgment. *Yes, for better or worse, I'm your dad.* Both of his parents were outdoorsy sixty-something silver foxes who looked ten years younger than they were, a matched set out of a Lands' End catalog, but his dad was holding himself a little more stiffly than Levi remembered.

It wasn't as if he hadn't seen his parents' faces in four years. They'd video chatted, and his mom loved Instagram. Since Cass's niece Miriam had moved home last fall, she'd been featuring his parents regularly on Blum Again, Miriam's popular Instagram account for her antique upcycling business. Levi combed through every picture she posted for a glimpse of his parents and his younger twin siblings.

He'd seen them, but it wasn't the same.

His parents were the backbone of Carrigan's, the unit that kept the whole thing ticking along. Mr. and Mrs. Matthews to everyone else, Ben and Felicia to each other, together with Cass, they had *been* Carrigan's for forty years. His mother was the head of the kitchen, his father the jack-of-all-trades, maintenance supervisor…His title changed, but he Fixed Everything. He also managed to be Dad to his own kids and every kid who wandered in off the street.

They were the backbone of Carrigan's, but they were not the owners.

At that thought, the memory of Cass, which was always in the back of his mind, rushed forward so strongly he thought he could hear her laugh and smell her perfume. He gasped her name. Then, shocking himself, he began to weep. His dad broke his stillness, wrapping his arms around Levi tightly. Levi felt a tear drop into his hair.

Had anyone taken time to check on their grief, as they kept feeding people, fixing things, having lost the best friend of their whole lives? He hoped the twins had and hated himself that he had not. If even he, who had hated Cass, was mourning her now, how must they feel?

"How long are you here?" his dad rumbled, his voice vibrating at a frequency in Levi that his body read as "home." He held Levi out at arm's length, gripping his forearms, looking him over.

"How long do you want me?" Levi asked, kicking the gravel, not answering because he didn't have an answer.

"I don't think we're the ones who get to decide," his dad said meaningfully.

"Why not? You're my parents. This is my...where I'm from. Why shouldn't your say be final?" His anger flared, and he was that feral cat, his fur up.

They both knew the answer to whose say was final.

Instead of leaving the Christmasland to his parents, Cass had left it to her nieces Hannah and Miriam, the farm manager Noelle, and, shockingly, to him. So, how long he stayed was up to the people—well, person—who did run Carrigan's these days.

As it had every day of his life, his future lay in the hands of Hannah Rosenstein. His oldest and best friend, the love of his life, the reason his heart beat. The woman who had chosen Carrigan's over a life with him. The woman who'd told him she never wanted to see or speak to him again when he left.

He'd returned to convince her they still belonged together. He'd never stopped loving her, and he was pretty sure she'd never stopped loving him, either. He was going to talk her into leaving this place with him, or letting him stay, whichever he could get, as long as it meant she took him back. He had no idea how he would bear living here, but he knew he couldn't bear to live without her any longer.

His dad cleared his throat. "Well. Whatever you all decide, your mother and I would love to have you for as long as you can stay."

"Aren't you mad at me?" he asked. He knew his dad wasn't happy with the way he'd handled, well, most things, for the past few years.

His dad shrugged. No one could put more meaning into a shrug than Ben Matthews.

"I will have some things to say to you eventually. Right now, I'm going to enjoy having my boy home for Passover. Besides, by the time Hannah's through with you, I figure it will mostly all be said."

Levi's dad pulled his hat off, ran a hand through his hair, put his hat back on. He cleared his throat again. "I'm going to let your mother know you're here. You talk to the girls."

He pointed with his chin toward the door to the kitchen. Levi followed his gaze, then nodded.

"I'll stash your bike," his dad added gruffly, and disappeared.

Alone, Levi brushed the tears from his cheeks and shook snow out of his hair. He gave himself a pep talk. *You can do this, Matthews. Don't be an asshole to anyone for at least five minutes. Ten, if you can manage.* He paused in the doorway to run two fingers over the mezuzah, then kissed them and walked in from the chilly morning into the warm, bright kitchen of his childhood home.

He was met with a wall of cold that rivaled a Siberian midnight.

The woman he loved, his soul made flesh, the person he had missed and yearned for and seen behind his eyelids every moment of every day since he'd left, was standing in front of him, arms crossed over her chest, eyes flashing knives. He took his life into his hands and leaned against the door frame, crossing his legs and grinning at her. (*Great job, Matthews. Ten seconds without being an asshole.*) He could hear her grind her teeth from across the room.

Anger was better than indifference, which was the response he'd feared the most.

He drank in the sight of her, finally here in real life—not just his memory or late-night Instagram binges. Oxygen reached parts of his body he'd forgotten existed. Her hair was piled on top of her head in a messy bun, the kind she wore when she was only with family, not putting on her Manager of the Inn guise. She'd gotten highlights or spent a long time out in the winter sun, because the honey blonde was shot through with lighter streaks than he remembered. Her eyes, in the kitchen light, were the color of whiskey, though they'd be amber in the sunlight and almost yellow in the glow of a fire. She had the most stubborn jaw known to humankind and curves that went on for days and days and days.

She stole his breath.

He noticed, belatedly, that his best friend, Miriam, was also there, standing next to her. On Hannah's other side was his least-best friend, Noelle Northwood. Unlike Hannah and Miriam, Noelle wasn't related to Cass and hadn't grown up coming to Carrigan's. She had shown up one day five years ago and been immediately accepted by Cass in a way Levi had failed to be all his life. She was the Diana to Hannah's Anne Shirley, a dapper butch tree farmer with a grudge against Levi a mile long. The dislike was very mutual.

Noelle's stance mirrored Hannah's, although her shoulders were thrown back, as if she were a bear challenging him at her den. While he'd been gone, the girls' whole world had shifted—they'd lost Cass and saved the farm from bankruptcy. Miriam and Noelle had fallen in love. They'd made an unbreakable unit of three—like he, Miri, and Hannah had once been—and he'd only heard about that unit secondhand.

He was realizing there might not be room for a fourth person in this triangle.

"Hi," he managed to get out, sounding grumpier than he'd intended. He'd meant to say "I'm home," but he'd choked. Something about being here brought out his surly side. Most of his loved ones thought surly was his only side but that was only at Carrigan's.

"It's about fucking time," Hannah said, then turned on her heel and walked away.

That had gone about as well as he could have expected, honestly. He wished Noelle hadn't witnessed it, adding to her ever-expanding list of Reasons Why Levi Was Bad for Hannah, but at this point the list was insurmountable anyway. He looked between Noelle and Miriam.

Kringle, a massive Norwegian Forest cat and extremely rare male tortoiseshell, pushed through the kitchen doors Hannah had just exited, chattering at Levi. He leapt onto Levi's shoulders, wrapping himself like an extra scarf, and chirped again, as if in remonstrance.

"Yes," Levi crooned to him, "I'm sorry I left you, baby. I'm here now."

"That's my cat," Noelle snapped.

Because he was feeling especially raw—and because he loved to fuck with Noelle—he said, "Oh, no, he was always mine, but thank you for cat sitting."

Noelle grimaced, disappointing him by refusing to take the bait and get into the fight he was spoiling for. She turned and left, presumably to follow Hannah.

He scanned the kitchen, which was a beautiful blue delft and in desperate need of upgraded appliances, and waited for the familiar itchy, trapped feeling to wash over him, but it didn't come. As he hung his leather jacket on its old peg and self-consciously fixed his hair, he could feel his ghosts, but as angry as the Ghosts of Levi Past were, the ones in his present had calmed.

Mostly. They were, he had to admit, a little lonely.

In the four years he'd been gone, he'd cooked on cruise ships and yachts, and in street markets around the world, and, most recently, competed on a reality show called *Australia's Next*

Star Chef, which had just begun airing. It had been exactly the life he wanted, filled with food, adventure, friends, and success. Empty of Carrigan's. He hadn't missed this place, but he'd missed his parents and his girl. And though they'd kept in touch, he'd missed Miriam.

Miriam Blum was Levi's oldest friend. She'd spent her child-hood vacations at Carrigan's, before leaving for ten years because of a rift with her parents. She was tiny, looked like a young Cher dressed as a Lost Boy, and had built a cult following for her prowess at upcycling antiques into weird art, like haunted doll heads covered in glitter glue or vanities decoupaged in women's suffrage cartoons. She and Levi had texted, written, and video chatted, but with first her, then him staying far away from Carrigan's, their friendship wasn't the way it used to be.

Miriam threw her arms around him and squeezed tightly. He slid up onto one of the tall bar stools at the kitchen island and patted the one next to her before slumping onto his.

She hopped up. "C'mon, Blue, I want to hear every detail of your life of high adventure as the world's Next Great Famous Chef." She sounded more alive than she had for the past few years. Lighter, more playful.

He groaned, and his head fell back. No one had called him Blue in a long time, unless he counted Miri's texts. It was a name that belonged here, even though he didn't. To the three of them when they'd been a trio. When he, Hannah, and Miriam were kids who were going to love each other forever, no matter what. He'd run away from here to stop being that person, but it was a name that swamped him with memories and he didn't want Miri to give up calling him that, to give up their shared past.

He reached over, pulling a piece of dried glitter glue out of her raucous dark brown curls. She always looked like a half-finished craft project. "I will tell you tales of derring-do, bad and good luck tales," he said, "tales of the high seas! Tales of faraway lands! But first, I need coffee."

She scooted off the high stool until her feet touched the floor and walked around the island to the coffee pot that he suspected, now that she lived here, was always on, and poured him a cup.

"Black?" she asked. "With three or four sugars?"

"I can't help who I am," he said.

She only shook her head at him. From under the counter, she pulled out a plate of dark chocolate–dipped macaroons his mom must have baked for tomorrow.

She set a cookie and the coffee in front of him, then planted her elbows on the counter and her head on her fists.

"Talk."

He skipped all the pleasantries because that's not what Miri was asking him. "What was Cass thinking?" he asked.

"I assume she was trying to get you to come home, since you didn't seem inclined to ever do so without drastic intervention," she said, bopping him on the nose with one finger.

"Hannah told me not to come back. I listened."

"That's a bullshit answer, but here you are," Miriam told him.

"You sent Cole to find me. In Australia. It seemed the least I could do."

Cole was Miriam's other best friend, an amiable blond giant who had usurped Levi's place in her affections. Cole looked like a surfer, dressed like a cast member on *Southern Charm*, and did something maybe illegal with computers. He was incredibly annoying and a little scary, which was how people usually felt about Levi. Levi shook off the thought—he and Cole were nothing alike.

"But you wouldn't have come back if you weren't ready," Miriam pointed out. "So what did he say that made you decide to come home? He never told me his plan."

He cleared his throat, trying to get around the lump that was suddenly there. "He handed me a photo, of the three of us as kids, in snowsuits. Cass called us her heirs on the back of it. I needed to know why. And he said Hannah asked for me to come home."

Miriam kept watching him, head cocked to the side.

"I couldn't keep running from the specter of Carrigan's forever," he said caustically, chugging his coffee. "Besides, the cooking competition I was filming ended, and I didn't have anywhere else I needed to be."

His parents, his demons, and the love of his life were all on this farm. Hannah had sent for him, asked him to come home. And he finally had something to show for himself. So, here he was, sitting in the place he swore he'd never come back to, committed to winning her back. Because he'd seen every corner of the earth, and not a single mile of it was worth a damn without her.

Blue, Age 11

※

I f Hannah were here, she would make him feel better. Even
Miriam would make his mood less bad, although Miriam
wasn't as good at fixing things as Hannah was. It shouldn't
matter that the other sixth-grade boys thought he was weird.
He *was* weird. He lived at the inn instead of in town, he was
always in trouble for some adventure that seemed like a better
idea than school, he was extremely into *Mastering the Art of
French Cooking* (Julia Child was a genius), and he didn't have a
crush on anybody. Why did anyone have a crush on anybody?
They were eleven.

Suddenly this year, all anyone had wanted to talk about
was "who you liked." He could have made something up and
told them he liked Miriam, but he wasn't going to lie about
something that didn't matter.

He kicked the stepladder on his way into the kitchen, then
scowled as he picked it up, because his dad would kill him if he

left it in the middle of the floor. He slammed open the fridge door, grabbing all the ingredients for mole poblano. If they thought him wanting to cook was "gay," then he was going to get better at cooking. And start wearing eyeliner. And burn his khakis.

Because there was nothing wrong with being gay, and even though he didn't *think* he was gay, he sure as hell was not going to try to convince them he wasn't. They wanted to mock him for being who he was and not fitting in? They would get the most obnoxious, over-the-top, not-fitting-in Blue Matthews possible.

The kids in Advent, New York, would think he was an alien by the time he was done.

He slammed his knife down on the cutting board when the kitchen phone rang, but he answered it the way he was supposed to. Not that it mattered, because customers never called this extension, they always called the front desk, but whatever. He didn't need to get his mom in trouble.

"Thank you for calling the Christmasland Inn. How may I direct your call?"

"You said there was an emergency but there can't be an emergency because I called the desk and Cass said you were just being melodramatic," Hannah said, without a hello.

"There *was* an emergency, which is that you and Miriam aren't here and I hate school and no one will go on Shenanigans with me," he said, but as soon as he heard her voice, some of his anxiety lessened. His shoulders relaxed down from his ears.

He didn't need any of the asshole kids at school. He only needed his friends, who actually understood him, and he would be fine.

Except they weren't here.

Miriam was trapped with her shitty parents in shitty Scottsdale, Hannah's parents were filming a documentary about a famous Guatemalan poet, and the only way he could usually talk to either of them was email, but his parents got mad if he tied up the phone lines dialing into AOL, so he could only email at night, and Miriam's dad read her emails so he couldn't say anything real anyway. He was basically alone out here in the middle of nowhere with a bunch of Christmas trees—*which was ridiculous* because they were Jewish, and he would never understand why his parents had stranded them all out here.

If they lived in a city, at least he might meet a couple of kids who weren't small-town rednecks obsessed with how everybody needed to fit into a tiny little box.

"Blue," Hannah asked, "did you zone out? I'm calling long distance from Guatemala City. Could you at least listen to me?"

"Ugh, sorry." He went back to chopping onions, the phone cord stretched out as far as it could go, the old faded pink plastic of the headset tucked under his ear. When were they going to get a cordless phone? Like, they were in the twentieth century. Cass always had to do everything "retro." It wasn't as charming as she thought it was.

"I should let you go, since I'm just being 'melodramatic,'" he continued, making air quotes with the hand that wasn't holding a knife.

"I can see you making air quotes from the other side of the globe, Blue Matthews. I know you're lonely and you hate going to school out there, but like, I don't even get to go to school! I don't even have the opportunity to pretend I want to be like all the other kids, because I don't know any other kids! Try to make friends with someone." Hannah sounded exasperated with him. "Or, I don't know, join an email mailing list with some other cooking nerds or something. I'm working on my parents, trying to convince them to let me do high school at Carrigan's. But in the meantime, I can't call you every time you're lonely. We can't afford the phone bill. You need to try talking to your mom or something. Or your siblings."

"Whatever." Levi shook his bangs out of his eyes. "My parents don't care. They just care if Cass is happy, not if I'm miserable. Which is not even fair, because we're not even family. We're the help."

"I'm not having this fight with you again, Blue. Just because you're not a Rosenstein doesn't mean you're not family. And your parents obviously do care whether or not you're happy. I'm hanging up. I love you," Hannah said, annoyed, her voice getting farther away as she moved the headset from her face. He didn't have time to respond before he heard the click.

The kitchen door swung open. Cass swept through, all silks and jangles and a trail of perfume.

"Are you crying, sweet drama boy?" she asked, walking over and putting an arm around him. They were almost the same height now, and if he hit another growth spurt, he would be taller.

He prickled, a cactus whose spines only came up when he was touched.

"I was chopping onions," he said defensively, turning away to dash a tear off his cheek.

"Can I... do something?" She sounded faintly horrified by the idea.

Why was she always pretending she cared about him? When he was little, he'd believed in her, believed she was like a second mom to him, but he'd heard enough customers treat his parents like servants to know better. When Cass's family was here, except for Miriam, no one paid him any attention, and it was like he was invisible. He might live here, but no one thought of this as his home. He hated being invisible.

"I'm not one of your misfit toys, Cass," he said sullenly. "I don't need you to save me."

"Oh, no, I just meant should I get your mother?" she said uncertainly. She brushed a little flour off his hair, then stuffed her hands into her robe. "If you're going to cook through your preteen emotions, make sure you clean up the kitchen and don't bother the guests." Cass sniffed, floating from the room in her cloud of feathers.

He felt sooooo much better and less lonely now. He rolled his eyes. She wasn't getting any of his mole.

Maybe instead of Hannah coming to Carrigan's, he could meet her parents wherever they were. He could cook for their production crew. Maybe they could all travel together. Then he could have Hannah with him all the time *and* never be stuck here.

Chapter 2

Hannah

Hannah was proud of herself. She'd handled seeing Blue again beautifully. She'd gotten in the last word, and there was no way he'd seen her shaking. But why did he have to be here? Just because she'd specifically asked him to come home and had in fact sent someone to find him?

And why did he have to look so unholy hot? It was like his entire being radiated hormones her body always responded to, no matter what her brain was saying.

She'd locked herself in her room, in the middle of a workday, under a tent of blankets, and was now repeating to herself over and over that she'd handled that really well. Her breathing was slowly returning to normal. She could feel her fingers again. Unwrapping her bun, she shook out her hair and wrapped it again, moving slowly and intentionally.

Levi had loved her hair. He'd spread it under his hands and over his pillow, playing with it mindlessly while they talked and getting tongue-tied when she took out her ponytail or her braid after a long day and brushed it all the way down her back. Since he'd left, she'd grown it out. She kept meaning to cut it short to spite him, but something in her obstinate, hopeful heart stopped her. She wanted to be able to break his heart and stop his breath, still, if it ever came to that. If he ever came home. And now he had.

She looked around at the room she'd completely redesigned since he left, so it held no trace of the life they'd built inside it, together. Her little tower. She'd had to make the space unrecognizable in order to breathe. She could have changed rooms, certainly. She lived in a hotel; there were several to choose from. She could have taken over Cass's old rooms when she died, or Noelle's when she moved with Miriam to the carriage house. But she didn't want to show weakness, to herself or anyone else. She didn't want to admit that every part of her missed him every day, even while she built this beautiful new life that brought her so much joy.

Suddenly, her best friend was banging on her door, demanding she be let in. *Ugh.*

"It's open," she yelled, scooting over in bed to give Noelle a place to sit. Noelle was a fat, dapper butch, often in flannel and suspenders and currently wearing a short-sleeved button-down with a ladybug pattern. Her auburn hair swooped up in a pompadour and her head was shaved on the sides. She kicked off her work boots at the door to expose neon yellow taco cat socks.

Noelle was the love of Miriam's life but she had been Hannah's best friend in the universe first.

"I brought a lot of ibuprofen," Noelle said. Hannah guessed she could forgive the intrusion. "I figured you were going to get a crying headache, and we should get in front of it.

"I also brought your planner up from your office, because I thought you might be feeling the urge to organize your day to within the minute, and I didn't want you to have to run across him on your way to get it." Noelle handed her the journal stuffed with color-coded flags.

Hannah hugged it to her chest. It would be better if she had her laptop so she could update her spreadsheets, but this would do.

"I love you," Hannah said, leaning over to touch her forehead to Noelle's. "You are my platonic soulmate and I could not live without you."

"I know," Noelle told her, kissing her forehead. "Do you want to talk about it?"

"Nope nope nope noooooooope, a world of nope. I am that gif of the nope octopus. I am only made of nope." Hannah shook her head. Noelle might be her number one person, but Levi...Levi was off-limits.

He wasn't off-limits to only Noelle. She never talked about him with *anyone*.

When she was younger, being in love with him was a secret she'd kept from everyone, him most of all. When they'd gotten together, their relationship was so precious, they wanted something that was just theirs, without Cass, the Matthewses, and everyone else in their lives inserting their opinions. Miriam had already stopped coming to Carrigan's by then and never knew they'd been in love until she came back last year. She and Levi had been chaotic at best, on the verge of falling apart, when Noelle moved to Carrigan's. Then he left and Noelle picked up all the pieces of Hannah's heartbreak, so she'd never really seen them happy together either.

No one here had, except for the Matthewses. It wouldn't be fair to dump her feelings about their son on them, so she'd kept the whole of it—the years of longing, the overwhelming out-of-control roller coaster of their relationship, the way she missed him—locked inside. She and Levi were an island nation, trapped in a civil war, and the only person who understood the scope of the casualties was the one person she couldn't talk to about it.

Noelle nudged her gently, interrupting Hannah's thoughts. "Do you want me to stoke your fire, then sit with you and go over all the things you could be doing today that would leave you too busy to see or talk to your ex?"

"Yes. That is what I want," Hannah declared, opening her planner on the blankets in front of her.

There was another knock, the pattern—two short knocks followed by three quick ones—that Miriam had been using since they were four years old.

"Your girlfriend doesn't believe I should be alone to wallow," Hannah complained.

"You're not alone, you drama queen, I'm here," Noelle said, ruffling Hannah's hair. "She's probably worried about you."

"She's probably worried about him," Hannah grumbled unfairly.

Miriam didn't wait for an invitation, just stuck her head inside, then slipped through.

"Babe," she said, her hands on the hips of her overalls, "what's happening here?"

"She's not talking about it," Noelle told Miriam.

"Is she leaving her room today to finish up preparations?" Miriam asked curiously.

"She's not," Hannah said, giving in to impulse and pulling her blanket over her head.

"I'm sorry, Hannah Naomi Rosenstein, are you missing work because your ex-boyfriend is in the same hotel as you?" Miriam was incredulous. "Nan, this is *Blue*. You're going to be hiding for the rest of your life."

She peeked out to glare at her tiny, paint-spattered cousin. "You know that I don't like it when my plans get upended."

Miriam laughed, folding herself into a chair by the fireplace. "I do know that about you, yes."

"Well, I always planned that Blue and I would take over Carrigan's together, but unfortunately while I was doing that, he was planning our great escape together, so it all exploded a bit."

Noelle snorted. "A bit."

Hannah stuck her tongue out but kept going. "Then I assumed I would inherit Carrigan's myself—"

"Because you had been running the entire inn side of the business for several years," Noelle supplied.

"Right, and because Cass explicitly told me I would. And then you came along, and you were the best farm manager in the world—"

"*Were*, past tense?" Noelle teased.

"Stop interrupting me when I'm trying to be honest about my feelings!" Hannah cried, and hit her best friend with a decorative pillow. "You were going to be my Blue, but better, because you're, you know, not Levi. The two of us were going to usher in a Carrigan's for a whole new generation."

"And then I screwed everything up," Miriam said, smiling.

"And then you made everything whole," Hannah countered. When Cass had left part of Carrigan's to Miriam, it had been a surprise, but a perfect one. Miriam and Noelle fell in love, she and Hannah renewed their sisterhood, and she brought new business and new creativity to the Christmasland. The old Carrigan's had been focused solely on Christmas-related business, not utilizing either the inn or the farm outside those few months, and business had been failing as the older, once-devoted guests had slowly stopped coming.

They'd taken a bold risk and launched Carrigan's All Year to save the business they all loved—hosting all kinds of events year-round to bring in a new generation of guests. Now they hosted weddings and summer hikes and Purim carnivals, and everything in between.

She, Noelle, and Miriam had worked their asses off, and the past six months had been chaotic, with windfalls coming right as roofs fell in, all of them leapfrogging from potential catastrophe to potential income stream with no time to rest. It had been thrilling but also left her constantly feeling like she was on the knife's edge of failure, about to lose everything she'd ever worked for.

"But we know all this," Miriam said. "What does it have to do with Blue?"

"Well," she continued, "we were finally starting to get our sea legs, and then here he is."

"Hannah"—Miriam pointed at her—"you *asked* him to come back."

Hannah scowled. "Only because we have legal business we need to take care of. He owns part of *our* farm, and I want it back."

"I'm sure that's totally the only reason," Noelle grumbled.

Her friends were so mean to her.

Miriam sighed. "Okay, can I circle us back around to the key point that, even if he didn't own the business, and even if you were totally over him, unless you're planning to fire Mr. and Mrs. Matthews, kick them out of their rooms, and ban the twins, you're never going to be rid of Levi Blue. Whether he wants to or not, he belongs to this place as much as you or any of us."

"I would die before I fired the Matthewses," Hannah objected.

"Obviously," Miriam agreed.

Mr. and Mrs. Matthews were the closest thing she had to stable parents, her adoptive aunt and uncle, who—unlike her parents—always lived in the same place, knew where they were going to be tomorrow, and never made major life decisions on a whim.

Cass had been her lodestone, her greatest fan, her inspiration, but the Matthews family was her home, as much as anything was. Joshua and Esther, their twins, were the siblings she'd always wanted. Levi was something else. She knew she could never be rid of him. No amount of organizing, or planning, or arranging her life could excise Levi Blue Matthews. They'd known each other all their lives.

She didn't know when she'd fallen in love, or when he had. They'd tried to trace their feelings back, and both had loved the other years before they'd ever admitted it. When Miriam had left them alone, Hannah and Levi had, without a buffer, with nothing to stop them from tumbling headfirst into certain disaster, done the only thing they could do—they'd fallen wildly, intensely, outrageously in love. They'd almost destroyed each other.

"Wait," Hannah said, suddenly realizing something. "What the hell is he doing while we're in here? Did you leave him to run loose in the inn?"

"I put him in the back cottage," Noelle told her. "The one where we put guests we don't actually want to talk to."

This was true. It's where they'd put Miriam's former fiancée, Tara, last year, right before they broke up.

"Right now he's helping his mom kasher the kitchen," Miriam said. "He tried to go on a whole rant about how obviously none of us considered how much work it would be for Mrs. Matthews to have all the Orthodox cousins here for seder, but Mrs. Matthews told him to shut up and clean something."

They were preparing for slightly more than one hundred extended Rosensteins to descend on Carrigan's for the first night of Passover tomorrow. Every corner had been ruthlessly cleaned, the sheets turned down, the mantels dusted. The great room they used as an event space and overflow dining was hung with navy blue bunting, wound through with tiny twinkling gold lights. Ferns draped over the massive curving staircase that led up to a landing, off of which branched the first floor of rooms. Tablecloths in blue, white, and gold had been laid out with the best china, the napkins elaborately folded.

It wasn't Christmas at Carrigan's, which was always a spectacle of kitsch. It was, instead, beautifully elegant.

Having the whole family for Passover had, ostensibly, been Hannah's idea, although it had been planted, fertilized, and watered by many aunts and uncles in the months since New Year's Eve once it became clear Hannah, Miriam, and Noelle would be able to keep Carrigan's afloat. The family wanted to celebrate Hannah and Miriam, see their vision for the new Carrigan's All Year, and be together for the holy days.

There were last-minute details to attend to, but she could

do them from her bed, with her door locked against the love of her life. And that's what she was going to do, as soon as she kicked everyone else out.

She woke up the next morning, having slept only in the most technical definition, with a very specific kind of hangover. The "please knock me unconscious so I can escape my own brain" kind, despite Noelle's ibuprofen. She was mad at everyone who didn't have an ice pick piercing their temple.

This day was going to go swimmingly.

A perk of managing an inn with full breakfast service that stocked only pastries from your family's famous bakery was you could order a perfect latte and bagel delivered to your room every morning. Normally she got a toasted whatever-the-guests-hadn't-wanted with schmear. This morning, what showed up outside her door was her perfect breakfast, her celebration bagel. Lightly toasted everything, with scallion cream cheese, whisper-thin-sliced onion, fresh tomato, lox, and capers. She burst into tears. Mrs. Matthews loved her so much, even after she'd broken the woman's oldest son's heart and driven him across the world.

With breakfast came Kringle. Technically he lived in the carriage house with Miriam and Noelle, because he was A Lot for the guests, but in reality he showed up where he felt he was needed. This morning he curled up with his giant head on her knee while she sat up in bed with her breakfast. She ate it, one slow bite at a time, the salmon melting on her tongue, and let her mind go blank.

He was somewhere outside her door. They needed to have a conversation, at least one, and it was probably going to be the most difficult one of her life. She reminded herself how happy she was now without him. She was doing work that showcased her skills and stretched her talents, kept her on her toes. If she stayed up every night imagining his face, if she couldn't hear his name without flinching, if some part of her existed only in suspended animation so her heart would not crumble to nothing, well, what of it? People survived heartbreak every day.

When she was as ready as she was going to get, she put on her favorite dress, a green wool wrap that made her feel invincible, and a lot of waterproof mascara. Noelle texted her that the coast was clear because Levi was "apparently on some kind of business call with his agent, which is the most asshole thing I've ever heard."

Knowing he wasn't in the kitchen, she dropped in to check on Mrs. Matthews, who was prepping enough potato kugel and charoset for an army.

"Just a sec, Ziva," Mrs. Matthews said into the phone as Hannah walked in. She'd been on the phone with Miriam's mom for days, trying to decide on recipes, quantities, and seating placements.

Her hand over the receiver, she said to Hannah, "Are you here to take the patented Hannah Rosenstein fine-tooth comb to my spread?"

Hannah knew she was joking, but she winced a little. Sometimes the line between getting everything right and anxious micromanaging blurred.

"You know there's no one I trust more than you—" she began.

Mrs. Matthews waved her off. "I know you, kiddo. And

this is a big night for you! You're allowed to be anxious. Even without my most troublesome progeny."

"I've just never hosted Passover," Hannah said, blowing out a breath, her shoulders relaxing a little, "much less for everyone I'm even tangentially related to. My parents used to go to whichever Rosenstein relative invited us when we were in the country."

"And when Cass was sick, we started making everything smaller," Mrs. Matthews murmured.

Hannah didn't say, although Mrs. Matthews knew, that she'd also slowly stopped going any farther afield than Advent because she had panic attacks if she left Carrigan's for too long.

"Remember last year when Noelle dragged the table all the way up the stairs and we set up seder next to Cass's bed?" Mrs. Matthews smiled sadly.

"The best seder of my life," Hannah said. "Cass got drunk on one glass of wine because of her meds and gave an impassioned anti-imperialist rant through her coughs."

Mrs. Matthews reached over, squeezing her shoulder. "You did good, taking care of her. I know what it cost you."

Hannah shook her head. "It cost me nothing. It was the greatest honor of my life. I would not have missed it for anything."

"Let's do this thing Big in her honor, yes?" Mrs. Matthews said, returning to her phone call.

"Go Big!" Hannah agreed, and left her to her cooking. What Go Big meant was rather than having any old giant seder for a huge extended family that involved Jews from across the religious spectrum, from Modern Orthodox to Reconstructionist, they were turning First Seder into a Matzo Ball. A full fancy-dress event. Throwing events was her job, so she shouldn't be nervous, but she was.

She was hyperaware that Levi was in the building some-where; the hairs on her arms rose with the anticipation that he might come around any corner. They hadn't seen each other since last night. At some point they would have to speak *some* words to each other. In theory, it would be easier before her family got here, but she wasn't brave enough yet, so she was avoiding him. She didn't want to keep him from his mom, or vice versa, so she slinked to the great room.

Just as she was pulling the measuring tape out of her work apron to triple-check that the bows she'd hung on the walls were exactly evenly spaced, her family showed up, en masse, loud, enthusiastic, chaotic, and vying for her attention. Having all the Rosensteins in one place for Passover meant, naturally, Hannah's parents were also going to be there. They'd been here for Cass's funeral, although Hannah had been so busy with everything else, she'd barely spent time with them. They were good people, who adored her and wanted nothing more than for her to be happy.

And she was mostly not mad at them.

She was mostly not mad about the years she spent travel-ing and hopping from school to school or being sporadically homeschooled. About how their inability to stay put had left her with an insurmountable need to stay rooted as an adult. If she'd had some roots to start out with, maybe the idea of leaving Carrigan's for any length of time wouldn't send her into a panic spiral. She was mostly not mad at her parents about it, because they hadn't done it on purpose, but she *was* a little salty.

When her mother, Rachel, disembarked from their Air-stream, she swept Hannah into her arms and began a monologue about their travels that—as far as Hannah could follow—took up exactly where they'd driven off six months ago after Cass's funeral.

"How are you, sweet girl?" her mom asked, holding Hannah's face in both hands. Hannah looked down at her mom, trying to decide how much to say.

"Blue's here" was what she went with, and hoped it was adequate.

When Levi left, Hannah didn't want to bother her parents or make them feel obligated to come back to Carrigan's to take care of her, so she'd made up a polite fiction about their breakup.

Her parents both adored and were exasperated by Levi in equal measure. She imagined them telling her she'd overreacted, that this was "just another Blue Shenanigan." Most of all, since her parents made their life traveling the world, she'd been afraid they would take his side rather than understanding hers. She told herself she was being the bigger person by not poisoning his relationship with them, but that wasn't entirely true.

She was rarely the bigger person where Levi Blue was concerned.

Her mom raised an eyebrow and patted Hannah's cheek. "Oh," she said.

She knew Rachel suspected a great deal, but they'd never acknowledged out loud there was more to talk about. Now—when they were surrounded by their entire family, in the hallway of her business—seemed the wrong time to break down sobbing in her mother's arms because the boy who'd broken her heart had come back and she had more feelings about it than she wanted to.

As they walked into the great room, Miriam rushed forward to hug her aunt. Hannah smiled at them.

Her father's voice boomed out over all the family din. "LEVI."

She looked up to find Levi looking at them, frozen in place. Their eyes met and she had to plant her feet to stop herself from walking straight into his arms.

When he'd walked into the kitchen yesterday, her body had responded to his nearness, she'd been enveloped with his essence, but she had been too busy keeping her voice steady to really see him. Now she saw him.

He was exactly the same, but so much different. He was deeply tan, and unmistakably closer to forty than thirty years old (what was time, even). He was standing up straight. His shoulders were, if not relaxed, not hunched in on themselves. Sometime in the past four years, he'd stopped holding himself like he was always waiting for someone to stab him. She hadn't even consciously realized that's what he'd been doing until now.

She watched him do a mental inventory and wince almost invisibly. He touched his hair, which was so high it was almost its own zip code. When he ran his hands over it, her scalp remembered the feeling of his fingers in her own hair, and she shivered. He lightly touched his argyle sweater vest, then his leggings, and lastly his not one but *two* oversized scarves.

She wished she couldn't still read the smallest change in his face and posture. She wished she didn't still find him so unrelentingly sexy. He'd always taken his clothes seriously, and he'd never dressed like anyone else in the little town of Advent, where he'd gone to school all his life. Black kohl eyeliner, leather jackets, an androgynous vibe that when mixed with his beautiful face seemed to say he was vastly too chic for small-town life and belonged somewhere cosmopolitan enough to appreciate him.

She'd appreciated him, more than any boy she'd seen in any corner of the world she'd visited.

He'd been a prickly child, serious and easily bruised, prone to transforming into a cactus rather than be vulnerable around people he didn't feel were worthy of witnessing his joy. She watched him mask his face now, put on a polite façade that was new. Blank, rather than scowling. Ironically, Levi *had* been mad at her parents for not giving her a more stable home growing up. For someone whose insatiable wanderlust had driven him from her life, she felt it was a precarious stance to take, but Levi lived on a knife's edge of hypocrisy.

Having gotten his face under control, straightening his vest and poufing his hair, he approached her parents. Her father wrapped him tightly in his arms, perhaps squeezing a little harder than necessary.

"Daniel," he croaked, from inside the hug. "Chag Sameach."

"I'm glad you're back," her dad boomed, as if he himself had been anything that could, even generously, be described as "back" since Levi left. "You belong here."

Levi stiffened. She remembered every rant he'd ever gone on, about how Carrigan's wasn't his destiny, that it was simply an accident of birth. About how he belonged in a city, in Europe, in a bustling kitchen learning from the world's greatest chefs. Of course, he'd been a fourteen-year-old snob, but the twenty-four-year-old resentful about being "trapped" out here in the middle of nowhere and the thirty-year-old who'd wanted to see the world hadn't been that different. All he said, though, was "You might be the only person who believes that."

"Nonsense," Daniel Rosenstein said, "Cass thought so."

"How long do we keep making decisions based on what Cass

wanted?" Levi asked, an edge to his voice. Ah, there was the Levi she knew, always ready to disparage Cass at any opportunity.

Cass, who had saved her life, given her a home, mentored her. Cass, whose last days she'd chosen to witness when it meant losing him. Cass, who she'd had to wake up without every day for six months now.

"Well, the girls moved the earth to make Cass's vision happen for Carrigan's," her dad pointed out.

"Everyone always did move heaven and earth at the whim of the great Cassiopeia Carrigan." Levi's voice didn't sound bitter, as she was so used to, just tired.

"We're going to talk more about this," her father told him, "as soon as I spend some time with my girls. Miriam and I have a lot of catching up to do."

He clapped Levi on the back, then walked off arm in arm with her cousin.

She shook off the feeling she always had near Blue—that he was sucking all the oxygen out of her life and all she could do was watch from the sidelines. Since the moment she'd realized she loved him, a part of her brain had portioned itself off, assigning itself the full-time job of Thinking About Levi. The moment they'd gotten together, that portion had taken over the rest of her brain. Their relationship had swallowed her whole, consuming her selfhood in the hunger of their love.

When he'd left, it had taken her years to get her sense of self back. The part of her that Thought About Levi had spent four years wandering around like a gothic ghost and she didn't have time for it right now. There was family to check into rooms and a Matzo Ball to throw. The Rosensteins, the big family she and Miriam came from, had invested in their idea for Carrigan's All Year when it had looked like they would lose the business. She wanted to prove it had been the right call. They were throwing a seder like none they'd ever seen, and she needed everything to go exactly to plan. Which nothing ever did when Levi was involved.

By early evening, the Ball was in full swing. Seder began at sunset, which wasn't until almost eight o'clock, so there was plenty of time for socializing. Silk and taffeta and satin swished through the Carrigan's great room in a luscious song, cousins and aunts and uncles as far as the eye could see. She'd been offered management positions at Rosenstein's Bread and Pastries by four different relatives tonight. Every time she looked up to find Levi watching her, she almost considered taking them up on it.

She bristled. She, Noelle, and Miriam had slain dragons to keep Carrigan's, and no one was going to drive her out, especially not Levi Blue Matthews. He might look delicious in an emerald satin smoking jacket with matching yarmulke, cigarette pants, and smudged eyeliner, but he wasn't looking delicious *for her*. He was here to settle business. Carrigan's was an annoying stop for him on his skyrocketing career and she wasn't interested in his deliciousness. She was absolutely not going to climb him like a lanky green tree, even if her hormones felt otherwise.

He must have seen the heat in her eyes because he stole toward her through the crowd, leaning down to whisper in her ear. "You can't look at me with those eyes, Hannah. It gives me ideas. Ditching all these people and finding a quiet place to be alone kind of ideas. Which I would support, but we should probably have a conversation first."

Four years, a couple of continents, one dead matriarch, thousands of tears, and the shattered remains of her heart lay between this moment and the last time they'd spoken to each other, unless you counted yesterday's five-word exchange, and this was what he chose to open with. As if they were picking up where they'd left off, except where they'd left off was her telling him to never come home again. As if he could just turn her on and they could forget everything else.

That's how they'd always handled things before. Relying on their physical connection to say the things they couldn't find the words for.

She deliberately kept her gaze over his shoulder, refusing to meet his eyes. She thought about lying to him, but it would never work. It never had; he knew her too well.

"We're not having sex or a conversation, Blue," she said through gritted teeth. "I don't know why you're here, but we're going to celebrate our peoples' freedom from bondage, then we're going to ignore each other until you leave again, and then I will be personally free from the bondage of you."

"You don't know why I'm here? Really?" he growled in her ear, low enough that no one else could hear, sending goose bumps down her spine. "I'm here for you. To fix things with you. And I'm not leaving again until we've settled things between us. With sex or a conversation, preferably both."

She was going to ignore how he was whispering in her ear that he wanted her back, because if she acknowledged he'd said it, she would never get through this night.

"Go talk to your siblings, Levi. They haven't seen you for four years." She gestured to where the twins were chatting with some of her cousins.

"They hate me." He pouted.

"So do I," Hannah pointed out. "But Esther and Joshua are not trying to throw a massive event at their place of business, so they can deal with you for a while."

"We're not done," he said, and walked away.

Of course they weren't. She'd told herself they were. But then he'd walked through the door, with his long lithe legs, swooping hair, and sexy beard, and shattered her careful illusions. She'd missed him every moment, even as she'd been praying to never see him again. Everything about him still set her nerves on edge, made her feel like the volume on her life had been turned up to eleven.

She shook her head, trying to dislodge him. He'd been living rent-free in there for far, far too long. No, they weren't done, but she couldn't think about that now. This was an event, and she was in charge.

She went to find her cousin, so they could get everyone seated.

She didn't find Miriam, who'd been carried off under a wave of matchmaking aunts wanting to know if they could help plan her wedding to Noelle, although they weren't yet engaged. Hannah could have saved Miriam, but she suspected Miriam had been waiting for this kind of familial attention all her life and was basking in it. Miriam's dad had been emotionally abusive and had kept her away from the Rosenstein relatives. It was only since she'd come back to Carrigan's last year that she'd been able to reconnect with them.

Instead, she found Noelle.

"I need you to distract me from obsessing about Blue," she told her best friend.

Noelle raised an eyebrow. "How is this night different from all other nights?"

"Did you just make a Passover joke?" Hannah was both delighted and distracted. "NoNo, I'm so proud of you!"

"Your cousin Ephraim is hoarding a bottle of Manischewitz, your aunt Talia wants to know who's single, and the younger kids got into the stash of Cass's boas, so there are pink feathers all over the floor. I feel we should eat," Noelle told her. "Is that distraction enough?"

"That's exactly what I expected to happen. And eating? Oh, honey, you've only ever been to reform seders, haven't you? We're not going to eat for several hours." Hannah laughed when Noelle's eyes went wide.

"Sometimes I wish I could still drink," Noelle muttered, wandering off to round everyone up so they could begin seder. She wasn't serious; Noelle had been sober for more than a decade, but Hannah understood how her family could make someone feel that way if you weren't used to them.

Eventually everyone was seated, and the seder began. The Haggadah they read from had been passed down through generations of Rosensteins. The youngest cousin had learned to read since last year, so it was her first time reading the questions. She had obviously been practicing and just as obviously had a flair for the dramatic.

She stood up on her chair, cleared her throat for silence, and asked in her biggest five-year-old voice, "WHY on THIS NIGHT do we RECLINE?"

Then she almost fell off the chair trying to act out reclining.

After, the plagues went on seemingly forever. She could see Noelle starting to fidget in her chair. Hannah hid her giggle behind a napkin.

"Stop laughing at me!" Noelle whispered. "Let my people go!"

Ziva, Miriam's mother, kicked them both under the table to get them to behave, which only made them giggle even harder.

It made her heart feel a peace she could only have in her community, practicing her faith.

As soon as everyone was bundled into bed, exhaustion hit her and she stole into the library to be alone.

She curled up in a big armchair, humming "Dayenu" to herself, barefoot in her ballgown, and closed her eyes to let herself reset. When she shifted, matzo crunched underneath her. It was the afikomen, which had gone unfound. Rain pounded against the windows, beating a heartbeat of the mountains, and Hannah found herself weeping along with the rain.

She didn't cry often, because it wasn't productive, and she was usually too angry for it, but sometimes it was the only way to clear everything out. She wept quietly at first, then louder, her body racked with sobs. For surviving Passover without Cass's overly dramatic version of "Chad Gadya," for the loneliness of being in the same house—the same room—with the love of her life, her oldest friend, but not being able to hold him, brush the hair out of his eyes, kiss his forehead.

She wept out of frustration for how much her body still wanted him, no matter what she told herself.

She didn't hear the door open over the rain, so when Levi appeared in front of her, kneeling down and cupping her face, it was as if she'd summoned him out of her thoughts. She didn't pause to remember who they were now. His face was inches from hers, and his hands were touching her, so she did what she'd done a thousand times before, as if by muscle memory.

She closed the distance between their mouths and kissed him.

He tasted like macaroons, and his beard was fuller than she remembered, but his lips were hers. Instantly, magnetically, their bodies were fused from head to toe. He was picking her up out of the chair, swooping under her and settling her in his lap before she even understood what was happening.

"Don't stop touching me," she breathed frantically against his mouth.

"What makes you think I could?" he groaned, his hands pushing the velvet of her dress up past her thighs.

"Oh, I don't know, the past four years?" she asked.

Levi grabbed her face. "Hannah," he growled, "I love you, but please, shut up."

She did shut up then, because his mouth was on hers, his hands were under her dress, and he'd told her he loved her as if it were nothing, as if this was not world-shattering information. As if, to his mind, loving her was as obvious as the sun rising.

She shut up because every thought had been driven from her head by his mouth.

This felt inevitable, building since the moment he'd walked in that kitchen door and leaned against the door frame, snow in his hair and fire in his eyes. The only possible end to them being in the same house again. No matter that they couldn't fix what was between them with sex, her body wouldn't believe that truth.

As long as he was touching her, the loss of him wasn't exploding inside her. A temporary cease-fire in the never-ending blitz of their breakup that was always bombarding her under the surface of her life.

She shoved his suit jacket off, pulling his shirt open, desperate to get her hands on his bare skin. If she could touch him, all of him, one last time, maybe . . . Aw, fuck, she didn't know what the end of that maybe was, except maybe she would feel different than she felt right now.

"I can hear your mind working, Hannah," Levi rasped in Hannah's ear as she lay in his arms after, staring out the window. "You're going to tell me that this was a mistake, and it never happened, and we're never speaking of it again."

Hannah was already getting off his lap and gathering her clothes, distancing herself, putting her armor back on.

"Why are you here, Blue?" She was so tired.

"You sent a giant blond man to Australia to find me, presumably to deal with the mess that Cass left when she gave me a portion of the business. You asked me to come home. I came."

Hannah held her dress in front of her, her arms crossed. "You've never done anything for another person in your life, Levi Matthews. You didn't do this for me, so what are you getting out of it? The truth, just like, two sentences of truth, for once in our lives."

"I made it. I have a show coming out, offers from TV producers for more work. I did what I set out to do. I made my dreams into a real career. I wanted to show you. I wanted to show *all of you* what I made myself into." He growled out "all of you," too much weight for those three small words.

"What are you even talking about?" She threw her hands up, irritated, and her dress dropped. Oh well, it was too late for modesty anyway. "You sound like you were trying to prove us all wrong about you, but who didn't believe in you? Me? Miri? Your *parents*? The twins? No, you know what? I don't want to know what fucked-up thing you've decided to believe in your head. You're not my responsibility anymore, and I'm happier not knowing you."

"Are you, Hannah? Because I'm not happier not knowing you. I'm not happier not having you in my life. I'm pretty fucking miserable, actually, if I'm being dead honest." He leaned forward to try to take her hand, but she moved away. He flopped backward in the chair.

"I'm not happy, no." She took a rattling deep breath. "I haven't been happy in four years, except in brief tiny flashes, and I'm angry as fuck about that. I'm so mad at you I want to scream all the time, that you left me here to Miss Havisham my way around this house while everyone who loves me tiptoes around me, careful not to say your name lest they upset my fragile balance."

She tugged on her hair, and bobby pins scattered around the room, curls falling out of her updo and down her forehead. She blew one out of the way. "Why can't you set me free, Blue?"

He looked up at her, tears smudging his eyeliner, his hair wild from her hands. "Because you're my wife, and I want our marriage back."

Chapter 3

Levi

Before, when he'd found her, she'd been weeping, but now she was furious, like a dam had broken on words she'd been stuffing down for years, and there were no tears at all.

"I'm not 'your wife.' I'm Hannah Naomi Rosenstein, my entire own human being. You have become the main character in the story of my life, Blue, and I hate it. I want to be the main character in my own damned life."

His heart broke, again. More, somehow, which seemed impossible. This righteous fury that crackled from her like an ancient goddess, he'd caused this.

He was home, having finally made something of himself, found himself. He wasn't the old Blue, a wrecking ball in the lives of the people who loved him while he worked out his misery. He was ready to fix everything between them. Maybe it was too late, and she was ready to walk away. But he couldn't let her, at least not without a fight.

"You're the center of the story of my life, Hannah. That's who we are. We're fucking tattooed on each other's souls."

"So what?" she asked him, her hands on her hips. "So we're tattooed on each other's souls. Who fucking cares? You think no one's ever gotten a tattoo they regret? It doesn't make us less of a destructive garbage fire, Blue. You have to have a better reason for us to try again."

He scrubbed his hands down his beard, then stood up so they were facing each other. "You asked me to leave and I left, but that made you more angry. What do you want? Me to leave your life forever? I can't. My parents are here. I'm not exiling myself again."

"I want you to call Elijah." Elijah Green was their lawyer, friend, and the best Scrabble player in the state. A tall, thin Black man with an impressive collection of argyle sweater vests, a stunningly beautiful husband, and very cute twins, Elijah was one of the people Levi found least objectionable in all of Advent. But right now, the sound of his name filled Levi with dread. "Ask him to transfer your shares to me, Miriam, and Noelle."

She stepped up so they were toe to toe and looked him right in the eyes. "And tell him to draw up divorce papers."

Her eyes flashed in the dark, like she was daring him to argue with her. Never let it be said that Blue Matthews backed down from a dare from his wife.

"Hell no," he growled.

"What are you talking about?" She gestured, waving her dress, her voice unbelieving. "We haven't spoken in four years. We may be legally married, but we're not married in any way that counts. No one knows we're married because for some reason it seemed like a *great* idea to keep it a secret from our family and friends. Just sign the papers and let us all move on with our lives."

"New York is a single-party divorce state, Nan," he pointed out. "You could have filed any time you wanted, without my signature, but you didn't. I don't want a divorce, and neither do you. And you could have told everyone you know. Don't blame me for that bad decision."

She wasn't giving him a chance to show her that he was finally someone who deserved her, and it pissed him off. They'd been figuring their lives out, but their road was always going to lead back to each other. The thought of getting a divorce made him want to vomit. He couldn't do it.

"I don't give a fuck what Cass wanted, and I wouldn't care if Carrigan's burned to the ground, but I'm keeping my shares until you agree to figure this out. Give me a chance to prove I've changed."

"You're proving to me right now that you haven't," she told him.

"I'm not giving you a divorce. Our story isn't over." He spat this out and watched her eyes narrow.

"Fuck you, Levi Blue," she said, shoving her arms back into her ballgown and slamming out the door.

Even for him, legendary screwup, that had gone poorly.

The next day, Miriam told him that his mother would love his help. He assumed this was Miri's attempt at getting him out of the way, since his mom would greatly prefer he stayed out of her kitchen while she was cooking because he was, she said, nitpicky and dictatorial and didn't know what he was talking about.

But he found himself wanting her company, the comfort of prepping mise en place, to be somewhere that didn't rub his skin raw and make him want to snarl at innocent passersby, or his in-laws. The kitchen at Carrigan's was the first place he'd ever felt at home in his skin, and he needed that grounding. It was ironic, because he'd always been so angry that Cass relegated his mom to the kitchen, made her the help instead of a partner, but given a choice of being anywhere in the inn, that's where he would always choose to be first. Even more, he needed his mom.

"Hey, Mom," he said. "Can I hide in here? I can chop or wash dishes. I promise I won't try to take over your duck."

His mom looked at him for a long minute, her silver hair swooping over her forehead in a way that looked exactly like his own. He could feel her assessing him and hoped he wasn't coming up too wanting.

"You have a matzo ball soup recipe you've been working on, right? Kind of Spanish-inspired flavors? You emailed me about it last year. You can make it, as long as you don't make your matzo balls too dense."

He was too stunned to argue with her that fluffy matzo balls were an abomination.

"You would let me make the matzo ball soup?" he whispered, floored.

"Well, you're here, aren't you? How often do we get a TV chef here to cook for our seder?"

She could brush it off, but this wasn't a small deal. Even

when she had been planning to turn over her position to him, when he and Hannah were together, she'd never let him cook something as foundational as this. She always said he was too focused on making an already perfect thing fancy, and he never knew how to let well enough be.

She wasn't wrong.

He unwound his scarf and pulled a headband out of his back pocket to tame his bangs, while his mom handed him an apron. She held out a hand for his bangle bracelets, and he piled them, clinking, into her palm.

The apron read *I'm Not Irish Kiss Me Anyway*. It was new since he'd left, like so much was. Spontaneously, he bussed her cheek and she giggled. His heart lifted. She was his idol, everything he wanted to live up to, and she was handing him the matzo ball soup and laughing alongside him in the kitchen. *Don't cry, Matthews.*

That night they had a less formal second seder, more raucous, and it gave him a chance to take in the glittering, transformed space. It was spotless, as was customary for Passover. Even without Passover, the space was different than the one that existed in his memory. Cass Carrigan had been a pack rat. Hannah Rosenstein made clutter terrified of her. The great room, which had once been home to a great deal of marginally uncomfortable, dusty furniture, was now a premier event space.

This was the first time Levi was seeing Carrigan's All Year in action. When he'd left, the inn had been nominally open for business during the spring and summer months, but all their energy and resources went toward the Christmas festival, which started on his birthday, November 1, and wrapped up on New Year's Day.

Now Hannah planned and coordinated weddings, reunions, local fashion shows, charity events, and a huge array of other creative offerings. The Carrigan's calendar was never empty, and he knew because he had a Google alert for when it got updated. She was a brilliant whirlwind of precise organization. He wasn't surprised by the fact that she was a terrifying genius. He was mad at himself, because she'd tried to tell him she had big dreams for this place, and he hadn't believed her. She'd proved him wrong, while *he'd* been trying, apparently unsuccessfully, to prove *her* wrong.

She'd made Carrigan's so much bigger. So much bigger that it excited him, made him want to see all the things it could be, but also so much bigger that all the room for him had been squeezed out.

"There's no space for you at the table," Hannah told him, walking up behind him, looking at the seder preparations.

"There are two empty place settings right there." He motioned.

"One of those is for Elijah the prophet, and one is for our lawyer Elijah. None for you." Hannah smiled, smug.

She walked away, and he sank into a chair (not one designated for an Elijah, corporeal or otherwise). He closed his eyes. She was so beautiful it hurt to look at her, and every time he did, he saw the worst of his mistakes reflected in her eyes. Had he honestly thought he could swoop in, blow his bangs out of his eyes, smile at her, and she would embrace him? He had spent so much time focusing on how he'd changed and so little worrying about how she had.

At the head table, his mother's mother's mother's painted enamel seder plate sat, as it always had, with a place of pride, already filled with bitter herbs, boiled egg, and maror. Along the tables were benches, couches, seats for lounging. On this night, they reclined.

His dad came up behind him.

"The furrow on your brow is scaring the children, Levi," Mr. Matthews said. "Also, this isn't your seat. Come sit with your parents and make a horrifying sandwich out of charoset and horseradish."

"Charoset and horseradish are delicious together, Dad. The sweetness complements the heat." He followed his dad to where his mom was already sitting. She looked up at him and her face lit up.

"You look beautiful, Mom," he told her honestly. "You clean up nice."

"Your mother is the most beautiful woman in the room no matter what she's wearing," his father said smugly. *These two.* Levi smiled to himself.

He loved Passover, loved the ritual and the meaning and the gefilte fish. He dipped parsley in saltwater and remembered that his faith stretched so far back through time and so far forward. He had been to seders in North Africa and South America and Poland, and every year he pretended he didn't want to be at home.

He looked around at the table. There were spots for his siblings, which they would love, since they'd worked so hard to avoid him last night, and he hadn't seen them at all today. There were also spots for Hannah, Miri, and Noelle.

"*Oh*, the owners have deigned to let us sit with them," he remarked.

"This table is for the Carrigan's family," his mother said, tugging at him to sit down and glaring. "That's us."

He sighed. His parents refused to admit that, to the guests and the Rosensteins, they weren't the Carrigan's family; they were the hired help. And, in the end, that had been true of Cass, too. If they had been family, she would have left the business to his parents.

"Also," she reminded him, "you're one of the owners."

He scowled. That wasn't better. Cass hadn't left it to him out of love, but out of some Machiavellian manipulation only she knew. If he was certain of anything, it was that Cass Carrigan had not loved him.

"Charoset alone is not a meal, son," Joshua said to his son, Grant. Joshua had stuck Levi's nephew and sister-in-law, Lydia, between them, in a move Levi had to assume was intentional.

He'd never been close to Joshua growing up, although he liked Esther. The twins had always had each other, and he was older and had Hannah and Miriam, so they hadn't bonded much. Still, there was a level of animosity now that he didn't really understand. What *had* he done to his younger siblings, other than be himself? They hadn't even talked much for four years. How mad could he have made them?

"Fine, but I'm not eating gefilte fish," Grant replied, poking at his plate.

His mother grinned and speared his fish from his plate. "More for me!" she cried. He made a fake gagging sound.

Esther was across from him, refusing to meet his eye, talking to a Rosenstein cousin about the incredible new off-off-Broadway show she'd seen, predicting it would be the next big hit, and where to get the best shakshouka in the city.

"You know the best shakshouka in New York State is in my

kitchen, baby sister." He couldn't stop himself from needling her. "I'm happy to go to shows with you whenever I'm in the city."

Her face turned to ice, and she continued as if he hadn't spoken.

His siblings had always been more successful than he was, both in their careers and at generally existing on the planet with other people. He felt a strong urge to growl at everyone that he was (sort of) famous in Australia. He didn't, because he refused to be the kind of person who told people he was kind of famous, even if he wanted to.

He'd left home to prove himself to everyone, had come back puffed up with his own success, and found none of them cared. They had no evidence that he wasn't the same old Blue, difficult and ungrateful and surly. He couldn't break the mold he'd cast for himself all those years ago by simply showing up.

"Why isn't Grant asking the four questions? Is it because he's not a Rosenstein?" Levi asked, already angry.

"No," his brother sighed, "it's because he's not the youngest anymore. He did it last year, but you missed it."

Of course he had.

"You could try apologizing to them, you know," his mother stage-whispered to him.

"For what?!" he whispered back, and his mom rolled her eyes at him. Was eye-rolling contagious when he was around?

He felt too raw to subject himself to their anger, whatever they were angry about, and not particularly interested in playing martyr.

"For what, Mom?" he repeated. "I left my childhood home to take a job seeing the world, a thing millions of people have done. I asked my fiancée to come with me, and not only did she say no, but she also told me to never come home. Yet somehow I'm the cause of all strife."

She brushed his bangs out of his eyes and adjusted his yarmulke where it was threatening to go flying. "For not being a very present big brother and letting your drama with Hannah get in the way of your relationship with them?" she asked gently.

His shoulders slumped, the fight going out of him again. He stuffed a spoonful of matzo ball into his mouth. Too fluffy.

At the other end of the table, the girls were telling Esther about their plans for the next couple of months, and he started listening.

"Obviously the Davenport wedding is our biggest event, and all the stuff leading up to that," Hannah was saying. "We'll have to hire some outside kitchen help for your mom, because it's a massive event, and she may have superpowers but—"

"Why would you hire someone? I'll be here," Levi cut in.

"You *won't* be here," Hannah said, her voice even. "You're giving us your shares and then you're leaving."

"You're giving them your shares and leaving?" his dad said, turning away from Grant.

"No, Dad, I'm not going anywhere." He reached over, squeezing his dad's hand without taking his eyes off Hannah.

"You're leaving," Hannah said, folding her hands with icy calm in front of her.

"You can't make me." He mirrored her.

"Why. Won't. You. Leave?" she asked through her teeth.

"Because. You're. My. Wife," he answered, much less calmly.

He heard Noelle gasp and remembered they weren't actually having this argument alone.

Oops! He'd never been the person who wanted to keep that secret anyway.

"I'm not your wife!" Hannah argued. "Stop saying that! We're not married!"

"Tell that to the state of New York."

"There was no rabbi. No chuppah. We signed no ketubah. The state of New York may think we're married, but we're not in the eyes of Hashem, which is what matters."

"We are to me," Levi said, trying not to let his voice break. "In my heart, we have been married every second since we took those vows, courthouse or not."

"You're fucking MARRIED?" Noelle boomed, pushing up from the table and knocking over a wineglass.

They both turned to look at her.

"No," Hannah said.

At the same time, he said, "Yes."

"We can talk about this when it's not seder," Miriam hissed.

"You lied," Noelle said, planting her feet and ignoring her girlfriend. "To all of us. How long have you been married? Why would you hide this from us? We spent four years changing everything in our whole lives, walking on eggshells, holding you while you cried so that you could get over this asshole and move on, but you were never going to get over him! You were married the whole time!"

Levi moved to stand between them, but Hannah put a hand on his arm, shaking her head.

"I am sorry I made our lives about my grief and that I took up so much space needing you," she said to Noelle. "I'm happy to unpack that with you later, when we're not surrounded by every one of my relatives." She gestured around the room.

Noelle was rooted and didn't budge. "That's not what I'm angry about, Hannah. We show up for each other. You shut us all out. And *you!*" She rounded on Levi. "You stay out of this."

This felt kind of unfair since he hadn't actually said anything to her. Yet.

"Maybe," Levi suggested, "it's *you* who should stay out of *my* marriage."

Mrs. Matthews stood up. "This is our seder," she said, steel in her voice. "This is not an appropriate conversation to have right now. Hannah and Levi shouldn't have started having it."

They both looked down at their shoes.

Noelle almost looked abashed, but she squared her jaw. "These two"—she gestured to Hannah and Levi—"were married this whole time, *in secret.*"

Miriam took Noelle by the elbow and led her out. "Let's get out of here before you say something you have to make amends for later."

Levi looked over at his mom, about to apologize, but she waved it away. "Please. We know. It's a very small town. People at city hall talk, especially to Cass."

They knew. Fuck. Cass had known. He stumbled backward. Cass had known, and she'd still told him in no uncertain terms that he should leave and never come back.

Fuck, he hated that woman, dead or not.

Chapter 4

Hannah

That was not the warm and welcoming family seder Hannah had envisioned. Currently, she was hiding in her office until all her relatives went to bed, because she didn't want to talk to her parents, or his parents, or any of her aunts. Once the hallway quieted down, she snuck through the dark out the side door and across to the carriage house, where Noelle and Miriam lived. Noelle had rehabbed it into a living space and studio so that Miriam could make art at Carrigan's full-time.

Kringle was sitting in front of the door, a giant guardian. His ear tufts swiveled toward Hannah as she tiptoed up, and he yawned.

"Am I allowed to knock?" she asked him. He chirped at her, sounding scolding.

"Why do I even let you live here?" Hannah grumbled, although she suspected it was the opposite—that Kringle let all of them live here.

She knocked anyway, in spite of his continued squawking.

Noelle opened the door, looked at her, and slammed the door again. Hannah knocked again.

This time, it was Miriam who opened the door. She was ready for bed, her hair wrapped in a T-shirt on top of her head, one of Noelle's flannels worn as a nightdress. She cocked an eyebrow at her cousin.

"Are you here to apologize?" Miriam asked, looking back over her shoulder at Noelle. "I'm not sure she's ready to hear it."

"I have absolutely no intention of apologizing, now or later. No one, not either of you, or anyone else, has a right to information about my relationship that I don't want people to have. I would love to have a *conversation* with my best friend, because I've had a difficult night, but I can tell I'm not welcome."

"You lied to me! Your best friend!" Noelle said from somewhere behind Miriam. "You didn't trust me with this huge information?"

"She didn't tell me, either!" Miriam pointed out, yelling over her shoulder. "No one tells me anything!"

Hannah sighed deeply, scrubbing her hands over her face. "I didn't know where we stood, or if I would ever see Levi again, and I didn't feel like I wanted to talk to anyone about that."

She heard Noelle blow out a breath. "You said we couldn't run this farm with secrets, Hannah. How could you hide this from me? No matter how much he fucks up, and no matter how much we show up to clean up his mess, you're always going to choose him."

"I'm not choosing him!" Hannah said, aghast.

"So you're getting a divorce?" Noelle asked.

Hannah paused.

Why was she hesitating? She'd told Levi she wanted a divorce, and she did. Didn't she?

"Talk to me again when the answer is yes," Noelle said. Hannah heard her clomp up the stairs to the loft bedroom.

"Okay. I guess that's that." She started to walk away. Miriam came after her, Kringle slinking along between Miri's legs.

"You can talk to me, if you want."

Hannah shook her head, her braid whipping. "I can't talk to anyone. You're Team Levi. Noelle's pissed. I can't talk to his parents about this because that would be unfair. Who's here, Miri? Who am I supposed to go to?"

"Why do you assume I'm Team Levi? Because I'm still his friend? We've been friends since we were born, remember? Am I supposed to hate him? Also why is there even a Team Levi?"

Hannah turned on her heel and glared at Miriam until Miriam threw up her hands. "Fine! Don't talk to me. Go talk to Marisol, or, hell, call Tara! She gives weirdly great relationship advice."

Marisol worked at the boutique in Advent and hung out with Noelle all the time, so she was out. Whatever Noelle had already told her about Levi was probably true but definitely not unbiased.

Tara Sloane Chadwick was Miriam's former fiancée, an icy blonde she'd left in Charleston when she'd moved home to Carrigan's and been swept off her feet by Noelle. She and Hannah had started to build a real friendship. They were both highly competent women other people thought were bitchy, going through shitty breakups.

It was kind of Miriam's fault. Miriam had fallen in love with Hannah's best friend, and now Hannah needed new friends.

She liked Tara. Tara was a stone-cold bitch on the outside but she had surprisingly insightful input on relationships. Also, she didn't live in their tiny bubble, which was amazing.

Unfortunately, she didn't think her friendship with Tara was up for middle-of-the-night freakouts about boys, and she didn't want to explain to yet another person that she was secretly married. So she was going to go to bed, because she had a very important client coming the next morning, and she was going to try to sleep without imagining Levi's hands all over her skin.

But if she imagined it a little, who would ever know?

When she got to her room, Blue was sitting on the floor next to her door, his knees up and his arms wrapped around them. His head was resting on the wall, which was covered in vintage parrot-patterned wallpaper. A parrot looked like it was about to nest in his hair. His eyes were closed, long dark lashes resting against his cheeks, those slashes of eyebrows relaxed for once. He looked the way he used to, when she would watch him sleep.

"LB," she said, trying to sound annoyed but only managing exhausted. "Haven't you caused enough of a scene tonight?"

His lashes rose, and he looked up at her, his face breaking into a smile. The kind of smile he saved only for her, the "I'm so glad you exist" smile. She instantly tensed, on guard against her own reaction to him.

"I wanted to check on you and apologize. I didn't mean to ruin your seder. I know you worked hard planning it." He didn't stand up, didn't try to get into her space. He just sat there, in the middle of their hallway in the middle of the night, being casually thoughtful. What was she supposed to do with that? "Is there anything I can do to make it up to you?"

She rested her forehead against the door. "If you really want to do something, it would help if you made yourself scarce tomorrow. I have the governor's daughter, Delilah Davenport, coming to tour in advance of her wedding festivities. I very much need you to *not* make a scene while she's here."

He chuckled sadly. "Aye aye, Captain. You won't even know I'm in the inn."

"I highly doubt that," she muttered, unlocking her door.

He stood up, shoving his hands in his pockets.

"Nan," he said quietly. He waited until she looked at him to say anything else.

"You asked me why I'm back, and I left out the most important piece of information, because it seemed obvious. I'm here because you're the love of my life, and every minute of my life that I've ever lived without you sucks so much more than any minute with you, even the worst ones. I just...thought I should say that. While we weren't naked, or screaming, or both. That I love you."

She froze. Him entreating her that he loved her was so much different than him yelling at her that she was his wife. So much harder to guard against, here in the dark.

It hurt, so she lashed out. "I believed you when you told me that once, and your version of love destroyed me. Your love is poison, Blue. I don't want it."

He blew out a breath. "Good night, Hannah. I'll try not to see you in the morning."

How many nights could she cry herself to sleep, she wondered, before she ran out of tears in her body?

The next morning was dreary, the snow having turned into a slushy rain, the sun in hiding. Her tour had been delayed by the bride getting a late start because, as she'd said when she called, "who gets out of bed on a day like this?" Hannah couldn't fault her for that logic. Still, she'd been on edge all day waiting to begin, wondering where Levi had holed up. Even when she couldn't see him, he was destroying her calm. She kept hearing his words from last night, echoing in her head.

Focus, Nan. Get through this tour. This is the most important event you've ever booked, she told herself once she was walking the governor's daughter around the space.

"Normally we set up the ceremony outside, but as you can see, we have lots of room both in the great room or the barn, depending on the size of the wedding, to move indoors in case of weather. The staircase provides a nice bit of drama for the bride, if you have a small enough ceremony."

As she was speaking, the kitchen door swung open, and Levi walked through in his leather jacket, holding his motorcycle helmet in one hand and shaking out his hair with the other. Had he been out riding in this miserable weather? How suitably melodramatic of him. He looked up and their eyes met. *Oh shit,* he mouthed.

Delilah Davenport followed Hannah's eyes and gasped. "Oh my gosh, you're Levi Matthews!"

Hannah put on her best "the customer is always right" smile. She was going to kill him.

"Chef Matthews, I read the article about you in *GQ* last month, and I watched the first episode of *Australia's Next Star Chef* a couple of days ago," Delilah gushed.

The cooking competition he'd filmed had just started airing.

His mother had made everyone watch the first episode the night before Levi returned, but Hannah had begged off. Instead, she'd watched it alone under her weighted blanket and Kringle. Levi's incandescence had lit up the dark room.

"Chef Matthews," Hannah said through only slightly gritted teeth, "grew up here at Carrigan's."

"My parents are—" Levi started.

Hannah interrupted, not trusting him. "The cornerstones of our staff and beloved members of our family."

The bride's eyes lit up, and she grasped Hannah's arm. "Is Chef Matthews joining the staff here at Carrigan's? Is there a possibility he'll be...catering weddings here?"

Hannah scrunched up her nose before gesturing between Levi and her. "This is Delilah Davenport, the daughter of Governor Davenport," she said. "Delilah is a long-time follower of Miriam's art who has booked Carrigan's for her wedding."

"I'm not sure what my plans are yet, but I will be in the state for the foreseeable future," Levi demurred, and Hannah narrowed her eyes at him.

"If you'll excuse me," he said, walking past them and shaking the woman's hand, "I'm going to change out of my wet clothes so I can get back to helping my mom in the kitchen!"

Delilah turned to Hannah, her eyes bright. "It would literally be an actual, no joke, dream come true if he could somehow do the food. I'm sure he's like, intensely busy with requests for talk show appearances and meetings with his agent about next steps and he probably, like, has to fly back to Australia to film wrap-up stuff once the finale airs." Delilah paused to take a breath. "But...I don't know, is there any way?"

Was he being inundated with requests for TV appearances?

Was he going to fly back to Australia? Why did the idea of that twist her gut into knots?

"I'll check in with him about his schedule, but I don't think he's planning to be here until June, unfortunately," Hannah said. *Please, let him not still be here in June.*

After the Davenport team bundled themselves off for a cake tasting—Hannah hadn't been able to convince them to order a Rosenstein's cake, although she suspected they would regret it—she headed into her office to find Blue sitting at her desk. Fuck.

She closed the door and banged her head back against it. "Are you just lingering in places now, waiting for me?"

"The place looks amazing. It's so . . . dust free. And Carrigan's All Year, it's really smart," he said, rearranging the pens on her desk. She gritted her teeth against the impulse to grab them and put them back in the right place. He wasn't answering her questions.

"It was Miriam's idea," she told him. "Carrigan's All Year, I mean. I would have kept doing things the way Cass had always done them until we went bankrupt, but Miriam saw that saving the place was a more fitting tribute to Cass than letting it fail."

"It has your organizational fingerprints all over it," he said. "Did I do okay? In there? I wasn't trying to get in your way. I thought they'd be gone already."

She wanted to think the worst, that he'd burst in on purpose, but given the late start, he probably had thought they'd be done, and he'd been uncharacteristically professional and circumspect.

"You were fine," she said grudgingly. "Now I have to convince Delilah that she'll be happy with someone other than the famous Chef Matthews cooking for her wedding, but that's not your fault."

He tapped a pen against his mouth in thought, and she snatched it away before it gave her ideas about his mouth.

"You have your troublemaking face on. Quit it. Whatever idea you have right now, the answer is no. Besides, Delilah mentioned that you probably have appearances to film. In Australia. Is that true?" She held her breath, waiting for him to answer.

"There are lots of places I *could* be, but none of them are more important than being here with you right now," he hedged.

Translation: he had a million places he could run to as soon as things got hard or didn't go his way.

"Get out of my chair, Blue."

"I love this chair," he said with a little smirk. "I have very fond memories of us—"

Yeah, so did she, which was why she wasn't going to let him finish that sentence.

"This is a new one. I burned that one!" she interrupted.

"You didn't burn all the furniture in this house we made, uh, memories on," he said smugly. "This beautiful antique desk, for instance, or the banquette in the kitchen, or..."

He trailed off, probably in response to the murder in her eyes. "Yep, I'm going. Gonna go see if my dad needs help with anything."

As he left, he squeezed by her much more closely than he needed to, and her knees almost buckled at the brush of his arm.

She threw the pen she'd taken from him at the door he closed behind him.

Blue, Age 14

It was his fucking birthday again. He looked around as he thought this, in case his mother somehow magically heard him cursing in his brain. But he should be allowed, like, one f-bomb. Because it was his birthday and as always, everyone was too busy opening Carrigan's for the season to notice. Except Esther, who had made him a card and stuck a candle in a piece of Rosenstein's coffee cake for breakfast, which was actually kind of sweet. She was the person he hated least who lived here.

He checked for his mom again. He didn't hate her, necessarily, but she kept them all here living in the middle of nowhere, so he hated her choices.

He'd spent his entire birthday outside in the cold carrying heavy trees to the cars of whiny locals. Kids he hated at school whose parents looked down on *his* parents for working for Cass, but then kissed Cass's ass.

"Oh, Cass darling, I'm so glad you're back from your travels. I just don't know how the farm runs without you!" they would say, and she would smile that smug, awful smile like she had a secret, when the secret was that his parents did all the work of running the farm. All while Cass swanned around the world, collecting lost people and telling them they'd always have a place at Carrigan's.

So generous. He rolled his eyes. Such a perfect birthday. No one had even thanked him.

"Oh, Levi," Cass had said first thing this morning when he'd stumbled downstairs. He waited for "happy birthday," or "good morning," but instead she said, "Remember that the coffee and pastries are for guests, dear."

He bared his teeth at her, taking a huge bite of the cinnamon roll in his hand and grinning before he turned to go help his dad.

Other things she had said to him today:

"Make sure you don't drop that tree."

"Don't scratch that car, Levi. What are you thinking?!"

And, when he'd been standing with Miriam and Hannah, she'd looked past him to say, "Miri, Nan, do you want to break for lunch?" Then she'd turned to him and said, "Don't you have work to do?"

Now he was hiding in his parents' apartment off the kitchen, reading a copy of *Gourmet* magazine while stuffing hunks of French bread dipped in thousand island dressing into his mouth. If he waited until everyone went to bed, he could sneak into the kitchen for an actual meal.

Hannah knocked on the door of the large closet he used as a bedroom so he didn't have to share with the twins.

"Get your jacket," she said, gesturing for him to come with her. "Wait, what are you eating?!"

He ignored this. "Where are we going?"

"It's a birthday surprise. Your parents said it was okay. Come on."

"Aren't you supposed to be finishing up whatever Cass needs and then celebrating opening day?" he snarked, grabbing his leather jacket. His prized possession.

"I opened the farm, and now I'm going to celebrate my best friend's birthday. Come ON, Miriam is already waiting outside."

Miriam wasn't usually there for opening day, because it was in the middle of the school semester, but she'd ended up here this year, because it fell on a weekend.

"What if I don't want to?" he sulked. "What if I want to hide?"

"It's a Shenanigan, Blue," she said, her hands on her hips.

He sighed, taking her hand and letting himself be pulled to his feet. "Fiiiiiine. I'm never forgiving you for forcing me to have fun. You're dead to me for invoking Shenanigans when all I wanted for my birthday was to be left alone."

"Shut up, Blue," she said, dragging him outside to the Carrigan's shuttle, which was being driven by one of the seasonal workers instead of his dad like usual. Cass couldn't even give him time off to take his oldest son out for his birthday.

They stopped between Advent and Lake Placid, at the winery that had opened a few months ago. He'd been asking to go eat there since, because he knew shitty little Advent could never maintain a place with great food for very long. Other tourist destinations in the Adirondacks got Michelin-starred chefs.

All they got was a dive bar with mediocre fried pickles.

(He would never admit to Ernie that they were mediocre because Ernie was actually nice to him. Even if she wouldn't let him experiment in her kitchen.)

"Holy shit, you guys, how can you afford this?" he said to the girls when he saw the menu.

"We've been saving up to surprise you for your birthday! We planned it. We told your parents they couldn't take you without us." Miriam rubbed her hands together. "We plotted."

The meal was life changing. He sat in front of each plate in the degustation menu and wept as he put them in his mouth. He knew he loved food. He knew he wanted to cook, it was all he'd ever wanted to do, but that night he knew he was never going to be happy until he went to culinary school.

Chapter 5

Levi

The day after the second seder was awkward. He'd intended to talk to his siblings, but apparently the whole "secret marriage" was more evidence that he was too much of a fuckup for them. They'd left, taking Grant with them, which bummed him out. He liked Grant, mostly because Grant was seven and not yet disappointed in him. He'd promised Hannah that he would stay out of her way while Delilah Davenport visited, and everyone else was busy or avoiding him, except Miriam, who *he* was kind of avoiding so he didn't have to answer hard questions.

So, he wandered around, haunting the inn that had haunted him.

He'd meant what he said to Hannah about Carrigan's All Year being impressive. Cass had opened the Christmasland on a kitschy whim, wanting to have a space where she could be the Eccentric Queen and collect people who worshipped her and never have to do anything she didn't want to, or deal with anyone who didn't adore her. She'd never wanted to deal with the boring parts, like worrying about money, and since she had a lot of it to burn through, she simply didn't. Instead, she let his parents worry about budgeting and Elijah worry about the legality of her decisions, while she wandered off to a foreign port whenever she wanted.

She'd left the girls a huge steaming mess, which he'd only figured out between the lines of his parents' and Miriam's missives, because none of them would speak ill of her. Maybe he should be glad she hadn't left it to his parents, but he couldn't be. His mom would have had the whole thing sorted in a week. But the girls were doing a great job with the shit pile they'd inherited.

Miriam's fandom, named the Bloomers, came on pilgrimages to see her Instagram-famous art. He was a closet Bloomer, never telling her how many hours he'd spent at sea reading her words and looking at her art, anchoring himself. Did he have a well-worn #BloomerNation tee he slept in when he was homesick? He didn't *not*.

The old barn had been converted to an event space, the Carrigan's logo brightly repainted on the side, that creepy mid-century modern reindeer rampant next to a jaunty Christmas tree. The actual reindeer, which used to live in the barn, now had a temperature-controlled outbuilding his dad had custom built. They were spoiled rotten.

Noelle's "work shed," bigger than many reasonably sized single-family homes, he did not venture into lest she murder him on sight and claim self-defense. It looked as shiny and well-maintained as ever. Because he was petty, he lured

Kringle out with the promise of some very high-quality Norwegian lox (Kringle was a fish snob) and carried him off to snuggle.

A small, miserable part of him had been hoping all of this would fail, and he could finally be free. And they would all understand that the Great Infallible Cass had been wrong sometimes. But they were killing it. They'd even managed to book a massive event with the governor's daughter's wedding, and he was proud of them.

Well, not Noelle, but everyone else.

When Elijah knocked on the door of his little back cabin the morning after Hannah kicked him out of her office, Levi was convinced he'd come to deliver divorce papers, and Hannah wasn't even walking the few steps out the back door of the inn to deliver them herself.

"Levi," Elijah said, surveying him from the doorway, "you look panicked to see me."

"I'm thrilled to see *you*, the human, who I like and missed," Levi clarified. "I would love to hear about your gorgeous husband and equally beautiful children. I'm a little panicked about you being here for work."

Elijah smiled and kissed Levi's cheeks as he walked in. "I'm very honored to be among the few people you like, and I'm not here about your divorce."

Levi let out a breath. "Then can I make you a cup of tea? I'm having chai but I have a bunch of options."

His mom must have snuck into the cabin at some point,

because he'd come back to full snack provisions and an electric kettle.

"I would love some chai. And I would love to show you pictures of the kids. They were very sad not to get to talk to you more at seder. They always think of you as the guy who sent the matching rocking horses."

"Ah, well, seder did not turn out exactly the way I expected, vis-à-vis getting to catch up with old friends," Levi said, clearing his throat.

Elijah laughed. "Yes, I did notice that. Jason always says he loves to come to a Carrigan's event because it packs more drama into a night than he can pack into a semester of high school theater class."

This, for some reason, made Levi laugh until tears leaked from his eyes. Every time he caught Elijah's eye, they both started laughing again.

Finally, after long, deep breaths, Elijah adjusted his tie and the sleeves of his shirt, which Levi remembered always meant he was going into Lawyer Mode.

"I'm not here about your marriage, but I am here for work—although I'm also supposed to pass on an invitation to dinner at the house, zero work involved." He leaned over and pulled something from the side pocket of his briefcase. He reached across the tiny coffee table in the middle of the tiny front room of the cabin, setting a small manila envelope in front of Levi.

Levi sat back in his chair, his face half hidden in his scarf, staring at the offering like it was a cobra.

The envelope had *Levi Blue* written on it, in Cass's print. He did not want this. Whatever was in it would only destroy him more, and he knew that, even in death, she was doing it on purpose.

"Cass asked me to deliver this to you upon your return to Carrigan's and to read you the following, as dictated by her: 'Just open it, you little shit. Don't be a chicken.'" Elijah looked up from his notes. "I would apologize for Cass, but it wouldn't do any good."

She was a witch, Levi thought, not for the first time. Not a Glinda witch. One of the witches that houses fell on and everyone sang about. But only he could see it.

He reached out, slowly, for the envelope, sliding his hand inside.

There was a napkin covered in writing. Cass never wrote on paper if she could avoid it, preferring to hoard napkins from her flights like a dragon and dole them out to the emotionally unprepared. Usually it was Hannah or Miriam who got napkins, sometimes his parents or siblings. He'd always wanted them, yearned to open one of her envelopes while she was away for the summer and smell her perfume, but things were never that simple between them.

There was also a ring. He pulled the ring out first. It had been Hannah's favorite.

"Does Hannah know I have this?" he asked Elijah.

Elijah shook his head. "No, Cass thought you might need it for something."

Why, *why*, would the woman who told him in no uncertain terms to leave her niece alone give him the engagement ring Hannah had always wanted?

He unfolded the napkin, spreading it on his lap, his fingers trembling as they traced the ink.

Kid

I spent so long collecting lost souls around the world, but I lost the soul closest to home. I thought I knew what was best for you, and Hannah, and I guess I still do think that. But I can admit I was very wrong about one thing—I should never have let you feel I didn't love you as much as any of them. I failed you, kid. I failed to protect you from others, and from my own ego when the help you wanted didn't look like the help I wanted to give. We could have been two misanthropes in a pod, Statler and Waldorf of Carrigan's, but I blew it, and I hurt you. You deserved better.

Whether you want it or not, I love you.

Cass

He looked up at Elijah, who was watching him. "You're going to get eyeliner on it," he warned.

Levi realized that he was, in fact, about to drip black kohl tears right onto the paper and run the ink.

"She never could leave well enough alone, could she?" he asked, sounding husky to his own ears.

"I don't believe she thought it *was* well enough," Elijah remarked. "I don't know exactly what happened between the two of you, and I'm not sure I would have fixed it quite the way she tried to, but : . . . well, again, apologizing for Cass doesn't do you any good, and she wouldn't have wanted me to. My job was to deliver this. I'm sorry if I've caused pain in doing so."

"You didn't cause it, Elijah." Levi shook his head. "This is a pain as old as I am, and it's on Cass's head, and maybe a little on mine. I would love, though, to take you up on that invite to dinner. Things are a little heavy around here. I wouldn't mind a night with friends."

"I'll text you some dates, then. Jason will be freaking out, trying to figure out what to cook for the famous chef."

Levi watched him let himself out, the napkin still dangling from one hand and the ring clutched in the other.

Fuck. Fuckity fuck fuck fuck. Fucking Cass.

He was still brooding late that night. It was too cold to sit on the porch of the cabin and stare into the abyss of the stars for hours, so he gave up and went to the kitchen. He wasn't sure if he was looking for a snack, his mom, or three a.m. cooking, but the kitchen was where he always ended up when he couldn't get comfortable in his skin. He pushed open the door to find Miriam already there, cooking something. He walked over and looked past her shoulder, into the pan on the stove. "Are you making matzo brei? It's the middle of the night."

"Categorically the best time for matzo brei. Plus I can't sleep." She shooed him away. "Go sit down. I'll feed you for a change."

"This is super weird," he said, sliding onto a stool.

"This is what I do," Miriam told him. "I stress-cook in the middle of the night, and someone wanders in to eat and bond with me. That's how Noelle and I fell in love, over three a.m. rugelach."

"What are you stressed about tonight?" He rested his chin on his hands.

She squished up her face. "I miss Cole," she said. "I've been distracted by Noelle, and Carrigan's, but I need my BFF. We've been attached at the hip since college. And Noelle and Hannah have a whole secret best friend life. I don't want to interfere with it. I just want mine back."

Cole had not just been in Australia to retrieve him but had, as Levi understood it, been doing something for work in New Zealand and had been entirely off the grid since the beginning of the year. No one could tell him what, exactly, Cole did for work, except that maybe it involved cybersecurity and they weren't sure it was technically within the law.

"Can I offer my services as your original BFF?" he offered. "I realize I am missing some ineffable something that Cole has, since everyone seems to adore him, but I don't entirely suck."

"What Cole has that you don't," Miriam told him seriously, "is pants embroidered with tiny lobsters."

"He was literally wearing lobster pants when I met him." Levi laughed.

"Socks?" Miriam asked.

"No!" Levi shook his head, grinning. "Not a sock in sight."

Miriam nodded. "There you go, then." As if that settled it.

"I don't even eat lobster; they're not kosher," Levi pointed out. "But also he has a yacht. And a few million dollars in a trust fund. And Hannah doesn't hate him."

"Did you just explain to me that shellfish are not kosher, LB?" Miriam cocked an eyebrow at him.

"Sorry, sorry, a function of having spent the last few years among the gentiles," he apologized. "You wouldn't believe the number of times I've had to explain kosher hot dogs."

"It's mostly the pants, though," she told him. "I can't

overstate the pants." She reached over to squeeze his hand, forcing him to meet her eyes.

"You and Cole are polar opposites," Miriam told him once he was looking at her. "You met him. He's bright and bubbling and all of his few, superficial emotions are on the surface of his skin at every moment. You're all brooding jagged edges and keep all your cards close to your chest while you're snarling at everyone. He's a golden retriever. You're an alley cat. If you were on a TV show together, people would ship you."

"So you've all replaced me with the furthest thing you could get from me. Neat." Levi showed his teeth.

"Oh, boohoo." Miriam rolled her eyes. "People are capable of having emotional attachments to a variety of human beings. How did this middle-of-the-night conversation become about your loneliness and not mine?" Miriam asked him jokingly, waving a spatula.

"Our lonelinesses are best friends, too." He scowled. "You used to let me whine."

"You used to not be thirty-six years old," she replied, but her tone was gentle. "I did miss your whining, if I'm being honest. I missed your face." She touched his cheek with her free hand, and he teared up.

"If you're going to sit here and eat my matzo brei, we should probably talk about why all you wanted all our lives was to leave this place, and you burned all your bridges as you left, but now you're sad because you showed back up and everyone's life went on without you." She put her hands on her hips, the eggs on the end of her spatula bumping against her apron, and he tried not to smile at her tiny self with her giant hair telling him what to do.

"Ugh, crap, give me a cup of coffee if I'm going to be genuine about my feelings." This was the problem with people loving you. He waited until she handed him a mug, then stared down into it. He took the plate she handed him and poured an ocean of maple syrup on top of his eggs. Plus some in his coffee. "I'm still so in love with her, Miriam. I still want a life with her, I always have. Every moment. But how I feel about Carrigan's hasn't changed, and neither has how Hannah feels about it."

"Also you are a TV star now, which complicates things."

"Yeah, I really loved the whole experience. I will tell you alllll about it when the NDA expires. We might be able to deal with all of that if she didn't hate me. I have no idea what to do about any of it except leave again, but I fucking can't because I'm a selfish asshole."

"Oh, my love. My Blue." She smiled sadly. "I hope that doesn't explode on you both." She refilled her own coffee. "I'm going to need more maple syrup for this."

Chapter 6

Hannah

For all of her life, Hannah's parents had stayed when she wanted them to leave and left when she wanted them to stay. Now was no different. They had originally been scheduled to stay through the entire week of Passover, but she was hoping she could convince them they weren't needed.

"I've been thinking," she said, braiding and unbraiding the ponytail high on her head. "Now that the family is gone, we'll be focused more on getting ready for the Davenport events, and you and Dad won't have much to do."

They were sitting in the dining room, which was mostly emptied out because the majority of the Rosensteins had left after the disastrous second seder, and now, on day five, Hannah both wanted time alone and would kill for leavened bread.

Rachel leveled a disbelieving look at her. "You're not at all trying to get rid of us because you don't want to talk about being married."

Her dad pushed back from the table, balancing his chair

on its back two legs. She stopped herself from telling him the chairs were vintage, and she couldn't afford to replace one if he broke it sitting like a middle schooler.

"I don't understand. If you were married, why you didn't go with him?" Daniel said. "You're an excellent travel manager, you know all the locations he was planning to go to, you would have been a great asset to him. And what a wonderful way to start your life together!"

Hannah let the braid she was fiddling with drop. She couldn't decide if she was more shocked that her dad hadn't asked her this years ago, when Levi first left, or that he'd asked at all.

"Daniel," her mom said, rolling her eyes, "Hannah hates travel. And she has a life here. Why didn't he stay here to take over the kitchen from his mother and start their lives together at Carrigan's?"

Her dad shook his head. "Surely she's gotten over that. As an adult, she must know we gave her a life no other child got to experience."

"Yes, I think that was the problem. She wanted to stress about what she was wearing to her friends' b'nai mitzvahs, not fix our budgets and spend hours on the phone trying to get us hotel reservations for the whole crew."

Rachel was right, although Hannah wished they would remember she was sitting here, but this was kind of what her parents were like. And, while they always wanted what was best for her, it never seemed to occur to them to ask her what that might be.

Her therapist said she should allow herself to be mad at them about it, that if she did, she wouldn't get her buttons so pushed when other people tried to make plans for her. But sitting here watching them, she wasn't mad at them, just exhausted. She was tired of hoping they'd be people they weren't, and tired of parenting them and herself.

Hell, she was tired of hating traveling. She missed seeing new things, and eating new food, and meeting new people. She wanted the experience of finding travel joyous, and she couldn't have that, because her parents had ruined it for her, which had doomed her marriage before it even started, and they were still asking what had happened like they were brand-new to her as a human being.

She set her head down on the table and groaned.

"Hannah, that can't be sanitary," her dad said.

"Please leave," she said. "I'm not even going to pretend. I love you both, it's wonderful to see you, and I'd love to have you visit again in July, or for Rosh Hashanah. But right now, please leave early. I don't, in fact, want to talk to you about Levi. I will talk to my therapist and my friends. Maybe Kringle if I can lure him back from Blue."

Her mom wrapped the end of the dropped braid around her palm and said, "I'm sorry we haven't really been the parents you can talk to about boy problems. We'll go. For what it's worth, we love you, and we love him."

"Thank you for the apology. And for leaving."

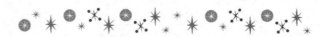

Levi peeked his head around the kitchen door into the dining room. "Are your parents gone?"

"You know they are," Hannah sighed. "You just watched them leave."

He didn't try to pretend otherwise, just walked in and sat down at the table across from her.

He smiled at her. "I like your ponytail."

"I'll kill you," she said flatly.

"You need me."

She barked out a surprised laugh. "The fuck I do."

"You're hosting the highest profile series of events Carrigan's has ever taken on," he said, leaning toward her, "and you need extra kitchen help. And the bride wants me."

"No." She shook her head hard enough that her braid whipped her. *This fucking hair.*

"The better this event goes, the better it is for the future of Carrigan's All Year," he pointed out. "Are you so drowning in business you can afford to turn down the kind of publicity a happy governor would provide?"

She tapped a fork on her plate, glaring at him. "You're not doing this out of the goodness of your heart. What do you think is going to happen, that I'm going to let you stay and be so overcome with gratitude I fall into your arms?"

"You're not letting me stay, because I own as much of the building as you do," he said, and her eyebrows lowered. "No, I do not think you will simply fall into my arms. Again."

She started to stand up, to make him leave. He held up his hands.

"Sorry. I want an opportunity to show you we can be happy together. You want me to leave. Right after the wedding, I have to be in Manhattan to film a pilot."

"Oh, so you are in fact planning to leave again the minute it's in your best interest," Hannah said.

"I am planning to go five hours away on a train for a week

or two and then come back when I am done," he said slowly, "because I already signed a contract with Food Network and my agent says I can't afford to back out of it. In the meantime, I will help with the events for the wedding, in exchange for a series of dates. With you. When the wedding is over, if you still want me gone, I'll give you the shares and make the city my home base. If you want to get back together . . ."

"I won't, under any circumstances, ever want that, but hypothetically, you would what? Give up your life dreams and move to a place you hate?" Hannah looked at him and knew he was completely full of shit. "You think you've changed because you got to be anyone you wanted to be out there, but back here, everything is the same."

She swept her hands around the room to indicate everything that was broken. "We want opposite things. You're determined to think the worst of everyone. We're still keeping secrets and pushing everyone we love away. You've been back for less than a week, and my best friend isn't speaking to me. There's no way for us to be happy."

She sat back, her arms crossed.

"Let's make a bet," he said, stretching his legs out in front of him, his head quirked at that angle he got when he was making trouble. "Let me take you out. I prove to you we can make a new love, or you prove to me that I should walk away forever."

She didn't want to go on any dates, but she also knew he would stick to a bet once he made it, and she knew she could outlast him if she had an end date.

"You scared, Rosenstein?" he asked. "I've never seen you back down from a Shenanigan."

She narrowed her eyes. Since they were kids, if one of them

said that magic word, they would all go along with whatever dare or game had been declared, no matter how terrible an idea it was. And even now, after everything, she couldn't make herself break with that tradition. For better or worse, a Shenanigan, once called, must be seen through.

He smirked. "I can see your evil wheels turning. I love your evil wheels."

"Two conditions," she said.

He snorted. "You can't negotiate a Shenanigan."

"Did I hear the words 'I hereby officially declare a Shenanigan' come out of your mouth? Because the rules clearly state that until you have uttered those words, the Shenanigan is not on." As if he could out-Shenanigan her. Please. He might pretend to be the King of the Shenanigan, but they both knew only one of them had thought up the rules to this little game.

"Fine. What are your conditions?" he asked, his arms crossed.

She counted on her fingers. "One, I will go on a single date. I don't have time or patience for more."

"Oh please, Hannah." He scowled at her. "You can do better than that. We can't find out if we should spend the rest of our lives together in one date. Ten dates."

"Are you kidding me?" she asked, aghast. "Three. Max."

"Six," he countered. "That's enough time to actually be sure."

"I will go on five dates with you. No more. This is final."

He pumped his fist, and she frowned. Damn it, he'd known she wouldn't agree to ten, so he'd manipulated her up to five. Point to Blue.

"It's a deal," he said. "What's your other condition?"

She smiled wolfishly. "When you leave, you sign the divorce papers."

"I do not love your evil wheels." He gritted his teeth, then relaxed. "Caveat. All five dates must be completed, in good faith. We will take turns planning them. During the time when we are on the dates, you must give dating me an actual chance. And if you call it off at any time before the five dates are over, the deal is off."

She pushed her sparkly purple glasses up to the top of her head and tapped her mouth. "This will be easy. By the time the wedding is over, you'll be running to get away. This is my home turf, LB, and you hate this turf."

He raised one hand, in the time-honored tradition of their childhood ritual. "I, Levi 'Blue' Matthews, hereby officially declare a Shenanigan."

It was done. Once those words were spoken, a solemn and sacred trust had been invoked, and neither of them would violate it.

"This is a catastrophically bad idea doomed to failure and heartache," she told him.

He grinned. "Catastrophically bad ideas doomed to failure are my favorite kind."

He was smiling at her. Not his TV smile, or his company smile, but the real Blue smile. Damn, that smile and the trouble it used to get her into. Years ago, before he was angry cactus teen, when he was a little boy who loved Shenanigans, that had been his only smile. Whenever that smile managed to make its way past his walls, she fell for it, because she missed it so much, and it never ended well. And now he was smiling like that at her, because he'd dared her and she'd fallen for it.

What had she done? Of course he would see her request for a divorce as a challenge. Of course he would decide, after years of not wanting her, that he wanted her back the minute she said it was impossible. She should have known he would.

But she *did* know if she gave him enough time, he would start looking toward the horizon. She knew nothing would ever keep him here for long, not even her. She needed to wait him out, until he got the urge to run. It shouldn't take long. She just needed to survive a couple of dates with her husband.

"I'm going to go plan our first date," he said, heading out of the dining room.

She rolled her eyes. "Maybe you should start planning what you're going to serve Delilah Davenport, because she'll be here for dinner with her team in two days."

He had to plan dinner, but *she* had to tell her fellow co-owners he was both staying and helping with an event, with her consent. She thought about putting off that conversation but decided she'd put off enough difficult conversations for the time being. She called them into her office.

Technically, as the events manager, she had the right to make unilateral decisions about these things. Technically, as an equal shareholder, Levi could stay wherever he wanted. Given how angry Noelle currently was at both of them, she was pretty sure neither of those technicalities was going to win her over.

"Okay," she said to her two best friends, standing in front of her desk and power posing to try to give herself some confidence, "I told him he could stay long enough to do the food for the Davenport wedding." She didn't explain who "him" was. She didn't need to.

"Delilah wants him because he's semi-famous in Australia or whatever, and the wedding is great publicity for us, and I felt guilty that I basically kept him from seeing his mom for years. And Mr. Matthews keeps watching Levi with these sad eyes and I can't stand it." Now she was rambling to fill up silence. She didn't tell them about the dating deal, because there was only so much information she could ask Noelle to ingest at once. Besides, there was no way it was going to change anything, so Noelle and Miriam didn't need to know.

Noelle had her arms crossed, and her mouth was tight. "First it was, I need to get him back to sell the shares. Then it was, oh oops, I forgot to tell my closest friends we're actually married. Now it's, oh he needs to stay a little while because his parents miss him." Hannah flinched. "If you want him here, tell the truth. Oh wait, you can't. You can't tell the truth about him. Because you two are a sick little secret club. Can't let anyone in, they might see how fucked up we are!"

Hannah's hackles rose. "Maybe it's 'can't talk to Noelle about this because I know she'll come to the worst conclusion no matter what!' Have you thought about that?"

Miriam put her hands up between them. "I am actually wondering why you got secretly married. You were engaged. Couldn't you have just gotten . . . not . . . secretly married? Regular married?"

"I honestly don't know." She sank onto her desk as she talked. "We got married on a whim, and only at the JP, so we thought, we won't really be married until we have a rabbi, but we'll have this little thing that's only ours."

Noelle made a disbelieving sound in her throat.

"Because when you live in a hotel with all your friends and family, everyone has an opinion on everything in your life, and no one ever lets you have a relationship between just two people," she said pointedly. Turning to Miriam, she continued. "Then he left, and we were broken up, you know? It didn't matter that legally we were married, except as a formality we were going to have to sever at some point. Honestly, I expected him to meet someone else and have me served with divorce papers from wherever he was in the world. I thought if you all knew, I wouldn't be able to hold anything together at all." She chewed on the bottom of her braid. "It doesn't even make any sense."

"Well," said Miriam, "I am a professional at keeping gigantic secrets from everyone I love, as you know."

This was true; she had disappeared for ten years and basically ghosted them all and refused to tell them why until the shit had very much hit the fan.

Miriam unfolded from her seat on the couch, sitting forward so she was looking at her cousin. "And it's my experience that some secrets are so huge we can't force them out of our throats until we've digested them some. They won't fit. And there are some realities we're not ready to face emotionally. We kept a lot of secrets from each other, you and I, for a lot of years. Maybe our family is bad at honesty? Like we weren't raised with those skills at all? But it's not actually helping any of us heal to be mad at each other for not doing things we were never taught to do."

"I love you," said Hannah, so relieved that Miriam was here.

"I love you, too, but gayer," Noelle said to Miriam. To Hannah she said, "Look, you two, this is what you do. You get insular and weird and you build a little fort you won't let anyone into. I'm worried this is one more thing tying you together. You're terrible for each other."

"One thing more or less tying us together isn't going to make that much difference, honestly," Hannah admitted. She didn't argue about the fort thing, because that part was very true. She'd done it on purpose, even.

"Can I remind you," Miriam pointed out to Noelle, "that

you hated me when you met me? Maybe you're not giving him enough of a chance."

Hannah shook her head. There was no denying that they were absolutely destructive as hell. "Noelle's right. Whether Levi is really as bad as she thinks or not, he and I together are awful. When the wedding is over, we're done."

Noelle scrubbed her face with her hands and shook her head. "I don't believe you, Nan. Cass was right about him."

"Cass was right about what?" Miriam asked.

"Didn't you ever notice they didn't get along? He hated Carrigan's, and Cass didn't like him much. I trust Cass's judgment. I don't trust him. And honestly, right now, I don't trust you, either," she said to Hannah. "You two do whatever dance you're going to do, but don't talk to me about it."

She stomped out.

"She'll get over it," Miriam said. "You know her. Fast temper, fast cooldown."

Hannah wasn't so sure about that. Noelle had spent a long time perfecting her hatred of Levi, and she'd trusted Hannah not to keep secrets. Still, she couldn't fix it now.

"Do you think she's right?" Miriam asked. "That Cass didn't like him?"

Hannah shook her head, denying it, even though something about the accusation tickled her subconscious. "I think we would have known that. We were his best friends. I'm his wife."

"Yeah, because none of us ever kept any secrets from each other," Miriam said.

"I'm going to deal with this later."

Right now she had to call Delilah Davenport to tell her she was getting the wedding chef of her dreams.

Hannah, Age 15

She'd finally convinced her parents she should move to Carrigan's to stay with Cass for high school. After a disastrous freshman year split between Nowhere, Iowa, and Bakersfield (which was a circle of hell), they were off to Nepal and she was off to the Adirondacks. All the Rosensteins would be there for Rosh Hashanah, Miriam would be there for Hanukkah, and before and after and in between there was Sukkot and Homecoming and Halloween and Spring Fling with Blue. Spreading out in front of her, as the road wound up the hill to the big wrought-iron gates, was day after day, weekend after weekend, of riding to school with Blue, getting into Shenanigans with Blue, fighting with Blue over nothing. They didn't have to hoard their time together, refusing to fight because they only had a few days. They didn't have to call each other in the middle of the night, leave voice mails that got cut off because they had so much to say. They could just be two wild kids who got each other the way no one else did, be Hannah-and-Blue. Best friends, forever, no matter what.

She walked in the front door and was immediately enveloped in Cass's caftan and perfume, a swirl of peacock feathers and maybe a boa. She couldn't tell, it was all color and movement and something tickling her nose. Cass held her face, turning it this way and that while her cascade of rings threw rainbows onto the walls.

"My Hannah girl, you are finally where you belong," she said, clucking at her nephew, Hannah's father, for having kept her away for so long.

"Her soul is drawn to Carrigan's. We must follow our souls," Cass had said when they'd called to ask if Hannah could move in. "I have been waiting for her. Her room is already prepared."

The Matthewses came out to greet her, Joshua and Esther peeking their preteen faces around the kitchen door to get a glimpse of the cool, sophisticated, world-traveling teenager who was moving into their home. As if she hadn't changed their diapers.

She was surrounded by chattering people, then someone took her bag out of her hand, and she turned to see who it was, and it was him. He was taller, thinner, and he'd grown his hair out long and had it in a low bun. He was holding a motorcycle helmet haphazardly in one hand. She knew from his letters that he'd bought a bike for himself from scraped-together tips, that he and Mr. Matthews were fixing it up together. Now the leather jacket he'd bought years ago wasn't just for show. His eyeliner was smudged like he'd slept in it, his jeans were ripped to shreds, his motorcycle boots were covered in paint.

He looked like some kind of bad boy out of central casting.

He was a mess, and he was so beautiful it stole her breath. He caught her eye and grinned at her, and her heart beat so fast she had to look away. She couldn't blush at Blue Matthews. She couldn't want to know how his hair felt, or his chapped lips. What was happening? Why was this happening, to her, in the middle of the Carrigan's front hall, surrounded by both their families?

She could never tell him. Ever. This wasn't really happening; she just wasn't used to seeing him like this, now, when they were both in puberty. She could never let it become a crush. He was her staunchest ally, her rock. She needed him. She made herself look back at him and smile, and he picked her up in his arms and twirled her around and she almost fainted from the way he smelled.

"You're here," he grumbled into her hair. Oh noooooo. His voice, how was it the same comforting sound that had lulled her to sleep a thousand times and also so sexy?

She could never, ever tell him. If she ignored it, it would go away.

"I'm here," she whispered back. Finally, all her plans were coming true.

"Now, Levi, take Hannah's bags up to her room and let her get settled in with her family. You'll have lots of time with her at school," Cass interrupted them, and Hannah had never been more grateful for anything.

She needed breathing room. Her body needed to calm down.

Cass wrapped an arm around her tightly. "Did you get a chance to read the copy of *Women Who Run with the Wolves* that I sent you? We're meeting with my Artist's Way group in a couple of days and I want you to join."

She had read *Women Who Run with the Wolves*, and she'd hated it. She didn't need to give up rational, logical thinking and listen to her intuition. She needed to make lists, then make plans from her lists, then systematically make those plans become reality through sheer organization and willpower. Which she'd just proven she could do.

Before she was whisked entirely away, Hannah smiled the little smirk she saved for Blue, and he rolled his eyes. They had a whole silent conversation in a moment.

I'll find you later, she thought at him.

I'll have food waiting for you, he thought back.

Chapter 7

Levi

Sleep wasn't happening after the adrenaline of convincing Hannah to agree to this very ill-advised dating plan, so Levi wandered the back acreage until the sun came up. Kringle wandered with him, pushing his giant body against Levi's legs every time Levi's brain started to free-spiral into worst-case-scenario futures. How did the cat know?

He wanted to get on his bike and ride as far as he could go before he ran out of gas, but he'd promised Hannah he would go to the weekly staff meeting that morning to talk about the Davenport wedding. Levi walked in with his fists already up. He was ready to fight for his right to be here, ready to go toe to toe to stay in a place he'd been running from all his life. Mostly he was ready for any fight at all, because his heart was still so battered from Cass's note.

Miriam and Noelle were in the big chairs facing Hannah's desk, so he sprawled out on the couch at the back of the room, doing his best impression of an insouciant wastrel, because it was highly likely to get a rise out of someone. All three of them ignored him while Noelle updated them on saplings or something, and Miriam talked about the registration numbers for her painting classes. He wondered if she would let him join one; they sounded fun.

He waited for his turn on the agenda, which Hannah had written in perfect cursive on the whiteboard on one wall. There were no details, not even his full name. It said:

IV: LB

"So on to item four," Hannah said.

This was it. Noelle was going to tell him to get out. Miriam was going to tell him that she loved him but he didn't belong here. Finally, he was going to be able to get into a fight.

"I'm excited for our budget that we don't have to hire anyone!" Miriam said. "We're not paying you, right, Blue?"

"We're definitely not," Noelle said, not turning to look at him. "I'm excited that he has somewhere to be right after the wedding. Hannah, did you give him the binder?"

Hannah pulled a binder out from a drawer in her desk, setting it with a thump in front of her. Miriam reached over for it and handed it to him.

It was color coded, because Hannah. He loved her competence. It had the timeline in both visual and list form, a breakdown of what needed to be done, when, by whom, plus vendor contact info.

"This is much more thorough than Cass's elaborate Post-it Note system," he said, remembering trying to help his mom cook for events where they didn't even have a full guest count.

"Yeah, Miriam decided maybe we shouldn't be in deep shit if we got audited, so she redid the books," Hannah said.

"And Hannah ran with actually having a calendar, like, on a calendar. Revolutionary!" Miriam said, blushing a little at the praise.

"The trees look healthier than I've ever seen them," Levi said before he realized this would mean admitting he'd been infringing on Noelle's territory.

Noelle glared at him, which was the first time she'd acknowledged his presence since he'd walked in. "What do you know about trees?" she asked him.

"I grew up on a tree farm," he pointed out, "and my dad knows a little bit about wood."

She scrunched up her nose, as if she were annoyed she couldn't argue with either of those things.

"You finally managed to get rid of that recurring fungus on the blue spruce. I'm impressed," he told her honestly. She was a huge pain in his ass, but she was a great tree farmer.

Noelle nodded. "Well. I can't have my trees sick." It wasn't warm, but it was probably the warmest interaction they'd had in years.

Miriam looked between them. "You know, the two of you might really get along if you let yourselves."

They both snorted. Miriam shrugged.

"Do you need to bring on help?" Hannah asked. "Because we might need to pay *them*."

He nodded, drumming his fingers on his thigh. "I'll definitely need somebody to sous-chef for day-of events. I have a friend, Nafil, who I know is off ship right now because he keeps texting me to meet him in the city for drinks. Maybe we can build him into the budget with the Davenport bill?"

"You have friends?" Noelle asked, feigning shock. "You should go meet him. And then not come back!"

He stuck his tongue out at her. He did have friends, even if coming back to Carrigan's felt like he'd cut himself off from the real world. This wasn't Narnia; he still had cell service, and he should probably start responding to some of the several "Hey dude you fell off the face of the earth" texts soon, before he actually didn't have friends anymore.

Nafil would be excited to hear about this cool project, anyway. Because it was incredible. His girls were transforming their home into something new, and big, and exciting. He didn't deserve to be proud of them, but his heart didn't know that.

"Okay," Hannah said, obviously trying to shuffle him out. "That should be everything you could ever need."

For reasons he couldn't explain even to himself, he wasn't quite ready to leave. Maybe it was because Hannah was hot when she was being In Charge. He stuffed his hands in his pockets.

"Before I put together a pitch for Delilah, or really do anything for Carrigan's, no matter how temporarily, it would help if I had a better understanding of the vision you all have for Carrigan's All Year. Not the business model—I understand 'use the big farm and hotel to host things throughout the year instead of only at Christmas' idea—but, I don't know, sell me on Carrigan's All Year like I'm a brand-new person who doesn't understand the magic of Carrigan's."

"You don't," Hannah said a little sadly.

Levi raised an eyebrow. "Oh, I know it's magic. I've just never been convinced the magic is benevolent."

"Ooh, can I do the pitch?" Miriam asked, bouncing up and down in her seat. "I'm so good at the pitch."

Hannah waved at her.

Miri took a deep breath, like she was preparing to sing an opera. "OKAY." She threw her hands out wide. "For sixty years, Carrigan's Christmasland has been a place families treasure, returning year after year to participate in traditions and bask in the atmosphere of a true Christmas spectacular. Couples have met, fallen in love, gotten married, and brought their children out to our farm to build snowmen, compete in the gingerbread house contest, swap cookies, and make ornaments that stay on our Carrigan's trees for *their* grandchildren. It's a place where dreams come true, sometimes even dreams you never let yourself admit you had. But, until now, Carrigan's Christmasland only held events to showcase its special brand of magic during the winter holidays. Now, with the newly launched Carrigan's All Year, you will be able to discover our little pocket of wonder in the Adirondacks for your class reunions, weddings, family weekends, and everything in between. If you have an event you'd like to host in the most beautiful place in the world, with incredible food, unmatched service, and a vintage atmosphere you have to see to believe, Carrigan's All Year is the place. It's the magic of Carrigan's, all year."

She finished with spirit fingers, and Hannah and Noelle clapped.

"Well?!" she asked him.

"Santorini, Greece, is the most beautiful place anywhere," he said. "But it's a very persuasive pitch." It made his heart raw, knowing this Carrigan's had always existed and he'd never thought he was invited to visit there. He looked up at Hannah. "Is that how you see it, too? This beautiful, magical place?"

Hannah scrunched up her eyebrows, her eyes showing her confusion. "Why else would I have worked so hard to save it?"

He shrugged. "Family legacy. Obligation to Cass."

"If I wanted to carry on a family legacy," she said, "I would have gone to work for Rosenstein's Bread and Pastry. I felt obligated to Cass for giving me my safe haven, but I wouldn't have made Carrigan's my whole life if I didn't love it for its own sake. I thought you knew that."

Their eyes were caught, and he forgot Miri and Noelle were there, as they both tried to tell each other things they didn't know how to say. He shook his head. "This is the wrong time to talk about this."

Hannah shooed him out. "You're right. We have real work to do."

He left the room feeling off balance. He was supposed to come back home changed and show them all who he'd grown up to be, but Carrigan's wasn't supposed to change without him. Miriam was happier, more present, more alive. Hell, Miriam was *here*. Noelle was smiling more and grunting at people less. She did still look at him like she was considering ways to drop him down the well without contaminating the water supply, but that was comforting, to be honest. Hannah was the boss of everything she was destined to be. Meanwhile, he was in limbo.

He was not the returning hero, and he hadn't won his girl back.

Like all of Carrigan's under the girls' management, the scope of events the kitchen needed to serve had ramped up fast. He estimated they needed a complete overhaul of the ovens and a walk-in refrigerator, at least, if they were going to viably transition to a large event destination. The part of him that loved a kitchen challenge wanted to sit down with Hannah to do a deep dive into her books.

It should be easy to write Carrigan's All Year off as something he wasn't interested in and no one wanted him to be involved with, but he was drawn to the partnerships Hannah had set up with food artisans from all over Upstate New York. The calendar for the year had wine and cheese pairing classes, beekeeping classes, olive oil tastings (he hadn't even realized you could grow olives up here), all with local ingredients.

The show he wanted to helm was all about people using their locally available ingredients to make their traditional dishes, and it tugged at him that she had created something so in line with his dreams here.

One of his best friends during the filming of *Australia's Next Star Chef* had been an older woman who ran a B&B with her husband in Queensland. Over many late nights in the contestant house, Levi had learned everything he probably should have learned from his parents, about how much work it took to run a place like that, and he'd begun to truly appreciate both his parents' brilliance and his wife's ambition. This first chance to see them in action, now that he had some distance and perspective, was illuminating and unsettling—because of how drawn he was to this work he'd disdained all his life.

He was sitting at the kitchen island, drinking a cup of coffee and reading the *Christmasland Circular*, imagining Hannah at all these food events without him, when his mom came in and began prepping for lunch around him. He was supposed to be finalizing the menu for the first Davenport event, the engagement party, and he stuffed the circular under his laptop, but she smirked at him. Busted.

She handed him a knife, a cutting board, and veg to prep.

"You need to order food for the engagement party, which is only one week from now. I started a list, but you'll want to go over it. I know you, and I know you'll have opinions."

This seemed unfair, because Delilah had specifically asked for him, so of course he was going to put his own spin on the event, although it was mostly already planned. He didn't say that, though, because whining to his mom about how things were unfair seemed like the opposite of proving he'd changed. Instead, he asked, "Isn't this all pretty last minute for a big society wedding? Engagement party at the beginning of May, wedding in the middle of June?"

His mother shook her head. "Ours is not to ask the rich to explain; ours is but to feed them and take their money."

"Aye aye, Captain," he said.

"You want a tomato sandwich?" she asked.

He had never wanted to eat anything more. No one made a sandwich like his mother.

"So your show is filmed, and you can't tell me if you won, but I'm guessing you got pretty far if you got a pilot off the publicity?" she asked as she got out ingredients. "What would you want the new show to look like? What are you envisioning?"

Whew. He was not going to have to talk about mooning over the Carrigan's event calendar. Or about the fight he'd had with his wife. Or the fact that he had a wife.

"I guess I envisioned it as being boldly Jewish, boldly modern, boldly who you are, where you are?" He could see the show in his mind, and he'd pitched it to Food Network already, but he felt silly giving his mom his elevator speech. "I'd be exploring Manhattan's diverse, multiethnic Jewish history, talking to restaurant owners, families, rabbis about what it means to them to eat Jewish food, and then re-creating traditional dishes from all over the world into modern food with bold flavors."

"Are those the kind of recipes you're pitching Delilah Davenport? She's going to be thrilled."

"Wellllll . . ." he said, and listed some of his ideas for her.

"Levi, these are the same old appetizers any CIA graduate leaves school with. Puff pastry with goat cheese and caramelized onion? I can buy this frozen at Costco." She wasn't wrong. It was delicious, but any other wedding caterer could do it in their sleep. "This isn't going to impress the Davenports. You need to bring Blue to this table. The whole Blue."

"I love your brain, Mom," he told her, and she blushed. He could feel the breath in his lungs reach deeper, and his world righted itself a tiny bit.

"You should update the Carrigan's menu while you're here," she said offhandedly.

He shook his head. "That's *your* menu. I'm not going to overhaul it and then leave." He did want to update the Carrigan's menu; he'd been imagining it for years. Had tried to go to Cass with his excitement and his new ideas, his big ambitions, and been told that's not what they did here, not what people came for. He'd been shut right down.

"Well, I'm not going to pass on my menu to whoever we hire to replace me. And it needs updating. Of the two of us, one is a relatively recent culinary school graduate who has cooked all over the world, and one of us is a grandmother who's been cooking the same dishes in the same kitchen for forty years."

The same incredibly delicious, perfect dishes that she was very territorial about. What was she up to?

"If I'm going to redesign any of it, it needs to have your fingerprints all over it," he said slowly. He wasn't sure he trusted this, and he was wary. "I would want to update some of the old recipes from when Cass first opened, make it go with Miriam's antiques and the aesthetic the girls are building. Appealing to young families and hipsters, but still a little nostalgic. Jewish as hell." He couldn't help it; his brain started designing a modern whitefish salad platter.

He chewed on his lip thoughtfully. "Hannah should help steer the new menu so she makes sure it dovetails with the rebranding. And she can figure out how to launch it to get the most local and tourist attention."

"Are you wooing your girl with PR strategy? Because it might work." His mother waggled her eyebrows at him. Oh, she was sneaky. This was all about matchmaking. "That's something to have brewing in your mind as you come up with wedding ideas. Right now, let's make a list of the events we need dishes for and come up with some sample menus you can pitch to Hannah and the Davenports."

"So, for the engagement party, Governor Davenport called

this morning to request some flavor of mandelbrot that Rosenstein's stopped making in 1978; then his wife called back and said not to make any changes without Delilah's express permission. If I mess up the delicate balance of this, Hannah's going to kill me."

"That's one you need to hand over to her. She's much, much better at diplomacy than you are."

He laughed. He was shit at talking to other people without starting a fight.

"I'm glad you're here, kid," she said, as if she could hear his thoughts. "And I'm glad you're throwing your whole heart in the ring. You've always been careful at showing your feelings, but it's easy when you're young to think that someone who doesn't show you their feelings doesn't have any. Sometimes you have to put it all out there."

"She must have known how I felt about her, though. She's the sun I orbit around." Levi pulled at his hair, the ramifications of what his mom was implying too big to believe.

She rested her head against his. "Did she? It's easy for you to say beautiful words about your love, but did you show her? Did you listen?"

He wanted to argue that there was no possible way that was true, but something stopped him. He *had* kept all his cards close to his chest, and he hadn't stayed when she needed him. He would show up big for this wedding. He would do anything if it meant she felt loved, adored, cherished beyond any measure.

First, though, he had to get her to speak to him, which she wasn't currently doing.

"I feel like I failed, not figuring this out when we were

twenty, like you and Dad. Like I wasted so much time we could have had together." He only whined a little when he said this, which he was proud of.

"You did have most of that time together, baby, just in a different way," she said seriously. "The people you were at twenty weren't ready for each other, and you had to do what it took to get ready."

"Are we ready now?" he wondered nervously.

"I hope you get a chance to find out."

He was going to make a chance. He needed to take his wife on a date so incredible, so perfectly nostalgic that she remembered what they were to each other, and so impressive that she understood he'd done what he set out to do with his life. He had an idea. He kissed his mom on the forehead and went to find his wife.

Levi rapped his knuckles on Hannah's open office door, and she raised her eyelashes at him. He had a flash of the way her eyes used to look when she saw him, the edges crinkling and the pupils dilating a little. That Hannah, the Hannah who looked at him with warmth, was overlaid for a moment over the Hannah in front of him, but it was incongruous. This Hannah, the one whose eyes narrowed when he walked in, was more beautiful than ever. There was a gray streak partly hidden in the blonde at the front of her high ponytail, and she had more laugh lines than she'd had when he left. She was doing her makeup a little differently now. All her clothes seemed more specifically bought for her personality, rather than things she thought she ought to wear as the manager of Carrigan's.

She carried herself differently, her shoulders back more often instead of at her ears, more settled into her body. He wondered if it was the difference between thirty and thirty-five, or if she was that much more comfortable without him around. He knew he felt better in his skin now, after everything he'd done in the past years, but he wondered if they would be able to maintain that comfort in close proximity to each other.

"You wanted something?" she prompted, and he remembered he was supposed to be breathing.

"Oh! Yes. I planned our date. Please be ready at seven the day after tomorrow."

"Where are we going?" she asked, her voice a little panicked.

"Dress nicely," he said. "It's a surprise."

"*Where* are we going, Levi?"

"Not quite to Lake Placid," he assured her. "I'll have you back before you turn into a pumpkin."

She thinned her lips. "I'm not getting on the back of a motorcycle for you, in a dress, in the snow."

"I'll figure out transportation that includes heat," he promised.

He begged his dad to use the truck, which made him feel like a teenager again. His dad grunted and rolled his eyes, but he did arrange transportation. Hannah was wearing a velvet jumpsuit that made him want to pet her, but he refrained with concerted effort.

They pulled up outside a restaurant with a Michelin star and a waitlist six months long that they had been to once, a long time ago.

She groaned. "You didn't."

He shrugged. "You up for a degustation menu?" he asked innocently.

When he gave the host his name for the reservation, he was rewarded with a dazzling smile. "Oh yes, Chef Matthews. Chef Harlow has a table in view of the passthrough reserved for you and asked that she be told when you arrived."

When they were seated, the chef in question came out to greet him. The two of them had met while working as dishwashers in the city during college. He'd called when he realized she was now in charge of the kitchen at the restaurant Hannah and Miriam had brought him to as a kid, the one that had changed his life.

"Bro!" she cried. "What is your famous ass doing in my little place?"

"Oh, sorry, which one of us has a Michelin star?" he asked, hugging her. "I'm here trying to impress a girl. You think you can help?"

Chef Harlow leaned over to shake Hannah's hand. "Hi. If this guy fails to impress you, feel free to take my number."

"Hey!" Levi said when Hannah grinned at her.

"There's no possible way he's going to impress me," Hannah said, "but I look forward to you doing so. I've heard nothing but great things."

"Levi reminded me it's still Passover, so I've designed a menu for you tonight with nothing leavened."

"Thank you so much for doing that for us, Chef," Levi said. "I know it's a pain."

Chef Harlow waved him off. "Anything for you, my dude," she said before leaving them.

"Who would ever have thought, when we first came here,

that I would be back as a friend of the chef's?" Levi rubbed the back of his neck, suddenly nervous that his sort-of career wasn't actually very impressive in comparison to Hannah almost single-handedly saving a whole business. "It's pretty great that almost anywhere I go in the world, I can convince someone much cooler than me to feed me a life-changing meal. One of the mentors on set has, like, one of the top-rated restaurants in the world and he—"

"What's your plan with all this, Blue?" Hannah cut him off. Her foot was tapping in annoyance, and she put her hand on her leg to stop it. "Did you bring me here to gloat about how you're famous now? Brag about the show?"

"Gloat about what?" he asked, sipping his water, trying to figure out what he'd done wrong this time. "Wait, are you mad at me for having a TV show?"

"I'm not mad about the show!" She slammed her water glass down. "I'm fucking livid that you have everything you said you were going to get when you left here, and you're in my home that you scorned all our lives, rubbing it in my face. You have this big, wide life full of adventures, you're on TV, you're famous in Australia. Obviously you were right to leave, and I was wrong. And if we were really 'soulmates,' you would have known I would be mad about it!"

He tugged at his hair in frustration, but his voice was gentle. "How would I have known that, Hannah? You haven't spoken to me in four years!" He needed to stay calm, because he wanted to prove to Hannah their dynamic had changed—which would mean not getting into fights every time they disagreed. He wanted to understand what was at the root of this. "I don't understand what's wrong with having a big, wide life full of adventures," he said, "but yes, I wanted things when I left here, I got them, and I came back here to show you, because you're the most important person in my life and I thought you would be proud of me. And, honestly, partly because I never felt good enough for you, and I wanted to prove that I was."

"But it's not fair," she said. Her voice cracked, and his hand moved toward hers of its own volition, but she pulled back like he might burn her. "What am I supposed to do to make *you* proud of *me*? You wanted to see the whole world and learn about the cuisine of every culture you could. You wanted to find your place in the great expanse, and I wanted to run a hotel. A really small hotel! One I didn't even have to fight for my job at! I could have been genuinely bad at running hotels, and I still would have gotten to be manager, because I'm family."

"That's bullshit, Hannah. If you'd been bad at it, Cass would have handed you your ass in an expensive handbag and told you to go find another job," Levi said.

She paused as the first round of food was set in front of them, smiling at the waiter.

"I felt like there was something wrong with me for not wanting more out of my life than this. And you always acted like Carrigan's was the worst prison, being stuck here the worst possible future." She dashed tears off her cheek.

"Which meant that what you wanted most in your life was anathema to me," Levi said, and Hannah shook her head.

"What I was doing with my life was small, and worthless." He shook his head, but she pleaded with him with her eyes to let her finish. He set down his knife and fork, folding his hands so she knew all his attention was on her. "I wasn't having great adventures, or making the world better, or having an impact. You said I was hiding. You made me feel like I was wasting my life in the worst way you could imagine: being at Carrigan's." He flinched, closing his eyes for a second, but he came back. He was a hell of a lot better at sitting through discomfort than he'd ever been. "What was I supposed to think? You were the Legend Levi Blue, larger than life. You took up so much oxygen in any room. I was barely even there. The mousy, neurotic girl in the corner, color-coding her life to try to make it stable. Why would you choose me if you had a chance?"

His breath rattled in his lungs. "How was I so bad at telling you what you meant to me? Why I needed to leave? I was so sure you understood why and that you just didn't love me enough to care."

She choked back a sob, stuffing a bite into her mouth.

"Hannah, you are the only thing in a room that makes it possible to breathe. You *are* oxygen. You're the one thing most in color in this whole world. I didn't choose to fall in love with you, because I'm not skilled enough at being a human to have made that choice for myself. Falling in love with you is the smartest, most emotionally responsible thing I've ever done, which is how you know I didn't choose it."

He pushed his hair out of his face. "I didn't run from us. I ran *to* everything else. Because even though I loved you with every cell of my being, even though being in love with you was the biggest thing in my life, you were the only thing for me at Carrigan's, and I knew I couldn't build a future that rested on loving you. That wouldn't have been fair, to either of us."

"I know!" she said, still crying. "And I wanted you to have the wide, amazing, international career you dreamed of. It's why I told you not to come back, so you wouldn't get trapped here, by us. By this suffocating love that keeps trying to take over our lives! I had to stay here, to keep Carrigan's safe, but I let you get out! But now you're back with everything, and I sacrificed all of that for nothing, because I *didn't* keep Carrigan's safe."

He sat back in his seat, a hand over his eyes. "And now I've blown back in, showing off my big fancy career that's so much bigger than Carrigan's, that's always going to take me away again. I was trying to show off for my girl, and I...Fuck. I'm so bad at this. How am I so bad at this?"

Levi had been very mad at himself about a lot of things in his thirty-six years, but he'd almost never been as devastated as he was right now, realizing how much damage he'd done to his wife.

He cut his very excellent food into very tiny pieces as he thought about what to say. "Look, yes, I want to gloat. I do. I want to crow to every kid who made fun of me in high school, 'Look at me, I'm fucking famous in Australia.' I want to gloat to Cass. She was wrong about me, and I'm mad as hell that I can't shove that in her face, to be honest with you. But no. I didn't bring you here to gloat."

"You keep talking about high school like you were some terrible outcast, not a hometown legend."

"To you this place was some sort of utopia, but you didn't grow up here." Why couldn't she believe him? "You know what the kids we went to high school with were like. You were there. I told you everything."

"You choose to remember everything bad that ever happened to you, but you refuse to remember anything good.

You've rewritten our entire life into this horrifying nightmare, erased every amazing time we ever had," she said. She sounded frustrated, and he was frustrated right back. Did she not remember all the times when he had told her about the awful town kids? How many times he cried and raged about growing up in this town?

"How am I supposed to know what to believe when everything I remember is so different from what you do?"

He swallowed. "Can you just believe that the way I remember it is the way it happened *for me*?"

"I want you to be honest with me about something," she said suddenly, tugging on her braid. "Did Cass not like you?"

"Um." He looked around the restaurant wildly. He'd been avoiding this conversation all their lives.

"Talk," Hannah demanded.

"Cass didn't . . ." He paused, trying to find the magic sequence that would make him understood. He started again. "Cass did not . . . like me very much. I mean, maybe she loved me once, out of love for my parents, or because I was an exceptionally charming small child." This was an attempt at a joke, because he had not been.

Hannah was twisting her napkin, looking a little sick, but now that he'd started, he needed to finish.

"But by the time I got older, she mostly thought what everyone thought, that I was surly and self-centered and whiny, that I didn't appreciate my parents or you, that I was always going to be looking for something without ever trying to find it because I liked being able to complain about not having it. It's not even that she was wrong—she wasn't.

"I was all of those things, but Cass . . . Cass saw the best in every lost soul. She saw into the depths of people she passed on the street and changed their whole lives with her insight. She saw the truth of people and I hoped she saw more to me than everyone else did, but she didn't. She saw the same disappointing Blue, and she didn't like him. And she really, especially, didn't like him for her niece."

He could see her brain pinballing.

"She told you we shouldn't be together?" she finally whispered.

"Oh yes." Levi nodded, blowing out a breath. "She told me we would be miserable together all our lives, because you would always be Rapunzel refusing to leave your safe tower, and I would always be either dragging you with me or abandoning you. She didn't think I deserved you, that I was too flighty and was going to ruin your ambitions. She said you were going to have Carrigan's one day, and if I truly loved you, I would walk away and let you."

Head in her hands, Hannah took long, shuddering breaths, then did some kind of tapping on her arms. He watched her, getting more and more afraid she wouldn't believe him or that she would and she would hate him for telling her.

"You kept all of it a secret so I wouldn't have to be mad at Cass," she choked out. "You must have stuffed it further and further down until you were full of thorns and barbs and pain."

He nodded. "So full I had to get out, so I could tear myself open and empty myself out and find something new to fill myself up with."

"I made so much fun of you for leaving to 'find yourself,' but you had to, didn't you?"

He shrugged. "I don't know what version of myself I could have become here."

"Was it just that?" she whispered. "That she told you to leave?"

He shook his head. "Do you remember that glamping trip she took you and Miriam on, the summer we were...twelve?"

Hannah nodded. "She said you didn't want to go."

"Hannah. It was hanging out with you and Miriam. It was being out in the woods. In a fancy camper where I could have cooked for us and brought my makeup. What possible part of that would I not have wanted? I remember the day she came to tell my mom she was taking you both, and she looked right past me like I wasn't there, and said, 'Of course Levi won't want to go.' That was kind of what it was like. All the time."

If Hannah's napkin had been paper, she would have torn it to shreds, working it in her hands.

"Are you sure," she asked as she tried to suck air into her lungs, "she was doing it on purpose? You know she was..." She paused, probably trying to find a way to describe Cass's idiosyncrasies that didn't make her feel like a traitor.

He pulled at his hair. "I knew you wouldn't believe me." He'd hoped she would, but why should she give him the benefit of the doubt at this point?

"I can't lose her!" Hannah cried. "If I believe everything you're saying, I'll lose her again."

"But you can lose me," he said. "Of course." He pulled his scarf in front of his eyes, like somehow he could say the hard thing if he couldn't see her. "I don't think she was deliberately cruel, ever. She was temperamental, and selfish, and kind of bad with children, and when combined with a sensitive little boy who was afraid of rejection, it . . . soured us. And the thing is, it doesn't really matter if she intended to harm me or not, because the end result was still that I was devastated by it. I'm sorry. I'm sorry the truth is that Cass was an asshole sometimes, and once she decided she didn't like you, it was done. But, Hannah, I didn't hide that from you. You knew that about her."

"I did know that," she whispered, so quietly he almost didn't hear her.

Levi reached into the pocket of his leather jacket and pulled out the napkin, which he'd been carrying since Elijah gave it to him. He placed it down in front of Hannah and watched her pick it up. She fished a pair of reading glasses out of her purse, peering at the slightly smudged ink.

"I've never seen Cass Carrigan apologize for anything," she said quietly.

"You wanted this place to be perfect, and it's not," Levi said. "It's not my fault that it's more complicated than you chose to remember."

"I'm going to take a Lyft home," Hannah said sadly. "So glad you decided the best way to win me back was to try to destroy the memories of the person I loved most. Enjoy the rest of your meal. Please give my compliments to the chef."

"I wasn't going to tell you!" Levi called after her. "You asked me!"

This Shenanigan fucking sucked.

Chapter 8

Hannah

When she got back to Carrigan's, she was still shaking with anger, her entire body a torch that had been soaked in gasoline and had finally lit. But now that it was burning, she didn't know how to put it out.

She paced the floor in her room, unable to be still, or sleep, or breathe. She might come out of her skin if she didn't talk to someone, but there was no one.

The old anger called like that ex who never quite manages to lose your number. It was as comforting as her best worn pair of sweatpants, the hoodie she pulled on when she was too cold with missing him. It had started to pill from being washed so much, but it had holes for her thumbs in exactly the right places, and she could hide her whole head in it so she didn't have to see the light when the world got too bright. She'd pulled that anger up into herself so many times in the past years that it had rewritten her DNA, had dyed her internal monologue a dull red and given her, instead of rose-colored glasses, bloodred garnet ones that painted her world like Dorothy's emerald glasses in Oz.

She was done being who she was with it, but she didn't know how to disentangle it from herself anymore. She had been wearing it like the Venom suit and its power had altered her; she couldn't go back to being plain Eddie Brock now. She found her restless feet taking her upstairs, to the top floor that used to belong to Cass. It was now a guest suite, recently vacated by her relatives. Miriam had decorated it with the million tchotchkes Cass left behind, kept it draped in tulle and white twinkle lights and feather boas so that walking into it felt like Cass might appear at any moment, beturbaned, waving a jeweled hand while telling a story about her wild life.

Hannah looked around now in the moonlight and hated all of it. She'd spent all her life thinking Cass saved her, but all that time, Cass had been destroying the person Hannah needed to survive. She picked up a vintage ceramic reindeer with crystals in its antlers that had the interlocking filigree C's from the wrought-iron gates out front, which stood for both Cass Carrigan and Carrigan's Christmasland, painted on its side in gold. It had been part of an early promotion for the Christmasland Inn, in the sixties. Guests who stayed left with a reindeer collectible. Hannah had loved it as a child; she and Miriam had played make-believe with it up here a million times.

"This will be yours someday. You have to protect the legacy I've left you," Cass told her over and over.

Her rage exploded out of her at the memory, and she threw the reindeer as hard as she could against the wall. Instead of shattering, it bounced. A scream erupted out of her, and she fell to the floor.

She'd been so mad at him for leaving without her, for abandoning her here with her fear when she found she couldn't leave. She'd been furious that he'd walked out on their marriage rather than wait for her to be ready to go with him. But she'd never been mad at him for wanting to see the world, build his career, find himself separate from Carrigan's. She'd been jealous, because she didn't have a self separate from Carrigan's. She'd wanted him to have the wide, amazing, international career he'd dreamed of. It's why, in the end, she'd told him not to come back, so he wouldn't get trapped here, by them.

She was mad at her anxiety for keeping her locked up in this tower instead of letting her see options, explore possibilities. She wanted to leave, but she couldn't. When she thought about leaving Carrigan's, she imagined all the things that could go wrong if she wasn't here to keep everything together, her vision got small, she forgot how to breathe, and she ran from it. This place had saved her from her parents' life that had made her miserable, though they hadn't meant it to.

She'd needed to save it.

She was mad that her brain made her see the whole world in black and white all the time, so it always seemed like there was an emergency to be solved, and she had to be the one to solve it, alone, right now. She was mad at falling in love with the one person who knew her best, because when things had gone wrong between them, she'd lost her person. She had Noelle, but she'd lost everything she'd built with Blue over decades because she couldn't stop herself from falling for him. She was mad as hell that their love swept over them and consumed her and left her so powerless and changed. Ironic that she'd fought so hard not to be taken over by their love but had opened the door and invited her anger in, and in the end it had done the same thing. Made her less herself, less free.

She had been mad at everyone and everything, but never at Cass. Never, for an instant, at Cass. Now, sitting on the floor in Cass's rooms surrounded by the tacky glittery crap Hannah had always loved so much, her body didn't have room for any more rage. She was going to have to give some of it up. She wanted to refuse to process anything Levi had told her, because she didn't know who she was if Cass wasn't her savior, but she knew in her heart she needed to let go of her anger at Blue or it was going to kill her.

He'd left because he had to, and she'd stayed because she had to, and they'd cut each other to ribbons trying to escape the hurt of that inevitability, but neither of them had been wrong.

She'd held on to this anger, fed it so she could get through, but now she had to work with him, had to do the most important event of her career by his side, so she needed to find some measure of peace.

Maybe these dates were a good thing, for more than just the divorce at the end of the tunnel. Maybe she could learn how to be around him again, without spinning out every time. Find some closure, so when he went away again, he wouldn't take any of her with him this time.

Stop being mad at Levi without getting back together, she wrote in the Notes app of her phone. And dust under Cass's bed.

The Davenport team blew in like a monsoon the morning before the engagement party, sudden and inescapable. Wedding planner, photographer, governor's social media manager, mother of the bride, several people whose jobs Hannah had not caught. All of them were arrayed in the kitchen, talking to Blue about the menu for the next day.

The warm delft blue of the kitchen glowed in the yellow light, and Levi looked...damn it, he looked perfect. He had that "haunted misfit fundamentally unable to make good choices" look, the kind of misunderstood antihero who made people contort themselves into pretzels to redeem him. She wanted to vomit.

He was standing behind the island, a towel over his shoulder and an apron around his waist, talking animatedly to the wedding planner about hollandaise, which he'd been trying for a decade to convince anyone who would listen was about to have a comeback. She could recite his hollandaise TED Talk from memory. His hair was defying gravity, reaching upward toward the sky in a way that seemed structurally unsound. His beard was trimmed neatly in contrast, and something about that contrast was annoyingly appealing. Everyone in the inn who liked men, at all, was making heart eyes at him and sighing under their breath while hanging on his every word.

This is what's waiting for him in the world, she thought. He can't stay cooped up here, where he's known, once the adulation leaves. He'll go where he's adored instead. What would stop him? *Not boring me with my day planners and spreadsheets and clipboard*. Not the type A hometown girl who knows him inside out. Who's always so fucking difficult. Who can't make her feel leave this damn hotel, even if she wanted to.

Which she did want to. She *wanted* to be able to go to all the places he'd been, as an adult, able to make her own agenda and see the things she wanted to see. She wanted to choose where she was, instead of letting her anxiety choose for her. And she was getting there, slowly, with her therapist and medication. She could get farther afield now than she could a year ago. Partly because Cass was gone, so the catastrophe her anxiety was trying to prevent had already happened—her staying hadn't prevented the worst, and somehow that had loosened her ties a little. But not fast enough for Levi. Not fast enough to let her go with him when he inevitably left this time.

She wanted to snarl at all of them, tell them he was taken, not just married but claimed in a way almost no one ever got to be, belonged to her in ways they wouldn't even begin to understand. It defied logic, and common sense, but some not-small part of her wanted to yell at all of them to get out of her inn and stop flirting with her hot husband.

"This is the most I've ever liked him," Noelle said, coming up next to her. She looked at her best friend, surprised.

"Aren't you mad at me?"

"Yeah, I'm pissed as hell, but I'm not going to give you the silent treatment. I'm not a child," Noelle huffed.

"Or the Noelle of six months ago who totally gave Miriam the silent treatment?" Hannah pointed out.

Noelle shoved her hands in her pockets and scowled. Oh, her best friend was so very much like her husband.

"This"—Hannah gestured at Levi—"is, like, everything you hate about him times eleven."

"Nah, he's brooding seriously, but it's because he's actually seriously passionate about food, which is kind of refreshing." She waved at where he was flipping a frying pan in his hand, like a pitcher tossing a ball up. "He's not being manipulative or whiny. He's comfortable in his skin instead of trying so hard it makes my skin itch. Also, he talks to everyone... like they're people. I've never noticed that before."

"What are you talking about?" Hannah asked, surprised out of her reverie. "How else would he talk to them?"

"I mean, he doesn't talk to women differently than he talks to men. He doesn't talk to production assistants differently from directors. I can't figure out..." Noelle cocked her head, watching him. "He actually speaks to everyone as his equal. It's making me reevaluate my life and I hate it."

Hannah laughed, but realized Noelle was right.

A very small blonde woman was staring up at him with adoration on her face, and he seemed totally unfazed by it. He just kept talking to her about bell peppers. It was adorable, which made her angry.

"He doesn't talk to me like that," she said. "I mean, he turns on that misanthrope smile, but it's calculated."

"Yes, to get in your pants. With you, he's actually flirting. Oh! Oh, that's it. He's not trying to have sex with any of these people. Also, I have to give credit," Noelle added, her shoulders hunched in annoyance, "his hair looks fantastic."

It did, damn him.

"Do you remember," Hannah asked, turning her head to Noelle, "when you were trying to decide whether or not to get together with Miri, and I told you if I had the choice to do it all over again, I would?"

"Yes." Noelle nodded slowly. "I remember that pivotal conversation that helped me make a major, life-altering decision. Why?"

"I was wrong, NoNo. I want to take it all back. Being in love with him is too hard."

"Yeah, because he fucking sucks, and you should forget he ever existed."

He turned from the conversation he was having, his eyes seeking her out as if they were two magnets. This is what it had been like between them for years, maybe always. When one was in a room in the house, anywhere in the greater Upstate New York area, the other knew. He raised an eyebrow, a silent communication in a language she no longer wanted to speak, and she turned away so he wouldn't see the tear tracks on her face.

Noelle followed. "I'm going to get sandwiches from Collin's diner. There's too much toxic sexual tension in this hotel, and not enough carbs."

"We have food here." Hannah sniffled. "Free food. Made by a chef who is *famous in Australia*." She said this last with a sarcastic hand flourish.

"A, we do not have sandwiches, because there's no bread in the entire inn. B, if we did, they would be traitor sandwiches," Noelle declared.

"Collin's egg salad *is* better," Hannah said. "Are you too mad at me to bring me soup back? I have to do this filming thing with Chef Suave over there."

"Extra pickle?" Noelle asked, knowing full well Hannah wanted an extra pickle.

"Maybe two." It was a multi-pickle day.

Governor Davenport was unable to be as involved in the planning of his daughter's wedding as he would have hoped. He'd decided the reasonable solution for that problem was to have a videographer follow Delilah around for the entire process. As a side benefit, he would be able to use the footage later for campaign material. Hannah agreed to this because she liked Governor Davenport's policies and wanted him reelected, and because the videographer promised to make Carrigan's look amazing on camera and she was hoping to use some of it for their own ads.

While Delilah and her betrothed wandered the grounds taking selfies with Miriam and going live from the reindeer enclosure, Hannah and Levi were meant to be explaining to the camera what Levi was preparing for the upcoming engagement party, while he demonstrated some recipes. The videographer and wedding planner had justified this terrible idea by repeating that it should be cake for Levi, a TV chef, to cook on camera. "Pretend you're filming a segment!" they said breezily.

This was all fine except that for reasons none of them had articulated to her satisfaction, they also wanted Hannah to appear in this segment, despite the fact that she couldn't even cook.

"Never underestimate the lure of a beautiful blonde!" the videographer said vaguely. Why she might want to be luring Governor Davenport was unclear. They arranged her braid over one shoulder so it glowed a dark honey under the lights and positioned her behind the kitchen counter, too close to Blue.

"Okay, Hannah," Levi began in a voice that was nothing like his own. His TV voice sounded like he'd invented a separate alter ego. Maybe he had. "Tell me what we're prepping for this week at Carrigan's Christmasland. What do we do on a Christmas tree farm in the middle of spring?"

"Well, the trees keep growing year-round, Levi," Hannah deadpanned, "so the farmers are still farming. But the Christmasland Inn hosts visitors and celebrations all year. This week we're celebrating a wonderful holiday about rebirth and welcoming the renewal of the world."

"Easter?" Levi asked, skeptical.

She laughed. "We're Jewish, dude."

"I know," he said seriously, pointing to his yarmulke. "So, what are we celebrating?"

"May Day!" She gestured, with jazz hands.

"Also not a Jewish holiday," he pointed out.

"Fair point." Hannah smiled at the camera. "We are hosting an engagement party tomorrow. The couple wanted something fun and informal. The groom is Welsh, and apparently it's a whole bank holiday there? So the bride asked us to plan a May Day festival, complete with maypoles, flower crowns, and morris dancers."

"I love Wales. It's so wonderfully eccentric," Levi said.

"Me too! Did you know Cardiff has two separate radical queer bookshops?" Hannah replied.

"Of course they do." Levi nodded, seeming unsurprised. "Point of clarification: Will there be dancing around bonfires in the woods?"

"There will be bonfires on the front lawn, because no fire is allowed near the trees," Hannah told him.

"Noted. So, what do we make to preserve the festival spirit of the holiday, while also presenting our guests with a gourmet experience? What says, 'let's rejoice that the world is fertile again'?" He cocked an eyebrow at the word *fertile*. Hannah swore she heard someone swoon off camera.

She propped her elbows on the counter and rested her chin in her hands, looking up at him with all the sweetness she could muster. "Well, Levi, since you are the chef, I thought it would be better if you told me the menu."

She didn't want to be having this much fun. But that was the thing about the two of them, when they weren't tearing each other apart, no one ever made her have as much fun.

"We need everything to be portable, so we'll have booths set up across the lawn with traditional May Day foods from around the world, updated with a Levi Matthews twist. Sticky buns, oat-cakes, grilled salmon skewers, miniature herb tarts, and more."

"Okay, I am looking forward to eating all of that," Hannah admitted, mock grudgingly.

"I appreciate your vote of confidence," Levi said. "The recipe I'm going to show you today is a twist on a traditional lemon shortbread, baked into a stick like a Pocky, then dipped in freeze-dried raspberry powder."

"This sounds complicated, Levi," Hannah said.

"Ah, that's the secret," Levi said, winking. Hannah rolled her eyes at him. "It looks very complicated, but it's actually easy enough for beginning home bakers, like yourself."

Hannah huffed in indignation, her hands over her heart. "Must you tell my deepest, darkest secrets? No Rosenstein publicly admits she can't bake!"

"Can you handle measuring the flour?" he asked with mock concern. "You're going to need to weigh it on the scale."

"I think I can figure it out," she said, sticking her tongue out at him.

"I'm sure you can. You run a very demanding, complicated business with ease." He looked into her eyes as he said it, and she felt her knees start to buckle. She looked away and dumped the flour into the bowl of the stand mixer. It poofed out at her in a cloud.

Levi caught her eye again, and they both started giggling. He reached over to wipe the flour off her cheek, and their gazes got trapped.

They fell into an easy rhythm, handing each other ingredients without needing to ask, seeming to understand where the other was about to be. All those years of being hyperaware of where he was at any time paid off. When he brushed an arm or a hip against her, she knew he was doing it on purpose, which didn't stop all her nerve endings from being raw at the touch.

When the videographer said she had enough footage, she left them to talk things over with the wedding planner while Hannah hid and took several long breaths to try to regain her equilibrium.

She needed to get away from him. The heat of him next to her while they cooked, the smell of him—still the same as when he left, and when they'd been twenty-five and she'd pined over him, and when they were fifteen and the sight of him had set her body on fire for the first time—all of it was making her hormones do things she hadn't even known they were still capable of.

He had once been irresistible in his surly, reckless self-centeredness, in his insufferable balance of whiny and cocky. That boy didn't appeal to her anymore; she'd inoculated herself against him, and she'd thought that would make her safe. Instead, he'd shown up grown, thoughtful, with his heart on his sleeve, and this version was irresistible, too. This version of the boy she'd loved every day of her life, who she'd never met, drew her in to the mystery. What changed him? How did he get this way? How did the Blue she knew become this loose-limbed comfortable man who smoldered instead of sulked?

This feeling of not being in control of her desires, of being pulled along by the tides of a love bigger than she could hope to contain, was what she hated about being near Blue. He had loved being pulled under by the current of the two of them together, but it had terrified her. It made her feel off balance. It wasn't her plan; it made her want to throw all her plans out and wing it. It made her someone different.

He deserved someone who wanted to fall with him and be swept under. He deserved to be a person separate from the destiny of their story, and so did she.

When all the various parts of the Davenport entourage had seen enough and been bundled back onto the train, she went looking for him to plead with him to do what was best for both of them, and let go of this idea he had of wooing her. They could be friends. They had been most of their lives. If they couldn't, he needed to leave.

"Blue, are you in here?" Hannah called out. She was standing in the kitchen. His apron was off its hook, the smell of potatoes and cheese came from the oven, prep for tomorrow was covering every available surface, and yet there was no sign of Levi.

"Pantry," he called out, and she followed his voice into the big walk-in pantry at the back of the kitchen, next to the door to the Matthewses' apartments. Levi was standing, hands on his hips, glasses pushed up into his hair (when did he get glasses? How hadn't she known?), wearing a pair of jeans she hadn't seen in years. She recognized the heart patch holding the back pocket onto the ass, because she'd sewn it there a lifetime ago. It had been before they started dating, but after she'd started whispering his name to herself in the night. His floral-print thermal shirt clung to his shoulders, the sleeves pushed up his forearms (thermals should be illegal, and so should Levi's forearms). She felt a rush of annoyance at him for being so unnecessarily hot, so she was scowling at him when he turned to look at her. His face was all serious contemplation, but his eyebrows shot up when he saw her face.

"What did I do?" he asked, and she was even more annoyed that he still knew her looks.

"Nothing, other than existing." She shook her head to clear the lust.

He waved her over, and she came to stand next to him. The fabric of their shirts brushed together and she got goose bumps. It was a mistake to be this close. The door shut behind her, leaving them alone together in the dimly lit pantry. The smell of his deodorant hit her with a profound sense memory of being naked and covered in his sweat. She breathed through her mouth.

"Shouldn't you be cooking for tomorrow?"

"Probably, but I needed an introvert break so I'm hiding for ten minutes, updating the dry goods inventory." He turned the tablet he was holding so she could see it. He seemed to have built an Excel spreadsheet to track all of their food expenditures, usage dates, recipes—it was extensive, and impressive.

"I did this while I couldn't sleep," he was explaining. "I can't seem to sleep here. I know my mom kind of runs the kitchen by vibes, but Miriam told me you three are trying to clean up the financial systems, and you're going to need..."

She should be listening to him, but she was watching how he lit up when he talked about running a kitchen, how his whole demeanor changed as he forgot to be on guard. She was sad, because she'd always wanted him to feel that way about Carrigan's, but she was also really, really turned on. He'd built her a spreadsheet so her business could be a success. A business he hated and actively hoped would fail.

She forgot her entire plan of begging him to just be friends.

"...you can obviously change any of the categories that don't work, but I think the formula I input will help—"

How could she resist that? She lifted her hand to his cheek, and he turned his face into her palm reflexively. His eyes widened as she tugged on the front of his shirt with her other hand. He wrapped his arms around her waist, burying his face in her neck. His beard scraped against her skin, and the pantry crackled with an electrical charge of want.

Hannah's hand slid around to his hair, yanking his mouth to hers. They melted together, exactly as they had that night in the library. This time, though, instead of comfort and muscle memory, it was frantic, incandescent want. Levi backed Hannah up against the door, and she wrapped a leg around his waist. Her internal monologue had completely fled in the face of her lust.

His fingers dug into her ass, and she moaned into his mouth. In between kisses, he mumbled, "I should tell you not to kiss me unless you're ready to be together, but I'm not going to stop you."

She took a deep breath. "We should not be fooling around in this closet."

"No room to make out on the kitchen counters right now.

Plus my mom might find us," he said against her mouth. He fit his body more fully against hers, and she lit up like fireworks.

She seriously had to stop having sex with her husband.

"What was that?" Levi asked as they got back into their clothes. "Not that I'm complaining. But. I'm a little confused."

She turned away, trying to get her bearings, and he braided her hair while he waited for her. How was he so calm, and why couldn't she be? "I don't know, I convinced myself I was going to use this time to find peace with you, and then there was so much touching, and flour, and the wedding planner was flirting with you! Right in front of me! And I did not feel peaceful."

"Are you jealous?"

She turned back, and he was grinning.

"Yes! It's awful." She glared at him. "Stop grinning! I was here, wasting away, while you were wandering the world, sleeping with who knows how many people. And now you're flaunting it in my face that you're beautiful and ooze charisma and people just...want you."

"Oozing charisma sounds kind of gross," he said somewhat nonsensically. He was trying to fix his hair but failing, so she stood on her tiptoes and fixed it for him.

"It is gross," Hannah assured him.

"Zero. I was sleeping with zero people," he said quietly, his face serious.

She froze. "What? Why not?"

"Um, because I was married, I guess?" he said.

She stared at him, flabbergasted.

"Look, Hannah, it's flattering that you think I could flirt with the wedding planner successfully, truly."

She raised an eyebrow in disbelief, and he raised a shoulder in response. "I'm never going to sleep with anyone else, I suspect. If it's not you, it's probably not anyone. That's not your fault or your responsibility, but it's true."

"You're not going to make me feel bad about ruining your sex life," she told him.

He started to answer, but she interrupted him.

"I'm sorry, that's not fair. I know you didn't come home so you could have sex again without feeling guilty about your marriage vows."

"I don't feel guilty. I don't feel sexual attraction for other people, but we can talk about that later."

She blinked at him. That was fairly crucial information.

"I came home because I realized the whole world meant nothing if you weren't with me, and your whole world is here."

That stung, that he thought of her as someone whose whole world was this hundred-some acres of land. But whose fault was that, really? She'd kept parts of herself quiet as a sort of test to him, to see if he loved her enough to guess them without her having to talk about them. And for a while, Carrigan's *had* been her whole life.

Still, whoever was at fault, he was wrong about her. Carrigan's might be the center of her world, but it wasn't the whole thing. She *had* wanted to see everything with him. Just, not then, not yet, not until she'd made sure Carrigan's would be safe to come home to.

"It's super convenient that you got to do all the sowing of wild oats you ever wanted and can now return to say it was me you wanted all along. You get everything you ever wanted, without any consequences." She looked up into his eyes, defying him to tell her what she already knew, that this too was unfair.

"I mean, living for four years wondering every day if I'd ever see the love of my life again is a consequence."

Oh. She hadn't thought of it that way.

He rested his forehead on hers. She let him. "Besides, you got everything you ever wanted. You got Carrigan's. What the hell is wrong with getting everything you ever wanted??"

She sighed, letting her body lean against his, taking comfort from his familiar warmth. She was doing a terrible job of being friends.

"How can we be everything to each other and know each other so little?" she asked, as much to herself as to him. "How can we know every breath the other has ever taken and still not be able to communicate?"

He kissed her forehead. "I have been asking myself that question for four years, babe. But I have an idea."

"Is it a terrible Levi Blue idea? Are there Shenanigans? Because I don't think that's going to solve our problems."

"You undervalue Shenanigans, but no." He took a deep breath, and their heartbeats synced. "For six years, whenever we got scared and our feelings felt too raw to talk about them, we either fought or fucked to try to get at the truth without having to actually sit down and be uncomfortable. I think we should agree to stop yelling at each other and try...talking."

All the wind was knocked out of Hannah. This was what she'd wanted, to find some way they could be at peace together, but she'd never expected him to put down his boxing gloves. How did he keep surprising her?

"Yes. You were the most important person in my life once, and no matter what happened or is going to happen, even if we're never an us again, I don't want to keep being unkind. I don't want to be on offense, or defense."

He smiled against her hair. "Hannah, I hate to tell you this, but I don't think there's any version of this world where there's no such thing as an 'us,' even if we're not together. We could be apart for fifty years, and on our deathbeds we would miss each other. That's just the story we're in. I know you hate it."

"I don't hate it, Blue. It scares me," she said into his chest. She wished she hated it. It would be easier if she hated it, if it didn't call to her like a siren song.

"I do have one condition," she said.

"Name it."

"We have to stop hooking up. If our defaults are fighting or fucking, we need to stop doing both."

He laughed. "Yeah, we do. It's really messing with my head."

"Speaking of hooking up..." She pushed away from him so she could see his face. "Do you want to explain this whole 'I don't feel sexual attraction for other people' thing?"

Levi surveyed the kitchen. "Do we have time for this talk?"

"For this, we'll make time."

"Come over to the porch swing and let me tell you about demisexuality." He threw an arm over her shoulder.

"I know what demisexuality is, Blue. I have two gay best friends and a Tumblr."

Chapter 9

Levi

"You like sex," Hannah said as they settled on the porch swing. "We've had a lot of it in the past decade. Some in the past hour, which I thought was great?"

She sounded so worried.

"It was! Better than great." He laughed a little. "Life-changing wouldn't be incorrect. I do like sex. With you. A lot." Levi held her eyes and pushed a stray hair back into her braid. "At no point have I ever been less than a very willing participant in our sex life. Way up on my favorite things list. I have zero interest in having sex with anyone else. I might if I fell in love with them. I've always been in love with you, so I don't know for sure."

"You're aware that you're allowed to fall in love with multiple people in a lifetime, right?" Hannah raised an eyebrow at him.

"I'm aware that is an experience many people have," Levi conceded, nodding. "It hasn't been true for me yet, but the next twenty years may bring things that the past twenty have not."

"I thought there was nothing new to learn about you." She laughed a little surprised laugh. "How did you figure it out?"

"The internet? I saw it in a fic, and I started Googling, and...realized that if I hadn't fallen for you, I would have been happy to be single forever. Maybe if I'd gotten to know someone else really, really well, the kind of trust we had, I might have wanted them, but otherwise..." He trailed off and shrugged.

She was quiet, watching his face. He started twisting his scarf. "Please say something!"

She put her hand over his, lacing their fingers together. He took a deep breath. "You said someone else. Do you think you could have fallen for a boy? Or someone nonbinary?" she asked, sounding only curious.

"I think it could have been anyone I felt that close to." He laid his head down on the back of the swing. "I've thought about this a lot, and I'm not sure gender matters much for me. If you told me tomorrow you were transitioning, you would have been a boy all along, and I would be in love with a boy; I would have been all my life. I would obviously feel thrilled for you, but you being a boy wouldn't change how I identify in any way. I don't know, it's not clear-cut. I've never loved anyone else, so I can't say for sure."

"So you're demi and pan? Maybe? But maybe just...?"

"Hannah-sexual." He laughed.

She frowned. "That's a lot of pressure, Blue." But she didn't unlace their fingers, so he knew she was processing out loud, and while he didn't love the response, he was willing to see where she went next.

"I don't mean it to be." He shook his head. "I'm not missing out on some crucial experience when I'm not experiencing sexual desire. My life isn't less fulfilling without it. I would have thought 'you're the love of my life and I don't want to divorce you' would be way more pressure."

She tipped her head back onto the porch swing and blew out a breath. "You're right. Your sexuality isn't a burden for me. I never want you to feel that way. It's not about me at all, and it's amazing, and I'm so excited for you that you know." She teared up a little, and his eyes welled up in response. "I wish the angry little boy mad at the world because he felt like a square peg would have had the internet to give him some language and community."

"You and me both." He nodded, choking up. "I think he still would have been angry at the world, but less angry at himself."

"I love that little boy. I never wanted him to be mad at himself for existing. He was perfect." She looked over at him, and some part of his heart blossomed where it had been barren before.

"And now?" he grumbled, because he was trying not to fully weep.

She ruffled his hair. "Now you're an asshole, and you make my life difficult."

"Fair," he said. He could work with that. Hannah liked difficult, and she kind of liked assholes. She kind of *was* an asshole a lot of the time, and it was one of his favorite things about her.

"Thank you for telling me," Hannah said.

He'd imagined this conversation, wondered how she would

react, tried to script what he would say. He'd never come out to anyone else, because it wasn't anyone else's fucking business who he had pantsfeelings for, but he'd known as soon as he first learned demisexuality existed, that first year he was working out on that first cruise ship, that he wanted to talk about it with Hannah, that she would understand what it meant to him. To have words for what he'd always felt and never been able to articulate. It didn't functionally change anything about his marriage but knowing changed everything about himself.

"No matter how it works out, I'm glad if I was going to love for the rest of my life, it's you."

Something occurred to him. "So, back to sex, do you still have your IUD?"

Hannah laughed. "Did it just occur to you that we should probably not get pregnant right now? Yes, I do. I do not prefer to ever be surprised by my period."

He was relieved, and also, just a tiny bit, disappointed. She was right that they probably shouldn't get pregnant. Right now. Because he didn't want to get into that, he asked, "Are you ready for the party?"

They worked well together as a professional team, he was finding, and it was something they could talk about that didn't feel like being put under an X-ray machine and having his darkest secrets revealed. Besides, he needed to give them time to talk about work. She needed to see him as someone who took her career seriously.

"Is everything completely organized and reorganized and triple-checked and ready to roll? Yes. Obviously, it's me." She pulled her hand away and his whole body protested the loss of her touch. "Am I having a little bit of anxiety over the governor being here and about leaving you in charge of the kitchen for a major event? Yes. But it's a good trial run for the wedding."

"You know I've run some kitchens, right?" he reminded her.

"I actually don't know, because I'm not clear on what you've been doing for the past four years except swanning about on a boat," she pointed out, "but I know for sure you have never run *my* kitchen, so the anxiety stands."

"Excuse me, I was making my fortune on a boat," he protested.

"Oh, I thought you were 'finding yourself,'" she teased him, doing finger quotes. "Who are you, Frederick Wentworth?"

He put a hand over his heart. "I am, after all, half agony, half hope."

"Batting your eyelashes and quoting Austen won't win me back!" she said, pushing him off the porch swing. He went, feeling lighter than he had in years.

"If you're done, and we can't eat in the kitchen because of the event situation, would you have time to have dinner with me? Maybe at the diner so I can see if Collin's egg salad is actually better than mine? I'd like a do-over of that first date."

"Once again I will ask, shouldn't you be cooking?"

Levi shook his head. "I'll be cooking all night. I don't sleep here, remember? Plus, a guy's gotta eat."

"This is going to count as date two," Hannah told him, bumping his shoulder with hers. "Just because you fucked up the first one doesn't mean you get special treatment."

"That's fair."

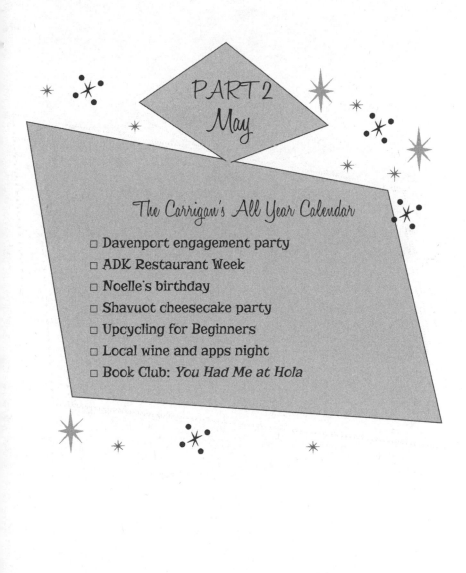

PART 2
May

The Carrigan's All Year Calendar

- ☐ Davenport engagement party
- ☐ ADK Restaurant Week
- ☐ Noelle's birthday
- ☐ Shavuot cheesecake party
- ☐ Upcycling for Beginners
- ☐ Local wine and apps night
- ☐ Book Club: *You Had Me at Hola*

Blue, Age 17

Levi sat on the floor of the library, his back up against bookshelves jammed helter-skelter with books, most of them poking him in vital organs in ways he expected were going to bruise. His crisscrossed legs were completely asleep, and he wasn't sure when he'd be able to walk on them again. He was supposed to be reading a book for English.

Instead, he was staring at the girl asleep with her head in his lap. The book was sitting open, facedown on the floor next to him.

Her dark honey hair was spread out in waves over his knees and the floor, her long lashes sweeping across her high cheekbones, her wide mouth slightly open. She was snoring faintly, and it was so cute Levi's body threatened to fold in on itself at the sound.

In the half hour since she'd fallen asleep, as he became increasingly uncomfortable, he'd thought about a thousand things he could do. Stay here forever, dying and calcifying so he didn't have to wake her up. Kissing her to wake her up. He ran a hand through her hair and banged his head against the bookshelf behind him. This closeness was killing him. He had never had any feelings for anyone else that might even approach what someone would call a crush, had rarely even thought about kissing anyone, much less doing anything more than that.

One day he'd woken up and the way he felt about Hannah, how she was the one person he wanted to tell about his day, and the one person he trusted to be himself around without all his armor, had morphed into her being the only person he wanted to see naked. He didn't know how other people felt when they had a crush, but the longer it went on, the more he was starting to suspect he didn't have a crush—he was in love. With his best friend. His one person. And she kept touching him, fitting her body up against his, her head tucked into his shoulder, her hair blowing its scent up into his nostrils and the heat of her curves destroying him.

Cass stuck her head into the library, and her eyes narrowed. She pointed at Blue. "Get out here."

He carefully moved Hannah, placing his hoodie under her head as a pillow, and slipped out the door.

As soon as the door closed behind him, Cass turned on him. "You should stay the hell away from her," she said, pointing at him with the empty cigarette holder she had taken to twirling between her fingers when she'd given up smoking.

"I can't stay away from her, Cass. She's my person." He set his feet, his body tensed for a fight.

"You're all wrong for each other," Cass argued. "It's going to end in misery."

Blue threw up his hands. "How can we be wrong for each other? We know each other better than any people on the planet."

"You're too close," she told him, waving the cigarette holder. "You're too tied to each other; there's no room to grow. To grow up." When she said "up," she gestured with her arms like she was a tree. Every damn thing had to be a stage with her. "You'll hold her back; she won't have any space to find herself. Besides, you don't have the same futures."

She threw her arms out more expansively, as if into the future.

"You want to get free of this place, study under great chefs, travel the world. She's already seen the world. She's destined to take over this place, be the next owner of Carrigan's. You can't take her inheritance from her, and you shouldn't try. It will only end with you both angry and lonely and everyone in the blast range will be picking shrapnel out of their hair for years. Don't do it, Levi. Stay away from her."

"I can't stay away from her," Levi whispered, barely able to get his voice past his throat.

"Then protect her from her own ridiculous feelings and don't let her know you return them, for the love of Pete."

He looked at Hannah's golden hair spilling over his sweater onto the floor. "You think she . . . you think she likes me?"

Cass snorted. "She's in love with you, and you're not going to touch her because you're no good for her."

His heart burst into flight at the idea that Hannah might be in love with him, back, and then plummeted into the ground at the rest of Cass's words. The thing they'd been dancing around for years. He knew most of Advent thought he was worthless, that the guests at the inn saw him as the help's son. That even

Cass and Hannah's family thought of him as an unwelcome nuisance and a lower class of people—Miriam's dad had called his dad That Handyman for years, and anytime he walked into a room where the Rosensteins were gathered, their easy familial banter got quiet.

He'd always wanted Cass to really see him, but to her he was just an emotionally messy, feral, dangerous boy who might hurt her Hannah. It didn't matter that she'd been at his bris, that he'd lived under her roof all his life, that she'd bandaged his knees and taught him to slide down the banisters yelling, "Shenanigans."

He wasn't good enough for her heir.

He wanted to tell Cass to fuck off, tell her she had no idea what she was talking about, but the thing was, she was right. He knew she was right. He didn't have anything to offer Hannah. He'd have to beg her for a job when she owned the place if he wanted to stay with her. He hadn't traveled to amazing places like she had, didn't know how to be anything except the angry weirdo in a small town.

Cass was right, he couldn't do anything.

"Go to culinary school, Levi. You have a bright future, far away from here. You'll fall for someone else, and so will Hannah, and you'll both be saved from breaking each other's hearts." Cass ended, sashaying off with a wave.

He was going to fucking prove to her that everything she thought about him was wrong, but until then, he was going to stay the hell away from kissing Hannah. Even if he had to renounce Judaism and join a monastery to do it.

Chapter 10

Hannah

They sat down at a booth in the corner, and Collin materialized beside them. He was a bear of a man with a huge red beard.

"Oh," Collin drawled in his deep baritone, looking down at Levi and then over at Hannah with a cartoonish "Oh shit" face. "Is this *the* Levi Blue Matthews?"

Levi raised an eyebrow at Hannah.

"Miri and I spent a lot of time here, talking about you, in the past few months," Hannah explained. "Also, Collin is friends with the twins, so who knows what terrible things Esther has told him."

"Well, my actual self can't possibly be worse than the version you and my sister have been telling people, so at least I get to start with a low bar and work up!" Levi did the world's grumpiest jazz hands.

"Speaking of, did you actually talk to your sister yet?" Hannah asked pointedly.

Levi grimaced. "No, but I'm totally going to. Eventually. Probably."

It was tragically comforting, all the ways in which he hadn't changed.

Collin cleared his throat, leaning against the back of Hannah's chair. "Are you going to order?"

"Give me whatever the special is, Col. You know I'm open," Hannah told him, waving a hand.

Levi pretended to faint onto the booth. "Did you just ask a human being to take your life out of your control and bring you a meal off the menu, about which you had not asked a million questions and made several substitutions?" he asked her. "Who *are* you?"

"I'm New Hannah," she told him, smiling at having surprised him, "and I trust Collin's food implicitly. He's never steered me wrong. I will even eat his gazpacho, in spite of the cucumbers."

Levi gasped and held his hand to his heart as if he'd been stabbed.

"I will have whatever your favorite is," he told Collin, "if I live through the indignity that my own wife has never eaten a cucumber in my food, no matter how I've prepared it."

Hannah glared at him for the audacity of that "wife" comment.

"My wife won't eat my borscht." There was a blush on Collin's cheeks as he said the word *wife*.

"Collin is a newlywed; he just married Marisol, who owns the boutique," Hannah explained to Levi.

Collin nodded. "After many years of pining."

"I know that dance." Levi smiled. "Sometimes, they're worth pining."

"Do you keep kosher?" Collin asked him, winking at Hannah.

"Not strictly," he said, "but I don't eat pork or shellfish. Thank you for asking."

"Many, many years of friendship with the twins has taught me something." Collin nodded and went to put in their order.

As Collin walked off, Levi said, as much to himself as to Hannah, "I like that guy."

"You don't like anyone," Hannah reminded him.

"That's patently false," he said. "I don't like myself, and I want everyone else to like me, and then if they don't like me it's devastating, and I always assume they're going to hate me, because I kind of hate me, so I get preemptively mad at them for making me feel bad."

What did she do with that confession? All her life, she'd wanted him to self-reflect, to find some peace with whatever the root of his unhappiness was. Now he apparently . . . had? In some ways he was exactly his old self, bursting in to proclaim he was back, no matter what anyone else wanted, and also, look how famous he was.

But this was very new. That he knew this about himself and that he could talk about it so casually, with so little angst.

"That's . . . a lot, Levi."

"I'm a lot, Hannah," he said, his elbows on the table and his chin resting in one hand. "I'm categorically too damn much, and sometimes so are you, which is probably how we ended up unable to quit each other. We're way, way too much for other people."

She shook her head. "You can't go around telling people I'm your wife. We broke up. Like, almost five years ago. People are going to think we're back together. Talk gets around fast in small towns."

He grinned at her, and she realized he'd done it to get a reaction out of her. *Don't stab him with a butter knife,* she reminded herself. *Collin will get mad.*

"It's a little weird that you're actually here now, in this diner. It's a lot weird that we're here together. This has always been a Levi-free safe space." She gestured around at the walls, covered in photos of old regulars. "There are no memories of you baked into the wallpaper."

"You know, we could change the Carrigan's wallpaper. It would solve several problems at once," Levi pointed out.

"You hush," Hannah told him seriously. "It's impossible to find reasonably priced vintage re-creation wallpaper covered in parrots. I know, I've looked. Everywhere."

"You could replace it with wallpaper not covered in parrots?" he suggested, holding his hands up in a shrugging gesture.

Hannah shook a fork at him. "How dare you." She was trying very hard not to smile, not to get into this banter with him, but it was like being carried out with the tide. And damn them both, it felt great. That was the part that made her the angriest.

His face fell, and she'd forgotten how quickly and mercurially his face could change from joy to abject grief. It changed all the air around him.

"What is that? What just happened?" she prodded.

"I forgot when I left that you were going to have a life here without me, be a whole person without me around that I would never get to see. Meet and befriend people I didn't know." He chuckled at himself and self-consciously fluffed his hair. "That's so ridiculous and self-centered, and the worst part is, now I'm jealous of everyone who gets to see that Hannah."

Ahh, there he was. Her whiny, selfish boy who wanted the world to revolve around him. She breathed a little easier.

"I thought you got a smug satisfaction out of being the person who had known me longest and best," she said, baiting him, but she was a little sad, too. He'd met so many new people, all over the world, and she'd never meet most of them. They'd all gotten to meet a version of him she'd never see.

"But as you pointed out," he answered, "I don't know *this* you. When you talk to me, I can see every wall, every mine-field, every memory you're trying to skirt. I don't get to meet the person you'd be if we'd just met."

"The same is true of you, isn't it? I don't get to meet the Levi who was never Blue." She sighed.

This man. Why was she even trying to talk him through this? This was a perfect opportunity for her to say, "You're right, we should stop doing this. You haven't changed, and I haven't healed. We're not going on any more of these dates." She should let him spin out and convince himself he was wrong and there was no chance for them. But she was a sucker for his bullshit, because it was her bullshit, too. They were a matched set. She held out her hands for him, and he took them, and her body said, "Finally."

Damn it. Her anger started to rise, to lash out, and she breathed. *We're finding peace*, she reminded herself.

"Here," she said, "we've never been on a first date before— if we're having a do-over—so let's do it right. How would we be if we were new? What should we pretend?"

Her shoulders relaxed as she tried to talk to him as if he were someone with whom she didn't have a lifetime of history. He flattened his bangs.

"What? What are you freaking out about right now?" Hannah toed him with her boot under the table.

"You have to actively try to be comfortable around me! Me, your oldest friend. You have to physically shift out of protect-yourself-from-Levi mode."

Hannah rolled her eyes at him. "You worked so hard to get me to agree to this date! Can you not prophesy doom for ten whole minutes? That's my job."

"I don't think you can call dibs on anxiety, Nan," he said, but he squeezed her hands.

She pinned him with her best "I see through you, Blue" face, which was pretty great, considering how many decades she'd spent perfecting it. "You wanted a date, let's have a date. What do people talk about on dates?"

"I don't know, I've never been on one." He looked uncomfortable. "Of the two of us, you would know."

"You've never been on a date?!" She dropped his hands in shock.

"I've been in love with the same person since I was fifteen, and as we've covered, this is our first date." He looked confused that she'd even asked. "Demisexual?"

"That makes sense." She nodded.

"Sooooo, what do people do on dates?" he prompted.

"Ask each other about their jobs, hobbies, families, books they've read lately, podcasts they listen to. Everything we know about each other already, I guess."

"I have no idea what books you've been reading lately. Let's do it. Let's pretend we've never met." He schooled his features into what she assumed he thought of as a "normal guy on a date" face, though it mostly looked constipated.

"Tell me about your work," he said in his douchiest voice.

"Well," she said, going along with it. "I'm the events and customer experience manager at a small Christmas-themed farm, event location, and inn that I inherited from my aunt. I run it with my cousin and my best friend."

"Oh, that sounds interesting, and busy. Do you enjoy it?" He leaned toward her, and her body ached to mirror the gesture.

"It's the only thing I've dreamed of doing all my life," she answered. True, if not the whole truth.

"That's not really an answer to whether or not you enjoy it," he pointed out.

She could say that she'd always thought she would be traveling the world with her husband on her vacations from work, not trapped in a self-imposed princess tower where her home was her work and her vacations, but they were supposed to be dating and not fighting.

Collin set down their plates. "You need a meat loaf plate," he told Levi.

"Oh man," Levi said, his eyes inhaling the plate of homemade mashed potatoes and roasted brussels sprouts, "you're so right. Oh, but wait, can I get a container of egg salad to go? I've been told it's better than mine."

"Best in the state, I'd say." Collin set down a burger in front of Hannah. "I'm trying this recipe out. It's a lamb gyro burger. You gotta let me know what I can improve."

"You're really going to eat tzatziki, huh? A whole new Hannah. One who likes surprises *and* cucumber."

Hannah cut her burger into neat quarters so she could pick it up without making a mess. "Do you remember telling me once that my problem is I'm mad that I don't get to write the script for life?"

Levi nodded. "Yeah, it was a mean thing to say. I'm sorry."

She waved him off. "Maybe there's a time and place for us to unpack every cruel thing either of us said to each other back then, but it's definitely not here and now. I bring it up because I've been working with my therapist, trying to process our breakup instead of staying stuck circling it forever, and one of the things she's having me do is inventory whether I'm mad about things you said because they were too true, or because they seemed so totally wrong."

He pushed his hair out of his eyes. "Okaaay."

She picked up one of her burger quarters and gestured with it. "So, in the case of the script comment, you were right. I was always trying to write a script so I wouldn't be so anxious about everything; then I would get more anxious when people didn't follow it. But once I started letting my life just happen every once in a while, I realized I don't actually *like* being in charge of every detail all the time, and I kind of enjoy surprises."

"Holy shit," he said, blinking owlishly.

"Too serious! What do you do?" she asked, back to their fake "first date" conversation.

He raised an eyebrow, like he noticed that she'd never answered his question about liking her job but didn't call her out on it.

"I'm a chef. I spent several years traveling the world via various cruise ship and yacht jobs and learning in kitchens wherever I ended up. Recently, I was on a reality show in Australia."

"Did you win?" she asked. The finale wouldn't air for a couple of months, and she was dying to know.

He waved a fork at her. "I'm not able to disclose that information, no matter how beautiful the asker."

She blushed, which was ridiculous. "What are you planning to do now? Back to the cruise ship life?"

He pushed his hand through his hair, then meticulously rearranged his bangs, then shook his head.

"It was something I needed to do, and I learned a lot about cooking and myself, but I'm getting a little old for that life. I'm filming a pilot for a show since I seem to do well on TV. That would allow me to spend more time in one place, see my family more. I'm not sure beyond that. I'm...uh...kind of waiting to see how some personal things shake out."

Oh no. He was not making her responsible for the rest of his life so he could throw it in her face later when he was unhappy.

"Maybe you should decide what you want to do with your life, and that will determine how your personal life looks," she said through clenched teeth.

"I know what I want to do with the rest of my life," he whispered, looking into her eyes. "I want to spend it with you."

"That's a weird thing to say to a girl on the first date, buddy!" she exclaimed, because she couldn't deal with his big sad eyes staring into her soul, saying he wanted her forever. She changed the subject, hiding back in their first date personas. "Are you into any podcasts?"

He cleared his throat. "I do listen to one where three guys play DnD with their dad. It's not bad. You?"

"I tried to get into true crime, but I ended up enraged about police corruption and the carceral state," she said.

"Fair." He twirled his fork, looking up at her from under

his bangs. "Do you have any hobbies, in between your busy schedule of managing a Jewish Christmas tree empire?"

"A first date would not know I'm Jewish, Blue."

"Your name is Hannah Rosenstein and you are wearing the hamsa necklace you got for your bat mitzvah from Cass," he countered. "A first date who was paying any attention to you at all would know you were Jewish. What are your hobbies?"

"Well, I grew up in the country, so when I need to blow off steam, sometimes I shoot skeet. I love to go trout fishing, although it's hard to find people who want to go with me." She took a bite of her food, smiling serenely. They'd been arguing about trout fishing all their lives.

"Oh, weird, you mean your friends and relations don't want to stand in a freezing cold lake in April catching their deaths of cold to catch three tiny fish they can't even eat? I find that shocking." His eyes twinkled.

"I will have you know I am an excellent trout fisherwoman," she told him, "and I often catch fish big enough to eat."

"Oh, do you cook?" he asked, even more mischief in his eyes.

"No, I do not. And I refuse to feel any shame about that. I have many other excellent skills."

His gaze went from laughter to heat in a flash, and she cleared her throat.

"Okay, let's head back now!" She signaled Collin for the check.

"Can I walk you to your door and kiss you good night?" he asked, smirking.

"Don't push your luck, my dude. You can walk me to the front door of the inn, then make yourself scarce."

"You're worried you're going to throw yourself at me. I understand. I'll protect your virtue."

He wasn't wrong.

In the truck, on the drive back up the hill to the farm, she looked over at him. "Hey, have you...have you gone to any therapy, about the bullies, and Cass, and everything?"

He blew out a breath. "I had a string of pretty bad experiences with therapists, and I got to a point where I couldn't go to one and be open to the process. We were mandated to see someone on the *Star Chef* set, and she could tell I was really uncomfortable, so she recommended a group setting, which worked out a lot better for me. Then I found an online support group for people who came out later in life, and I Zoom into that, and we work through a lot. So, not in the traditional sense, but also yes. It just turns out I do a lot better when I'm not one-on-one with someone I'm afraid is judging me."

"You should talk to Noelle. She's mad as hell at Cass. You two could unpack a lot together. Your little Cass Was Kind of a Bitch support group."

Noelle didn't think Cass had done enough to protect Miri from her home life. Hannah had never understood why Noelle couldn't let the past go, now that Cass was gone, but she was starting to get it.

He laughed. "At least with Noelle I would know ahead of time that she was judging me."

Chapter 11

Levi

The day of the engagement party, Levi was grateful for the trial run it provided when he was in the middle of making frantic notes about ways they would need to seriously streamline service the day of the wedding to make their kitchen, built to serve a twenty-five-room inn, feed a massive party. He was walking servers through how he needed them to schedule running trays back and forth between the food booths on the lawn when the bride flagged him down. He immediately put on his Interacting With Guests persona, a whole character he'd built that he could slip into so he didn't have to leave his soft or his pointy edges visible to the public.

"Chef Matthews! I'm so thrilled you ended up being available for this. The menu is beyond anything I could have imagined. You're a genius." She threw her arms around him, and he tried not to tense. Why did strangers always want to hug him?

"Hannah is a genius. I'm a guy who can cook." He extricated

himself and mentally smoothed out his wrinkles, since it would be rude to actually brush himself off. "I'm gratified that you asked me to be a part of your big day. Or big days, rather."

"Yeah, politicians' kids don't really get to do small low-key weddings. Part of the package. I personally wanted a *Flight of the Fordham* wedding, but the gov said veto." She rolled her eyes, but her tone when she talked about her dad was loving.

"Wait, you're FlightCrew?!" Levi asked, distracted from his fake public persona. "Who do you ship?"

Flight of the Fordham was a cult favorite space opera. Now in its thirteenth season, *Fordham* had a massive, devoted, intense group of fans. Many of those fans watched in large part to follow the relationship arc of Captain Singh and his first mate, Jax Jordan. Unlike many of its brethren shows, *Flight of the Fordham* had not merely teased the possibility of a gay love story between its leads but had actually delivered. The characters had fallen in love, gotten married, and neither of them had died. As a result, their fans would follow them to the ends of the earth, and those fans included Levi.

Levi was not embarrassed to be as rabid a member of the FlightCrew as anyone on the internet, or to have read more hours of CapJax fanfic than he could track. There was nothing to be embarrassed about because fandom was awesome, and AO3 had gotten him through some dark times in the past few years.

He just didn't usually talk about it with guests. Or anyone.

"Obviously CapJax. I'm not a monster." Delilah laughed.

He leaned in and whispered, "Please email me your favorite fic links as soon as we're out of this party."

"Oh my gosh, we have to do a FordhamWing salute for my

Stories. It will be legendary." She pulled out her phone, and he dutifully posed with her.

"You know," Delilah said after, "you come off very suave and grouchy on TV, but you're kind of a ball of geeky anxious energy wrapped up in scarves and eyeliner in real life."

"You noticed that, did you?" He smiled. "I'm genuinely very grouchy, but suave, never."

"Like recognizes like, my friend," she said. He suddenly felt much better about this event. It was so much easier to cook food for people you didn't hate.

"I need to get back in the kitchen to make sure everything is rolling out on schedule," he said, shaking her hand, "but you should try the scallion pancake tacos with pickled carrots and cilantro oil. You're going to be very into them."

"I am going to do that right now," she promised, and he pumped his fist a little. He was used to planning menus based on hypothetical customers that were eaten by people he rarely spoke to. Executing large-scale service for events was stressful, but really getting to know the client, building a menu around their tastes, was fulfilling.

He suspected that when she was satisfied everything was rolling smoothly outside, Hannah would be by the kitchen to check on him. She had probably scheduled her party rounds to within the half minute, to make sure she circulated to every server, touched base with both the bride's and groom's parents, and got several candid shots of everyone for social media (they had a photographer working, but Levi knew Hannah wouldn't trust them to get everything exactly the way she wanted it).

As sure as the tides, out swept a round of German-inspired cocktails and in swept his wife. She was wearing a yellow sundress with tiny blue roses, a crown of pink roses in her hair. She looked like a very sexy cupcake, all round stomach and soft arms. He wanted to unwrap her and lick her.

"It's too cold out there for that dress," he groused at her, because he was annoyed that she was so cute.

She nodded at him emphatically. "Whatever asshole let these people talk me into planning an outdoor event on the first of May is fired."

"You're firing yourself?" he asked, handing her an extra scallion pancake, because he knew she hadn't stopped to eat in several hours. She shoved it in her mouth and reached out her hand for something else. He handed her a mushroom tart.

"These are actually great," she said, as if she hadn't haggled with him over the recipes for hours and tried every test batch. "How are things going in here? Any unforeseen problems?"

"I mean, there are always unforeseen problems, but nothing I can't take care of. It turns out I am trained to run a kitchen," he reminded her. "I'm keeping a list of things we can tweak to run better next time, so when we debrief, we'll already have it."

"So hot, so smart," she said, distracted by looking down at the next thing on her list. "Why hasn't some nice Jewish girl swept you up and married you?"

"She has," he said pointedly.

"I walked into that one," she admitted. "Can Nafil take lead for a bit in about twenty minutes?"

When Levi had finally called him, Nafil had jumped at the opportunity to work together again. He'd called Levi every curse word Levi had ever heard for going off the grid, but he'd shown up this morning ready to seamlessly integrate into the kitchen. Levi trusted Nafil with his life, and also his knives, which was kind of the same thing.

"Nafil can take lead in any kitchen in the world, but I can't leave mine right now. You wanted me to run this event. I need to run it my way." He barked an order at a passing server.

"And I am the event coordinator, and I need you to circulate amongst the guests, who are asking about you. *Australia's Next Star Chef* is going viral and people are very interested in you," Hannah said.

"Get out of here, old man!" Nafil told him. "You're just holding me back!"

Hannah smiled beatifically at Nafil. "I like you. Do you want to take over the kitchen at Carrigan's?"

Nafil waved her off. "Maybe if I were getting too old for the yachting hours and had a hot wife here, I'd be as interested in settling here as Matthews. I have a little brother, though. He's half the chef I am, but since I'm twice the chef Matthews is . . ."

"Why are all my friends mean to me?" Levi asked out loud, as inside he thought, *Why do my friends think I want to work at Carrigan's?*

"Because you're an asshole and you only like mean people," Hannah told him. "Are you coming out to greet guests?"

Levi growled a little. "Give me a couple of minutes to get everything ready."

She nodded.

"Wait," Levi called after her as she turned to leave. He didn't miss the flash of fear in her eyes, or the way she'd sort of half taken off her "talking to Levi" mask and had to quickly slip her face back into it as she turned back.

"Take my jacket" was all he said, handing her the ancient leather biker jacket hanging on one of the kitchen hooks. "It will look cool with your dress, and you won't freeze."

She shrugged into the worn leather, and his heart skipped. She'd worn it before, countless times. He'd bought it when they were thirteen, at a vintage shop in Queens while they were on a trip to the city for something, and it had been too big for both of them but that hadn't stopped her from stealing it. He'd always loved when it made its way back to him, smelling of her old lady rose soap and sweat.

Now, when she pulled the waist-length rope of her hair out of the collar and tugged on the sleeves to get it to sit right, he was hit with a wrecking ball of nostalgia and lust. The jacket wasn't too big anymore; it hugged all her perfect ample curves, and the contrast between it and her sundress made her look like some sort of good girl gone bad fantasy. He didn't even have those fantasies, he didn't have sexual fantasies at all, except about his wife, apparently, at the worst possible times.

"This jacket always did look better on me," she said, and he didn't argue. He wondered if he really heard a catch in her voice, or if he'd imagined it.

They managed to get through the engagement party without anyone freezing to death or running out of food. It was exhilarating, collaborating with Hannah, watching her work her magic. Her almost superhuman competence was breathtaking.

It had been fun, he realized, the whole thing. A lot of fun, which surprised him.

"Okay," Hannah said, hands on her hips, standing in front of the giant sheet of paper that had been hung over the book-shelves in her office. In Hannah's neat cursive it said:

1. *Compliments*
2. *Feedback*
3. *Plans:*
   ◦ *Immediate needs*
   ◦ *Medium-term needs*
   ◦ *Long-term needs*

"Blue, welcome to debrief. Here's the structure—immediate needs are, like, we gotta fix this before the next event, medium-term needs are we can't fix this before the next event but we have to get started on it ASAP, and long-term needs are also stretch dreams; that is, what would we get if we had all the money and space in the world? Who wants to start with a compliment?"

Noelle raised her hand. "Levi kind of killed it out there," she said, to his surprise, shrugging nonchalantly.

"Agreed." Miriam nodded. "Food was great, speedy, no one noticed any issues."

They went on, threw around ideas for cold passed apps for the wedding since Levi now knew they wouldn't have enough ovens for their original plan, tweaking their service sheet.

After a few hours, Miriam and Noelle wandered off to bed while he and Hannah stayed up into the witching hours, a pot of coffee between them, brainstorming long-term dreams. It was everything he was great at and everything she was great at, the first time in their lives their brains had gotten a chance to go wild bouncing off each other, collaborating and learning from each other.

It was exhilarating, in a way he had believed nothing at Carrigan's could ever be.

The changes Hannah was making, the future of this kitchen, were going to be an incredible project for whatever chef they brought on when his mom retired, and for the first time in his life, instead of wanting to run screaming from it, he was envious that he wouldn't be involved. Someone else was going to have this time with his Hannah but would never be able to click with her the way Levi did. He didn't know what to do with that. He couldn't stay working here, but he could never leave Hannah. And none of that took into account what Hannah wanted, personally or professionally.

Hannah eventually left for her own bed, and he found he was too full of thoughts to stay inside.

The walls of the old inn closed around him until he couldn't see to the other side of his brain and he needed air. It was partly his own panic and some of it probably the wallpaper that might be slightly molding. Parrots. Honestly. Picking up a cup of coffee and wrapping far too much scarf around his neck, he started off into the Hundred Acre Wood of his childhood, prepared to be charmed by its beauty or, at least, distracted by nostalgia. He didn't realize, until she found him under the trees, that he was hoping for Miriam's company.

"What are you doing out here, Miri-belle?" he asked, bumping his shoulder against hers. "Do you never sleep, either?"

She smiled at the long-forgotten nickname. "Getting some quiet in the trees. Letting my soul stretch out. Hoping to watch the sun rise. You, Bluebird?"

"The same, I think," he said, a peace settling over him as she rested her hand in the crook of his arm. They walked silently next to each other, existing in spring in the mountains.

"Are you used to it yet?" he finally asked. "Being here?"

They had both left, in some way, to save themselves, and she was the only person who could understand what the leaving had cost.

"Not really? While I was gone, I dreamed about being here, but I never thought I would be again, so I kind of constructed a fantasy version of Carrigan's in my head. Carrigan's, through a filter. It helped it hurt less, to look at it sideways in my memory. But now I'm here, and it's like I've laid my childhood version, and my pretend version, in layers over the actual Carrigan's." Miriam shook her head, laughing. "I don't know what I'm saying. But it helps if I envision it as A New Adventure."

"Might be easier with a new love than an old one," he pointed out.

"Might be easier in a place I visited on school holidays, not the home I grew up in," she agreed.

He looked out over the mountains, thoughtful. "The weirdest part is trying to figure out who I am here. The person I used to be at Carrigan's is gone, and he wouldn't be welcome even if he still existed. I can't be the person I was out in the world, because that person didn't have any past."

"Why the intense self-reflection? Other than you being you." Miriam leaned on him. He kissed her on the head, thinking about how to explain.

"I got an email today from my agent. He's in talks with Food Network about market testing my brand, or something."

Miriam smirked but listened.

"Miri, the actual fucking words 'culinary bad boy' were used." He grimaced.

Now Miriam laughed at him. "Oh, come on, Blue. Hipster hair and beard? Leggings and giant scarves? Brash, opinionated beautiful boy with an overinflated idea of his own talent and a chip on his shoulder about being working class? You're a literal *Top Chef* villain."

He scoffed. "First of all, my idea of my own talent is not overinflated. But more importantly, I'm horrified by that guy. I want to throw that guy off a cliff. I'm not a Type. I didn't go to work for some"—he waved his arm around, looking for the right words—"French guy! I worked in street food stands. I don't think kitchens work better when we give our staff PTSD, and I've never done coke, even once. I'm a fully realized creation, my own human. I don't have...you know, tattoos of bacon!"

Miriam threw back her head and cackled, her giant mane of dark curls blowing in the wind. "I mean, your mother would explode if you either got a tattoo or ate bacon, so no. I'm sorry you're having an identity crisis, but, like, where's the fire?" She turned to him, her tone gentle. "Maybe you're becoming a real adult and having to decide who you want to be. Possibly getting a Food Network show isn't an emergency situation. What are you actually scared of?"

He scrunched his shoulders up to his ears and hid his face in his scarves. Why did she see him? It was awful to have lifelong friends.

"I gambled everything on this idea that I could find myself out there, that there was a myself to find and I couldn't find him here, and that whoever I found would be worth the sacrifice."

He stopped and turned to her. "I invented this entire new me out of whole cloth, and I don't know if he's good enough. But he has to be, because I lost everything to find him."

"Good enough for what, Blue? For who?" Miriam asked, capturing his hands.

"All of Carrigan's thinks I'm bad for Hannah, that we're bad for each other," he reminded her.

"But no one thought that *before* you left, LB. And if you left to make yourself good enough... where did that come from? Who made you believe that?"

"Have you met me? Have you met Hannah? She's a fairy-tale princess if the princess could lead an army into battle on a whim," he said, and it wasn't a lie. That was true, too. "No one's good enough for her."

"That's not an answer," Miriam told him, but she kept walking with him in silence.

No matter how much he didn't want to answer her question, he had to. Mostly because otherwise, she'd hear it from Hannah or Noelle, and she deserved to hear it from him.

"There's something I have to tell you. About Cass. And I don't want to," he said finally, picking up a stick and tossing it as far as he could.

She listened to him as they walked, her arms wrapped around herself, and when he was done talking, she sat down on the ground in a pile of pine needles, her knees against her chest, her face buried under her hair. Levi knew this was a massive blow for her. Her parents had been horrific, although her mother was coming around, and Cass had been the only family Miriam was close to. Cass had seen her talent, had supported her art career. Cass had given her a whole new life.

"You okay under there?" he asked, lifting the curtain of Miriam's curls and peeking underneath.

"No," Miriam said, sucking in a deep breath, "but I don't need to make your grief about my own childhood trauma. I do have a therapist, after all."

She held out her hand, and he pulled her up. She wrapped her arms around his waist, her head resting under his as they hugged for a long time.

"For what it's worth," Miri finally said, "you're one of my favorite people in the universe and one of the people I most admire and respect. You've always been exactly enough for me."

"It's worth a hell of a lot," he assured her, kissing her hair, as the sun came up and bathed them both in brand-new light.

Hannah, Age 20

The instant she turned in her last final, Hannah was on a plane home to Carrigan's from Amherst. She got to the airport so early that she managed to get on standby for the earlier flight into JFK, so she was there three hours before anyone expected her. When she got off the plane, she thought about dropping in on Blue, since she technically didn't have to be anywhere yet, but she shook off the impulse. He was in the middle of his finals week, at the end of his junior year in culinary school, and every time she talked to him, he sounded so busy with friends, and work, and being intoxicated by Manhattan.

He was bound by the electricity of the city, its frenetic energy that matched his own. He was always full of stories of things that happened at four a.m. Why would he want boring, needy Hannah to show up from a home he had all but disowned and interrupt his life?

She knew he hated when he had to explain to people what his relationship was to Carrigan's and the Rosensteins, and food people always wanted to ask her about it. What was it like, being a part of a hundred-year baking legacy, a household name brand, at least in Jewish households? It always raised Blue's hackles, because he felt the Rosensteins had never let him in as part of the family. It was only sort of true; some of her extended family was snobby and weird about who counted as family and who didn't, but it wasn't about Blue. It was just that families are weird, and hers was really big so it had a lot of opportunities for weirdness.

She didn't want to risk seeing him pretend to be excited she was there, so instead of going by his apartment, she headed to the train station. Besides, Carrigan's was calling to her, and every minute that she was away hurt.

When she walked in the front door, no one was there to greet her, because it was a summer Tuesday, and no one thought she would be there for hours. She got to stand alone in the foyer and drink in her home. The curving staircase, the great room with the soaring ceilings and three times as many antiques as ought to be able to fit in the space. The sound of Mrs. Matthews's voice coming from the kitchen competed with the hum of a far-off vacuum cleaner and the filtered-down music from whatever one of the twins was watching in the entertainment area on the landing. She breathed deeply and got goose bumps.

All the tension she carried when she was elsewhere left her body. All of the constant low-grade whir of fear that never left—the fear that somehow, when she was finally free to come home, home wouldn't be here anymore. She never felt comfortable, completely, when she wasn't on the one hundred sixty acres of Carrigan's property, even when she was happy. Even when she was having fun.

She was always worried she'd dreamed Carrigan's, and she would wake up and it would never have been there.

"Hannah-Nan-Banan-NanNan-Mo-Hannah!" Miriam's voice came, jubilant, from the kitchen. "You are EARLY!"

Miriam's curls came bounding, bouncing with their own life.

"Doesn't Northwestern get out in mid-June?" Hannah asked. She wasn't sorry to see her cousin, but she'd been looking forward to some Carrigan's time to herself.

"*Yes*, technically that's true," Miriam said, doing jazz hands with fingers covered in paint, "but I had a self-created long weekend and I knew you were coming home. I missed you. Tell me everything! Is hospitality management everything you dreamed?"

"We talked on the phone last week and emailed yesterday, Miri. There's nothing new to say," Hannah pointed out, but Miriam waved her off and dragged her to the kitchen, where they settled in on the old circular booth and Mrs. Matthews gave them cookies.

"I like it a lot," Hannah told her cousin. "It turns out living in hotels around the world for most of my childhood has given me a lot of Opinions about how they should be run."

"You?! Opinionated about how things should be run? I'm shocked. This is my shocked face," Miriam teased.

"This summer, Cass is going on some kind of river cruise down the Danube and I get to practice being in charge while she's gone. I'm getting credit for it as an internship, which is kind of cheating, but I'm not going to argue." She tried sounding chill about it.

"Are you sure you want to come back here? I mean, I love Carrigan's, too, but...is Cass pressuring you? My dad is desperate for me to come work in the family business, but I'm taking a couple of years off and moving to New York, trying to figure out if business is really for me."

Business was absolutely not for Miriam, and they all knew it, but none of them knew how she was going to get herself out of that expectation on her father's part. He was very scary.

"No, Cass actually wants me to work other places first. She's definitely not pulling a Richard."

"Okay, but do *you* know you don't have to be here for Carrigan's to function?"

"Uh, logically? Yes." She knew it wasn't a rational fear, that Carrigan's would float away into another dimension if she wasn't there to anchor it. The fear had started being noticeable as soon as she'd left for college, although maybe it had started when she was a kid and that's why she'd been constantly trying to get back. She would lie awake in her dorm bed imagining Cass was sick, or Mr. Matthews had taken a fall, or the reindeer got out—anything that could go wrong, and she knew in her bones if she were there, it would have been prevented. She'd even tried to talk to a counselor at her college's student health center about it, but they hadn't helped much. "I can't shake the anxiety that I have to be at Carrigan's, keeping it safe, making sure it keeps going."

Hannah knew she was a little tightly wound for a twenty-year-old. Or, probably for anyone. This didn't bother her. She liked to be organized, to have a plan, to know what was going to happen next. She liked having agency in her life, and not being surprised. She didn't need to have taken Psych 101 (although she'd aced it) to understand that her childhood of adventure had made her a little controlling about knowing what was coming next in her life.

That was fine. *We all grew the anxieties of the soil in which we were planted.* These were simply hers.

"Okay, well, you know I'll always be here if you need me. And Blue, too. We're your crew forever," Miriam said, squeezing her hand. "And now you're here for the whole summer!"

She was here for the summer, and soon she would be done with school. She would never have to leave again if she didn't want to. Then, the only thing in her life to ever knock her off-kilter would be Blue Matthews. But he was going to graduate from culinary school, travel the world, and only come back to see his parents.

She would have a chance to get over him, to finally be okay with the fact that he was never going to love her in the way she loved him. She was going to find her equilibrium around Levi Blue Matthews if it killed her. That was the last step in her plan to have a surprise-free life.

Chapter 12

Hannah

The Davenport engagement party had gone better than she'd feared—in fact, better than she'd hoped. Levi had been professional, present, charming. He'd been the person she'd only ever seen him be on TV (watching *Australia's Next Star Chef* every week was an exercise in heartbreak, as she saw the version of her greatest love and oldest friend that he'd never been able—or willing—to show her). She'd been telling herself he would never be his whole self at Carrigan's, but he was proving her wrong.

And maybe proving himself wrong. She wondered if he noticed.

Carrigan's All Year was still a precariously growing business, even with the governor as a client. So, they had to participate in things around the Adirondacks that would raise their profile, and the week after the engagement party was ADK Restaurant Week, seven days of highlighting food from all over the region.

To join, restaurants around the Adirondacks offered special

prix fixe menus. The Christmasland Inn had never participated before, both because it was outside the scope of what the inn did while Cass was alive and because it wasn't in Mrs. Matthews's wheelhouse. It was, however, very much in Levi's wheelhouse.

He'd asked if he could do something, even though it was last minute—suggesting a special dinner for the tourists who were staying at the inn, one he could open up to anyone in the area. Since it was fine with Mrs. Matthews, and dinner was her area, Hannah said yes.

"He's doing an event," Noelle said, bursting into Hannah's office the day they announced the event on social media. "Just like that? You gave him an event?"

"Blue is a famous chef who is currently here and was bored, so he is making dinner," Hannah said slowly, "which his mother, whose kitchen he's using, agreed to."

"Blue?" Noelle closed the door behind her a little more violently than necessary. "Blue is cooking? Not Levi?"

"Is there a difference?" Hannah asked, not making eye contact, because she knew there was, and she didn't know why she'd called him that.

"You know there's a difference. Blue is the boy you used to love. Levi is the man you're divorcing."

"Slip of the tongue," Hannah lied, to both of them.

Noelle crossed her arms over her chest. "Do you remember six months ago, when you almost murdered your cousin for infringing on your Carrigan's events territory?"

"It's not the same thing, NoNo. He's here. He cooks. There's a local cooking event. We need to participate in local tourist events. It's an easy call to make. Also, you both wanted me to chill out about being so territorial. So I did! We all rejoice."

She straightened the Post-it pad on her desk, lining it up with the edge of her desk calendar.

"I would be thrilled that you were letting someone else take point on an event if it were not Levi. Because it's not just cooking dinner. He's making space for himself in his mother's kitchen, doing the things he was supposed to do before he abandoned you, supporting your dreams for Carrigan's All Year. It's sneaky. He's trying to win you back!"

He was absolutely trying to win her back, although she wasn't sure he was aware enough to realize that supporting Carrigan's All Year was a much better strategy than taking her on dates. The real question was, what would happen if she let him and then he realized he was trapped here again?

"I'm not going to turn down an opportunity for business, good press, and networking because the person bringing them to us is Levi," she hedged. "He's here. I'm making the best of it. I suggest you do the same."

"He stole my cat!" Noelle complained.

"Is your girlfriend happier?" Hannah countered. Noelle didn't answer, only shoved her hands in her pockets. "Look, he and I had some pretty big talks. I understand why he is the way he is sometimes, a lot more than I ever had. Maybe you could try the same thing."

"Oh, I'm sure he sold you a very good sob story." Noelle frowned. "She promises she won't fall under his terrible spell again," she muttered to herself, "and then she lets him run events."

Noelle wasn't wrong, but she wasn't right, either. Hannah had been prickly when Miriam came back and started making decisions, for a lot of reasons. One, she was a control freak. Two, Miriam had never done any work running Carrigan's, and she'd been gone for ten years, so she had no frame of reference for the big picture. Three, Miriam had been planning on staying at Carrigan's and making huge lasting changes to the way they did things. This had made Hannah territorial, because she was the manager and had spent her whole life training to take over Carrigan's.

Levi was different. Not because she loved him, but because he'd grown up working on the farm. He knew more about how Carrigan's ran than anyone besides her and his parents. And, unlike Miriam, he *hadn't* missed a decade. He still knew all the regulars' names, remembered where the extra towels were stored and who to call if something was wrong with the plumbing that his dad couldn't fix.

No matter how much he hated it, Carrigan's was in him at a cellular level, and she knew if he made a choice, he would understand its potential repercussions. Besides, he wasn't staying and trying to make big waves. He was going to be gone as soon as the wind changed, off to make a career for himself.

"He didn't sell me a sob story, and I can't talk details to you. There is something we have to talk about, though. We have to talk about Cass and Blue."

"Yeah, Miri told me." Noelle hunched her shoulders, folding in on herself a little. "I guess I always assumed Cass gave Levi shit as an adult because he's a pain in the ass, but the way she treated him as a kid, even if she didn't do it on purpose..."

"Yeah." Hannah just nodded. "Yeah."

"I fucking hate that on top of all the other reasons I'm mad at her, now I have to be mad at her on Levi Matthews's behalf."

Cass had saved Noelle in a thousand ways, had given her a

job, brought her and Miri together, had been their North Star. Cass had been the most important person in all their lives, their eccentric, misanthropic, meddling angel.

Blue had let them think that Cass was infallible rather than disillusioning them. Blue, the most selfish boy in the world, had kept all his pain inside that this adult, who he should have been able to trust, had torn him up. He'd kept all of that inside because he thought he deserved it, or because he thought they wouldn't believe him, but also because he loved them and he didn't want to take Cass away from them. And in the absence of that information, he had allowed everyone to think the worst of him.

"You really didn't know? All of it?" Hannah asked, because she didn't know how to focus on the rest of it.

"I knew Cass didn't like him," Noelle said, "but I assumed that meant he wasn't likeable, not that Cass was wrong. Fuck. I hate misjudging people, and now I'm going to have to make amends to him. Can I go back to an hour ago when I didn't know all of this?"

"Only if I can go back, too."

Noelle looked over at her and winced. "You've been processing all of this without me, because I've been mad at you."

Hannah nodded. "I have learned so much in the past month that's changed everything I thought I knew, and I couldn't bounce it off the person whose opinion I trust the most. But I'm keeping you forever, so you have a long time to be there for me."

"I still think he probably sold you a sob story," Noelle said, reaching over and weaving her fingers with Hannah's, "but I'm sorry I reacted like an asshole to the whole marriage secret thing. I'm just scared for you."

"I'm scared for me, too! Join the club." Hannah laughed. "And you should ask him. About the sob story. Judge for yourself."

Noelle scowled. "That would mean having a conversation with him."

The show Levi was filming a pilot for was apparently called *Living Bold*, which was a really douchey name and made her heart hurt that he'd obviously purposefully chosen the initials LB. It was about bold new takes on traditional Jewish flavors, and that's what he highlighted for the ADK Restaurant Week dinner. He made tiny shooters of richly flavored shakshouka with quail eggs, saffron rice with pomegranates, chicken cooked in sumac and wrapped in grape leaves, babka- and tahini-flavored ice creams.

Hannah talked to the guests about the differences in culinary tradition between her mother's Sephardic background and the Rosensteins' Ashkenazi background on her dad's side. Mr. Matthews gave the longest speech she'd ever heard him make in her life, about the varieties of baklava.

Watching Levi with his dad charmed the hell out of her, because Ben Matthews was very high on her favorite-people-of-all-time list, and she didn't want to be charmed.

She also didn't want to feel guilty about keeping Mr. Matthews from seeing his son for the past four years, while she was being melodramatic about her breakup, but she did feel guilty. All the time, whenever she saw them together. She wanted to fix it. Wanted to take away the hurt she saw flash across Levi's face when his dad walked more stiffly or mentioned something offhandedly that Levi had missed.

"Nan!" he said when the event was over, after shooing off the last of the Restaurant Week guests. (Did they *all* have to flirt with him? How were so many people watching an Australian cooking competition?) "Let's go on a date tomorrow! I heard about a bowling alley in Lake Placid called Bowlwinkles that has mac-and-cheese wedges with ranch dipping sauce. We have to go. Pleaaaaase? You know you love to kick my ass at bowling."

She did love to kick his ass at bowling, but she was currently having way too many Feelings to be alone in a bowling alley with him, with fried carbs and cheese. She would make out with him. It was inevitable.

"I can't tomorrow," she lied. "I have to go to trivia."

When Miriam had learned that Elijah Green's husband, Jason, ran a pub quiz at Ernie's, the dive bar on Main Street, she had declared him her favorite person in Advent and immediately made herself a staple there. Every Tuesday night, weather permitting, every millennial in the area congregated in the tiny, wood-paneled bar. There were bitter rivalries established, but Miriam and Jason were an unstoppable force, always coming in top three. The bartender, Sawyer (also the president of the Chamber of Commerce, and recently the sole mayoral candidate), was the MC, and a secret tribunal made up the questions.

Hannah almost never went to trivia, because with Miriam and Noelle there, she felt someone needed to stay back at the inn to keep an eye on things. This Tuesday, however, she pleaded with Noelle to swap with her.

"Please, please, I know you're mad at me but I'm trying to avoid my husband, and I need your help," she begged, batting her eyelashes.

Noelle folded her arms over her chest and raised an eyebrow. "I notice you call that man your husband a lot, for someone who insists she's not really married."

"See? I need time away from him! He's so hot when he's feeding people and my defenses are getting low. Save me from myself." She looked up at Noelle with big puppy dog eyes, designed to get Noelle to crack.

"Fine. Take my girlfriend on a date. But you owe me," Noelle agreed, wandering off and mumbling about delaying an inevitable train wreck.

So Hannah took her cousin on a date to pub quiz to avoid a date with her husband. Miriam and Jason immediately retreated into an intense trivia bubble, and Hannah smiled at Elijah.

"I haven't heard anything from you," he said surreptitiously. "Are you . . . filing for divorce?"

"I mean . . ." She raised her hands in a helpless gesture. "There's not a rush, right? He can't leave until after the wedding, anyway."

Elijah laughed, holding up a hand. "I'm sorry I asked. That's more drama than I want to get into. Let's pretend we never brought it up."

Hannah looked between him and Jason. Jason was beautiful to a degree usually reserved for magazine covers and runways. He had a chiseled jaw, locs down his back, and dark skin with high cheekbones. Elijah, looking like an old-time accountant and also somehow improbably chic in his wire-rimmed glasses and bow tie, had a casual hand on his husband's back, and they orbited the other without noticing. Jason was busy talking to Miriam, and they weren't drowning in each other. They'd figured out, Hannah assumed over long years of practice, how to be together comfortably, without everything feeling like broken glass or fireworks all the time.

She wanted that. She'd found peace, sort of, without Levi, but now a part of her wanted to see if she could find it *with* him. More of her than she wanted to admit.

Sawyer sauntered over, a compact package of pure swagger with a giant handlebar mustache and a side shave. He set down a massive basket of fries.

"Where's Chef Emo?" he asked, looking around as if they'd hidden Levi under a table.

"Not invited," Hannah said, "although I wish he were so he could hear you call him that."

His eyes lifted to the door and his eyebrows shot up.

"Does he know he's not invited?" He gestured with his chin.

Hannah followed his eyes, the hairs on the back of her neck already telling her he was in the room.

He had his hands stuffed into a ridiculous Lloyd Dobler trench coat, his hair combed up to the sky, and he was glowering, daring anyone to bother him. This was patently absurd, as he was not only a celebrity in a tiny town but had also gone to school with every single person in the bar since he was five. His wild Shenanigans had been talked about in increasingly improbable tales throughout town.

As he tried to make his way to their table, he was stopped every foot by someone hailing him to remember this time or that and ask him who won the show or about Australia. Whoever he was speaking to got his undivided, laser-like focus.

He nodded seriously as he heard updates on siblings, relatives Hannah was certain he didn't remember, and the minutiae that made up gossip in a small, remote town.

She watched him, worried he was going to be rude to these people she and Miriam and Noelle had worked so hard to build working relationships with. He wasn't, though. He wasn't charming, not in the way he was on camera. He didn't smile easily (or at all), didn't have a quip or an anecdote in his back pocket designed to put people at ease.

Instead, he was present, and genuine, in a way he maybe had never been before at home. He felt, much more keenly than his siblings, the difference in being part of the Carrigan's family and being the child of the cook and handyman. This, combined with his peers' distrust of his own disinterest in fitting into the mold, and his general dislike of people knowing his business, had made him a cipher. This made people all the more interested in finding out everything about him.

And, of course, in any and all gossip about whether the two of them were getting back together. As he made his way to them, he caught her eyes and grimaced. She laughed. He'd hated that, but he'd done it anyway.

"People are going to be talking about their encounter with The Legendary Levi Blue for months. You just gave this small town so much gossip."

"Why do they care?" he asked, seeming genuinely confused rather than angry. "They all hated me in high school, and I've never had a conversation with any of them."

"Did they hate you, or did you hate them?" Hannah asked, not questioning his recollection, but wondering if it had been so cut-and-dried.

"If they didn't hate me, they probably should have stopped calling me a faggot," Levi pointed out. "Although none of those people are here tonight. Which is best, because I wouldn't have been polite to them."

Sawyer smiled, a little feral. "Those ones know they're not welcome in Ernie's establishment."

"If most of them didn't hate me, I was a very lonely, angry teenager for no good reason," Levi grumbled, and Hannah shrugged.

"We all were. It's developmentally appropriate," she told him. "And you weren't surly for no reason. Some awful things were said and done to you, and you were trying to figure out who you were, and we kind of all thought you were just being melodramatically weird and angry, which, in retrospect, was extremely shitty of us. We should have trusted you that it was actually bad, that you were really being hurt."

He shrugged back at her. "I'm starting to think both things can be true. That some of them were awful, and no one really believed me, *and* that I was so used to having my defenses up that I couldn't see any of the non-awful people, except you and Miri."

She leaned over to squeeze his hand. "That might be what happens when one of the adults who's supposed to be your biggest supporter, isn't."

They stared at each other, and she thought Levi might kiss her.

Sawyer leaned down so they could hear him but no one else could.

"Whatever you do right now is going to be reported to the whole Adirondacks in about fifteen minutes, so if there is something going on between you, I wouldn't let on unless you're ready to go very public," he said, winking at them.

"There's nothing to go public with," Hannah said.

"I don't give a fuck what they think they know," Levi said.

Elijah looked between them and took a swig of his beer. "You two are messy as hell."

"We have much more important things to discuss than your drama," Jason told them. "Specifically, Levi, do you know anything about geography? Like, at all?"

"I do, in fact," Levi said, smiling at Jason. "It turns out traveling the world makes you better at remembering where all the parts are."

"False," Miriam said. "Hannah is worse at it than any of us."

"Thank God," Jason said. "We need you to fill out this visual round." He shoved a map in front of Levi, along with a pen, and Levi immediately did as ordered.

"You can come to trivia forever," Miriam told him.

Hannah's heart turned over. She didn't know what they were doing, where this could possibly go except inevitably off a cliff, but her heart was a traitor and wanted to believe in a version of the future where Levi was around to come to trivia.

At the end of the night, when they'd won, Hannah leaned over to whisper to him, "I'm counting this as date number three."

He gasped in indignation. "You're playing Calvinball, Rosenstein."

She smirked. "You knew what you were getting into when you married me, Matthews."

"You can count it as a date, if you want, but I'm not going to. I'm still taking you on three more." He smirked back.

"Ugh." She scrunched up her nose. "You're the most infuriating person I've ever met."

He nodded emphatically. "I'm the most infuriating person *I've* ever met as well. But I didn't marry me."

"I'm trying to divorce you," she reminded him.

He raised an eyebrow. "Are you?"

She refused to engage with that question. "Okay, I'm going to leave with Miri, bye!"

"Did you know," Levi said, throwing his arm around Hannah's shoulder while she was trying to update guest contacts the next morning, "that New York State has a festival called RampFest that is all about the foraging and eating of ramps?"

"Why are you giving me this information, LB?" She looked over at him, then quickly looked away so she wouldn't get mesmerized by wanting to touch his beard.

With her mouth.

"You run a farm. That makes you a farmer," he pointed out, obviously thinking he sounded reasonable. His arm was still around her, and the feel of it was doing very fascinating things to the lower parts of her anatomy, which was probably inappropriate given they were at the registration desk in the front hallway. "There will be other local farmers there with whom you can network. Talk supplying local ingredients to the kitchen. Maybe meet some chefs who might want to do guest spots before you hire a full-time person."

"Noelle runs a farm," she countered, "and is a farmer. I run a hotel that sits on a farm. I am a hotel manager. I do not farm in any sense of the word."

"Ah," Levi said, waving a finger, "but I do not want to go on a date with Noelle, for a variety of reasons, not limited to the pertinent facts that she hates me, she's in love with my best friend, I'm in love with her best friend, and she is a lesbian."

"You want to go on a date to...forage for wild onions? Is that what you're asking, here?" She pushed away from the desk so she could look at him.

"Doesn't it sound thrilling?" he asked, without irony. Wild vegetables were genuinely thrilling to him.

She shook her head vehemently. "It does not. It sounds cold, and we could buy leeks at the store. Or ramps from the farmer's market that someone else has already picked! I know, let's go on a date to the farmer's market. Where they have coffee. And sometimes cute puppies."

He pouted. "Foraged ramps taste better."

"Where is the RampFest," she asked, "and when?"

"It's in Hudson, in three days."

Her stomach dropped, and her anxiety skyrocketed. "I can't go to Hudson in three days."

"You can! I checked your schedule." He clapped.

She chewed on the end of her braid. "No, Levi, I *can't* go to Hudson in three days. I can't go farther than Lake Placid unless I meet with my therapist first and take a couple of Klonopin, and I need at least a week to prepare. It's a whoooooole thing, as in, it's new that I can even leave Advent without having panic attacks so bad I can't move, but I still can't do it without advance warning."

He dropped heavily onto the stool next to her. "Oh."

She nodded. "Yeah."

"This seems like, uh, critical information in the puzzle of why-you-couldn't-travel-the-world-with-me," he said quietly.

"I mean...yes and no." She shrugged. "I wouldn't have left, with Cass's health unsteady, even without the anxiety, but I'd already been having panic attacks about travel and leaving Carrigan's and excusing them with wanting to be where you were or needing to learn the business, or whatever."

"Why didn't you tell me?" The way he said "me," she knew he meant *me*, your best friend, your soulmate, the person you told everything.

"I..." She took a breath and prayed for courage. "I thought I could handle it, and then I was hurt that you didn't somehow magically know? Like if you'd been paying enough attention to me, I wouldn't have had to tell you? My brain was always looking for evidence that you didn't love me as much as I loved you, and it would sometimes manufacture it. But then I thought I was letting you go to live the life you needed, so at least one of us could be free."

"And then you stayed here and got madder and madder at me that I was free?" Levi asked. His voice wasn't accusatory, just confused.

"It's not...logical. Or healthy. I'm working on it in therapy." She looked over at where he was curled like a fern perched on the stool.

Would this be the thing that finally cut their ties? Him thinking she was broken because her anxiety disorder had manifested in convincing her the farm would burn down if she was gone for more than four hours? Would he finally realize they could never have a real life together?

"So, the farmer's market," he said. "Do they have eggs? Because I think we need a new local egg supplier, and my dad said no to chickens."

Her eyes welled up a little. Why wasn't he running away? And why was she so relieved?

"Yes. There is an egg supplier. Yes, your dad is correct that we cannot have chickens."

"All right! Let's go on a date to the farmer's market!"

Watching Levi talk to the egg guy, get rapturous about the depth of color on some radishes, and hug the first harvest of arugula to his chest felt like being let into sunlight after years of living underground. She didn't need him to thrive, but when he cried from happiness over fiddleheads, her body turned toward him and soaked up his smiles.

As he was getting more comfortable back home, his defenses were coming down and he was becoming more and more alive. Part of her wanted him to keep those walls, because a fully illuminated Levi was an irresistible force. She needed him to keep all his defenses, to remind her he could never be truly happy in her life.

"The best festivals," she explained as they sat with quiche at the rickety little plastic tables watching all the people go by, "are in fall. The grape festival, where you can get grape pie, the pickle festival, the cream cheese and garlic and sauerkraut festivals . . . August through November is a great time to eat in Upstate New York."

"There is both a cream cheese and a bagel festival, I recently learned," Levi said around a mouthful of quiche, "and I feel like that's a real missed opportunity for a collaboration. Hey, this quiche is great. The perfect amount of nutmeg."

"Rosenstein's, of course, has a presence at the bagel festival," Hannah said, stealing a bite of his quiche. It was better than hers.

"But not the cream cheese festival?" he asked.

"We don't make cream cheese." She shrugged. He tried to block her fork with his when she went for another bite. "Until you give me a divorce, buddy, half this quiche is mine."

"Tell me more about cool shit in Upstate New York. What do you love about here? As an adult?"

This was . . . a tricky question. She did love it, very deeply, but she couldn't leave, so she'd made the best of it. She couldn't tell him she'd actually rather be at the farmer's market in Vietnam, because she didn't want to admit to him that he might have been right, and there might be more world to see. But she felt disingenuous trying to sell him on a place that was too small for her some days, and would be for him, too, eventually. Their lives were fundamentally incompatible—he could not thrive in the only place she'd ever been able to blossom.

Except he was, sort of, thriving here. And was she really still blossoming?

They were sitting on the ground with puppies in their laps when the words she'd been trying to keep stuffed inside burst out of her. "Why don't you think I'm broken?"

"What are you talking about?" he asked, trying to disentangle a puppy from one of his scarves. "Why would I think that?"

She huffed. "Because I can't leave."

"I think lots of people have really fulfilling lives in one

place. If being a hermit is what calls to your heart, I want to support that. Because I want to support your heart. Even if it doesn't call to your heart, there's nothing broken about having an anxiety disorder and dealing with it. Which it sounds like you are."

It was so much kinder than anything she'd ever said to herself about the situation, and she hid her face in her puppy so he wouldn't see her cry.

Later, as they walked toward the car, he asked, one arm slung over her shoulder and the other loaded down with produce, "We had fun today, didn't we?"

"We always have fun, Levi. Especially when we're not fighting or fucking, which we've decided we don't do anymore. That's who we are, fun, fighting, and fucking. The three Fs of our marriage." She wasn't even exasperated that he didn't see the problem with this, just sad.

"Fun is good," he pointed out. "I get the feeling you didn't have a ton of it the past few years. Hell, we weren't having a ton of it at the end."

She sighed. "No, I didn't. You had all of mine."

"Oof. Fair."

She shook her head, stopping his long strides so they could look at each other. "It's not even... That's not the problem. I mean, I guess I could be mad about it, because I'm great at being mad at you, but I wouldn't go back and make a different choice. The problem is that fun isn't enough. It's not enough to build a life and a marriage on."

"We have enough to build a life on, Hannah. We have shared history; we love each other. Fun doesn't hurt, though!" he sang, pirouetting away, bags flying out around him.

"What about the fact that we still want opposite things?" she called after him.

"We'll figure it out as we go!" he said, and she sighed.

She still couldn't handle his We'll Do It On Vibes, and he still wasn't listening when she said she needed more. It was a good thing she was on this date to make peace with her divorce and not to restart her marriage, or his answer might break her heart.

"Do you think Noelle might want to go to RampFest with me?"

Chapter 13

Levi

Noelle had not wanted to go to RampFest with him, but he was glad he'd asked. He wasn't sure they would ever be friends, but he could make the attempt. Maybe if he stopped making Hannah miserable for long enough, Noelle would forgive him. He knew Cass's animosity had colored Noelle's opinion of him, but he didn't believe she was a fundamentally unfair person, so the longer he stayed, and changed, and didn't pick fights for fun, the more likely it was that they could find a middle ground.

The part about not picking fights was a problem.

He couldn't stop thinking about Cass's napkin, about the audacity it had taken to treat him like an annoying afterthought all his life and then use him in her elaborate melodramatic game of redemption. He didn't know how to feel about her apology, such as it was. He asked his dad out to dinner, because his dad was smarter than he was, and interested in Levi's emotional growth, though Levi couldn't figure out why. There was a good Thai place a couple of towns over. He knew Ben Matthews would never say no to Thai food.

"You're mad at me," Levi started once they had their food, and his dad harumphed into his ginger ale.

"I'm frustrated with you. You went away, fine, you needed to make a career, figure out who you were. You screwed up your marriage, okay, that's your business. But your mother had to chase you down to talk to you, you never returned any of your kid sister's texts, and you lied to Miriam about you and Hannah. It's like you shut off anyone who would have told you any truth."

Levi didn't argue with him because he wasn't wrong. Miriam accused him of being self-centered and only ever wanting to talk about his own problems, and he'd been home for a month now without putting any effort into repairing his relationship with his siblings, distracted by saving his marriage.

"It's fine if you stay mad at me——"

His dad, the most stoic man he'd ever met, rolled his eyes at Levi. "Son, you would rather I be mad at you, and you get to mope about it, than go tell people that you might have handled yourself poorly and ask for forgiveness."

"Esther doesn't need me. She's got her own lab. She's got a life," he said instead of acknowledging his dad's point.

"Do you remember when you were younger? When she was a kid who looked up to her cool big brother? She still wants that."

"She has Joshua," Levi protested.

"Joshua is her twin," his dad argued, "and the younger one, even. He's not a big brother. He would be bad at it. He's good at being the baby. You were cool, and interesting, and didn't care what anyone in this town thought of you. She was a science nerd with no friends because she lived at the snobby hotel. She was a queer girl in a small town who cared what everyone thought. She needed *you*. And when you leave and never call, when you come home and don't even try to apologize..."

Levi winced. Being five years older meant he had never been in high school with the twins and hadn't really known if they fit in there.

"Dad, I don't know how to reconcile what other people remember of that time with what I remember. I wasn't the Legendary Levi Blue, or whatever Hannah calls me. I was a kid barely making it through without getting the shit beat out of me."

His dad put his fork down. "Your sister sees the chosen child. The one we wanted to take over the Matthews legacy at Carrigan's. The one who got away with leaving the family and building a career around the world. She thinks you wore eyeliner every day to your tiny rural high school because you could, and not because you had to."

"They have careers," Levi protested, not sure where to start or how to process any of that. "Both she and Joshua have incredible careers. Away from Carrigan's."

"In the city," his dad explained, "a train ride away. Either of them can be here at any moment, and often are."

"I'm confused," Levi said, holding up his hands, "which, yes, I know I would be less confused if I had been paying attention for the past ten to twenty years to people around me who were not Hannah. Did she want to be able to travel without worrying about you guys? Did she want to stay at

Carrigan's and take over something? She doesn't give a rat's ass about botany. She's wanted to be a marine biologist since she was three and found out about whales."

"Do you think she works with whales now?" his dad asked. "She lives in the most populous city in the United States."

"I mean, it's an island?" he said hopefully, and his dad shook his head. "So she's in Manhattan to be close to the family, and I've been off. But, Dad, I didn't ask her to do that, and I'm guessing you didn't, either. Everyone thinks I'm making my life choices *at* them."

His dad raised an eyebrow. "Weren't you?"

"I didn't leave *at* anyone. I had no idea who I would be if I got to *choose*, if I might be, I don't know, pleasant and interesting instead of combative and withdrawn. I wanted to know who I actually was."

"Levi." His dad shook his head, frustrated. "Everyone builds their personality by reacting to their circumstances. None of us are tabula rasa. We all have to figure out how to be our adult selves."

"I know. I don't know what's wrong with me." He flexed his hands to stop himself from pulling his hair out.

His dad laid his own work-worn hands gently over Levi's. "Tell me what you remember."

Maybe this should be getting easier, this tour of pouring out his childhood to one loved one after another that he was apparently on, but it wasn't. Every time he opened up his wounds to bleed all over someone he'd been trying to protect, it hurt, even if he was maybe also letting those wounds finally heal.

"Some of the families would talk about me when they thought I couldn't hear, or even when they knew I could. How

I was high in the instep for thinking I would ever be more than a short-order cook, and I was too big for my britches for talking about taking over the kitchen at Carrigan's and marrying the heir like we're in some kind of bizarre medieval drama."

"They were rich assholes, Levi. The world is full of rich assholes. Why did you listen to people whose opinion wasn't worth the paper they wiped their asses with?"

"Does that include Cass?" Levi asked, leveling his father with a stare.

"What are you talking about? When was Cass ever unkind to you?"

"Do you really not know how cold she was to me? That she told me to leave Hannah alone because I would never be enough?"

His dad sat perfectly still, his face ashen. "Levi. Tell me what you mean."

Up to this moment, there had been two possibilities in Levi's mind: (1) his parents had known how Cass treated him and did nothing to stop it, which would be an awful thing to discover of parents he idolized, or (2) they had completely missed her behavior, which meant they hadn't been paying attention, which was a slightly less awful but still bad thing to learn.

It turned out he was glad it was option two, but now he had to explain again.

"You know that Cass was sometimes...quixotic...about her preferences," he began diplomatically.

"That's putting it mildly," his dad agreed.

Levi folded his hands on the table, holding them tight so they didn't shake. "At some point, she went from being charmed by my idiosyncrasies to having her feelings hurt that

I wouldn't let her mentor me and collect me like one of her lost toys. And it's not even that I wouldn't. I *wanted* her to, but I didn't know how to ask or let her in. I didn't realize that if I was closed off, she would take it as a personal affront and decide I was ungrateful."

"But you were a child, Levi. She was an adult." His dad looked angry, but not, Levi thought, at him. "And she was our best friend. We trusted her with you. With all of you."

"I know." Levi nodded. "Now, I know that she probably shouldn't have . . . but at the time, you know, I thought she was right."

"What did she say? Or do?"

"Little things . . . leaving me out of conversations or invitations, forgetting gifts, letting me feel invisible." He shook his head, trying to remember all the tiny ways he'd felt unwelcome in his home. "She didn't do it on purpose, Dad. She wasn't a monster. I never thought that of her, and I don't want you to. I think I just disappeared for her. And then when Hannah and I fell in love, she was so angry at me. She felt I was defying her because she didn't want us together. When I left, she told me good riddance, that I'd never been a true child of Carrigan's anyway. It was . . . an ugly scene. I said some things, too. My heart was broken over Hannah, and somehow I thought it was Cass's fault."

"I'm sorry I didn't know how Cass made you feel," his dad said, voice thick. "I would have stopped it. I would have told you that you were my perfect boy and told her she needed to get her head together."

"I didn't want you to have to choose, Dad," Levi said, tears streaming down his face.

"I would have always chosen you, Levi. I hope you know that."

He hadn't really been sure, but looking at his dad's face now, he was.

"And then she left me a fucking napkin. Telling me she was wrong, asking for my forgiveness. But why didn't she call me, Dad? On any Yom Kippur, or any random Tuesday? Why didn't she ask me to come home?" His eyes filled with tears, and his dad caught his hands again.

"I'm so sorry," his dad said. "It was my job to protect you, and I didn't. Not from her, and not from the kids at school."

"I have never, for a minute, held that against you. You and Mom are the best parents anyone could ever ask for," Levi assured him.

"I hope that's not true; you deserved to ask for more. But the good news is, you can be a better dad than I was," he said seriously, pushing Levi's hair out of his eyes and running his fingers over his son's forehead. Winking, he switched his tone from serious to teasing. "If you can win your wife back."

An awareness had been building in Levi, since he and Hannah had talked about birth control, of how desperately he wanted to be a dad to his and Hannah's children. Hearing his father bring it up made it feel all the more real. Another piece of their future he was fighting like hell for.

"So, about that. I have a new plan. I want to learn how to stop picking fights. Do you have any advice? You're never mad. Except at me, I mean."

His dad laughed. "Levi, I'm always mad. My grandson is growing up in a world with a climate apocalypse and rapidly rising antisemitism. Most of the kids I've helped raise to adulthood are queer, and homophobic laws are passing every day.

I'm so mad I'm made out of fire. But I can't fight any of that if I'm fighting with my wife about whether she proves that she loves me in the right way."

"How do I stop feeling unlovable? So I don't need her to prove it all the damn time?"

"Asking the big questions, son. I think you'll have an easier time believing we love you when you see that we *believe* you, about all the things that happened that made you feel this way. It's not all on you."

The middle of May brought Noelle's birthday, and Hannah, whose love language was Organizing People's Lives, had taken a brief break from organizing the Davenport festivities and their guests' activities to plan a birthday party for her best friend. Levi couldn't tell if Noelle *wanted* a birthday party, but Hannah wanted to throw one, so he was cooking for it. When he'd pointed out that Noelle hated him and probably did not want him cooking her birthday dinner, Hannah had threatened to do it instead, and he'd broken.

"What's your deal, Blue?" Noelle asked, walking in while he was prepping.

"Like, in general?" he asked warily. "I'm terrible at social interactions and often prejudge people as having the worst possible intentions, without getting any information first? That's probably my primary deal."

"Oh no, that much is clear," she told him, and then, after a moment's thought, said, "Have you ever heard of rejection sensitive dysphoria?"

He shook his head.

She shrugged and said, "Huh."

"What's my deal that you're specifically mad about right now?" he prompted her.

"Oh, right, so Hannah said you had some deep talk, secrets were spilled, understandings were reached, and now she 'really sees your past in a different light,' which, I gotta tell you, looks an awful lot to me like some gaslight-y rewriting of the past to serve your own ends, and I know you would never try to manipulate my best friend into getting back together, would you?" She stared hard at him.

"She didn't tell you what we talked about?" he asked, looking back down at the food he was cooking so he wouldn't have to meet her glare.

"She did not," Noelle answered, "which also fucking worries me. None of the secrets you two have ever kept together have been healthy."

He set his spoon down and met Noelle's eyes. "I didn't ask her to keep secrets for me, if that's what you're asking. She didn't tell you because she's not an asshole, and only assholes out people."

Noelle shook her head like she was trying to process the last thing he'd said, or maybe follow his brain dump. He was used to only speaking to her in as few words as possible, so she didn't usually get the Full Levi.

"Out you as what?" she asked skeptically.

"Demisexual. Maybe pansexual? It's up in the air."

"You like sex," Noelle told him. "We live in a very old hotel with very thin walls. I have heard you like sex."

"Not that it's your business, but I do like sex. With Hannah," he confirmed. "There are a whole lot of ways to be demisexual. It's a wide spectrum. Mine is, apparently, sex is great if I'm in love and holds absolutely no interest for me if I'm not."

She hummed, crossing her arms over her chest. "This annoys me, because I always thought you had a whiny woe-is-me attitude about feeling like an outcast because you were an average straight boy who wanted to think he was the victim of something, but I imagine you actually did grow up with some real angst about why you weren't like everyone else, and now I have to factor in your lived trauma to your attitude, and I would prefer you remained a cartoon villain."

"If it helps, I still am a whiny outcast boy with an unearned woe-is-me attitude. I'm just a queer one?" he offered.

"Welcome to the rainbow umbrella, I guess," Noelle said grudgingly, holding out her hand. He shook it.

"This absolves you of nothing in our past but I'm no longer specifically mad about anything you've done this week," she told him.

"Super fair. Do you want to test this risotto?" He held out a spoon. "I made it without wine so you could eat it."

"Obviously," she said, taking the bite.

"You know," Levi said as she was eating, "I spent a long time casting her as the villain in our breakup. It took me . . . too long to realize I was being wildly unfair. She couldn't leave, and I should have seen that. How self-centered do I have to be to know someone all my life, be their oldest friend, and still fundamentally misunderstand who they are when it's not who I want them to be?"

He'd picked up a bunch of basil as he was talking, rolling into a tube and chiffonading it, the rhythm of his knife matching the rhythm of his words. As if this monologue had played over and over in his head, and he was familiar with its tempo. Which it had, and he was.

"Why are you telling me this?" She looked at him suspiciously.

"I don't know," he said, gesturing at her with a handful of basil. "You're the person who loves her as much as I do? We're Team Make Hannah Happy, and you suck less at it than I do?"

"Sometimes," Noelle said, waving her spoon back at him, "and I can't believe I'm even vaguely taking your side here, we hope so hard for something that we convince ourselves it's possible. You hoped Hannah would go with you, because you needed to go and you couldn't imagine your life without her. You constructed a future for the two of you, and some part of you knew that if you ran it by her, she would shoot you down. That wasn't actually the asshole part. Now, never calling . . ."

"She told me she never wanted to hear from me again!" he protested, not very convincingly.

She scowled at him. "A convenient excuse."

"Do you think she can ever forgive me?" he asked, and heard the anxiety in his voice. He hadn't meant to ask, or even to admit, to Noelle of all people, that he worried over it.

"I think she's already forgiven you. I don't think that's the part of your past that's standing in your way." She bopped him with the spoon, and then added, "This needs more acid. The flavors aren't complex enough yet."

"Thank you, Gordon Ramsay," he said grouchily, because she was right.

"She's not worried about how I left . . . She's worried about how we were when we were together?" He nodded.

Noelle did a golf clap. "You see? You listened. If you want to win her back, which you should not do because you are literally the worst person I've ever met and you'll never be good enough for her, you should show her that you two together can be different. Give her evidence. Let time take time."

"I've been in love with her for twenty years, Noelle." Now he was absolutely whining. "I want my heart to stop feeling like it's stabbed every time I'm in a room with her. How much time is time going to take?"

"Levi, my dude, she's going to pierce your heart every day forever." She patted him on the head. "I've got work to do. You might want to do some, too."

"Wait," he called after her. "Miriam says you might be able to help me with something."

"Are you really asking me for a favor on my birthday?" she asked, half turning back to him.

He huffed out a laugh. "I...um...I have some anger, at Cass, that I'm trying to figure out how to deal with. Miri said you were the person to talk to about that."

Noelle turned her whole self back, a fist on her hip, and studied him. "Yeah. Yeah, I guess I am. All right, some day that's not my birthday, come find me and we'll form the two-person Mad At Cass Carrigan Support Group. You bring the snacks."

"I can do that," Levi agreed. "You can read the emotionally manipulative napkin she left with Elijah to give me after her death."

"She fucking didn't," Noelle said, shaking her head. "I should be surprised, but did you see the one she sent Miriam?"

That night, everyone gathered for dinner in the dining room. His risotto was correctly praised as excellent (he'd managed to screw it up on *Australia's Next Star Chef* and it had almost sent him home, so getting it right for his family was a small redemption). Everyone sang very loudly, including Kringle.

Miriam looked at Noelle with so much love shining on her face, her feelings could probably be seen from space. Aliens were going to make contact, and someone was going to explain to them they hadn't intentionally been signaled—it had just been dopey lovesick sapphics.

The Rosenstein's home office had sent a rainbow tie-dye cake with rainbow confetti in the frosting, and Levi felt more than a twinge of jealousy. They sure as hell had never sent him a birthday cake, even when he'd been dating Hannah. He knew Noelle was fundamentally an easier person to like than he was, but damn. His best friend, his parents, his siblings, his in-laws. His wife.

Everyone liked her better except his cat. It was dawning on him a little that proactively living his life as a fuck-you to everyone was incompatible with being liked back by people you genuinely liked.

This made him surly and snappish, and his dad had to kick him under the table and tell him to stop snarling at people. Being more pleasant to his loved ones was obviously going well.

Elijah and Jason came with their twins, Jayla and Jeremiah. They were overwhelmingly cute and reminded Levi of when Esther and Joshua had been little and he'd been intent on being a good big brother. When had he forgotten that vow to himself? Maybe he could be a good uncle to the Green twins. And, you know, his actual nephew if Joshua would let him. Jason gave him a hard time about when he was going to come over for dinner, and he was surprised the invitation had been genuine rather than a polite fiction, so he set a date for the next week.

Collin, of the better-than-average egg salad, came with his wife, Marisol, a boutique owner from Advent. According to his mom, who was his source for all Advent gossip, Marisol and Collin had danced around each other for years and finally gotten together at the Carrigan's Christmas Eve tree lighting. They'd wasted no time getting married. Levi felt a certain affinity for them, having also jumped into marriage.

Marisol ribbed Noelle about getting her ass handed to her in Spite and Malice, and they had a rapid-fire conversation in Spanish mostly about how he was a shithead but Noelle was trying not to kill him.

"Lo aprecio," he said, because it seemed shady to let them talk without cluing them in that he was, after several years in commercial kitchens, fluent in Spanish.

Noelle glared daggers at him. Marisol threw back her head and laughed. Levi liked her.

He also liked Ernie, the owner of the dive bar on Main Street, where trivia was now played. He'd adored her grandmother, after whom both she and the bar were named and had spent many hours sitting in a dark corner of the bar sulking.

Along with his high school English teacher, Mrs. Acosta, the original Ernie had been one of the adults who always checked on him. At the time, he'd been too much of a feral cat to appreciate their interference, but as he looked back on that time and tried to remember the good parts, he had a lot of memories of one or the other of them keeping an eye out for him.

The new Ernie, a stunning young Black woman with lipstick the red of dark summer cherries and box braids, asked
him about behind-the-scenes secrets of *Australia's Next Star
Chef* and they gossiped about what the judges were actually
like offscreen.

For several hours in a row, he wasn't miserable at all.

He didn't feel the way he did when he was traveling, like he
could put on whatever persona felt right that day, but he didn't
feel the way he usually did at home. He didn't feel stuck inside
an ill-fitting Halloween costume, several years too small. He
wasn't obsessing about how everything he said came across. He
was just there, and it wasn't going terribly. He would never be
at home without having to mask at all, because being at home
meant all the old dynamics he'd grown out of, but for an hour
or two he retracted his claws and stopped expecting everyone
to hate him because of who he used to be.

Blue, Age 23

I t's my fucking birthday!" Levi yelled as he threw back a shot.

Laurence cheered, and their buddy Short Darren whooped from his place on the couch. They were celebrating in the shitty, cheap apartment Levi shared with four other recent CIA grads. The Culinary Institute of America might have prepared them to work in world-class kitchens, but there were thousands of talented young cooks in New York City, and even if you had a great mentorship, you couldn't afford your own place. Or to drink in bars.

The landline rang, the handset buried somewhere in the couch cushions. Short Darren fished it out and answered, "Wooohoooo!"

"No one named Blue lives here, dude! Blue's not even a name!" Short Darren dissolved into giggles while Levi grabbed the phone from him.

"Hannah?" he asked breathlessly. He'd been waiting for her to call all day. Hoping.

"Who's Hannah?" Laurence yelled in his ear.

"Blue, buzz me up!" came Miriam's voice instead.

"What do you mean, buzz you up?" He was, perhaps, a little buzzed already.

"What do you mean, what do I mean?" Her laugh cracked up to him. "This is New York City. How many definitions of 'buzz me up' are there, you nerd?"

He dropped the phone and buzzed her in, then barreled out the door to start running down the six flights of stairs to the street.

Wow, was he too drunk for this. But Miriam was here!

He met her halfway down, in the middle of the rickety old metal staircase. She was bundled up like she was going on an Arctic expedition, and he was wild haired and out of breath. They hugged each other and rocked and sat on the steps and cried. This was the longest they'd ever gone without seeing each other, in all their lives. They had missed each other at Carrigan's, had been busy working all summer.

"What are you doing here?" he finally asked.

"It's your birthday!" she declared, as if that explained everything.

He put his hands on his head in a vain attempt to keep it attached to his body. "What are you doing in New York? I thought you had some kind of fancy gallery internship."

"I do! In Manhattan! Surprise!" She threw her arms up.

"You're here? You live here? What?!" His brain couldn't process any of this.

"Hey!" Laurence yelled down the stairway. "What are you doing down there?"

"Come and meet my friends!" he said. "We're celebrating."

"I don't want to drink with your college bro friends, Blue. Come get food. Come on, we can go somewhere super fancy we would never splurge on, like that time when we were kids." She pulled at his shirt.

He shook his head. "I can't leave my friends! They came to celebrate with me—*wait*. I have an idea. It's so much better than a fancy place. Come up so I can get my jacket."

They ended up in a tiny Tunisian spot he'd found by accident last year, that took an hour to get to by train, was smaller than Levi's living room, and served food that made him feel like he was having an out-of-body experience.

"I'll never be able to cook like this!" he wailed as he stuffed more flatbread into his mouth.

"You're not Tunisian!" Short Darren laughed at him.

Miriam watched him, a little smile on her face.

"What? What's happening?" He wiped his face. "Is there couscous in my beard?"

"You're happy here," she said. "Happier than I've ever seen you."

"You've never seen me outside of Carrigan's," he said, tipping his beer at her.

"Well, that's changing now," she declared. "We're going to have every adventure this city will allow us, Blue. No Carrigan's necessary."

She looked down at her buzzing cell phone.

"You answer this," she said, handing it to him. Hannah's number flashed on the screen.

He suddenly panicked. "I can't! I'm too drunk! I'll say something maudlin! You have to pretend I'm not here. No, wait. Pretend you've never met me." He handed it back.

Rolling her eyes, Miriam answered the phone. "NAN, my Nan, my favorite most beautiful cousin." There was a beat of silence. "Why, yes, I do know a birthday boy, and I think he wants to talk to you."

She put the phone up to his ear, and Hannah's voice sang "Happy Birthday" to him, making all the hairs on his body stand up. Suddenly he wanted to cry from missing her, and with relief that she'd called, and also to beg her to be here, to be his birthday present. He wanted to scream from the rooftops that she should be his girl, but he wasn't quite drunk enough for that. Not with Miriam's curious eyes on him.

Over the sound of his own thoughts and the din in the tiny restaurant, he heard her shout, "I LOVE YOU, BLUE MATTHEWS!"

And even though he knew he couldn't tell her the truth, that he loved her back the way she loved him, he couldn't keep all his feelings in. When he shouted back at her, he was telling her everything. "I LOVE YOU, HANNAH ROSENSTEIN."

It was the most true thing he'd ever said in all his life. Now he wasn't sad anymore. He was free, he was surrounded by his friends, full of food that was delicious beyond belief, he loved Hannah Rosenstein and she loved him, even if she would never be his. And it was his fucking birthday.

Chapter 14

Hannah

Watching Levi interact with locals at trivia and laugh with her friends at Noelle's birthday made it impossible to pretend he hadn't changed. He was working on Carrigan's events without making snide remarks about wanting the business to fail, he was showing up at staff meetings and not picking fights with Noelle, even for fun, and he wasn't wandering off to mope when things didn't go his way. That was a low bar to ask him to clear, but he was clearly doing what was, for him, an immense amount of emotional labor, while complaining about it very little.

She decided she also needed to at least appear to be trying, if only so he didn't win the breakup by seeming healthier.

In this vein, she suggested their fourth date be the Gardiner Cupcake Festival. It was much farther away than she usually liked to go, and it was the kind of event he loved so it looked like she'd thought about him. (Actually, she'd mostly picked something huge and public where they couldn't get into trouble. It was definitely not so she could spend a day wandering in the sun with the love of her life, enjoying his smile.)

"Are we actually going to drive hours to Gardiner just to eat cupcakes?" Levi whined. "What does the Hudson Valley have that we can't get in the Adirondacks?"

For a person who had spent the first thirty-six years of his life trying to escape the Adirondacks, the man was getting a little defensive about his home territory. Also, for a man who had been known to drive all night to eat in one specific diner in New Hampshire because he heard they had the best breakfast in New England, he was remarkably grouchy about the drive. He could find anything to complain about.

"Mostly a cupcake festival," Hannah said dryly. "Where they have some fascinating flavor combinations, and where we can get inspired for the family reunion we are hosting soon. The matriarch of the family has requested cupcakes that will, and I quote, 'make my baby sister eat her hat with jealousy.'"

"Are you sure you're okay to go to Gardiner?" he asked, holding her eyes.

That was the whole point. Couldn't he see that? He made her itch to be back out in the world again, and she needed to start somewhere, so she was starting with the Hudson Valley. "I'm okay. I went over the whole thing with my therapist. I have a plan in case I have a panic attack. I'm ready. I want cupcakes."

"Eat all the cupcakes!" Levi raised his fist in a poor Allie Brosh imitation.

The day was stunning, all warm and shimmering golds and blues, the air so beautiful it hurt to breathe. The festival smelled like buttercream frosting, and a band was tuning up. Hannah was alone with Levi and ten thousand cupcakes.

"Can I buy you a cupcake, cupcake?" he asked.

The first booth had beautiful cakes, but all the flavors were fairly pedestrian. She nodded and smiled at the owner but moved on. The next booth had several floral flavors, with candied pansies and the smell of herbs mixing with the sugar. Levi moved up beside her, brushing a hand along her back. He hummed happily while he looked over the options. The proprietor glanced at them and then did a double take.

"You're Levi Matthews," he said, holding out his hand for Levi.

Levi nodded. "Guilty as charged." How was her human cactus so smooth at making small talk with strangers these days? When did he get *actually* charming instead of charmingly grumpy?

"I'm Jake Shi." He pointed to the sign on the booth. "I run Cake in a Cup."

"Oh!" Levi said, delighted. "I read an article about your transition from food truck to storefront. I'm excited you're here."

"I'm Hannah Rosenstein," Hannah added.

Jake's eyes got wide. "Of Rosenstein's Bread and Pastries?"

She nodded. "I don't work for Rosenstein's, but yes. I own an inn." She heard a note of pride in her voice and smiled. She would have wished Cass immortality, if she could have, but she had to admit, owning the inn felt pretty great.

"That's right, Levi. I heard through the grapevine you were back at your family inn. I hadn't realized there was a Rosenstein connection." He paused, obviously hoping for an explanation.

"His parents have run the inn for years, alongside my aunt, who recently passed," Hannah provided. "We grew up together." True, if not the majority of the truth.

"Cool! What a powerhouse culinary space that must be. And congrats on the show, dude!"

Truly, did everyone watch Australian TV?

Levi nodded, distracted by the cupcakes. "Can I try a thyme and blackberry, and a rosewater and honey? Oh! Nan, they have lemonade with a lavender buttercream. That's perfect for you."

She prickled. He had loved to feed her, once. She did want a lemonade cupcake with lavender frosting, very much, but she didn't want him to know her palate so well. She took it from him as if it might shock her and peeled the paper back, her eyes suddenly locked with his. He was watching her, waiting to see if it was good, and she couldn't look away.

The cake and frosting burst in her mouth, the tartness of the lemon balancing the floral note of the lavender. It wasn't too sweet, with a little bite, and she was angry that Levi had been right. This cupcake was amazing. She was about to have a food orgasm while Levi watched.

She was trying to figure out how to extricate herself from this intense stare when the band changed songs, and Levi froze. She smiled a little when she recognized the first notes—they were playing the Highwomen's "Crowded Table."

"When this album came out," she said, "I was so mad I couldn't talk to you about it, because I knew you were the only person who was going to love it as much as I did."

He went even more still; then his hand came up to adjust his scarf, shaking.

"I listened to this song over and over and over when it dropped, because it reminded me so much of you," he finally choked out.

Hannah looked at him closely. The man she knew had a vulnerable side, somewhere, but he always covered it up with wit and bravado and a heavy dose of fuck off. He was aggressively defiant toward anyone he thought might see his feelings, and he wasn't always able to turn it off with people he trusted. Hannah knew he had been having honest conversations with Miriam, and with her, for that matter, since he came home, but this...this man in front of her with his grief and regret written all over his face, in public, in front of strangers? This was not the Levi she knew, and that worried her.

This Levi was much, much more fascinating. She didn't need to be any more fascinated by Levi Blue Matthews.

"Come dance with me," he said as she shoved the rest of the cupcake in her mouth to distract herself.

She balked. They'd never danced together, unless you counted dance parties where they stole the Matthewses' records and played them on Cass's old turntable in her rooms when they were little. Human cacti don't dance. She couldn't handle having his body pressed up against hers, so she made a desperate bid to distract him.

She pulled open her purse and dropped a small spiral-bound notebook into his hands. Levi looked at it quizzically.

"What's this?" he asked, his fingers winding with hers as he stroked the cover.

"This," said Hannah, "is a list."

"Oh, well"—he winked at her—"I should have known. What is it a list of?"

She turtled her head into her shoulders. Now that she'd brought it up, she wasn't quite ready to tell him everything.

She bit her lip, then smiled at herself. "I started keeping it a few months after you left, because no matter how angry I was, I kept thinking of things I wanted to tell you, or jokes only you would get, or new things I wanted to hear your opinion on. I was annoyed that I couldn't get the ghost of you to leave me alone, so I started writing all those things down. Every time I couldn't say something to you, I wrote it in there."

"So, lots of cursing, then?" Levi smiled—his self-mocking half-smile, the one that was mostly cat.

She laughed. "No, I cursed at you out loud. Usually on the back acreage, at the top of my lungs. I didn't want to remember the things I called you. I let the mountains take them."

Levi opened the book at random and ran his fingers down her tiny, neat print lettering.

"'The new hipster kosher place in Rochester,'" he read. "'I rewatched *Fringe* and it mostly held up.'" He snuck her a glance and added, "I'm really gonna miss Lance Reddick."

She nodded. "May his memory be a blessing."

"You know that I missed you every second, right?" He looked deep into her eyes, and her breath caught.

This wasn't better than dancing, after all.

"Not just us together, but you, my favorite person, my anchor. I went to find myself, but I didn't realize...I didn't realize how much of me I would lose without you, or how much of me was missing until I saw you again. I'd built a life around all the holes."

"I know what you mean," she said. "That's still about you, though, LB. You're still trying to keep or lose me to find yourself." She breathed deeply, trying to dislodge the ache in her chest. She should be rejoicing that he was still too self-centered to love her for herself, instead of grieving it. "Do you want tacos?"

He cocked an eyebrow. "Yes. I'm breathing. I obviously want tacos."

"Let's go get some before we get a little too maudlin," she said, pulling him along.

"I still want a dance," Levi said quietly as he walked with her to the food truck.

"Hasn't your father ever told you," Hannah asked, "that you don't always get what you want? He tells me that all the time."

"Of course," Levi answered, "but he also told me that if I try, sometimes I get what I need."

She attempted to rally herself back into Business Hannah, chirping at Levi about his extreme weakness for marzipan and chatting up the other owners of Upstate food establishments with whom she would, eventually, like to have a working relationship. Only every time she started feeling more herself, Blue would brush up against her, or hold a cake to her mouth for her to taste, or trail his fingers along her hand as they were walking. He was doing it on purpose, using her attraction to him to cross her internal wires. It wasn't a fair play. She had to figure out a way to get back at him, to make him want to wave a white flag and give up this outrageous idea that somehow they could get back together.

She'd have to come up with it later, when the warm breeze and sunshine and vanilla sugar and beautiful man near her were not dulling her will to do battle.

She looked up from her haze to find Levi had moved on to a Filipino woman with purple yam cupcakes, and if she didn't catch up, Blue was going to eat them all without sharing.

Finally, after they'd eaten a truly alarming quantity of buttercream, Hannah dragged Levi to a picnic table and made him sit still long enough to drink a cold brew coffee.

"You must always balance your sugar intake with large quantities of caffeine," she told him primly. He reached over, wiping a little frosting off the side of her mouth with his thumb, and then sucked it off. The sight of his thumb in his mouth made parts of her body feel things she was not excited to feel in public.

She needed to gain back some equilibrium. He was pushing all the way into her comfort zones and personal space, using every tool he had to disorient her. She just needed to get some of the power back.

Chapter 15

Levi

Hannah was sitting across from him at a picnic table, her hair shining like a halo in the sun and the freckles on her shoulders calling to him like a siren song. She leaned her elbows on the wood, her head tilting toward his. When he wiped frosting off her lips with his thumb and sucked on it, her eyes sparked with a challenge. He felt a tiny victory. His inner asshole (which, to be fair, was also mostly his outer asshole) did a fist bump.

He'd gotten to her, and now she was going to get him back. He could not wait.

Their foreheads nearly rested together. She smelled of roses, always, because she used a soap, lotion, and shampoo all from the same company that had been supplying little old ladies for a century and somehow was still in business. She'd been using them since they were teenagers, right around when Levi had realized that, while he wasn't generally interested in sex in the way boys his age were told they were meant to be, he was desperately in love with Hannah. He'd never been particularly like other children, so he wasn't overly concerned about being unlike other teenage boys.

Living in a small town meant that the few boys he knew teased him about being gay when he didn't profess interest in girls, and he'd leaned into that by starting to wear eyeliner and care about fashion, because it annoyed and confused them. He was ashamed of a lot of things in his life, but people assuming he was gay had never been one of them.

He'd found that he felt more himself in eyeliner and leggings and clothes his classmates deemed "too girly" than he'd ever felt in the khakis and polos his peers preferred.

When he and Hannah got together, all of Advent had been baffled. Several well-meaning elderly ladies had quietly ceased their machinations to set him up with Sawyer Bright. For the first time, he'd understood why people cared about sex, or went out of their way to have it. And all of that—figuring out that sometimes his body really did do all those things people talked about—was wrapped up forever in the smell of Hannah's rose soap.

"Where did your brain just go?" Hannah asked, looking up at him through her lashes. She brushed the edge of his lips, right in the crease, the softest drop of a touch. It was an exact mirror of what he'd done to her a few minutes earlier, but instead of the contact being tinged with sex, it was both gentler and more cutting.

He was left starry-eyed and shaken. How did she do that? She had his whole heart in her hands, and it made him breathless all the time. Suddenly, he was feeling less victorious about goading her into playing this game with him.

"I was thinking about your soap," Levi said. "I was in a rose garden in London and the smell overwhelmed me with missing you. I spent that whole night looking at pictures of you on social media and wallowing."

"I get that way about crème brûlée," she whispered, her voice husky. "Remember the month you made nothing but crème brûlée, trying to perfect it? I can't eat one without crying anymore. It's annoying."

He wanted to have a very long conversation about fancy pudding and maybe nudity, but instead he moved his body out of her physical space and chugged the last of his cold brew. "Do you remember the time we took my motorcycle—"

She cut him off. "Shut up, Blue." Her eyes flashed, hot.

She did remember, then.

They had driven up into the mountains, into the night, to a big clearing under the stars, with nothing but a blanket, and they had been much louder than they could ever be at home. On the drive back, they'd stopped for pie at a little all-night diner and hadn't left until they'd tried a slice of every flavor.

"I miss that bike." Levi sighed. He wondered what exactly had come of his bike, now that he thought of it.

"Wait," Hannah said, "you showed up on a bike. Whose bike was it? You left yours at Carrigan's."

"Oh, it's Laurence's."

Hannah looked at him. "Laurence, like, your roommate Laurence from college? Is he in the area?"

"Yeah, he lives up on St. Regis Mohawk land, with his family." Levi nodded. "He just got off a stint as the guest chef at the Smithsonian National Museum of the American Indian, and now he's launching a program to bring traditional food knowledge to Indigenous kids who grow up in urban areas."

"Um, Laurence is a badass, firstly," Hannah said. This was true. Laurence could cook circles around him. "Secondly, why haven't you been hanging out with him? Have you even gone to see him?"

"I mean, I saw him when I borrowed the bike?" Levi realized that he probably should also return the bike at some point, having had it for a couple of months. Or maybe he could buy it off Laurence.

Hannah poked him. "You should invite him to dinner, or trivia, or to one of the events!"

"I don't know if he'd want to hang out," Levi said, running his hand through his hair. "He's super busy. I don't want to bother him."

"LB, the dude lived with you for many years. He didn't have to. He could have gotten another roommate. And I knew you in college, you were hard to live with. He's your *friend*. You need friends."

He did need friends. It was great having Nafil come in for the wedding events, but that wasn't enough—Nafil would be back to the city and then on a ship soon. He missed his Manhattan kitchen crew and the other contestants on *Australia's Next Star Chef*. They'd all formed a bond during filming; then he'd left to the other side of the world.

"Elijah and Jason invited me for dinner," he pointed out.

Hannah raised an eyebrow. "Are you going to go?"

"Yes! Why does everyone think I'm not going to go? I promised the twins I would let them beat me at Uno."

He knew if they were ever going to work as a couple again, they both needed to have their own lives. They couldn't survive being as tangled up in each other as they'd always been. Hannah had a career, a big group of friends, a fulfilling life.

He'd come home committed to either leaving with Hannah or staying at Carrigan's with her, and it was obvious she wasn't leaving, so he needed to get serious about planting roots.

That meant building his own support system here, aside from his parents and Miri. Returning his friends' texts, instead of just thinking about it. Part of his unwillingness to come home had been a deep fear that he would lose the person he'd managed to become out there in the world. He hoped connecting to his chef buddies would help him remember he was an entity separate from the weird kid who grew up at the inn. From the kid who wasn't quite good enough. He was going to go see Laurence and have dinner with the Greens.

He might even try to hang out with his sister.

Laurence was a dynamic, incredible chef, and Levi was itching to taste what he was cooking these days. When Levi called, Laurence immediately invited him for dinner and Levi headed out like a shot ("My mom's coming over, too, so keep your fucking potty mouth under wraps," he was warned). The St. Regis land was a short, beautiful drive from Carrigan's.

"I brought cookies," he said as way of greeting as a small child opened the door.

She yelled behind her, "Uncle Lo, there's a dude here who looks like he escaped from a TikTok!" Then she turned back to him and neatly lifted the box of cookies out of his hands. "I'll take those."

"Those are for your grandmother," Laurence said, coming up behind the child and taking the cookies. He eyed Levi.

"That seems like an unnecessary amount of scarf, my man."

Levi shrugged and was pulled into a hug. "If you hadn't called me soon, I was going to drive down to that farm of yours and demand satisfaction. What the hell, bro? You've been home for almost two months!" Laurence scolded but also ushered him into the kitchen, where an older woman sat drinking a cup of coffee.

"This is my mom," Laurence said, handing her the cookies. "This is my asshole friend Levi, who has not yet invited us to stay in the Victorian mansion he owns."

"I brought cookies," Levi repeated. "You have a beautiful home."

"Are they Rosenstein's?" Laurence asked, and Levi nodded.

"New recipe. They sent them over to us for a trial. They're decent. I figured you'd get a kick out of eating something no one else had ever tried."

He'd finally found his voice. He hadn't expected to be choked up with emotion from seeing an old friend. He'd always been obsessed with food, but the surprise for him about becoming a chef was the camaraderie. Everyone knew everyone in the food world; there was no hiding in a corner being a disconnected grouch. Everyone talked shit about everyone, everyone gave everyone a leg up, everyone drank until the sun came up with everyone. Levi would have thought he'd hate it, but he'd craved it like breathing.

He didn't realize he'd been terrified that he wouldn't be able to have that up here until he'd walked in this door.

"Sit down," Laurence said. "Peel some potatoes." Levi

obeyed, catching the peeler Laurence tossed at him. "Tell me what's new."

"Well," Levi said, "I'm married, to begin with." Laurence threw a towel at him, and Levi laughed. "Do you really want to hear all this bullshit?"

"Hell yes, bro," Laurence told him. "I'm gonna hand you a beer and proceed to dump five years of bullshit on your ears as soon as we're done eating. It's called reciprocal friendship. Also, don't curse in front of my mother."

"Fuck you," Laurence's tiny beautiful mother countered.

"Hannah says you should come over, for literally any occasion, or all of them," he told Laurence.

Laurence's eyes got as big as dinner plates. "You married Hannah? Start talking right now."

He settled in and told Laurence about Hannah (date dare and all), and Laurence told him a long, complicated story about a girl. He tried to provide thoughtful feedback, and Laurence laughed at him for thinking he knew anything about love. They ate one of the top five best meals Levi had ever had, and Laurence's mom apologized that it wasn't very good. Laurence's niece showed them the dance choreography she was learning for school.

All his life at Carrigan's, he'd felt undeserving of real friendship—or incapable of attracting it—and being back had sucked him into those old worn thought patterns. Having this friendship, here, healed a part of that little boy's hurt. He looked at Laurence and silently promised both his adult and child selves that he wouldn't isolate himself from his friends again, no matter how lost in his head he got.

Chapter 16

Hannah

The day after the Cupcake Festival, while Levi went to hang out with Laurence, Hannah was supposed to be prepping for Delilah Davenport's bachelorette party, but she wasn't.

Instead, she was hiding in the same way she'd been hiding all her adult life, by doing room turnover and making every guest room at Carrigan's absolutely, unassailably perfect. She pulled hospital corners so tight she could hear the sheets creak. Kringle was helping by walking through every room and yelling at the top of his lungs, presumably because he couldn't find Levi.

Each week, they'd been watching him compete against some of the best chefs in the southern hemisphere. His parents put the show on the big TV in the lounge, and everyone gathered around to see if he'd been eliminated. It was down to the top five now, from sixteen original contenders, and he was still strongly in the running. The Chef Matthews on her TV was dynamic, snarkily hilarious, addictively watchable. She didn't think it was because she was in love with him; he had a star quality that screamed that cooking on TV was his destiny. She understood why Food Network was desperate to get him in to film a pilot.

While they watched, he filled them in on backstage friendships, dramas, the people who'd hooked up, the bonds he'd formed. She watched his face light up while he watched people he obviously thought of as family. Every week, she'd watched him and wondered, *How can he be happy here?* Not only because he hated Carrigan's, or because of his wanderlust, but because he was obviously made for a life he couldn't have if he stayed. She'd already let him go once, tried to get him to leave for good so he could be free, and he'd come back telling her he wasn't interested in freedom.

But watching him on TV made her more scared than ever that no matter how much he said she was his future, she could never be future enough.

He wanted her to choose him, but how could she if it kept him from this?

Miriam swept into the room she was working on, her hair flying in front of her. As a person with an objectively absurd amount of hair on top of her head, Hannah appreciated that her cousin was committed to having more hair than her head seemed able to support. She wondered if it was somehow Cass's influence that they both felt compelled to have some part of their appearance that no one could ignore.

She winced, thinking about how Cass had always said every woman should have a signature. A scent, a lipstick, a type of hat. One thing that would make people remember them even when they weren't there. She'd taken that as an unquestionable truth, as she'd taken so many things Cass said, and here she was, with iconic (and annoying) hair and smelling like roses, only to remember that not everything Cass said was trustworthy. How many decisions had been guided by their flawed belief in Cass's wisdom?

All of them had made choices because of their faith in her. It made Hannah want to reevaluate, not just her hair and her perfume, but her whole life.

"I've looked in twelve rooms for you! How are you so fast at turnover?" Miriam panted. "Noelle said you'd fix my scheduling problem."

Hannah waited while she caught her breath, then threw her a corner of a comforter. "What's the scheduling issue?"

Miriam put the blanket on, poorly. "My Upcycling for Beginners class is scheduled to start at five on Thursdays but if your local wine thing is starting right before dinner, we won't have room in the dining room for people from my class who want to stay to eat. Also, apparently some people want to do both instead of driving up here for only an hour."

Overbooked classes was a good problem to have, and guest logistics was something she could fix in her sleep.

They tossed around some ideas while Miriam tried to help her finish turning over the room. In truth, she slowed Hannah down, but it was still kind of nice to have the company. Part of why she'd been so broken when Levi left was that Miriam was gone, too, and with them, everyone who had truly known her all her life. She'd lost both the people who understood exactly who she was, and then she'd lost Cass.

But now Miriam was back and, awkward as it sometimes was trying to reintegrate into each other's lives after a decade, her presence made Hannah feel less off-kilter. Less like she had to somehow stuff Levi into the gaping wound of her soul in a desperate attempt to staunch the bleeding.

"So...Blue," Miriam said into the silence of a new empty room. "I assume you're thinking about Blue, anyway, because you kind of trailed off and are staring into the corner."

Hannah sighed. It always came back to Blue. "What about him?"

"You're going on dates or something? How is *that* working out?"

Hannah laughed helplessly. "I don't know, he called a Shenanigan...He's so dead set on the idea of proving he's different now and that we could be different."

"Well," Miriam said slowly, "he does kind of seem like he's grown up a lot. I mean, I don't know how you were together before, but I don't see this destructive supernova Noelle seems to see. Actually I'm not sure Noelle even sees it anymore, she's just kind of a mother hen."

"Can I ask you something?" Hannah said. "Not to put you in the middle, but...you're the least biased of everyone here, and you know us the best."

"Oh, now I'm a neutral party, and not Team Levi?" Miriam ribbed her.

Hannah rolled her eyes. "I apologize for implying you love him more."

"It's fine, Blue can make anyone their worst self. Or their best. It's a special skill, really. What's the question?"

"What *do* we look like to you, from where you're standing?"

Miriam tilted her head back, her hands in her hoodie pocket, rocking back and forth on the heels of her Chucks.

"Both of you are always in motion, always buzzing and

spinning and planning and working. And when you're to-gether, you're still. Like the magnetism between you interrupts your constant movement, forcing you to be in the moment. It's probably really uncomfortable. I myself avoid being present in my body whenever and however possible. But it might be crucial to your happiness."

Hannah shook her head because wasn't that how they'd gone wrong before? "I don't want him, or anyone, to be crucial to my happiness. I want to be complete, by myself. Just Hannah."

"I don't know if that's how we work, Nan," Miriam said. "I mean, I get it. I empathize. But we're an interconnected web of existence sort of people. It takes a village to raise a Rosenstein girl."

"Thanks, I hate it," Hannah grouched.

"Hey, you asked."

Hannah threw a pillow at her.

"I know I already kind of recommended this, but I feel like you might need a friend who's not at Carrigan's to talk to about this, and I know you and Tara are buds now because you're both like . . ."

"Deeply anxious, control freak blondes with complicated families?" Hannah supplied.

"I was going to say more competent than the normal person, but sure," Miriam said. "Anyway, not that I won't talk to you about it, but, you know, the more friends the better!"

Miriam left her alone again, but now she was done turn-ing over rooms and she didn't feel better. Because she was feeling raw that Levi was off having friends, even though she'd told him he needed friends, and because she desperately didn't want to deal with the Davenport bachelorette party, she called Tara.

"Sugar," Tara drawled, "I'm so glad you called. I was about to call you. I need you to do something for me."

Tara was a dyed-in-the-wool Southern belle who never asked for anything without twenty minutes of circular small talk, so Hannah knew she must be desperate.

"I'm a little swamped right now, Tara, with the huge-deal celebrity events and the prodigal husband thing," Hannah pointed out.

"You know that I would not ask for your help right now if this were not an emergency," Tara told her, "but you have got to get this whiny man-child off my couch and up to Carrigan's. I can't handle him right now. I need Miriam to take custody of him."

"Wait," Hannah said, "Cole's in the country? Does Miriam even know that? Why is he on your couch instead of at his house?"

The last Hannah had heard, Cole was in New Zealand working on a top-secret cybersecurity contract or something. She knew Miriam hadn't heard from him in months because she complained about it every day.

Tara sighed dramatically. "That is all information you will have to ask him. I cannot have a gigantic man living in my home. He smells weird and I'm dating again, and women look askance at him, understandably. He keeps trying to get me to have long, emotional conversations about our childhood. I'm pulling my hair out."

Cole and Tara had grown up together since birth. They had shared baggage that put hers and Levi's to shame, although of a much less romantic and much more felonious variety.

"I'm not sure having him here is the best idea. He's kind of a chaos Muppet, and we're already pretty full up."

"Don't you have something he could do?" Tara sounded exhausted.

Cole *was* exhausting. Like an enthusiastic puppy, if the puppy were six and a half feet tall. "Some of Mr. Matthews's repair work, for instance?"

"Do you think it's a smart idea to give Nicholas Fraser III a power tool?" Hannah asked, skeptically.

"Well," Tara said, "he is good with a sailboat. It's not like he's never held a tool. But perhaps if you need anyone's financials hacked or a global banking system taken down?"

"I'm fresh out of hacking needs," Hannah said. "Maybe Noelle will have an idea. I could make him take tourists on boat tours, I guess. I don't know. Why did I become responsible for him? He's your and Miriam's friend."

"It takes all of us to keep Cole alive, Hannah, and you've been drafted," Tara said. "Get him off my couch. I'll call you later to hear about whatever is going on with Levi, and I do want every single sordid detail."

"I'm not going to forget you said the words 'dating again,' Tara Sloane," Hannah warned instead. "Is it the hot redhead at the cafe who Miriam told me about?" She heard Tara choke on her drink.

"Miriam needs to stop telling tales out of school," Tara said primly.

"Okay, I'll plot a heist for you *if* you do a favor for me."

Tara hummed. "I cannot agree without knowing what the favor is."

Always the lawyer. Hannah sat down on the bed she'd just finished perfectly making, wrinkling the sheets. "I need some advice. I have to throw a bachelorette party for Delilah Rose Davenport."

"What's the problem? Is she awful?"

"She's not, actually. She's great. That's what I need you to help me figure out. I don't know why I'm so stressed about this. I'm good at event planning. I've planned several larger parties with bigger stakes at Carrigan's."

"That's true. At New Year's, you threw a party that saved the entire farm," Tara reminded her.

"We've done multiday events for large groups." Hannah chewed on her braid. "I wasn't this nervous about the engagement party."

"Are you having feelings because you never had a bachelorette party, just skipped right to a secret elopement?" Tara asked.

"I don't think so?" Hannah mused. "I'm not really a bachelorette party kind of person."

Tara hummed. "Okay, so tell me about the event."

"Delilah requested a slumber party theme, including facials and massages, makeovers, and horror movies, so we're partnering with a nearby spa to have several aestheticians and massage therapists set up in the great room downstairs, along with nail art stations. The barn is now a movie theater with a drop-down screen and projector, and the women are going to take turns doing each other's makeup."

"Did you go to a lot of sleepovers as a kid?" Tara asked, and Hannah laughed.

"Not unless you count staying with my cousins. I've only seen movie versions of them."

"So you never got the experience of seeing someone else's house, eating the dinner their mom made, seeing what sort of shampoo they kept in their bathroom or how many kinds of mustard they kept in the fridge," Tara guessed.

"What if I'm re-creating it wrong?" she worried, lying back on the bed. She was going to have to change the pillow covers again. "What do people do at sleepovers?"

Tara laughed. "I stopped getting invited to sleepovers in about the fifth grade, when it became apparent to some of the moms that I had a crush on their daughters. But I have a theory. Your problem is not that you've never been to a sleepover."

Hannah sat back up, wrapping her hair up and out of the way. "What *is* my problem?" she asked. "Because I've been trying to figure it out all week and I can't."

"Your problem," Tara said, "is that you're afraid all these women are going to judge you as small town and boring."

Hannah began to protest, but Tara cut her off. "You're living in a place you've known all your life. You're in a will-they-won't-they with your childhood sweetheart. You haven't made new friends in years, unless you count me and Marisol."

Miri always said that Tara argued in lists. Apparently, she also gave pep talks in lists.

"I do count you both," Hannah said. "Also, Elijah and Jason!"

"How long have you been friends with the Greens?"

Hannah thought about it. "Ten years."

"That's not new," Tara told her. "You're not stressing about a childhood you missed out on, or a bachelorette party you never had. You're stressed out about trying to look cool in front of a bunch of women."

"You really think I'm having a freak-out because I'm not cool enough?" Hannah asked. "That's so embarrassing. I'm too old for that."

"How often did you feel cool enough for the cool girls growing up?" Tara asked.

"Never," Hannah admitted, "but look at how cool I am now. I have an amazing business. I have great clothes. I live with a giant magical cat."

"You have a hot TV star husband," Tara supplied, and Hannah froze.

"He's not really my husband," she halfheartedly protested.

"Okay, your hot TV star, secret half-married ex, whatever is going on between the two of you," Tara drawled. "But you're right. You are cool. How are you going to believe it?"

"I need to feel unstuck, like someone who makes wild, impulsive decisions sometimes," Hannah said.

"Wild, impulsive decisions like getting married on a whim?" Tara suggested.

Hannah worried her lip. "That was years ago, and I haven't done anything like it since. Also, I'd prefer something a little less legally binding right now. A small act of rebellion."

"Tattoo?" Tara offered.

"Too permanent. Kind of a religious gray area." She flicked the end of her braid, which had once again fallen over her shoulder. The braid she'd cultivated for years, that hung down her back like an anchor, weighing her down with all the ways she'd tried to make Levi want her enough to stay.

She was sick of taking care of it. She was tired of it in her way, in her mouth, weighing down her head, the time it took to deal with it. She hated the comments people made, wanted to be something other than the woman with the Rapunzel hair. She had started to grow it out as some sort of tether, some rope to keep him bound to her, even as she pushed him away. As penance, for cutting the ties of fate that bound them in an impossible love. She'd taken garden shears and hacked at all the threads tying them in a hopeless tangle to each other, but on her head, she wore all the threads at once. As a beacon in a storm, bright enough to lead him home.

She was fucking sick of it. She didn't need to do penance, and she didn't need to keep a candle lit for him. He'd made his way home, inevitable as a salmon swimming upstream. And she was mad enough at Cass right now that she didn't want to keep her One Thing. Also, she kept sitting on it, and it took a literal fortune in conditioner to maintain.

"I need a haircut," she said. Tara whooped. "And I don't want to be blonde anymore."

"Well, my friend, for that you need to talk to my former fiancée. Your cousin must have someone up there, with all that hair."

"Okay." Hannah stood up, brushing herself off. "I'm going to see if she'll take me. Maybe I can get Noelle to come with. She's kind of still not talking to me, but who can resist a makeover?"

"Text me pictures," Tara said. "And come get this fool man off my couch. You owe me."

"I'm right on top of that, Rose," Hannah quoted at her, and hung up.

Okay. She was going to roll into this bachelorette sleepover with incredible new hair, a hot TV star sort-of-ex-husband, and a plan to kidnap a grown man.

She was obviously cool.

Hannah: MIRI I NEED YOU. ALSO NOELLE. EMERGENCY.

Both Miriam and Noelle came running into the guest room, where Hannah was back to lying down on the bed, her braid hanging off the edge. She'd gotten overwhelmed by the entire thing and had to lie down again.

She looked up at both of them.

"I need you. To take me. To get a haircut. An amazing haircut. A traffic-stopping haircut," she told them as they gaped down at her, "and dye."

She was worried they would tell her a haircut wasn't an emergency, but they both knew her better than that.

"Right now?" Noelle asked.

She nodded.

Miri chewed on her lip thoughtfully. "If you're doing color, we have to drive into Lake Placid. You know Myrtle stopped mixing color last year after the Incident. But I know a guy. It's going to be amazing."

"Are you doing this for Levi?" Noelle asked.

"No," Hannah said, sitting up. "He actually might hate it. I'm doing it because I'm tired of being stuck in the person I was when he left. I want to be Hannah, today."

She put herself in Miri's hands. They piled into Noelle's vintage restored red Chevy truck, Miriam in the middle because she was basically child-sized, and they bounced along the old highway, the Chicks turned up loud. They ended up in a tiny salon in a strip mall.

"How did you find out about this place?" Hannah asked.

"Believe me when I tell you that every curly haired person in the greater Adirondacks area knows about this place," Miriam said, "if not right away, then eventually."

When Hannah sat down in the chair, the hairdresser crossed his arms. "I will cut this off for you. I'm happy to cut this off for you. But you need to look me in the eye and tell me you're ready. There's no going back once we start."

Hannah looked him in the eye in the mirror and nodded. "Take all of it. I don't want to feel it brushing my shoulders. I want it long enough to clip back, but that's all I care about. I'm thirty-five fucking years old. I want a bob."

He looked at Miriam, and Miriam nodded. "Trust her. She's ready. She needs to be free."

"You wanna donate this? There's a lotta wigs in here," he asked, holding her hair up.

Hannah nodded again.

"What the hell else am I going to do with it, keep it as a memento? Braid it into a rope?"

He shrugged as if to say, *People are weird about their hair.*

When he'd sectioned it into ponytails and took the first big snip, right at her collarbone, she breathed in more deeply than she had in years. The feel of scissors on her hair was magical. The sound of them gave her tingles all over her body.

"You okay?" he asked, looking at her as she shivered.

"I'm more than okay."

"Fantastic. We'd be screwed otherwise."

Hannah's hair had been long all her life, certainly never above her shoulders in her memory. The feeling of weight lifting off her head was incredible. And as she watched, something started to happen. The freed locks sprang up into waves.

"Do you have curls in there?" Miriam asked in delight.

The hairdresser ran his hands through the shorter pieces, considering. "They don't know how to curl right now, but I bet if you did some work, you could retrain them."

"You still want color?" Noelle asked. "This is already more change than you usually like to deal with all year."

"Hell yes."

While she waited under the dryer, Miri went next door to get them bubble tea, and Noelle read celebrity gossip to her from year-old magazines, complete with commentary. When Hannah saw the final product, instead of a honey-gold braid down her back, she had red waves that stopped above her collarbone.

In the truck on the drive back, she ran her fingers through the ends and felt them brush deliciously against her neck. She suddenly felt her throat constrict. Levi Blue had loved her all her life, but what if he didn't love, or want, this new version of her?

"Having second thoughts?" Miriam asked.

Her whole being felt freer, and she thought the freedom might be part of what was causing the panic. She was always the one holding everything down, never the free one.

"If he doesn't still love me after a haircut, I guess I wasn't actually the sun around which his soul orbits, or whatever. Which I should probably know now."

"He's going to like it," Noelle grumbled. "You look hot. And he's not the kind of guy who stops loving his wife because of her haircut."

"Noelle Northwood!" Miriam clapped and bounced in her seat. "Did you say something nice about Blue?"

Noelle harumphed. "He's not...that bad." This, coming from the woman who'd once told the love of her life that she "wasn't the worst person Noelle had ever met," was high praise. "I still think it was unhealthy of you both to hide your marriage, but I am willing to allow that Levi himself is...ugh. He's fine. I don't like him. But he's fine."

"You like him," Miriam teased. "You text each other *Flight of the Fordham* GIFs. He made the special granola that only you eat because you're a monster who loves raisins. You let him shave the side of your head the other day."

Noelle threw up her hands. "Fine! He's my friend! Which I hate! He's going to like your hair. The question is, do you want him to?"

Did she? She'd spent four years casting him as the villain in her heartbreak, because it had been simpler than recognizing that neither of them had been wrong, that they'd needed opposite things—and also they'd both been wrong and broken each other's hearts. She was mad at Cass, and herself, but she wasn't mad at Levi anymore.

In the place where that anger had been, grief swept in to fill all the holes. Grief that she'd been given a love beyond anything she could ever have imagined, and she'd pushed it away because it had made her feel trapped. Meanwhile, she'd locked herself in Carrigan's like Rapunzel in a tower, refusing to come down, pretending it was her choice instead of her fear choosing for her.

Her prince had come to her window and offered her the whole world, but she'd sent him away, then raged at him that he'd left her.

She wasn't ready to jump back in, but she wasn't ready to be done either.

"I'm scared," she admitted.

Noelle nodded. "Mir, do you have paper and writing utensils on you?"

Miriam pulled a sketchpad and a giant pack of colored pencils out from her purse.

Hannah quirked her head. "You keep colored pencils in your purse?"

"You keep colored Post-it Notes in yours," Miriam pointed out. Hannah couldn't argue. "Okay! Ready to write. What am I writing?"

"We are going to make a list of Hannah's fears about Levi," Noelle told them.

"You might need a bigger notebook," Hannah deadpanned.

Miriam poked her in the side with a pencil. "Start talking. What are you afraid of?"

"Oof. Okay."

She took a deep breath and tried to let herself actually listen to the constant maelstrom of thoughts she usually kept tightly muted. "I'm afraid that I'll give myself to him completely and he'll realize this place *is* truly toxic to him and he has to leave forever, and I won't be able to follow him, and I won't ever be okay again."

She reached behind her to grab the end of her braid to chew, before realizing it was gone, and ended up chewing on her thumb instead.

Next to her, Miriam drew a sketch of a broken Hannah and Levi on a plane.

"I'm afraid that I never got to choose my life, that I got so swept away by being in love with him from the start I never got to see what my life would be like if I'd gotten another choice."

"Wouldn't you probably still be at Carrigan's, but single?" Noelle asked.

Hannah huffed. "Maybe I would have fallen for someone easy, uncomplicated. Someone who didn't challenge me and make my life harder every day!"

Noelle barked out a laugh. "You would not. You would have been bored out of your mind. Lots of people have that kind of love, but you would have chosen someone else like Levi."

"Except no one's like Levi," Miriam said quietly, shading in a sketch of Hannah wrapped up in one of Levi's scarves. "It's not as if you fell in love with some guy and let your life run away with you. You fell in love with the Legendary Levi Blue...and then you *didn't* let it run away with your life. You *didn't* let it overwhelm you. You still chose the life you wanted."

"I never said my fears made sense," Hannah argued, although she'd never looked at it quite the way Miriam just put it.

"Okay, fair," Miriam said, "but I do have a question. Nan, you're afraid of him leaving you and you're also afraid of him staying and being too much. Those seem..." She trailed off.

"Contradictory?" Hannah finished for her, and Miriam nodded.

Hannah laughed a little. "I think all of it is just being afraid of loving him too much, and it manifests in whatever way it can fuck with me best, on any given day."

Miriam drew a giant human heart with a tiny Hannah underneath it, carrying her away like the house in *Up*.

"So we know what you're afraid of. What do you want? Do

you want him to love your haircut? Do you want him to walk away?" Noelle asked.

Hannah groaned. "How do I know what I want? All the things my heart wants, my head tells me are wildly unsafe."

"I don't want to tell you how to feel," Noelle said, which was patently absurd because Noelle had been trying to tell her how to feel for their entire friendship, "but are you open to the possibility that maybe you could be together in a way that didn't fit into your very narrow specifications of safe but still worked?"

"Or was even more wonderful?" Miriam added.

"That makes me hyperventilate," Hannah said honestly.

Noelle chuckled. "Okay, let's start with a different question. You said you're afraid because you didn't choose him, but now you have a choice. You might not be able to stop loving him, but in terms of your future, he's put it in your hands. If you could choose, of all the people in the world, would you fall in love with the exasperating, angry, egocentric, beautiful man with the unholy culinary talent?"

She'd told Noelle that if she could choose to do it over again, she wouldn't love him, but that had been because she was desperate to stop being in pain. When she thought about all the people she could have loved, and him, there was no contest. She nodded. "I want him to like my haircut. I want *him*."

"Well," Levi said when she walked through the kitchen door, "I can tell what you did today." He was smiling a little, the smile that used to mean he'd been surprised by her and was pleased, and she thought she saw a flash of heat in his eyes.

He put down his knife and looked at her a long time.

"I was going to ask how you feel," he said, "but I can tell by the look on your face that you love it."

"Do you...like it?" she asked, more nervous than she wanted to be.

He cocked his head, still smiling. "Do you want me to?"

She shrugged, trying to seem nonchalant.

His smile grew into a grin. "I would like anything that made you glow like that, because I love how you look when you know you're fucking hot. Also, I'm super impressed by you, as usual."

Hannah's shoulders crept up. "All I did was get a haircut, Blue."

He shook his head. "Our hair is a big part of our identity, and you've been living with the kind of hair that people often see, then never see the rest of you. Letting people see all of you is pretty brave."

She teared up a little, because of course he got it. Levi, more than maybe anyone she'd ever known, played with how his outward presentation affected the way people treated him. He was never not aware of what people were thinking about his hair, his clothes, his projected self-image. It was his armor and also his defiance.

Her hair had been her armor, and now it finally felt like her defiance.

"I was a little worried you only wanted me for my hair," she whispered.

He came around the kitchen island and brushed a wave out of her face, tucking it behind her ear.

"I want you for your Hannah-ness. You could put you in any package in the world, banish me to the ends of the earth, tell me you never want to see me again, and I would still want you. I know, I tried it. But don't you want me to stop wanting you?" He cupped her cheek, and she couldn't look away from his eyes, the green specks in the gray that only she knew were there.

She stared into his eyes for a long minute without answering. "I thought so, but I had convinced myself I could excise you from me, that I needed to find a Hannah without Blue, and I don't think that person exists. If you took away all the parts of me that only exist because of growing up with you, because of loving you in any way, I would be Swiss cheese." She swallowed, bringing up every ounce of her bravery. "And that's *okay*. There are lots of things I have that are only mine, but there's also...no me without loving you. I can't love you without wanting you, and the idea of wanting you, if you don't want me back, makes me want to scream."

"Where does that leave us?" he asked, and she could see in his face that he was trying not to hope.

She put her hand over his on her face, and their fingers laced together as if they'd been built to. Inside, equal parts of her screamed to tell him they were forever no matter what and to run as far away from him as she could get. She knew he was waiting for an answer. She didn't have one, except that she didn't ever want them to be what they'd been when they'd split up.

She wanted something new, something they'd never been before.

"I don't understand how we can ever be together. You can't stay. I can't leave. Nothing has appreciably changed about our future. Can you tell me how we're going to make it work?" she pleaded.

"I can't." He shook his head. "But I can tell you that I want to figure it out more than I've ever wanted anything else, some way that makes us both happy, and I refuse to believe that's impossible."

She breathed in deeply, past the overwhelming panic, and told him the truth.

"I love you, and I want you, but I can't try again unless we have some idea of how it's going to work. I want to tell you that we'll go with the flow and see if we can be in love as the people we are today, but I can't. Levi, I can't survive it again. I need a plan. Even if the plan doesn't work, even if we have to throw it in the trash and start over, I can't just jump in again."

He blew his breath out and pulled one hand away to flatten his bangs, in the way he always did when he was nervous and trying to hide it. She clenched her hand to stop herself from fixing his bangs the way she'd done all her life.

"I am more in love with this version of you than I ever have been before, and I believe we *can* be something new as we are, today," he whispered. "But I hear you saying that's not enough."

"It's not that *you're* not enough, Blue," Hannah assured him, because she knew his brain gremlins. "It's that I barely survived last time. Even if we would be better for each other now, and I think we would be, does it have a built-in expiration date, because there's no way for us both to get the life we want?

I can't do that. And if we can't answer that question, we're not ready."

He was still looking down at her, the hair falling in his face, his eyeliner smudged and one dimple trying to destroy all her good intentions. But then he nodded.

"Okay. Maybe we're not ready. But will you do something for me? Will you believe, with me, that we might be someday? Will you not give up on us yet?" he asked, his eyes holding hers, his fingers tangled in her own, their hearts beating in unison.

"Yes," she said, and his face split into a grin. "Yes, I will believe we might be able to make this wild love of ours work again someday."

He jumped in the air, pumping his fist. He grabbed the back of her head and kissed her hard, just for a moment. "You're not going to regret this!"

"Don't make me," she said.

"Oh!" Mrs. Matthews exclaimed, coming into the kitchen. "Hannah, I love your hair!"

PART 3
June

The Carrigan's All Year Calendar

☐ Delilah's bachelorette party
☐ Davenport wedding
☐ Pride Carnival
☐ BYO Antiques to Ruin class
☐ Prep for Bloomer Fest + MiniFordhamCon
☐ Book Club: *Natalie Tan's Book of Luck and Fortune*

Hannah, Age 25

When they opened the Carrigan's Christmas Festival on November 1, Hannah had already been home for a month, after rage-quitting her assistant events manager job at a hotel in Chicago after the fifth time that month the manager threw her under the bus for something that was absolutely his fault. She had promised Cass she would get five years of experience running hotels out in the world after college before committing to coming back to run this tiny inn, in the middle of nowhere.

She knew Cass had only love for her niece in mind when she talked her into that promise. She wanted to make sure she wasn't clipping Hannah's wings, wasn't forcing her into the family business unless Hannah really wanted it. It was appreciated, since the actual business that the rest of their family ran, Rosenstein's Bread and Pastries, was full of aunts and uncles constantly trying to get her to join them.

But she'd seen the world. She'd spent her whole childhood seeing it, and she didn't want to go anywhere.

Every day that she wasn't at Carrigan's was painful and getting more so. The panic she felt that something would go wrong without her was increasing with every year. Carrigan's Christmasland was her harbor, and she was ready to put down anchor for good. So, two years ahead of schedule, here she was, working another Carrigan's opening day.

Unlike the last few years, when he'd been busy with school or work, Blue was here, too, resentfully spending his birthday helping out his mom. Not resentment at his mom, who he adored, but at the imposition on the life he wanted to be leading, which wasn't here at Carrigan's. She'd expected him to be far away as soon as he finished culinary school, off to apprentice with some French chef who was as much of a smug asshole about food as he was, or working in some Michelin-star restaurant he would brag about forever.

She loved Blue, more than almost anyone, far more than she ought to, but even being in unrequited love with someone half your life couldn't make you oblivious to all their faults. Blue Matthews loved his own talent too much and Carrigan's too little to still be here. Yet, here he was, working under the bright lights of the kitchen to make sure his mom's kitschy, old-fashioned appetizers that didn't properly showcase his culinary genius went out perfectly and on time.

When they finally closed down for the night, she found him alone in the kitchen, wiping down all the counters and cleaning the knives.

She stood in the door and watched him, his long limbs and strong hands moving in a careful, precise dance. He'd learned it while they were apart, each at school, and it fascinated her to watch his body move in ways she'd never seen before. In the month they'd been back, they'd settled into their old friendship like slipping into a cool pond on a summer day, all at once and easy but with each wave, a thrilling little shock to the system.

"Little boy Blue," she said, "I thought I might find you here."

He looked up, and the shadows cast by the overhead light in the dark night made his eyes look hot, but Hannah knew better than to trick herself into believing she saw interest in Blue's face. She'd spent too many years parsing every glance, every word from him to see if there was a crumb, even a scrap of evidence that he felt about her the way she did about him.

He flung his dishtowel over his shoulder and came to lean on the other half of the doorframe, one foot up, his arms crossed over his chest.

"Cass shouldn't work you so hard," he said, his face the sullen mask it always was when he talked about her aunt. "She doesn't pay you enough. She's taking advantage of how much you need this place."

She wouldn't let him dim her glow from a successful opening day. He could be as mad at the world as he wanted to be, but they were twenty-five freaking years old, and she was over his brooding teenager shit ruining her mood.

Actually. He wasn't twenty-five, not as of this morning. She nudged his black leather boot with a battered Chuck Taylor.

"Hey. Happy birthday, you."

"You remembered." He ducked his head, and his hair swooped down into his eyes. She stopped herself from reaching up to brush it back.

"Have I ever forgotten your birthday? It does come on opening day every year." She raised an eyebrow. This boy. As if she hadn't spent a thousand hours imagining giving him a birthday kiss.

"The year I turned twelve you didn't call or send a card, I seem to remember."

"We were on an island in the Pacific with spotty mail service, and my parents wouldn't let me use the sat phone to call you and sing to you!" she protested.

"I thought Miriam would be here by now," he said, scratching at a burn scar on his arm, which he'd gotten trying to fry sufganiyot when they were nine.

"Cass says she's not coming this year. Something about her dad? She wouldn't tell me, but it sounded serious."

He frowned, his brows slashing across his forehead.

"She promised me," he said, then shook his head like he was trying to shake off the disappointment.

"I'm here?" Hannah offered, wanting him to say that she was just as good, that even though she was always trying to organize their Shenanigans into an itinerary, she was just as much fun as her cousin.

He scowled harder. "I know, that's why I need Miriam here. She's supposed to be my buffer."

Hannah's heart sank, her brain scrambling for some meaning that wasn't as cruel as it sounded. He was her person, her best friend, her middle-of-the-night call. He couldn't mean he needed Miriam around to be able to tolerate her. She couldn't even begin to restructure her entire understanding of her life in the face of that possibility.

"A buffer for what, Blue?" she asked, angry at herself when her voice came out choked, but proud that she'd raised her eyes and looked at him instead of down at her shoes.

He glanced up, and she followed his eyes to the mistletoe hanging in the door frame above their heads. He pushed his foot off the wall and loomed over her, hooking an arm around her waist and pulling her into him so their bodies were flush.

What was happening?

She had literally had this dream. He was looking down at her with open longing in his face, and she thought Cass must have spiked the hot cider again, and now she was somehow hallucinating.

"From my constant, obsessive need to kiss you every second that we're in the same room," he explained, as if this were obvious and not the wildest and least likely answer he could possibly have given.

"Why would you ever stop yourself from kissing me?" she whispered, hypnotized by the green flecks in his eyes that she'd never noticed before. How had she never noticed?

"I can't remember anymore. It seemed so smart, but now you smell like roses and I can't think about anything else."

"I always smell like roses," she whispered, her brain too scattered to say anything else.

He rested his forehead against hers and growled low in his throat.

"I've spent the past ten years trying not to kiss you, Hannah, but if you don't move, I'm going to stop trying."

She held his gaze as she put one hand on the back of his neck and pulled his head to hers. She kept her eyes open as their lips came together, because she needed to know this was real. She wouldn't miss even a second in case he came to his senses afterward and it never happened again.

What started as a hard, declarative kiss, the answer to a dare, changed as their bodies fused. Blue picked her up and held her against the doorway, her toes barely grazing the floor.

She had done a fair amount of kissing, and everything else, in college and after. None of it had felt even remotely like this. She had been imagining this kiss for a decade, and nothing compared to the reality of his lips and hands on her. This was her Blue, the one person who lived entirely inside the confines of her own soul.

She was kissing him, and he was kissing her, and the hurricane of love that swept through her left her unable to breathe.

Blue pulled back, startling her.

"Are you okay?" he asked. "You stopped breathing. Should we stop? Did I do something wrong? I haven't... I'm not... I don't know that I'm very good at this."

She held on to him to keep him from pulling away and to keep herself upright.

"It was perfect. I just—" She tried to stop herself, but the words flooded out of her, her dam broken. "I'm just so fucking in love with you."

He picked her up for real this time, all the way off the ground, and swung her around. He grinned, that old Levi Blue Shenanigans grin, and kissed her so hard she saw stars. He laughed out loud, and she realized she hadn't heard that sound in years, not in this kitchen, anyway. Maybe when he'd been away at school and called her.

"Hannah Naomi Rosenstein, I love you more than I have ever loved anything or will ever love anything."

This was it for her. She knew it in that moment down to the very atoms of her being.

Chapter 17

Levi

Levi watched Hannah navigate the social intricacies of Delilah's bachelorette party—a large group of women who all knew the bride but didn't necessarily know each other and were mostly a little tipsy—as if she'd been born with the skill. Everything she did was thought out, and he knew it sometimes gave people the impression that her bun was wound too tight. When he left, he'd only ever known her to unwind in front of a very select group of people, himself included.

Even then she could sometimes be kind of mean, which he personally thought was hot, but probably wasn't a professional asset.

This Hannah had obviously put an enormous amount of work into becoming gregarious, effervescent, easy with strangers. She would have to be, to event plan successfully, and he knew her well enough to know she was going to be successful, come hell or high water. She steered clashing bridesmaids into activities that kept them occupied, swapped out drinks for virgin substitutes without anyone noticing, and made sure no drama came near the bride.

The morning after the party, all the women slowly rolled out of their beds, stumbled through coffee and Rosenstein's pastries, and headed to the airport, gushing praise for the party.

Levi was sitting in the dining room, finally eating some breakfast now that all the guests were fed and gone, when his mom entered.

"You seem lost in thought, my sweet boy. Where is your mind?" she asked, sitting down beside him.

He laughed. "Hannah. As usual."

"And what about Hannah?" his mother prodded, jostling him a little with her elbow.

"She managed to be both a part of the fun and the person running the show, without the participants noticing she was holding herself separate. It was masterful." He sipped his coffee, staring off into space. "I'm so damn impressed by her."

From the corner of his eye, he saw his mom smile a sly smile. "We're very proud of her. And of you, too. Your dad and I noticed that the two of you seem to be a very effective team."

How was this brilliant, successful, incredible woman ever going to choose him as a life partner? He'd asked her to decide, after their dates were over, if she wanted a divorce or if she wanted him. At the time, he'd been convinced that he could win her back, but now that he'd spent weeks watching her work, he couldn't imagine what he brought to her life that she didn't already have, except chaos and tears.

And they only had one date left for him to figure out how the hell they could ever make it work.

He was spared further parental interrogation by Noelle, who popped her head around the corner. "Boss lady needs you for something," she said. "I suspect it might be a diabolical plan."

Levi dropped his fork and headed toward Hannah's office, stopping only long enough to rearrange his scarves and fluff his hair. Diabolical plans were his love language. Was his wife trying to woo him?

He walked into her office, about to ask what she needed— and stopped.

Involuntarily, he shut the door behind him, leaning against it to catch his breath. Hannah was wearing a cream satin blouse with a plunging V neckline and a big bow. It was tucked into a gray tweed pencil skirt, and her hips and ass were going to be his actual death. She was sitting on the edge of her desk, her legs crossed, a heel hanging off one swinging foot. Behind her, slung over the back of her chair, he could see a matching tweed blazer.

How could he have so little interest in anyone else's physical body, and so much in hers? It was like he'd saved up his desire, all his life, and the need only surfaced around her, but then it all did. A lifetime supply of wanting. He swallowed, hard.

"Blue, you're turning an interesting shade of red. Is there something wrong?"

"I think I'm blushing," he admitted. He walked forward, drawn to her, setting his hands on either side of her hips, not quite touching. He was shaking, just a little.

"I asked you in here because I needed something," she said, suddenly sounding a little short of breath.

"I know, but you look edible and I'm distracted." He slid his hands over her blouse, squeezing her waist.

She put her hands on his shoulders and skated her finger-tips up to his neck. His hands, seemingly on their own, landed on her thighs, and he was pushing her skirt up so he could stand between her legs. She gripped the hair at the back of his neck.

"Chef Matthews," she whispered into his ear, "do I look like the kind of woman who's going to go for a fast, filthy, lunchtime quickie on top of her desk?"

"Yes," he groaned, "you very much do." Then he moved himself away with an enormous effort and stuffed his hands in his pockets. "But you needed something from me, and Noelle mentioned a scheme. I have to know."

She whined in the back of her throat before rearranging her bow and fixing her glasses. He watched her school her features back into a mask of normalcy, but she couldn't turn off the heat in her eyes.

"What did you need, Nan?"

"I need your help with something slightly shady," she said. His heart skipped a beat. It gave him a zing all the way down the tips of his fingers that she was asking him on an adventure.

"You had me at shady." He pulled up her extra chair and settled his elbows on his knees. "I was starting to wonder if you still had a shady streak, or if you were too grown up for it."

"I was busy helping Cass die and trying not to lose the business, but I am still very capable of making trouble."

There was a sore spot there, and it was a well-earned one. He kept thinking of New Hannah as more laid-back, more comfortable in her skin, having had all these wonderful times growing into herself without him. But he kept forgetting that while he'd been eating his way through self-actualization, she'd been holding everything here together by her finger-nails, and a lot of New Hannah was grief and self-preservation and sheer stubborn unwillingness to let the ship sink. He had missed all the fun she'd had, but he'd also missed all the opportunities to show up for her when she most needed a partner.

It was amazing that she was even willing to try to figure them out. It was a huge risk, to trust him enough to try again. The fact that she was willing to plot mischief with him? That was a gift he couldn't even begin to process.

"I'm sorry I teased you about not being fun. You're my favorite mischief partner."

He batted his eyelashes at her, and she huffed in amused annoyance.

"Cole is in some kind of trouble and he's ensconced him-self on Tara's couch," Hannah explained, clearly deciding to move on. "I promised her I would kidnap him and bring him to Miri."

He steepled his fingers. "I have so many questions. Why are you talking to Tara? Does Cole want to see Miri? How did we get involved in this mess?"

"Did you forget how Carrigan's is?" Hannah asked him. "Everyone's business belongs to everyone. We're involved be-cause the situation needs fixing, and we are available. We're getting Cole because he's one of ours. Also, I talk to Tara because she's my favorite of all of you except Noelle."

"And you can't go because it's several hundred miles away."

"Yeah, there's not enough Klonopin on the Atlantic sea-board." Hannah shuddered. "I would need months to prepare, and I'm too busy with the Davenports. But thankfully I have a world-traveling husband who is keen to show that he's a useful part of the Carrigan's team."

He rested his hands on his knees and grimaced. "So, to be clear, you need my help to kidnap a six-foot-five grown-ass man who is having a tantrum and hiding on his friend's couch."

"Yes. Although I think he might be lying about his height, I suspect he's closer to six-seven. It's fitting because he came to get you and told you to get your ass home, and because no one knows more about throwing a tantrum and hiding out than you." Hannah looked at him over the rims of her purple sparkly glasses.

He wanted to run his hands through her new red waves and pull her into him, forget about their friends' drama and the commitments that tied them so tightly to everyone they knew. When they'd been together, he'd spent so many hours wishing he could be with Hannah separate from the enormous baggage of Carrigan's. But here, in her office, with her dressed as the Boss and coordinating a full grown-up Shenanigan, he felt struck by lightning.

There was no "them" without Carrigan's, and if he wanted her, it would have to include every single emotional entanglement and complicated baggage of this place.

He was going to have to unpack the shit out of that revelation at a later time.

"I don't even know how he found me in Australia. Everyone on set had signed an NDA, and we were filming out in a tiny little town to try to keep press from camping outside for photos." Levi rolled his eyes at the memory of a blond giant, larger than life in every way, wandering in and getting his way.

Hannah laughed. "I guarantee he made himself comfortable in the production company's emails."

"Cool, that seems totes legal." Levi scowled.

Hannah shrugged. "I haven't known him long, but I have learned his idea of what information he's entitled to is based less on a moral or legal compass and more on what information he can access, which is all of it. I asked him to go get you, and he went."

"He flirted with the craft services guy until he somehow ended up backstage, sitting next to me while I got my makeup and hair done," Levi told her. "He was just there suddenly, taking up a huge amount of oxygen, telling me I was a dick for running away from the best girl he'd ever met."

"That guy's the best," Hannah said wistfully. "Do you know, when we met, he told me I looked like Mae West?"

Levi cocked his head. "I always thought a hotter Christina Hendricks in *Mad Men*."

"Christina Hendricks wishes she had my ass," Hannah joked.

Levi nodded emphatically. "*Exactly.*"

"Focus," Hannah said when Levi's eyes drifted down her blouse. "Cole."

He shook his head, trying to remember what he'd been saying. Right. Cole in Australia. "The creepiest part was how much it sounded like my own internal monologue, yelling at me."

"You owe him." Hannah pointed at him.

He scrunched up his nose. "Eh."

"I hereby officially declare a Shenanigan," she said. Well. That was that.

"I'll go get him," he said, sighing dramatically. "In spite of the mortal wound he dealt me when he stole my best friend out from under me, and despite his being twice my size and extremely annoyingly enthusiastic about life. Is there anything I need to know about this operation?"

"You need to be there and back in twenty-four hours. Give me your phone. I'll give you Tara's number."

He loved her bossiness so much. He could watch her be the boss forever. What was he going to do if, after all, she decided they still weren't ready and they never would be?

He handed his phone over and watched her type.

"Levi. Am I your phone background?" She raised an eyebrow. "Yes?"

"You're a dork."

After he slipped his phone back in his pocket, he snuck his hand behind the nape of her neck and brought their heads together. Her pupils dilated.

"Rain check on the quickie on the desk?" he asked.

She whimpered. "I thought we weren't fooling around anymore."

"We have a lot of life left, Hannah. No expiration date on that rain check."

He went to leave and then turned back. "I want you to know that I see you including me in Carrigan's business. I know it's hard for you to let anyone be part of the team, me especially."

Hannah looked at him over her glasses. "You're Team Carrigan's, Levi Blue, whether you like it or not. This place is the Jewish Christmas Hotel California."

Even two months ago, the idea that he might never escape from Carrigan's Christmasland would have sent him into a panic spiral. Instead, he replied with the Team Carrigan's motto. "Ride or die."

The next day, Levi flew into Charleston, where Tara and Cole lived, at lunchtime. He stopped at an old friend's restaurant before he went to Tara's. His excuse for this was that he didn't want to show up empty-handed, but actually he would never miss a chance to pick up a fried green tomato sandwich.

He expected some drama on Cole's part, given that he was being kidnapped, but all Cole did was grab the bag of takeout from Levi's hands, say, "Oh thank God," and go to pack his bag.

Tara looked him up and down, laughed, and shook her head, her perfect blonde bob swinging. "You're Hannah's kryptonite, huh?"

"I would have said Hannah was mine, but I'm certainly Hannah's something."

"Well, good." She nodded, her Southern accent like molasses. "You look like you're made out of pure unadulterated chaos, and she needs a little. Hurt her again and I'll fuck you up."

"What is it with Miriam dating women who threaten to kill me?" he groused.

"Miriam has impeccable taste," she said before disappearing back into her office.

"You have a lovely home!" he called back after her. Cole dragged him out to the car and didn't stop dragging him until they were at the airport. Levi was no longer sure who was kidnapping whom.

"So," Cole said as they stood in line at an eerie airport coffee shop that was the kind of liminal space where you felt your very selfhood floating away, "you and Hannah are back together."

Everything Cole said was alarming, generally. His exuberance, seeming omniscience, and closeness with everyone Levi loved made him constantly disarming. This pronouncement, his knowing about Levi and Hannah when even they weren't sure, was not necessarily *more* alarming than anything else Cole had ever said to him in their short acquaintance. But, under the unnerving fluorescents of the airport, it somehow felt like Cole might have been inside his brain.

He turned to look at Cole, who shrugged happily.

"You're less green around the gills than the last time I saw you," Cole said. "And you keep smiling to yourself. I got the impression you're not often pleased about whatever's in your brain."

Levi thought about this. It wasn't surprising that his demeanor had changed, and he wondered that his mom hadn't noticed, although maybe she was keeping it close to her chest. She was wily.

"If it doesn't work out, will you get a divorce?" Cole asked nonchalantly as he bit into a bear claw.

"You know that you don't have to run full background checks on everyone you know, right?" Levi pointed out.

"Don't I?" Cole replied, the world's most affable master criminal. "How else will I know how to help my friends, Levi?" He wiped the donut off his face and winked.

"You can call me Blue, if you want," Levi grumbled.

"No, I never knew Blue. I am happy to be friends with Levi."

Who was this guy?

"I do have a question, though," Cole said once they were seated, stretching his legs all the way out in the airport chair that was way too small for his frame.

"Sure," Levi replied, giving in to the force of nature that was Nicholas Fraser III.

Cole put his hands behind his head, the wingspan of his elbows stretching out improbably far. "What are you going to do if you stay together? You're happier out in the world, from what Miriam has told me, than you ever were before."

"Except for the whole not having my wife thing, which truly and profoundly sucks," Levi pointed out.

"Sure," Cole conceded. "I've never been in love but that sounds like an impediment to happiness. But like…are you going to move home? Let your parents retire and move into their apartments, and live at Carrigan's for the rest of your life? Do you want to be head chef at Carrigan's? Didn't you run away from your entire life to avoid that?"

Levi wouldn't have had this conversation with anyone he knew better, and maybe not in any place more tethered to time and space, but somehow here with Cole it felt reasonable to have a calm, logistical conversation, about the fate of the entire rest of his life, with a near-stranger.

"Hannah won't seriously consider being back together until we figure that out, but I'm worried there's not a good answer. What the girls are doing with Carrigan's All Year is *very* cool, and I honestly think it's something I would be proud to be a part of, but living at Carrigan's again? The thought gives me hives."

"Look," Cole told him, "as a person so adept at avoiding my

own feelings that I didn't realize I was gay until I was thirty-five, I empathize with this level of refusal to deal with reality. But I do recommend you maybe think critically about this."

Cole toasted him with his coffee cup, then proceeded to give an unprompted lesson on how Levi should deal with being famous on the internet, which apparently he was an expert in because he was beloved by Miriam's fandom, the Bloomers. He talked without breathing, through boarding, takeoff, the flight, landing, deplaning, and getting from the airport to the train station.

On the train into Advent from Manhattan, Levi had been worn down enough by Cole's relentless cheer to attempt his own foray into connection, opening with "So, I didn't know you were gay."

"Nor did I!" Cole said happily, shrugging expansively. Although perhaps, given the breadth of his shoulders, it only looked that way. "I thought I was a Very Good Ally who never felt any romantic connection to the women I dated, no matter how much I wanted to."

"But you slept with them?" Levi asked, baffled.

Cole nodded, talking around the sandwich he'd procured from somewhere in his bag. He offered half to Levi, who shook his head. He preferred not to eat sandwiches of unknown provenance. "Sex is fun, with anyone. I just couldn't connect, you know?"

Levi shook his head. He did not.

"I had these big hopes for a great romance, but it never clicked for me," Cole said. "Then I met a guy. I mean, not in the normal 'I met someone' way. I literally shook his hand and he smiled at me. Boom. All of a sudden everything lit up. It made everything make a lot more sense, actually. But it turns out there was a limit to my parents' tolerance of my behavior, and that limit was telling them I was gay."

"I'm sorry," Levi said.

Cole shook his head. "I'm not! My parents suck and being gay is awesome."

Levi looked at him. "You're kind of a chaos gremlin, you know," he observed. Without judgment.

"Well"—Cole pointed between the two of them—"pot. Kettle."

When they finally made it to Carrigan's, Cole said, "Don't think you're escaping our friendship."

As much as it galled him, that truth seemed inescapable. They were going to be friends whether Levi liked it or not.

The screech of glee Miriam let out upon seeing her best friend startled Kringle so badly he leapt several feet in the air. It was a hell of a lot more enthusiastic than the welcome he'd gotten.

He was annoyed until the moment Cole said, "So I'm gay," and Levi realized Cole needed that overwhelming joy right now.

Hannah winked at him and mouthed, *Thank you*, and he lit up inside like a damn firefly. He would do anything for her.

For her, he was going to figure out a plan, one that didn't include either of them being miserable for the other.

Hannah, Age 28

"D o you want to go to Rio for Rosh Hashanah?" Cass asked from where she'd draped herself on the chaise longue in the corner of the great room, artfully arranging her feathered robe around her, one arm hanging gracefully to the floor.

Hannah looked up from the laptop she was working on, where she had been playing with a new layout for the *Carrigan's Christmasland* circular. August was their dead time, and everyone else took it as a time to rest, but Hannah hated resting. Besides, it had been dead during the spring and summer. She was extremely well-rested, and she was committed to making this Christmas Festival their most successful ever. Which started with updating the circular that hadn't been redesigned since the mid-eighties.

"What's in Rio?" she asked.

Cass huffed. "Well I don't *know*, that's why I want to go see."

She really fucking didn't want to go to Rio, or anywhere,

for Rosh Hashanah, unless it was maybe to the Rosenstein's home office in the Quad Cities. However, she couldn't go there because they hadn't invited Blue.

"I want to stay here, with our family, and spend the holy days in the woods. You know how many holidays I missed because we were traveling," she said through gritted teeth.

There was no use telling Cass that she hated traveling, because Cass loved what she loved, and she refused to believe everyone else didn't also love it.

"When I went to save you from that horrid hotel in Budapest and brought you home to be the heir of Carrigan's, I did not intend for you to never leave again, Hannah Naomi," Cass chided.

This was absolutely not what had happened. Cass had come to surprise her one summer, then Hannah had gone back to traveling with her parents, before eventually settling at Carrigan's for the end of high school. Also, it had been a very nice hotel. But the spirit of the memory was true, even if the history was incorrect. Cass had tried to give her a home, not a hermitage.

It was just, if she stayed here, she didn't have to worry about whether it would be there when she got back. Besides, she'd made a promise and a plan: to never again live apart from Blue. And she was carrying it out.

Actually, thinking of Blue—

"You should take Blue," Hannah told Cass. "He'd love to go to Rio."

Cass scowled. "I don't want to take Levi to Rio. I want to take you, my heir. My protégé. Levi will complain and want to eat at every street food stand and obsess about his hair the whole trip. He's not any *fun*."

Blue was, by any measure, much more fun than Hannah was. She was the least fun person she knew. Her favorite hobbies were obsessing about the future and filling out varieties of planners. Which was sort of the same thing.

As they were getting ready for bed that night, Blue brushing his teeth and she brushing out her hair, Hannah said, "Cass tried to get me to go to Rio for Rosh Hashanah. Isn't that absurd?"

"You should go," Blue said from the bathroom after spitting out his toothpaste. "What else are you doing?"

"Uh, celebrating the High Holy Days with my family? Running the inn?" Why did he always make her work sound disposable?

"Cass ran the inn for decades while still managing to travel all the time."

"Well, I'm not Cass," she said defensively. Maybe Cass was brilliant enough to run a successful business while spending half her year around the world, but Hannah needed to focus on operations here. She loved guest management, making sure everyone had everything they needed.

Also, she hated travel.

"I told her she should take you," Hannah told him.

He snorted, and she turned around from where she was sitting on the bed to look at him. "What? Why not you? With Miri gone, it's just you and me from the original crew. I can't go, and I don't want to, and you would love it."

"Yeah, I'm sure we'd have an amazing time, the two of us," he snarked. "Why don't you and I go to Rio, and leave Cass here to run the business she still owns?"

She shook her head. He always looked for a reason to be mad at Cass.

"What, Nan?" he demanded, his hackles obviously up. "What about us having an epic romantic trip to Rio de Janeiro pisses you off?"

"Why does it have to be some epic romantic trip? Why can't we eat kugel in our second-nicest sweaters and then sleep in our own beds? This isn't a fairy tale, Blue! We're not in some sort of fated love story! We're just a regular couple, trying to figure out what the fuck to do for the holidays!"

"We can have any life we want!" he yelled. "And I want more than kugel in our second-nicest sweaters!"

This fight wasn't about Rio or kugel, and she knew it. And he knew it. It was the same fight that they kept picking at, a scab they couldn't let heal over. But she couldn't stop herself. It was like, once she'd started them on this track, there was no way off the train but to ride it to the end.

"There's nothing wrong with a fairy-tale love! People wait all their lives for the kind of love we have. People write songs and poems about it, yearn for it, die for it. We get to have it! Why do you hate that so much?"

He was pacing in their small room, tugging at his hair. He didn't understand how being Levi's Hannah had overwritten her whole identity, how desperate she was to be allowed to find herself.

Why didn't he know her enough to understand that?

"I didn't choose it!"

He went still. "I know you wouldn't have chosen me if you'd had a choice, Hannah. You've made that perfectly clear."

"Shut UP, you absolute asshole." She wanted to scream into the night forever. "IT IS NOT ABOUT YOU. I never got to choose! Anything! I went from being stuck with my parents to falling in love with you, and I never got to see who I would be if I were just Hannah! Would I have flirted with a bunch of people and gotten to know myself better in the middle of crying over breakups? Would I have gotten really into yoga? Would I have joined a choir? I don't know who I am because I was always obsessing about you!"

"Why don't you ever ask yourself who you would have been if you hadn't fallen in love with Carrigan's, Hannah?" he demanded, still stalking the room like a caged cat. "Because it's not me who's keeping you from finding yourself! You're not tied to me—you're chained to this fucking farm."

A tiny voice whispered that he was right—that she wasn't *choosing* Carrigan's, she just couldn't leave. She lashed out, as much at the voice as at him.

"Carrigan's IS who I am," Hannah cried. "Why would I want to be free of that?!"

"Why would you want to be free of me?" Blue thundered.

"I don't want to be free of you. I just. Want. To. Have. Had. A. Chance. To. Choose. You."

Hannah didn't even know how they'd gotten into this fight. She never understood how they ended up screaming at each other. No matter how hard she tried to not bring up subjects that would explode on them, somehow they both always ended up with all their claws out, trying to see which one of them could draw the most blood.

Stomping up to him, she pulled his mouth to hers. He pushed her back up against the door, and they fought with their tongues until they forgot about fighting.

And Rio.

Chapter 18

Hannah

The sun rose over the trees the morning of the Davenport wedding, into a sky so blue it seemed improbable. A breeze kept the temperature from being too hot and sticky but there wasn't so strong a wind as to blow anything over.

It was a day designed for a perfect June wedding on the front lawn.

"If I liked Delilah less, I would be really annoyed that her wedding, which costs the same as a Manhattan flat, has also apparently been blessed by the gods with perfect weather," Levi said as he sat on the front porch swing with his morning coffee, a hand on her knee.

"Don't say that!" Hannah shrank back in horror. "You'll jinx it!"

"I don't think that's how meteorology works." He smirked, like an asshole.

Three hours later, as they were putting the last tiny finishing touches on the chairs and aisle runners, a wall of black clouds stampeded across the sky so fast it looked like all the electricity in the world had gone out. She looked up and muttered, "*Damn* it, Levi."

But she didn't have time to run back to the kitchen to destroy him for cursing her. She had to move the biggest event of her career inside. Which she'd planned for because she'd planned for everything.

Everyone at Carrigan's, from temporary catering staff to the day maids, was roped into helping. The couches and settees in the great room of the inn were whisked into Noelle and Miriam's living room in the carriage house through the back door, while white wrapped chairs were whisked inside, ribbons tied around the backs trailing behind. The fireplace that traditionally hosted battles between the Carrigan's nutcrackers at Christmas became an explosion of ribbons and flowers to act as a backdrop for the officiant. Buntings were hung from the rafters and lit up with tiny fairy lights.

The cavernous room was transformed into a magical faerie queen's summer bower in seemingly the time it took to blink.

"Young lady," the governor said, coming up behind her as she relayed orders through her earpiece, "you are a marvel. You are truly excellent at your job."

Hannah turned to deflect the compliment graciously, because she'd long ago learned that it was off-putting to people when you agreed with them about how great you were at your job, but the man wouldn't let her.

"Oh no, I've seen a lot of event planners at work. Very few of them make it look this effortless or make clients this comfortable. I know this must be a high-stress job for your crew, as you're in your first year of ramping up events, but I want you to know, if the rest of the day is as smooth as everything leading up to it has been, I'll be recommending Carrigan's to everyone I know for their event needs."

Hannah tried not to choke at this. No pressure or anything, just make sure the reception was a masterpiece and they would have more business than they knew what to do with. Although she did know what to do with it, she had an extensive five-year plan with budget projections and could recite a dozen dream projects that kind of income would help launch.

She positioned herself in the back of the room and watched the wedding planner send the groom and groomsmen down the aisle on her exacting beats. She was glad Delilah's mother and the wedding planner had insisted they hire a day-of planner's helper to take care of the hundred thousand emergencies that arose on any wedding day. Hannah could do wedding day coordination but trying to put out bridal fires and make sure her team was in place might be a superhuman act of organization, even for her. The woman they'd hired was both excellent and relatively local. Hannah was already planning to talk about collaborating with her on future weddings.

As Delilah walked down the aisle to the instrumental version of the *Flight of the Fordham* theme song—a compromise Hannah had orchestrated between her and the governor—Hannah could hear Levi's voice over her comms getting the reception service ready, making sure everyone was in place. She loved how calm and measured he was with the staff he oversaw.

Delilah floated up to her waiting groom on a cloud of tiny blush roses, which decorated the hem of a gown that made her look as if she ought to be reclining on a chaise longue in a forest bower. In Hannah's ear, Levi's gravelly voice, like some sort of accidentally erotic ASMR, told someone they had to get everything perfect because they couldn't let Hannah, Miriam, or his mom down, and Carrigan's had a lot riding on this.

Goose bumps rose on her skin, and she brushed a tear away.

This man, who had made her dreams feel so insignificant, who had hated Carrigan's for so long, was putting the people he loved first and working his ass off for something he knew mattered to them, even if it didn't matter to him. He was putting her needs in front of his wants, without even pausing. It was everything she'd ever asked him to do, and it terrified her. She wanted so badly to ask him to stay, but it was almost time for her to decide, they were almost out of dates, and they still didn't have anything close to a plan for how to not explode again.

And if he still couldn't hear her, when she'd told him what she needed, it would really be over.

She kept half an ear on the comms to make sure she didn't need to slip out to take care of something but kept the rest of her attention to the vows. The governor was a devout Episcopalian, and the priest they'd chosen to do the ceremony was, Cole assured her, known as kind of a maverick badass among in-the-know Episcopalians (of which, she'd learned, Cole was apparently one). She was currently reading a Mary Oliver poem, as if Hannah needed more reason to ruin her mascara at this wedding.

What would they have chosen to incorporate, she wondered, if they'd had a real wedding, with a rabbi and a chuppah, if they'd had months of premarital counseling and time to work with their parents about what traditions they most wanted to incorporate? What pieces from her mother's Sephardic background would they have found room for? What parts would solely have been for them as a couple?

She had begun to plan their real wedding, after they'd eloped, but had never finished.

Watching Delilah marry in a ceremony that fit her relationship exactly, that celebrated their family, their faith traditions, and—even within the enormous constraints of a political society wedding—their personalities, made Hannah long for what they'd missed. Would they get a do-over? Could they?

"Hannah, I need you!" Blue's urgent voice cut through her wandering thoughts. Immediately she moved out of earshot of the guests.

"I'm on my way, LB. I've got you covered."

"I never doubted. Can you get me eyes on the cake table?"

The ease with which they worked together made her heart ache. This thing they were doing, where they used their past connection to make amazing new things happen in their passions and careers…it made her feel like their love was opening doors for their future that would never have existed otherwise.

It made her feel free instead of trapped. Rooted and safe so she was able to explore into the stars. Before, they'd always been making themselves less to stay together, but this version of them, they made each other more.

Blue, Age 31

L evi walked into the kitchen ready to fight. He was angry at the morning light and the ancient oven Cass refused to replace, the electric smell of summer hanging thick in the air. He was sick and fucking tired of this place, of being stuck here in the same old dynamics, in the same literal walls he'd been born in, in the middle of fucking nowhere, surrounded by the same trees and the same sky and the same bullshit drama. He was suffocating inside this version of himself no one would let him grow out of, and out of spite, he kept leaning all the way into it, getting pricklier and sharper and more cutting because fuck them, it was already who they thought he was.

He wanted to hop on his bike with Hannah on the back, wearing his leather, and roar off into the sunset, never to return. Since he couldn't, he was looking for someone to get into a screaming match with—Noelle (fucking Noelle) or Cass or anyone who got in his way, and—

He stopped.

Hannah was in front of the open fridge, in a pale blue sundress and flip-flops, eating olives out of a jar with a fork. She looked up and caught him staring, a whole olive frozen on the way to her mouth.

"These aren't guest olives," she said around it.

He was poleaxed by her. This woman, always so in control of every aspect of their lives, standing with her hair down, sneaking pimento olives like some sort of Nigella Lawson fantasy come to life.

"Marry me," he said, before he even knew the words were going to come out of his mouth.

She very carefully chewed and swallowed the olive in her mouth, then set the jar down on the counter, like she feared she was hallucinating, or the laws of physics might not be working.

"Can you run that by me again?" she said, blinking at him.

"You're my favorite person I've ever met in my whole life, and the best thing that's ever happened to me. The me with you is the best version of me, and I want to be your husband." The words all came out in a rush, all the things he'd been bursting with, unable to figure out how to say, spilling out of him as the dam broke.

"If the you *with* me is the best version," she said with a sly smile, "I would hate to see the you without me."

"Hannah," he choked out around his heart, which had lodged in his throat. "Will you marry me?"

She stared at him. "You're serious?"

"Yes?!"

She looked at him for a long beat, and he tried to read

her mood. Was she angry that he hadn't made the proposal a bigger planned deal? That he'd waited so long? That he hadn't waited long enough? They'd talked about "someday when we're married" so many times, but never had a conversation about how that someday would become soon or now.

As he waited, his soul left his body and the voice in his head—sounding a lot like Cass—told him what a fuckup he was, reminding him that everything he'd ever done in his entire life would not make him good enough for Hannah Rosenstein. His palms sweated and some part of his brain wondered if it would be awkward to wipe them on his scarf. He settled for scrubbing them through his hair.

Fuck, his hair probably looked like he'd stuck his finger in an electrical socket. Had he brushed it before he'd come down here? *Damn it, Blue, way to propose without even brushing your hair.*

Suddenly she was in front of him, pulling on the ends of his scarf.

"Hey. Where did you go just now? Already regretting asking?" Her voice was light, but something in her eyes was anxious. He focused on her face, taking it in his hands.

"Never. You could wait to say yes for ten years and I would never regret asking. Asking you to marry me is the single most right decision I've ever made, and probably ever will."

She set her forehead against his, and he breathed in her rose scent.

"I don't need ten years. I could marry you today and it would be the smartest thing I've ever done."

He grinned slowly. The zing went through his body that said, *Do A Shenanigan.* He'd never, ever ignored that zing, even when he should.

"Today, huh?"

"Yeah, but I don't think we can get a rabbi *or* a ketubah by sundown, and it's Friday. Also, my parents are on Easter Island."

"Wait, really? Haven't you always wanted to go— Nope! I'm not getting distracted. We can go get a marriage license today. You know Ernie is a minister. Then when we have time to get all our family together, we'll actually get married. You know, one for us, as a secret, and one for religious purposes. And my mother."

"This is a profoundly terrible idea made entirely of chaos," she told him, her pupils blown.

"Yes, because it's mine."

She kissed him hard, quickly. "Let's do it."

Every cell in his body paused in a way they had never done before. All his life, he'd vibrated on a slightly higher frequency than anyone around him, and he felt himself stop.

Yes.

This.

This was where he was always supposed to end up.

They tripped down to Advent, to the tiny courthouse to get a license from the judge right as she was trying to lock up early and take a Friday afternoon nap. They stumbled, love drunk and giggling, into Ernie's as she was getting ready for the Friday night tourist crowds, and she married them in the kitchen in the back, saying if they split up, she didn't want them to curse any of the booths. They slipped into their room quietly, their laughs smothered in each other's hair, and made love in a conflagration, a slow desperation to show each other that this was it forever, that they were each all in.

Later, in the firelight, Blue sat up in bed, his knees tucked up under his chin.

He was watching his wife sleep, the waterfall of her golden hair encroaching on his pillow, reminding him of Strega Nona's pasta pot. On the table next to her was her bullet journal, filled with sketches and notes for when Hannah officially took over guest management and Blue took over the kitchen. It was a smart plan, one that would potentially put Carrigan's Christmasland on the map as a culinary destination.

It was an impossible plan.

Even if he could stay here, even if he could breathe inside these walls, Cass would never let him take over. Carrigan's was her baby, and she had hand-chosen Hannah as the heir. She could barely acknowledge Blue was in a room, and since they'd gotten together, she told him once a month to leave and give Hannah a chance at a real life.

He had to get out of here.

He had to convince Hannah to go with him.

Chapter 19

Levi

The Davenport reception was a lot. A lot of money, a lot of food made from outrageously expensive ingredients, a lot of famous people. Levi expected to mostly hide in the kitchen, but after dinner service, Delilah had come and dragged him out to show him off.

The finale of *Australia's Next Star Chef* was about to air, and he was in the top three. Everyone wanted to know if he was going to take home the trophy.

He was tired, hot, frustrated from trying to run a huge event out of a kitchen that desperately needed upgrading and wasn't up to this kind of volume, even though they'd set up a catering tent outside the back kitchen door to accommodate it. Consequently, he mostly stood around with his arms crossed over his chef's whites, scowling at people. People loved this (yet more "culinary bad boy" stereotypes to overcome, yay), which made him even grouchier.

The saving grace of the event was Delilah herself, who was charming, funny, and bursting with happiness. He watched her greet every new loved one with apparently genuine joy, overflowing with pleasure at being able to share her love with so many other people she loved. He might kind of hate all the guests, but he really liked the bride, and all of these people were going to bring Carrigan's business.

That was his job right now. Send out a great meal and make Hannah's life easier by making Carrigan's All Year a successful event destination.

Hannah, who'd organized all of this with beautiful, terrifying efficiency. Hannah, who was multitasking so fast he thought she was going to start levitating from the speed of her movement, a hummingbird goddess. Hannah, whose voice, calmly, meticulously issuing orders in his ear all day, was exhilarating and fascinating and strangely sexy. Hannah, who he'd loved since the day he was born and who had transformed into this woman so brilliant it was hard to look directly at her, and from whom he couldn't turn away.

Delilah's maid of honor gave a toast and talked about how in college, Delilah had been dating a guy off and on that none of her friends liked, because every breakup was a big, dramatic event that left Delilah emotionally devastated. Then she'd met the groom and realized love didn't always have to be painful and turn you inside out, that you could love someone who was easy to be around, who brought you peace.

It was a beautiful speech, and it made Levi want to go hide and cry. Was he that person standing in the way of a love that brought Hannah peace?

He tried to imagine either of them falling for someone else, really falling, the way Delilah had obviously done, and all the work that would take, how much untangling it would require to be ready for someone new. Hannah had said that taking out the parts of her that loved him would leave her Swiss cheese, and he trusted her to know her own heart, but he still worried.

Because worrying that no one could love him was the well-worn record always playing in the back of his mind when he was trying to sabotage something good, a little voice in his head whispered. When he actually listened to his gut instead of his asshole head, he believed they were building something entirely new and healthy out of the materials of their past.

A new house from reclaimed brick. An upcycled antique, a Miriam Blum piece. Strange and held together by glitter glue, but beautiful.

In the inside pocket of his coat, his phone was buzzing. He ignored it. It was his agent, trying to get him to Manhattan ASAP. Levi had already told him twice today that he would call back later. His life away from Carrigan's, the life he had burned down his marriage in desperation to get to, was waiting right outside the gates for him to pick up again.

He would have to call back. Soon, because he did actually want to sign a contract for a full season of his show. He just had no idea how they were going to navigate fostering this new, delicate relationship if he had to be in Manhattan. Yes, it was a train ride away, but it put them apart after they had just now found each other again.

He knew he didn't want to stay at Carrigan's—the wall-paper and ghosts still made him itchy—but he wanted Hannah, all the time. He wanted to smell her and hear her and taste her. He was starving to hear every thought she had, about everything. He had spent thirty-two years knowing everything happening in Hannah Rosenstein's head, and he'd been cut off cold turkey, and now a little taste made him want everything again, right away.

With no interruptions, even if the interruption was his own TV show.

He wanted to bring Jewish diasporic cuisine to the world, wanted to get paid to talk to people about what he was most passionate about. Hell, to be honest, he liked being a little famous. It made him feel like he'd finally shown everyone who didn't like the full Levi Blue that they could go fuck themselves. Which was probably not the healthiest reason to start a career, but queer spite had taken a lot of people a long way, and he was not above admitting he was driven by it a little.

He also really wanted to hang out with his parents more, because he wanted to build a better friendship with them as an adult. Which he could do from Manhattan, he supposed, but in Manhattan he couldn't stop by to have coffee with his mom on the porch in the mornings or help his dad with projects that needed extra hands, at the spur of the moment.

And he wanted to be more available so Esther didn't feel like she needed to be as tied to New York.

Cole popped up beside him, dressed as a waiter and bouncing on his toes. It was alarming—no one that hulking should have that much energy.

"How did you get roped into waiting tables?" Levi asked.

"One of the servers got food poisoning and it turns out I'm

very skilled at front of house!" Cole chirped happily. "Also it was an easy sell because Sawyer is bartending and I wanted him to see how hot I look in this tux. I look hot, right?"

He did a little half turn, and Levi laughed. "You do. Simply wander past the object of your affections looking great until he comes to you. Is that the plan?"

"I mean, I certainly can't flirt with him," Cole said, as if this were obvious.

"You flirt with everyone, Cole," Levi pointed out. "You flirted with both my parents and the minister within the past twenty-four hours. You flirt whenever you're breathing."

"But I actually *like* this man," Cole explained patiently.

"I appreciate you interrupting my own wallowing about my love life with your absolutely inexplicable and self-manufactured drama, Nicholas," Levi said, patting him on the back.

"Oh good, it worked! You looked mopey." Cole grinned.

"Get out of here!" Levi said. "Go serve food! Or talk to Sawyer! You brat."

"Oh no, I was serious. I absolutely cannot do that. Have you seen his mustache? It's so dreamy." Cole shook his head. "I've never liked a boy before. I'm fully unequipped to deal with it. But I will take another round of cake out. Have you had some of this cake? Mediocre compared to your meal. They should have gone with Rosenstein's."

Why were they friends? he wondered again as he watched Cole walk off.

His phone was still buzzing. What would he say, if he answered it? Whenever he thought about what to do about the future, how to make life work at Carrigan's, he came up against the emotional brick wall of Cass. He didn't want to stay because he didn't want to be reminded of Cass. He wanted a show to prove to Cass that he was worthwhile.

Until he started actually putting his relationship with her to rest, he wasn't going to be able to move forward. He'd have to go see her.

Tomorrow. After he cleaned up the kitchen and slept.

Levi stood outside the carriage house, having knocked, and waited while someone inside cursed Kringle for being underfoot on the stairs. It was drizzling, a cold, morose rain that made him miss Australia. He felt like he was starring in an emo music video against his will. He was starting to worry that his eyeliner would run when the door opened to Noelle in her pajamas, her hair sticking straight up in the air.

She scowled when she saw it was him. "You woke up Kringle," she snapped. "We were having a snuggle."

"Is Miri here?" He caught Kringle as he tried to escape into the woods to decimate the local blue jay population, scooping all thirty pounds of him to his chest. Kringle happily wrapped himself around Levi's neck.

"She's in the studio working, and she'll lose her shit if you interrupt her." Noelle waved him in. "But she hasn't had a cup of coffee in an hour, so she'll be in soon, lest her clock run down like Tik-Tok of Oz."

He nodded. "Ah yes, I had somehow forgotten that she can only make art, or function, when caffeinated beyond the normal limits of human existence."

"When I first met her," Noelle told him, "she asked me

to put espresso in her hot cocoa. It was cute but also deeply disturbing."

"That's Miri in a nutshell." He finally remembered to look around him, at the newly renovated carriage house. "Holy shit, Noelle, this place looks incredible. You did a great job."

"Yes," she agreed, "I killed it."

Over the fireplace, a huge painting hung. Levi had seen photos online of the painting Miriam had auctioned off at New Year's as part of the girls' plan to save Carrigan's from bankruptcy, but he'd never seen a Mimi Roz in person. She'd been a brilliant painter under a pen name in her early twenties, before abandoning it and remaking herself as an artist of up-cycled antiques. Of the Carrigan's crew, only Cass had known about both her paintings and the reason why she'd stopped.

This painting, the one Miriam had chosen to keep for herself and give pride of place on her mantel, was terrifying and magnificent. It was of Baba Yaga. She reminded him of Cass a little, and also of Hannah. An untamed forest witch of immeasurable power who drew people to her, apologizing for nothing.

He found his hand over his heart and realized he'd gasped out loud.

Behind him, Noelle laughed. She came up beside him and handed him a cup of coffee. "You've met our house witch, I see. What do you think of her?"

"She's my favorite thing I've ever seen, probably."

"You should see the one she painted for me, of La Llorona. It used to be down here, but it felt too personal for all the Bloomers to see when they came on tours, so I moved it up to our bedroom." She motioned at the loft.

"Oh, that's new," he said. "That staircase is beautiful."

"I built it myself," Noelle told him. He knew she had; Miriam had gushed about it.

He looked down at his hand in confusion. "You made me coffee."

Noelle gave a long-suffering sigh. "Sit, hang out with Kringle and Baba Yaga. I'm in the middle of something. She should be in here any minute."

Levi did exactly what she suggested. He sat in the love seat facing the fireplace, and he contemplated wild forest witches until he heard Miriam come in from the studio.

"Levi Blue!" she exclaimed in delight.

He hugged her tightly, and she hugged him back, both of them trying not to spill hot coffee on each other. Kringle complained that neither of them was hugging him.

"Did you see how cool my kitchen is?!" She pulled him into the room to point out all the new appliances. "Noelle made me a little baker's paradise."

He made appropriate—and unfeigned—noises of appreciation about her new KitchenAid and admitted that the oven was extremely good.

"What's up, though, why are you here?" she asked. "Are you going to steal my oven for the main kitchen? I told your mom I was buying her one for her birthday next year."

"You're bad at birthday surprises"—he started a list with his fingers—"you know I'm going to need to have input on that oven, and I would never steal someone else's kitchen equipment. What are you up to for the rest of the week? Do you have a chunk of free time?"

She opened her phone and checked her calendar app. "I

have a BYOB sculpting class on Tuesday night, and the Ohio Bloomers are coming for a tour on Wednesday, and then Thursday I'm on dinner duty because Noelle goes into the city for an AA meeting...I'm free right now? Today? What do you need?"

"I want to go visit Cass's grave," he said. "I need to see it. I hoped you'd go with me. But we don't have to do it today. I'm sure you have stuff."

"I already did stuff! I ruined a very old antique and posted it on Instagram and immediately sold it for a totally outrageous amount of money!" she assured him happily. "I'm free for the whole day. ROAD TRIP TO THE CEMETERY!"

She ran off, muttering about stealing Noelle's keys so she could take the vintage cherry-red Chevy truck that Noelle had restored and loved almost as much as she loved Miriam.

"Noelle will kill me if I take her truck, Mir," Levi protested.

"But she won't kill *me*," she sang, hopping around to get her boots on like a tiny fae creature. "You're not taking the Chevy. I'm taking the Chevy—you're coming along for the ride. We'll stop for Michigans and poutine at Clare and Carl's on the way back and we'll sing too loud the whole way there and you can be Simon and I'll be Garfunkel and it'll be *so fun*, Levi!"

"But in this scenario, I'm actually driving, right? Because you definitely don't know how to drive stick."

"Oh, ha, yeah, I don't even know how to drive automatic. You're definitely driving. But the spirit remains, I'm the one who technically borrowed the truck." Miriam pirouetted away to find her coat.

He sighed. Only Miriam, who had managed to have a meet-cute at a funeral, would think a cemetery adventure made for a fun day. But he was glad she was the one going with him, so he wouldn't sink into melancholy he couldn't get out of, like Artax in the Swamp of Sadness, giving in to the Nothing. "Thank you for coming with me."

She kissed him on the cheek and hustled him out the door. Her enthusiasm for his company rubbed off some of his pointiest edges so he could sit in his own skin without injuring himself on them.

"Didn't you used to be like . . . more chill?"

Miriam shrugged. "Yeah, I used to be in a trauma-induced fugue state, so I didn't really feel things except through making disturbing but adorable art. But now I feel things! It's better."

"Is it?" he teased, winking.

"Do you want to talk about your secret marriage?" she asked once they were on the road.

"Do you want to talk about your secret painting career that you hid from me *while* we were living together in Manhattan, or the reasons it ended and you disappeared for a decade?" he countered.

"Touché, Blue. Let's stop for coffee and donuts instead!"

Levi had imagined a thousand responses to standing on Cass's grave. Sadness, anger, regret, more anger. He had not expected to be overwhelmed by a wave of grief that felt like he was drowning. As soon as he clipped a yarmulke into his hair and stepped through the gates of the cemetery, his steps were leaden.

When he turned a corner and saw the grave marker, he

sank to his knees, unable to move. On top, in Hebrew, it read *Rivka bat Gavriel*, and her dates of birth and death. Below, in English:

Cassiopeia Carrigan, Famed Eccentric,
Extraordinary Pain in the Ass

He clasped his hands to stop them from shaking and recited the Kel Maleh Rachamim.

Cass had been the biggest, brightest star around which his life had revolved, at least until he'd kissed Hannah for the first time or eaten the first meal he ever cooked by himself. She'd introduced his parents, given them their life's work, been their closest friend and co-conspirator. She'd felt unfulfilled by the life her family assumed she'd lead, so instead she'd struck out on her own, making a life wildly outside the confines of what anyone could have imagined for her. At every turn, she'd figured out how to be free in whatever way she was able, and how to do it without cutting ties with anyone she loved. In fact, she'd loved more people than anyone else Levi had ever met.

It had hurt him in the deepest, most secret part of himself that she couldn't seem to love *him*.

To his young, worshipful self, her approval—or lack of it— had seemed like an absolute, unquestionable judgment on his worth. She was so much bigger than life, had lived so much and done everything she ever wanted: Who was he to question her opinion of him? It had never once occurred to him to ask if she could be wrong.

If she, a fallible human, could have looked at him and drawn the wrong impression. If he hadn't helped her do it, a little, by asserting loudly, over and over, that he was all the things she thought him to be, even if, as the adult in the situation, she should have seen through his childish, defiant posturing.

"How do you deal with this, Miri?" he finally asked when he could speak again.

She shrugged, staring at the grave marker. "Am I dealing with it? I just put one foot in front of the other. The enormity of the years I gave up with Cass will swallow me whole if I look at them straight on. So I try to keep her baby from going bankrupt, love the girl she picked out for me, and hang out with your parents and listen to stories about her. I don't know what else to do."

"I love the only girl she ever wanted me to stay away from, and I'll lose my whole self if I try to stay here," he said. "Where does that leave me?"

"Doing the exact opposite of what your family told you to do, which is the most Cass legacy imaginable," Miriam answered.

He chuckled. She wasn't wrong.

"What if Cass was right all along? Not about me, but that the two of us can never be happy together? What if we're bad for each other?"

There it was—the fear that had kept him from being able to move forward toward a concrete plan for their future. What if Cass had been right, all along?

He was saying it now, out loud, to Cass as much as to Miriam, or maybe to the wind.

Miriam sat next to him on the ground and curled her tiny body underneath his long limbs. "Maybe you were, Blue, but you're not now. Who are you *now*? Who are you together, now? Because I see two people who understand each other, have fun together, collaborate brilliantly together. I see two compatible people who happen to know all of each other's history, want each other badly, and love each other passionately. Do you know how rare that is?"

"Hannah accused me recently of being a melodramatic jerk who loves misery," he said, sniffling. "It's possible I'm being hyperbolic right now."

Miriam wiped some eyeliner from his cheek where it marked a path from his tears. "You're both melodramatic jerks who love misery, which is part of how you ended up together. But you're also not blockheaded enough to throw away a once-in-a-lifetime love because of something Cass said, or because it took you some practice to get good at relationships."

"You exploded your entire life because of something Cass said," he pointed out.

"I exploded my entire life because it wasn't working, and a pretty girl turned my head," she corrected. "Cass was the excuse."

"Do you really think we can ever make it work?" he asked.

She reached an arm way up and patted his hair. "I do. I mean, I never knew you as a couple, but I've known you both all our lives, and I've never seen something you couldn't get through together. I see you together now, and you seem incandescent with happiness, honestly. Like a very beautiful cactus night-light glowing away."

"How am I going to convince her that we're right this time?"

"Did she tell you what she needed to be convinced?"

Levi sighed. "Yeah, but I don't know how to give it to her. If I knew how to fix the problems between us, I already would have. I feel like she wants an answer before we have a chance to work together on the problem. My messed up brain, and her messed-up brain, got us where we were before, and maybe as a team we could figure it out, but I feel like we need—"

Miriam stood up, brushing leaves and grass off her paint-spattered overalls. "You have your plotting face on, which is great, but it's starting to rain again." She pulled him up beside her. "Can I recommend you continue to plot whilst buying me a hot dog? I cried too much and now I'm hangry. Plus, you can tell me about hanging out with Laurence! Is he coming to visit? I miss him."

He went with her because she wasn't wrong. He probably would plot better after a hot dog.

"Are they kosher? Because you know for them to be kosher—" he jokingly started to explain.

"GET IN THE TRUCK, BLUE."

Hannah, Age 31

"Y ou're a fucking coward," Blue snarled, his hands fisted, knuckles turning white.

He'd come to their room at the end of a perfectly normal day, where they'd split a bagel and talked about redoing the Carrigan's menu, and then he told her he'd been offered a job cooking on a cruise ship and had negotiated so she could come as well, and when did she think she could leave?

"When do I think I can leave?! I fucking don't think I can leave. Cass is sick, Blue. I can't miss the last years of her life. I'm finally being given actual responsibility. This is what I've worked for all my life!"

Somehow they'd ended up here, screaming at each other on opposite sides of their bed.

"I'm not the one running away from my family and my future!" Hannah spat. She was so angry she was shaking, and terrified. How had he done all of this planning and applying for jobs, without even asking her?

Had he been so miserable here, with her, that he couldn't even talk to her about it?

"I'm not running away!" he shouted. "I was fucking born here. I've lived in these goddamned walls all my life. I'm finding a future. I'm MAKING a future. You're locking yourself up in here like it's fucking *Grey Gardens*. I will die here. I will wither away and become nothing. I. Can't. Have. A. Future. Here."

"It's almost Rosh Hashanah! You want me to leave right before the holidays?" She was incredulous.

"And then it will be Yom Kippur, then Sukkot, and then it will be Hanukkah and Tu B'Shuvat. It will always be almost another holiday, and we'll waste our lives here!"

"I'm *not* wasting my life. You knew what I wanted, what my plans were. Why did you marry me knowing you were going to leave?" He had to know she couldn't leave Carrigan's right now. She knew he'd always wanted to live somewhere else, see the world, but he'd asked her to marry him.

She'd thought that meant they were settling down. *Here.*

"I thought you would go with me! Hannah, it's been us all our lives. We've always had each other's backs, us against the world. I thought *you* knew me well enough to know I could never stay here," he shot back.

How dare he accuse her of not knowing him? It was like he'd never even met her!

"We'll be a team. We can dream up where we'll go, research together. I can learn from chefs and work in kitchens all over the world. I'll be able to learn things I could never learn here, or anywhere in the States." He was getting more and more excited as he talked, his anger fading.

"What do you envision I will be doing while you're cooking

in all these kitchens?" Hannah asked him, stunned. How could he possibly be this selfish?

"Play tourist, see the world, I don't know!"

He had his hands shoved in his pockets, his tell that he knew he was wrong and didn't want to admit it. He *hadn't* actually thought about what she would be doing when he was imagining all of this. He kept saying he loved her more than anything, but all he loved was the idea of them.

All he could envision was himself.

"I *hate* travel, Blue. I've already seen the world, and I'm done. I'm a hotel manager. It's what I've always wanted to do, it's what I got a degree in, it's what I've always worked toward. I can't be a hotel manager on a ship. You don't even see me. How can you ask me to travel?"

"Of course I see you. You're the only thing I see!"

She threw a pillow at him. "You see yourself at the center of an epic love story. It wouldn't matter if it were me next to you, or a cardboard cutout, as long as you got to be Fated for Something Special."

"That's bullshit." He caught the pillow and threw it back at her. "I know you. I know you hate to travel *with your parents*. Where you had no agency and no consistency. Where you were getting uprooted every time you got comfortable, never choosing where you wanted to go, never free to see whatever interested you. This would be different. It would be *us*," he pleaded.

"I thought you knew," she cried. "I thought you knew me well enough to know *this* is my dream." Damn him. He'd never cared about her dreams, only his own. "I've never wanted anything but being with you and taking over Carrigan's."

"Well, it seems you want one of those things more than

the other," he said bitterly, crossing his arms. "I should have known you would always choose Cass. I should have known you would never choose a whole life when you could be safe in your little princess tower in this molding hellhole where you get to make all the plans and everything always goes exactly the way you say it will."

In that moment, she hated him.

"Get out, Blue. Get out of here, and don't come back." She flung open the door to their room and gestured out into the hall. "You don't deserve Carrigan's. You don't deserve me, or Cass, or the future we planned. Get out and go 'find yourself' or 'be free' or whatever the fuck you think you need."

"You're the one who sees our love as a trap!" he yelled, slamming the door she'd opened into the wall and wheeling on her. "I have never felt caged by us."

"Just by everything I love and everything that matters to me," she accused.

"I have a right to have my own feelings about the place I was born, Hannah! You don't get to own how people feel about Carrigan's."

How fucking dare he.

"Get. Out. You're done here. We're done." She turned away so she wouldn't have to look at his face while she said it.

She heard him grab his jacket off the coat rack by the door. "We can't be done, Nan. We'll never be done."

"Don't call me," she choked out. "Don't write. I never, ever want to see you again."

"You can't mean that," he pleaded. "This is *us*, Hannah."

"That's what I thought, too," she said quietly, "but it's clear the only part of us that matters to you is *you*."

The next day he was gone.

He'd taken his clothes, his leather, but not his bike. She assumed he'd given some explanation to his parents but none to the twins, or Cass, or anyone else. She couldn't believe he'd actually fucking left. He hadn't waited for her, hadn't loved her enough or known her enough to just wait until she could get up the courage to leave with him.

He'd called her a coward, and he'd been right, and she hated him for it.

And she wasn't sure she'd ever stop hating him, and that destroyed everything she knew about herself, her life, her past, and her future.

Chapter 20

Hannah

Hannah had, uncharacteristically, taken to her bed for a full forty-eight hours after the wedding, her legs aching and her brain empty. Delilah was off on her honeymoon, the governor was happy, and every one of their guests had checked out. She was going to sleep until her adrenaline levels normalized.

In the late morning of the third day, her phone chirped. She ignored it. It could wait.

Her room phone rang, a number no one had. She reached over for it without raising her head.

"*What.*"

"Come on a picnic with me," her husband's voice said. Her whole body shivered at the sound.

"I'm the most tired I've ever been, Blue," she mumbled into the receiver. "I'm not going outside."

"But it's beautiful out and we need to celebrate and I'm testing the guest baskets," he said. "Bring your helmet."

"I thought you gave Laurence back his motorcycle?" she asked.

"I did, but did you know my dad has been keeping mine in perfect condition the whole time I was gone? That guy loves me." He sounded very smug, although if Mr. Matthews was her dad, she would be smug about it, too.

Why did he assume she still had her helmet? She did, of course. They'd gotten into way too much fun trouble on that bike for her to get rid of it, even if she'd shoved it in the back of her closet with all her other Blue detritus. She pulled it out and hugged it to her.

For the first time in years, she climbed on the back of his bike, wrapped her arms around his waist, and let the wind whip past her as he drove them out into the woods. Her lungs felt more filled with air, her nerves more alive, than they had in all that time—and her skin, pressed to his, more on fire than she thought she could survive.

It *was* beautiful outside. There was a riot of birds, a cacophony of small forest rodents, and a waterfall of sunshine. Levi had laid out a blanket with a picnic lunch—sous vide egg bites, pasta salad, quick pickles, salted maple hand pies. The food baskets were part of the new Carrigan's All Year branding: Come visit spring through autumn, get a hand-packed basket to take on a rented bicycle or ATV out into the one hundred sixty acres of the farmland, and picnic among the Christmas trees.

They sat under the almost-summer sun (absolutely drenched in mosquito spray) and she reached out instinctively for his hand to weave their fingers together. Levi had his head in her lap, and the sun caught in his eyelashes. He was dappled in light and quintessentially Blue. His hair was death-defying, his eyeliner smudged, and his shirt read *Abortion Is Health Care*. His jean shorts were cut off and fraying, and he was wearing a silk robe like a vest that he must have stolen from Cass years ago.

He was a forest fae, for a moment angry at no one. His face at rest, when he was not defensive or snarling, was so beautiful it was difficult to process, all slashing eyebrows and cutting jawline and eyes like fog. She was mesmerized by him, which would have annoyed her, but he was looking at her like she was magnetic and also edible, so she didn't mind very much.

The boy she'd loved all her life had been reckless, caring more about protecting his tender heart than about how his spinning out hurt the hearts of those around him. He had been all sharp edges and whip fast lashing out. Now he'd come back, grown up in a way she never would have believed, cautious and thoughtful, ready to atone for how his behavior affected everyone around him. She would never have dreamed this version of an adult Levi could exist.

She still didn't have a fucking clue what they were going to do, now that their fifth date had arrived. He hadn't proven to her that they could have a life together, and she hadn't proven to him they couldn't, so their dare was at a standstill. Their future was shrouded, and it might still destroy her, but in this moment, in this sunshine, he was hers.

"I love you," she told him, because she could. He opened his eyes and smiled so big she thought his face would split. "I also know you brought me out here on this picnic because you want to talk about something."

He sat up, tucking his long legs under his chin and hugging his knees. Her fingers missed his. "You know that the show finale is about to air," he began slowly.

She nodded. "Yes. Tomorrow. Your dad has invited everyone in Advent over to watch it in the barn." She had been very pointedly ignoring thinking about what happened after that.

"I'm going to come in second, very fairly, because the winner cooks absolute circles around me in the last challenge."

"I'm sorry," she said, but he waved her off.

"I'm not. If I'd won, I would have been contractually obligated to be in Australia for a lot longer, and I wouldn't be here now." He smiled at her, his real Blue grin. "Here is much better."

Never, in all her life, would she have believed he could say that, and mean it, about Carrigan's Christmasland. "So why do I sense there's a but?"

"Because you know me," he admitted. "You know I pitched *Living Bold* to Food Network, and we're scheduled to film the pilot. When they saw what a fan favorite I was..." He rolled his eyes at this, but he *was* a fan favorite. She'd been right that his charisma and beauty made people around the world adore him. She just hoped she'd been wrong that he would leave to chase that. "They asked for a full season order."

"I mean, you have to do it, right? You have to take it. I've watched you on this show. You're bizarrely great at cooking on TV." Her shoulders were hunched, her body tensing for him to break her heart.

Levi chuckled. "Yeah, it's weird, right? I hate talking to people, but I love talking to a camera about what I'm cooking. It's like I'm able to turn off the part of my brain that's obsessed with how people are going to respond to what I'm saying."

"You're great at talking when there's no possibility of anyone talking back." Hannah elbowed him a little so he would know she wasn't serious.

"That's not inaccurate." He put an arm over her shoulders, and she relaxed into him. "And thankfully, I have this face, so people want to put me on camera."

"I'm so glad you found a way to save yourself from the curse of your own beauty."

"Astonishing that I manage to look like this and be the less attractive person in my marriage," he said, and she snorted a laugh.

"It's amazing, that out of all of this, this catastrophic pain we caused, you found a career you would never have imagined." She pulled back so she could look up at him, but wrapped his hands in hers to keep him close.

He looked out at the mountains for a moment, and she thought he was distracted, but he finally said, "I wouldn't go back and undo what happened. If I did, we would never have learned how to tell each other the truth when it was hard. And I would never have learned...that my version of what I think needs done is sometimes missing major information. I would never, ever have gotten my head out of my ass here. I didn't even get it out of my ass out there!"

"So now you have to go film in Manhattan," she said. Anxiety flared inside her. Was he making plans for them, again, without asking her?

"Well, I have some sway right now, because of the show. They want to use the finale buzz to start hyping *Living Bold*, so I can maybe push for the contract to look how I want. Or, how you want. Because I'm not telling them anything until you and I figure out how I can make it work. I obviously want to take this show, but my priority is doing that while staying married."

The anxiety became a wave of panic. "Doesn't that confine the future of your career?"

He shrugged. "So? I already have more career than I ever dreamed of. If someday there aren't any shows left to film, I'll find a kitchen and beg for a job. Maybe Chef Harlow needs a sous."

"I'm going to keep you from your dreams," she whispered.

He shook his head. "No, Nan. You're the best dream I ever had. But I need you to tell me if you also want to stay married. We've done our five dates. Shenanigan successfully concluded. What do you want?"

She held his face in her hands. "I want to spend the rest of my life with you. And we still don't have a plan. I feel like if you leave to film without one, we'll keep kicking the can down the road until we end up exactly where we did last time. I want to be your wife, and I don't want to give you more ultimatums, but, babe, if we don't take the time to figure this out now, I don't know that I can keep believing we ever will. It's now or . . . maybe never."

Nodding, Levi rested his forehead against hers. "I would like to negotiate for a sixth date."

"Now who's playing Calvinball?"

He kissed her forehead and sat back. "Hear me out. I think we should go on a sixth date—to a marriage counselor. We probably don't have the skills to figure out how to build a new, healthy marriage that's different from the way we used to be, but we can ask someone to help us."

"Ask for help? Us?!" Hannah faked incredulity, because she needed some lightness in this, and because she was worried. "You hate therapy, LB."

He shrugged. "I love you more. I want us to figure this out together, as a team." His eyes were big and beseeching. He hadn't said, *I want this my way, let me talk you into it.* He was saying, *I want to do this a way we decide together.*

She cocked her head. There was no way that forcing him into therapy that made him uncomfortable was going to help, but…"What about a rabbi?" she asked. "I know a freaking great one."

Levi's face broke into the kind of joyous grin she'd forgotten he was capable of. "I would love that so much."

The moment crystalized around her, time frozen in the sun.

He wanted to go with her, together as a couple, to her religious mentor, her most trusted spiritual teacher, and seek counsel as a team, as members of their shared faith. This, more than anything before, pierced her heart. It was like he had the blueprints to her princess tower, and he knew exactly where to plant the dynamite.

She didn't say any of that. Instead, she wiped a tear off her face and said, "If you embarrass me in front of my rabbi, I will personally put you in a human cannon and shoot you back to Australia."

"That's fair." He nodded. "Just so we're clear, which part of my personality do we find embarrassing? Because I personally think all of it, but that seems unsustainable if we want actual feedback from them."

"I mostly meant you should not tell tales about my extremely awkward adolescence," Hannah said, "although perhaps you might wear full-length pants."

"I do understand the concept of dressing for shul." He winked at her. "I think your entire adolescence was incredibly charming, but I'll keep the amusing anecdotes to a minimum."

"Your personality can stay." Hannah brushed his bangs out of

his eyes. "I'm coming back around to it." His grin lit up everything inside her. Holy shit, he was trouble when he smiled.
When he wasn't around, she wondered how he'd managed to
talk her into quite so many bad ideas over the years, but this
was the answer. She had no recourse against that smile.

She suddenly realized something. "Blue, holy shit. You
came in second in one of the biggest cooking competitions in
the world."

His grin turned smug. "Fuck yeah I did. I'm a *really* good chef."

"Will you do something for me, Blue?" she asked, her heart
caught up in his eyes, her hope bolstered by his.

"Anything in the whole world."

"Will you kiss me?"

"I've kissed you several times recently, and none of them
were great for either of us emotionally," he said softly.

She nodded. "I know, but all of those times were kissing so
we didn't have to talk about our feelings, and I want to kiss
you only because you're my person and we're in love and we're
trying like hell to figure out what that means, but we're going
to figure it out together. Kiss me because even if it's going to
blow up in our faces once and for all, you love kissing me?"

He sucked in a breath, and his eyes welled up, then his face
was on hers and his arms were surrounding her completely,
and his lips were her only lifeline. This kiss was the first time
in so many years that they'd kissed not to fight or escape, or
because they were wrestling with things they couldn't say. It
was the first time in a long, long time they were kissing not to
lose themselves but to find each other.

It was bittersweet and aching and she tasted every kiss they'd
missed, every dream of each other they'd woken up from

sweating, every phone call they hadn't made. It was their first kiss again, but a hundred thousand times better and worse. Because they knew each other's bodies, likes, needs, and they knew everything they'd left and maybe lost forever.

His eyes glittered with unshed tears as he pulled away, and her nails caught in the hair on the back of his neck, trying to keep him from leaving.

"So I know we decided we weren't going to fool around until we figured out what we were doing, but does this count? We're figuring it out, right?" Hannah asked.

Levi laughed. "That might be moving the goalposts a little, baby. Besides, I love you so much, but I don't want to have sex on this blanket. There are so many bugs. Maybe we can try, I don't know, having sex in a bed? With pillows? Or finally get that quickie on your desk."

"Both?" Hannah asked hopefully.

"Both is good."

"Okay. Rabbi first, sex later." She nodded. "That's probably smarter anyway."

"Cockblocked by our own emotional maturity," Levi lamented.

"I truly never thought I'd see the day."

Rabbi Ruth was Hannah's favorite person outside of the Carrigan's crew. They walked with the aid of a cane topped with a wolf's head that Hannah thought was the coolest thing she'd ever seen, and always spoke very thoughtfully and purposefully. They never said anything they weren't sure of.

When they'd been called to the local congregation, Hannah had been worried that they would face immense pushback from the community, but the members of the congregation would probably have fought a lion for their rabbi. Hannah certainly would have. She had been avoiding services so she wouldn't have to face Ruth's knowing eye, one that could immediately suss out trouble, and she'd missed them desperately.

She threw herself into their arms when she saw them, and the rabbi laughed at her.

They looked Levi up and down and cocked an eyebrow at Hannah. "Is this the reason you've been avoiding us? You didn't want to have to answer questions about the long-lost Matthews boy?" They looked at Levi some more. "You have your mother's smile. I like your floral yarmulke."

"Do you want to swap?" Levi touched his self-consciously. "I made this one. I can make more. I didn't realize you knew my parents."

They grimaced. "I do not want to swap because I don't like other people's hair touching mine. It's gross. If you have an extra, I will take it the next time you come to services. I'm not technically your parents' rabbi, because they belong to a synagogue in Plattsburgh, but they're often here, and I adore them."

"They are the actual best. Did they tell you terrible things about me?" Levi asked, flattening his bangs. Hannah grabbed his hand to stop the nervous gesture.

"They did not," Rabbi Ruth said, "although both Noelle and Esther did."

Levi shrugged a little at this, and Ruth gestured at the two of them to walk toward their office. "Come on back, tell me what's going on. I can't wait to hear this one. All of you, Cass's kids, you're always in the middle of something."

"I love them," Levi whispered to Hannah as he followed them into Ruth's office. "I want them to be my rabbi."

"We can arrange that," Hannah whispered back.

Ruth closed the door behind them and gestured to a chintz sofa covered in pillows.

"So," Ruth began once they were seated, "Cass told me you were secretly married. I assume that's why you're here? And judging by the handholding, it's going better than it was?"

"We're working on it," Hannah said. "But we've hit a stumbling block."

"Is it the fact that you're *secretly* married?" Rabbi Ruth asked, a hand on their walking cane. Hannah watched them stretch their bad leg out a couple of times before settling back into their chair. "Or the fact that you both still want very opposite lives?"

"It's not a secret anymore, thankfully. Mostly the latter."

"We don't really know what to do with that part. The part where we want diametrically opposed things."

Rabbi Ruth hummed, and Hannah wondered what that meant. "Do you? I wonder. Do you both want to remain married? Or to become fully married?"

Levi bit his lip and smiled a little sadly. "Nothing else has ever made sense to me, but that's up to Hannah."

Hannah nodded. "That's what I'd like to work toward."

"What would it take for you to feel ready for that?" Rabbi Ruth asked. "What would need to happen before you could say, yes, let's commit to this for real?"

"I need us to face the hardest things about us, the fact that we feel opposite ways about our home, and our interfering families, and even our love story. The fact that we don't talk to each other when things are scary and then get mad that the other person can't read our minds. I need us to puzzle all of it out, no matter how uncomfortable it is or how scared we are and think of solutions. As a team. Because every time we've put it off or assumed that being in love would be enough, we've hurt each other."

"We're getting better at that," Levi said. "Or we're practicing."

Rabbi Ruth nodded. "I think you've already done extraordinary work getting where you are, and I wouldn't bet against you. Perhaps you can ask yourself, what things have you assumed to be true that might not be? What things have you needed in the past that you might no longer require? What coping mechanisms, or old ways of thinking, are no longer serving you in moving your marriage forward?"

They continued. "I'm sorry I don't have a more immediate fix, or answer, for you. I can't make a bullet-pointed slideshow of what you ought to do next. If it makes you feel better, all marriage is basically one day at a time."

"I don't actually find that comforting," Hannah told them.

"And how are you feeling, Levi?" Rabbi Ruth asked.

A Cheshire cat grin unfurled on his face. "You just helped me more than you can imagine." To Hannah, he said, "We have to go home. There's something I have to do."

She sighed. "Is it another damn Shenanigan?"

Chapter 21

Levi

The day after their date with the rabbi, everyone Levi knew, and several people he didn't, were set to show up to watch him lose *Australia's Next Star Chef*. Before they got there, though, he needed to talk to his dad.

"I finally figured out what I need to do...which is what Hannah told me explicitly I needed to do, several times. But I need to do it *big*."

"What is it with you all and your grand gestures?" his dad kvetched. "Miriam and her painting. Noelle and her building a cabin."

"Mine is better. Dad, I need your help with a Shenanigan."

"I thought you'd never ask."

Later, Levi addressed the small crowd he'd gathered in the barn before the screening. "Everyone, I've asked you here because

Hannah and I spent many years having our relationship in a vacuum, and I don't want to hide anymore. Is any of this any of your business? Probably not, but this is Carrigan's, so this is how we roll. Cole is coming around with buckets of popcorn, and I will ask you to turn your attention to the screen." He paused. "Dad, the lights and projector?"

Mr. Matthews nodded, turning off the overhead lights and turning on the projector that stood by the door.

Miriam brought out a microphone and set it to the side of the screen, giving Levi a thumbs-up before sitting next to Noelle and grabbing her popcorn.

"Babe, will you come up here?"

Hannah looked at him very skeptically but came to stand next to him. "You're really going all in on this lack of privacy thing, huh?"

"Shh! Let me do my big ridiculous thing. It'll be great. You're going to love it."

Onscreen, a PowerPoint came up. It was titled:

How We Are Going to Make This Work

"You made me a PowerPoint?" Hannah asked, sounding perplexed but touched.

"You asked for a plan. It won't be up to your standards but allow me to present it."

He straightened the lapels of his leather jacket and began. "I thought our love was epic, and that's why it was important— that it spanned years and continents, that no one had a love like ours."

"Are you quoting Logan Echolls at me?" Now she sounded incredulous.

"Yes." He nodded. "Bloodshed, lives ruined, it seemed fitting. I thought that being fated for each other made us special and meant we should be together. But then I looked at my parents, and Miriam and Noelle, and Elijah and Jason—the most in love, happy people I know, the loves that I would hold up as storied for the ages."

He took a deep breath, grounded himself. "I realized they're not special because they were fated for each other. They just work hard at being partners. Our story...it isn't special. We're just two schmucks in love. You asked me why we should be together, if not because of fate, and I want to answer you. Because I do think we should be together. Not because we're two perfectly matched melodramatic assholes who love to wallow in our own misery—"

"Although you are!" Noelle called out, throwing a piece of popcorn at him.

"Although we are, yes, thank you, Northwood." He ran his hand through his hair. "Look, I could give so many reasons that would make sense. We share a home, we share a past, we have an exciting vision for a shared future. Those things are precious, but if we weren't right for each other, they wouldn't move the needle. I asked myself, am I trying to win my wife back because breakups hurt and I just wanted to make the hurt stop? And the answer is, yes, it sucked, and hurt worse than anything I've ever gone through, but that's not why I thought we should reconcile."

"Are you going somewhere with this, Blue?" Hannah folded her arms. "Because right now I'm actually less convinced we should be together."

"Yes. Thank you. I was doing a dramatic lead-up, but I might have gone on too long. Good note." He took another deep breath, holding her hands. "You and me together, Nan, we're fire and gasoline, and I want to spend my life lit up. You are an evil genius, and I am your getaway driver, and apart, neither of us plays those roles that were made for us. We're like puzzle boxes that unlock each other's best—or worst, but most interesting—selves. We're both obsessed with being the most competent person at our jobs, and we both need partners who value that in each other. Even though we've heard, or been there for, each other's every story, we keep surprising each other and always will. We're happier and more creative and have more fun together than with anyone else on earth. We see each other, in our entirety. I think."

"I think so too," Hannah whispered.

"You have to talk into the mic!" Elijah yelled.

Hannah rolled her eyes but leaned over into the microphone. "I think so too."

"Okay. Glad we're on the same page. So, we're in love. We're good for each other. We make each other happy. We want to be together. But, as you've pointed out, we want very different things from our lives. Here's where the plan comes in."

He flipped to the next slide on the PowerPoint.

> 1. I cannot own Carrigan's.

"I love you, and Miriam, and even Noelle, in spite of either of us. I love the work you're doing, and I'm proud of you, and I'm excited to be a part of making it a success. I'm working on forgiving Cass. But, babe, no matter how I turn it over inside of me, I can't own shares in this business. It makes my skin itch. It makes me want to scream and throw things. It's like a rock stuck in my shoe."

When she didn't say anything, he continued. "What I'd like to do, and I've already talked to my parents about this, is sign over my shares to them, and they can...sell them to you and retire or give them to Grant or whatever you all decide. Without me. I'm sorry, but I have to do this to move forward."

Hannah blew out a breath. He watched her. This was the part he'd worried most about, and if she wasn't on board, he wasn't sure how the rest of the presentation would go.

"I get it," she finally said. "If you can't move forward with the shares, we'll figure out what to do with them."

He almost crumpled in relief.

"Okay. Next slide." He clicked again.

---

2. Immediate issues: Filming options.

"Food Network wants me to film a full season, in Manhattan. I have several options. I can get a place halfway in between for the duration of the show so I can commute both there and here. I can take the train in on the weekends. I can ask them to film at Carrigan's if you want."

This time, Hannah answered immediately. "I do not want them to film at Carrigan's—that seems incredibly disruptive— but I'm on board with looking over the other options and deciding what makes the most sense. You're only filming for a few weeks, right? That seems surmountable."

"Correct. And that leads us to slide three." He changed the screens.

> ### 3. Long-term issues.

"Now, the network has a lot of ideas about traveling shows. They have some vision of me as the discount-rack, off-brand Anthony Bourdain."

"You should be so lucky," Hannah said.

"Right? So, the problem is, I don't particularly want to spend my life traveling without my wife. You have a very busy professional life here, and a dislike for leaving the greater Upstate New York area. However, you've expressed that you would have liked to come with me, so I don't want to assume I should turn down all offers of adventure."

"I do want to travel, with you," Hannah agreed warily, "but I'm not sure I want to be at the whim of a film crew, again, with no agency over where we go, and for how long. That's kind of what I hated most about my childhood."

"Aha! Okay." He squeezed her hands, and she squeezed back and nodded at him to keep going. "There are several options, again. You could be contracted as a producer, or travel manager, or whatever title makes the most sense, so that you would in fact be the person telling the film crew where to go, rather than the other way around. Or you and I could go on scouting trips and I could do the filming trips separately. Or I could say to hell with filming travel shows, I film in New York, I travel for fun."

Chapter 22

Hannah

There's something wrong with this plan," Hannah said, and Levi froze. She told herself to be as brave as he'd just been.

"I think you're right to give the shares to your parents. I understand why you wouldn't want to take something you believe your mom and dad should already have had. I *want* to travel with you. Maybe not right away, but someday, I want to be able to go to the Grand Canyon with my kids and find the best croissants in Paris. The thing is . . ." She blew out a breath. "We've both been trying to figure out how we could make this work at Carrigan's, because Carrigan's has been the immovable constant. I couldn't leave, and you couldn't stay. I don't know if we *can* make it work at Carrigan's. I try to imagine moving into your parents' rooms after they retire, and you cooking full-time in the kitchen instead of eating every food of the diaspora . . ."

"I would do it if it meant we got to be together," he said quietly, hugging her tightly. "I would film here, travel from here, and hire help. Bring in visiting chefs. I like the Adirondacks a hell of a lot more than I expected to."

"You would wither here. You told me that once, and you were right. You would wither here, and, Blue, so would I." She knew as she said it that she was right, and her voice got more confident as she went on. "I couldn't have left when you did. I can't beat myself up about that, any more than I've already done. I don't think I would go back and make the choice to leave with you, knowing what I know now. But now... I don't need to be locked in this tower anymore. I'm not a princess to keep safe, and I can't hold everyone up by my hair anymore. You found out who you are outside of Carrigan's. I want to find out, too. Who I am. Who we are."

"What does that mean?" he asked, pushing her hair back. "What does that look like? Hannah, we own Carrigan's. It's your life's dream. I can't ask you to walk away from it."

"You're not asking me to, and I'm not talking about walking away." She shook her head, thinking out loud. She didn't, historically, love to think on her feet, but she did love to brainstorm and problem-solve with Levi. "I don't want to sell or quit working here. I just don't want to *live* here. I want to, I don't know, get a place in Lake Placid and commute in. I want to build a little house with you, filled with brand-new IKEA furniture that Cass never owned and we built poorly, and Miriam Blum originals, and kitchen gadgets I think we don't need. I want to go with you sometimes when you travel, and sometimes not, and go into the city with you to film sometimes, but not all the time, and I want us to have lives that intersect and hold each other up but don't keep each other in places we can't thrive."

She waited for him to say something, but he was just looking at her and crying, so she kept going. She couldn't stop now.

"I want us to go to shul on Friday nights, and marriage counseling with Rabbi Ruth, and have the next generation of Rosenstein-Matthews babies to ask the four questions and find the afikomen. I don't know if you ever want to be a part of running Carrigan's again. It would make me sad to have a Carrigan's with no Blue, to not get to collaborate with you, but we would make it work."

He stared at her, his eyeliner smudged under his lashes.

"What are you thinking?" she finally asked.

"I guess that we both must have grown up a hell of a lot in the past few years, if you're considering moving out of Carrigan's and I'm considering staying. I don't want to live here, you're right. Like I really, deeply don't," he admitted. "But I like being involved. I like brainstorming with my mom about the future, and bouncing wild, creative ideas off Miriam, and working side by side with you. Being a part of the inner workings, it's helping me rewrite the past. I don't want to cut myself out. I love watching you work too damn much."

He nestled his face into her hair, and she breathed deeply for the first time that day. "I want to, I don't know, hire someone to do the day-to-day cooking for the guests, but act as the advisory chef and plan and execute the menus for big events. I know it would help out Carrigan's All Year if we could advertise that, for a little more money, someone could have TV's Chef Levi cook for their wedding or whatever."

"You don't have to do what might be best for Carrigan's

All Year if it's not best for you, or us," Hannah said, her hope soaring.

He nodded into her hair. "I know. But I've spent all my life doing what's good for me at the cost of my family's feelings and our relationship. This would be a chance for me to see your big, beautiful dreams up close and support them. It doesn't always have to be a question of me versus the entire world."

"Gosh, Levi, who could ever have guessed that that was true?" Hannah teased, just a little.

"So how many kitchen gadgets is too many to fit into a little house?" he asked. "Because we might have wildly different ideas about the number."

She shifted so they were looking at each other. "Do you want to do this? Honestly? After everything, do you still want to try?"

"I told you I do." He nodded. "More than anything. I mean, it's going to be a lot of work, and we can't just put everything we did to each other in a closet, lock the door, and pretend it's not there. But do *you* honestly want to, Nan? You wanted a life where you could be Hannah, not half of Hannah and Levi. Are you just getting back together because it hurts to be apart, because it's too hard to fight against us while you're still so tired from losing Cass and trying to save Carrigan's?"

She laughed, so relieved and delighted she couldn't help herself. She threw her arms around his neck.

"I do genuinely want to. I want to grow up with you. I want to get to know everything about the person you've become and fall in love with him, too. It's not easier to give in and be with you, Blue. It's so much harder. It would be easier to say we're never going to make it work, sign the papers, let

Hannah and Levi be something we used to be. Because if we're together, I have to grow, and change, and compromise, and be on a team where I don't get to make all the rules, and things happen that I can't control. It would be easier to just stay a spinster, growing old as the head of Carrigan's, picking up lost souls like Cass did, but never letting anyone near mine. That's not what I want. I want you."

Mrs. Matthews and Esther cheered. Jason and Elijah applauded. Collin whistled through his fingers.

"I forgot they were here," Hannah whispered, but the mic picked her words up.

"We know!" Elijah yelled.

Levi turned toward them. "Okay, everyone, since you're here and you've got popcorn, let's watch this finale!"

After the show ended, there were congratulations, and condolences, questions about what was happening next, explanations about *Living Bold* that got progressively more pretentious as Levi got slightly tipsy, and a lot of food to be eaten.

"So," Mrs. Matthews said, sidling up next to Hannah. "Now that you two have reconciled, are you going to stop avoiding me?"

Oof. Hannah grimaced. "I wasn't—"

"Don't lie to me, Hannah Rosenstein. You've barely spoken to me since Levi came home. I miss you. You're as much my kid as he is. More, some days." Mrs. Matthews poked her gently in the ribs.

Hannah nodded. "I'm sorry. I felt so ashamed, every time I

saw Ben's face light up or saw you hug Levi, that I kept you apart for so long."

Mrs. Matthews snorted. "We saw him all the time. You didn't keep us from anything, and you weren't the only party involved. I don't know where all you kids got your black-and-white thinking. I'm not mad at you, and I never was. I'm mad at Cass, now that I know the whole story, but I'll work that out. And if you try to give me the silent treatment again, I'm *going* to be mad at you."

"No more," Hannah agreed. "I promise."

"Also maybe, since you're my daughter-in-law, you can start calling me Felicia? Or even Mom?"

Hannah teared up. "Please don't make me ruin the rest of my mascara."

Mrs. Matthews stretched up on tiptoes to kiss her on the forehead. "All right, go find that son of mine."

Hannah was, in fact, impatient to find Levi and drag him away from the party. She wanted to get her husband alone, and naked, and his delicious food and adorable self-satisfied smirk were not helping. They were officially, without question, one thousand percent back together, and she was very done waiting for marital relations to resume.

"Hey, Levi," she said, coming up behind him and setting her chin on his shoulder. He was standing on the edge of a group of Advent residents, listening to a lively debate about the final challenge.

"Hey, Hannah?" he asked, leaning over to kiss her hair.

"Do you remember how we were taking a couple of rain checks on various nude activities?"

He purred like a satisfied cat. "I do remember. Do you

want to do that thing you like with your office desk and the spanking?"

She choked. "I do want to do that, very much, but I was thinking right at this moment, maybe we could just go back to your cabin and lock ourselves in. Bed. Fireplace. Jacuzzi tub."

He smirked down at her. "Is it gauche to sneak out of your own party to have sex with your wife?"

She bit the side of his neck, lightly, although it would look to anyone watching like she'd just nuzzled him. "I don't care."

"Meet me there in ten," he ordered. "You leave first. Don't be wearing clothes when I get there."

Oh. She shivered. She'd forgotten how much she loved it when he got bossy.

When they emerged, eventually, the next day, Miriam and Noelle had called an emergency shareholders meeting, which just meant Noelle sending Hannah a text:

Noelle: please put on pants and meet us in the library

Hannah sat on the window seat, and Levi sat on the same chair where they'd hooked up the first night of Passover. She studiously avoided his eyes so she wouldn't get distracted by the memory.

"Okay!" Miriam clapped her hands, bouncing a little in the chair she was folded into like a pretzel. "We're very excited you're back together and that Blue is not going away again forever."

Noelle was leaning against a bookshelf, her booted feet crossed. "I'm ambivalent about both these things."

Miriam rolled her eyes. "She's excited. But! We need to have a serious conversation about what to do with Levi's shares, with the Matthewses obviously, and we need to talk about inn operations with Hannah off-site."

"Now, I know you're not going to love this," Noelle began, "because I remember very clearly that you freaked out so much about ceding control to Miriam that you screamed at her about napkins—"

"Hey, I eventually did replace those broken napkin holders," Hannah protested. "And I apologized."

Noelle glared at her, and she stopped interrupting, although she was very nervous about where this was going. "You've been the guest and the events manager, but as we ramp up Carrigan's All Year, you've spent more and more time running point on events, and you don't get to do guest experience. Miriam does some of it, but we run an inn that is regularly fully booked, and it's a big job. Basically, at this point, you have two full-time jobs."

"And you can't do two full-time jobs anymore if you're not going to live on-site," Miriam finished. "We both feel, for your emotional and physical well-being, and for the business, we probably need to hire someone for either guest management or events. We don't care which! You choose!"

Panic began to rise in Hannah's body. So she breathed in through her nose and out through her mouth and tapped her hands on her knees in a rhythm while she tried to remember how to think. Nothing they were saying was untrue. They weren't trying to take her agency or Carrigan's from her. They loved her and were trying to keep her from burning out. She closed her eyes and asked herself what she really wanted, what she envisioned in her best possible version of their future.

If she was going to do any of the adventuring that she and Levi talked about, she was going to need less on her plate, but it was more than that. Miriam taking over some of her duties six months ago had opened her time up to rest, see her therapist more, take a long bath sometimes. In other words, she'd visibly seen her quality of life improve. She didn't want to give up all control, because she loved Carrigan's and being in charge sparked joy, but she could envision a life where she wasn't in charge of *everything*, and the thought gave her nothing but relief.

"You know what?" she said, her voice only squeaking a little, "I don't want to do two full-time jobs, period, no matter where I live. I don't want my entire identity as a human to be my career. It's absurd that my husband had to declare a Shenanigan to get me to go on a single date with him. I want to go to breakfast sometimes, somewhere that's not our dining room. I want to read a book! That's not about hotel management! I want to, like...be less shitty at trivia because I've interacted with the outside world more. I want to have friendships, and kids sometime soon."

She got a full breath all the way into her lungs and looked around at her cousin, her best friend, and her husband. She was safe. Everything was okay.

"In a vacuum, without Levi here, I would probably say that I wanted to just do guest services, but I love our teamwork. I love working events together, it's really...fun? And energizing?"

"Why do you sound so baffled by that, babe?" Levi asked, mock offended.

She elbowed him. "I want to be an events team. Maybe there's a spare Rosenstein cousin we can poach for guest management."

"Okay, real quick events-related question," Levi said, raising his hand. "Do you want to plan a wedding for us? Because I'd like to have one so you'll stop telling people we're not really married."

"Is this the time, Matthews?" Noelle asked him. "She's going to need like a week to recover from giving up any of her job responsibilities."

"Hey!" Hannah complained. "But also, fair."

"I am getting on her calendar early, because scheduling things tells her that I love her," Levi explained to Noelle. To Hannah, he added, "I know you used to want a chuppah covered in flowers and a long lace veil."

She was touched that he remembered that.

"We should order a new glass to break; it's probably bad luck to use the one we ordered before but never used."

"I broke it," Hannah said sheepishly. "I threw it off the bridge over the stream at the back of the farm. I threw a lot of stuff for a few months."

Levi laughed at this. "What do you want now? A big wedding with everyone? Just us, a ketubah, a chuppah, and a rabbi? Something in between?"

Thinking about their wedding was like stretching an atrophied muscle. "I want everyone there. Or maybe not *every* Rosenstein, but our core crew. My parents. But, Blue," she said, meeting his eyes, "I don't want to plan it."

He startled, his eyes wide.

"I've planned so many weddings since you left. I threw

my life into planning other people's weddings, planning other people's everythings, because my life was so out of control. I just want to show up to a beautiful wedding, say my vows, and be married. More married. Officially married."

"You actually don't want to plan it?" Levi asked, shocked.

She shook her head. "I know, you think it will make me twitchy to give up control of something that big, but I just don't want to be in charge of all the labor all the time. My dream wedding would honestly be one I just showed up at. I know most people would not want to be surprised by their own wedding, but as long as we'd already decided we were getting married for real, I wouldn't want to worry about the actual planning of it, like, at all."

"Huh," said Levi. "I would not have guessed that."

"I wouldn't have either!" Hannah said. "I'm just so sick of planning weddings! And I already planned ours once and had to mourn it."

Miriam looked at Noelle victoriously. "See, I told you that when he wasn't making her miserable, he made her much better at relaxing."

"That's not his personality," Noelle argued. "That's just orgasms."

Levi winked at Hannah. "You wanna go relax?"

"Gross!" Noelle cried out, but Hannah just waved at her as she followed her husband out the door.

Chapter 23

Levi

A week later, the front lawn of Carrigan's was hosting its first Pride festival for the last weekend of June. Usually, Carrigan's held a Fourth of July festival, but the Carrigan's crew had debated the ethical ramifications of throwing a celebration of independence on stolen Mohawk land and decided to invite some drag queens instead.

Levi wandered out onto the lawn in a brand-new scarf (weather be damned) in demisexual pride colors, gifted to him by Cole, who was very, very excited for his first out Pride. He found Laurence chatting to Elijah, having a fierce debate about the local college basketball team.

"I was hoping to find both of you!" He went to shake hands, and Elijah gave him a bear hug instead.

"Hannah stole my mom and my kids to go stuff them full of candy apples," the lawyer said, "and my husband has been commissioned to settle a debate between a bunch of teenagers."

"Hannah has been talking about how excited she is to see your mom all week." Levi grinned.

Elijah laughed. "Why does everyone love my mom best?"

"Welcome to the club!" Levi turned to Laurence. "Are you ready for this showdown? I'm looking forward to getting my ass handed to me."

Noelle and Hannah had schemed up a live cooking skills competition between the two of them, in a tent off to the side of the fairway, with a livestream and lots of hype. The purpose was mainly to have something interesting going on where people could sit down, and the prize was just bragging rights, but Levi found himself full of excited nerves. He had cooked alongside great chefs, and even better untrained home cooks, but this was against one of his best friends, in front of his family. It mattered more.

Laurence pushed his sleeves up over his tattooed forearms and winked. "I'm glad you're prepared. I also think you probably have some places to be, Mister Famous in Australia. Some guests may need you to schmooze them."

"Oh no, my wife has officially banned me from any schmoozing activities. Apparently the number of f-bombs I drop is 'off-putting' or something." He shrugged.

"Your wife is very wise," Laurence noted.

Jason Green emerged from the crowd. "I finally got rid of my students," he sighed dramatically. "Speaking of teenagers, and Pride..."

"Why do I get the feeling you're about to ask me for a favor?" Levi said, worried now.

"Did you know that I'm in charge of teaching sex ed to those hooligans?" Jason began.

"The high school has sex ed? Is it more than the one class Hannah and I got about how we were going to get pregnant and die of AIDS if we ever had sex?"

Jason shook his head, laughing. "Oh no, the high school refuses to teach sex ed, so a big cohort of local families got together and wrangled me into teaching it. We hold it at the UU church. And yes, it's a lot more than one class. Every year, I have a panel where I invite a spectrum of LGBTQIAP2S+ folks to speak to the students about their experience. I'd love for you to join."

Levi twitched a little. "You want me to go talk to the children of the kids who bullied me, about how it's actually totally fine to be queer? Why don't you ask Cole?"

"You don't have to come if you're not comfortable," Jason said. "I definitely understand. But Cole's not from here, so he can't speak to the experience of feeling isolated and alone up here. And he's not the Legendary Levi Blue. I have a lot of weird little queer kids who would benefit from it, if you're up for it. It's not until next semester, so think about it."

"Ugh," Levi groaned. "I'm going to go eat fried food and forget this conversation." But he knew he wouldn't, and that if he asked his support group, or Rabbi Ruth, they would all probably tell him to do it. He would worry about that later.

Jason pointed at Laurence. "You're still coming to trivia next week?"

Laurence nodded. "Wouldn't miss it," he said around a mouthful of corn dog.

"And you"—Jason pointed at Levi—"are coming to Gay-b-que on the Fourth?"

Levi also nodded. "Noelle told me I would no longer be queer if I didn't show up. With potato salad."

"That is correct," Jason agreed. "Doomed to a life of heterosexuality, all for want of a side dish."

"I'll be there. If I've finished cleaning up from this madness first."

The lawn had been set up as a classic carnival, with rides and fried food stands and games of chance. Kids—and Cole—were screaming bloody murder on the Zipper, and Levi's stomach turned over just watching it. Noelle was down at the end of the long center aisle, holding a funnel cake the size of her head and wearing a rainbow bow tie with a short-sleeved button-down in the lesbian pride flag colors. She waved when she saw him and pointed to a booth where Miriam was failing to knock down pins with a baseball. Levi gave her a thumbs-up and kept moving, feeling the need to set eyes on all his people and make sure they were okay.

The twins were passing out handheld sparklers and glow bracelets to everyone who came by. His parents were with his nephew.

A presence was suddenly at his side, and he looked down as Hannah's arm snaked under his elbow. He dropped a kiss on the top of her head, breathing in the smell of her, roses, sweat, and sunshine.

"Hi, babe," she mumbled, nuzzling her face into his shoulder.

"Aren't we supposed to be Professional at this Work Event?" he asked, teasing her a little.

She grinned up at him, shrugging easily. "Who's going to fire us? Besides, no one's looking at us. They're all drunk on lemonade slushies and turkey legs and being outside."

"What about you? Are you having fun, or just stressing out?" He tucked an invisible hair behind her ear.

"Right now, I am seventy-five percent stress, but as soon as the showcase is over, I think I can be seventy-five percent fun." Hannah bit her lip, and Levi leaned down to nip it.

"Can I help with the fun?"

"What are you proposing?"

"We've never been on a Ferris wheel together," he said. "Come with me. After the showcase."

The Ferris wheel clicked into motion, swaying them gently. Hannah clutched at the bar.

"I shouldn't have let Miriam book the rides. I don't know whether anyone checked the safety record of this wheel and this operator," she squeaked. Blue rumbled a laugh.

"Stop freaking out," he said. "We're probably not going to die on this carnival ride. And if we do, what better way to go than together, on the Carrigan's front lawn?"

She glared at him, and he grinned. He wrapped her hand in both of his and brought it to his mouth in a kiss. She broke eye contact, and he looked around them, around at the world beneath them, as the car made its way slowly up over their one hundred sixty acres. He could see past the farm to the wilderness of the Adirondacks beyond, and he breathed deeply.

This was home, here, in this place and with this woman. He hadn't ever thought it could be, but somehow it was. He looked down at their still-clasped hands, where Hannah was running her free finger over his forearms, tracing scars.

"Most of these are from hot grease, but that," he said as she got to a particularly long one, "is a long story involving a jungle, which I'll tell you after we have been married for about fifty years, because it makes me sound like a total doofus."

"I used to know all your scars," she said, "the one on your chin that you got when we were four and playing fort. The line behind your ear from sledding. The time your leg—"

"Oh, we don't talk about that one. It still makes me woozy to think about."

"Imagine how your parents must have felt."

He shuddered. "Does it make you sad? That my skin is so different than it was when I left?"

She thought about his question for a long minute, then shook her head. "We are both in new skin, yours just shows more, on the outside. I look forward to spending hours and hours getting to know this new skin. I get to be naked with a whole new you."

"Hours and hours, huh?" He took one of his hands off hers so he could wind it around her curls. She leaned her forehead against his and then squeaked when the chair rocked beneath them.

"We should get off this Ferris wheel and get started on this naked thing," she said. "Or just be on the ground. That would be fine."

"What if we got started on the whole rest of our lives thing?" he asked, pulling a box out of his pocket.

He felt her stop breathing. He really hoped that was a good kind of stopped breathing.

The box he opened held Cass's ring. Every now and then, Cass had let them play in her jewelry box, and Hannah always put this ring on her too-small fingers and said she was going to have it someday when she got married.

She looked up at Levi with huge eyes. All his cockiness was gone, and he knew his whole heart was in his eyes.

"Where did you get this?" she whispered. "I looked for it after the funeral, but it was gone."

"Cass gave it to Elijah with the napkin. She must have known I'd be back someday and would want to ask you to marry me."

"You haven't, though," she pointed out.

"I haven't what?"

"Asked me to marry you," she said, and he gulped. "You're not going to get out of this the easy way."

"Hannah Naomi Rosenstein, you are the only person I have ever loved, or will ever love. You are the most extraordinary, brilliant, fascinating, competent woman I've ever met, and I know you could choose to spend your life with anyone. If you choose me, I promise I will do everything in my power to be worthy of that choice. I will be your partner, your teammate, your ride-or-die. I will coax you into adventures and listen to you when you tell me what you need and want. I want to get turned on every time I see you with a clipboard and help you execute the most elaborate possible schemes. I want what my parents have, with you. Will you marry me?"

"Levi Blue Matthews, I would marry you this very moment if we had a rabbi handy with a ketubah. You are always going to be my partner and my ride-or-die. I could love someone who wasn't you, but I don't want to. I want you."

Levi finally, finally let out the breath he was holding and put the ring on Hannah's finger, his hands shaking.

"Please do not drop my aunt Cass's antique diamond ring down a Ferris wheel, Blue. I'm pretty sure it would be a bad omen."

He took her face in his hands and kissed her, and the Ferris wheel stopped at the bottom. They broke apart sheepishly as the ride operator came to lift the seat bar.

"So, funny thing," he said as they disembarked, "about the rabbi and the ketubah."

She blinked at him.

"There is one…on the back lawn. Also a chuppah, and a lot of chairs, and your parents, and my parents, and your entire extended family, and Noelle might have bought a tux and there's a dress upstairs for you that Marisol picked out." He breathed out the words in a rush.

"If you want it. I mean. We don't have to get married right now." He sped up, if that were possible, while she looked at him in shock. "But you said you didn't want to have to plan a wedding, with everything else you have going on, so yeah, we could get married right now. Tonight. If you were serious."

Hannah took a deep breath. "I can't believe you pulled off a secret wedding." She grinned at him. "We got back together, like, two minutes ago."

"I have learned event planning at the foot of the master. Also, Miriam helped a lot. So, you want to do it?"

She'd never made him so nervous in all their lives. Not even the first time he'd asked her to marry him.

"I'll go get changed," she said, and he picked her up and swung her around, whooping.

"SHENANIGANS!" he yelled to anyone around to listen.

Elijah and Jason's twins acted as flower children, dancing up the aisle full of cotton candy and mischief. Noelle stood as

Hannah's best woman, and Miriam was Levi's groomswoman. The two of them were making such outlandish heart eyes at each other that Levi glared at Noelle, leaning across Rabbi Ruth to whisper, "Just ask her already, or I'm going to. Your ass better get moving if you want a Carrigan's Christmas wedding."

Noelle shushed him. "She'll hear you!"

Levi smirked.

"I already have a spot marked off for you in my calendar if you ever get your act together," Rabbi Ruth added, and Noelle blushed.

Hannah walked toward him, and he thought he might astral project from happiness. His face already hurt from the unfamiliar act of smiling so much, and they hadn't even started the ceremony yet. He heard Rabbi Ruth's voice, as if through a dream, telling them to walk around each other, to kiss. When they lifted him up in his chair, he truly thought he might fly.

He looked at Hannah. She was so radiantly beautiful he forgot to breathe, until his father yelled over the music, "I'm proud of you, kid. I'm glad you're home."

He was, too. Home, and glad.

Epilogue

A little more than a month before Cass's yahrzeit, they were sitting in the tiny lemon-yellow kitchen of their quirky little married apartment on a very rare Friday night off from Carrigan's, picking at the ends of takeout by the light of the Shabbat candles. Levi had his legs stretched out all the way to the other side of the tiny vintage Formica table Miriam had found for them, with Hannah's feet in his lap.

A bright late-summer moon shone in, August just turned to September, the long busy days inching to the High Holy Days again, their first time in this new place.

Their apartment was part of an old Tudor revival mansion in Lake Placid that had been segmented into flats. For reasons that escaped logic, the owners had built the kitchens into the faux tower. As soon as she'd seen it, Hannah had known they had to live there, because Cass would have loved it so much. The memory of Cass brought a sharper pain these days, with more teeth than it had, but she couldn't pass up something that would have so delighted her aunt.

Besides, she might have cut off all her Rapunzel hair, but she could still eat her yogurt in a tower like a princess.

The rest of the space—a cluttered efficiency with very quirky antique furniture, some Carrigan's, some Miriam's, from every era and an equally antique radiator that Hannah feared might not hold its own against winter nights—reminded her of a set from *Barefoot in the Park*. They weren't really newlyweds, but they were newly married, and they did need the space to themselves.

She understood now why Noelle had been so quick to build Miriam a place for them to live in the carriage house, apart from the main house at Carrigan's. It felt impossibly small after living in the hotel for most of the past twenty years, and it felt gigantic at night when they left the bedroom doors open and had all that space to themselves instead of a cramped hotel suite.

It felt like a choice she'd made out of joy instead of fear, even if it also felt like a long damned commute when she had an early morning event at the Christmasland.

Levi hummed contentedly from his seat, and she looked over to see him watching her with a soft, easy smile. She would never take it for granted how comfortable they were together, again, finally. Well, she probably *would* take it for granted, but she hoped she'd remember quickly. There was no "of course" about her and Blue, no matter how inevitable they had once seemed. It had taken marriage counseling and therapy, and they still sometimes found themselves falling into old patterns and having to fish each other out.

She was smiling lazily back at him, thinking she should mention the shabbat mitzvah of a husband bringing his wife sexual pleasure, when their phones both rang.

"I thought you turned yours off!" Hannah said, kicking him lightly.

"I thought you turned *yours* off." Levi raised an eyebrow at her.

"I only left it on because Noelle was maybe going to really, really need me to give her a pep talk . . ." She picked up her phone to peek at the caller ID. "It's her. Should I? Can I?"

"Mine's Miriam," Levi said. "Put them both on speaker."

"I'm sorry we're calling on Shabbat," Miriam called out, "but I knew Han wouldn't have her phone off and I know you have us on speaker!!"

"You're interrupting takeout and makeout. What do you want?" Levi grumbled, but he was smiling.

"Are you ready?" Noelle whispered, loud enough for them to hear.

"We're getting married!" they both said at once, the words echoing from both phones.

Levi let out an unholy squeal of delight, and Hannah dissolved into giggles.

"Noelle finally got up the chutzpah to ask you!" she cried out.

"NO! I got tired of waiting so I asked her. I tied the ring to Kringle!" Miriam singsonged.

Levi had tried to bring Kringle with them, but both the cat and their landlady had objected strenuously.

"I had a ring hidden in a haunted doll, but she is so impatient!" Noelle grouched. Levi laughed, and Hannah smiled at how far *those* two had come. They almost never threatened each other with death anymore.

"What am I planning for you? When is the most fabulous sapphic wedding in the history of New York State happening?" Hannah's voice was champagne in her throat. After this terrible year that she thought would break her, she would not have imagined she could feel this much joy.

"What do you think, Nan?" Miriam laughed. "We're going to have a Christmas wedding at Carrigan's, of course!"

Acknowledgments

First, to the real people I love named Hannah and Levi—thank you for the use of your names. Hannah, you told me if I named a character after you, I had to give her a lot of feelings about her hair. Well, here we are. May you each find a love as eternal as this one, if less melodramatic.

My editor, Sam Brody, and Forever EIC, Amy Pierpont, for being willing to go along for the ride with me when I pitched this "and they're secretly married" book. Leni Kauffman for the most beautiful pansexual panic cover (who's hotter?! I can't decide!). Copyeditor Carrie Andrews and production editor Anjuli Johnson for patiently fixing my timeline since "Carrigan's takes place in a pocket universe and time works differently there" is not a good reason for not knowing what day of Passover it is. Estelle Hallick and Dana Cuadrado, the most badass marketing team in publishing.

My absolutely brilliant agent, Becca Podos, for breaking open a crucial part of the plot. This would never have come together as a book without them. This book also owes a great debt to Therese Beharrie, who first made me realize they needed to be married. Many, many people read this book at some point over the past four years and fixed it when it was broken, especially Anita Kelly and Skye Kilaen. Rachel Fleming, Candace Harper, and Ky J. Harrison loved and cheerled Hannah and Levi's story even when it was a total mess I was holding together with duct tape, which kept me writing it until I could (hopefully) do it justice.

My online communities of writers, including the HoliGays, the Broken Circle, and our little Contains Insufficient Heterosexual Representation Discord: thank you for being a constant source of support and inspiration. Jake Arlow slept on my shitty inflatable mattress and dealt with my terrible cats just to support my book launch. Kait Sudol sat through the entirety of *Get Over It* for the same reason. I'm very lucky in my friends.

Jennifer Rothschild gives incredibly insightful sensitivity reads. My kid sister who read to double-check my portrayal of Hannah's anxiety disorder. Hannah's anxiety is a mix of ours and is true to our experiences, though it may not be true to anyone else's. Similarly, I've tried to portray one tiny, single splinter of the vast, myriad experience of demisexuality. If I have done so poorly, that is on my head and not on that of anyone who read the manuscript.

My big brother inspired me to write a poufy-haired chef with an epic love story, although unlike Levi, Stephan is both universally beloved and capable of communicating with his wife.

Joni Mitchell for writing *Blue*, which made this impossible book possible (also Flamin' Hot Limón Cheetos, same reason).

Writing a second book is really hard, and this one was no different. The readers, bloggers, bookstagrammers, and everyone else who messaged me to tell me how much they loved *Season of Love*, loved Carrigan's, and couldn't wait for Hannah and Levi's story kept me going. All the writers who blurbed it, booksellers who hand sold it, and librarians who invited me to your book clubs live in my heart every day. Carrigan's isn't just my place now. It's all of ours, and I'm so thrilled that I got to write us all another chapter in the story. I will never get over the fact that I get to share these little pieces of my heart with all of you, and they resonate, and you share little pieces back. Books are such a miracle, aren't they?

Always, always, bolstered by my personal Team Helena, which begins with my husband, kid, and mom, and extends further than I could ever list.

If I forgot to thank you, it's not because I don't love you, it's because this book ate my brain.

Levi's career owes a great debt to *MasterChef Australia*, which owes a great debt to Jock Zonfrillo. Z"L

Lastly, and always, I'm sorry about Levi.

You're invited to Miriam and Noelle's wedding!

(Don't miss Tara's search for a plus-one—and maybe more!—as the big day approaches!)

Available Fall 2024

About the Author

Helena Greer writes contemporary romance novels that answer the question: What if this beloved trope were gay? She was born in Tucson, and her heart still lives there, although she no longer does. After earning a BA in writing and mythology, and a master's in library science, she spent several years blogging about librarianship before returning to writing creatively.

Helena loves cheesy pop culture, cats without tails, and ancient Greek murderesses.

You can learn more at:
HelenaGreer.com
Instagram @BlumAgainCurios